All Souls' Day

Cees Nooteboom, born in the Hague in 1933, has built up an imposing oeuvre of novels, collections of poetry, short fiction and travel stories, many of which were first published in magazines and newspapers. With his novel *Rituals* he won both the Dutch Bordewijk Prize and the Pegasus Prize for Literature, while *The Following Story* was awarded the European Literature Prize in 1993. An inveterate traveller, Nooteboom lives by turns in Germany, Spain and the Netherlands.

All Souls' Day

— CEES NOOTEBOOM —

Translated from the Dutch
by Susan Massotty

PICADOR

First published 2001 by Harcourt Trade Publishers, New York

First published in Great Britain 2001 by Picador

This edition published 2002 by Picador
an imprint of Pan Macmillan Ltd
Pan Macmillan, 20 New Wharf Road, London N1 9RR
Basingstoke and Oxford
Associated companies throughout the world
www.panmacmillan.com

ISBN 0 330 39260 3

Copyright © Cees Nooteboom 1998
English translation copyright © Susan Massotty 2001

First published by Atlas Uitgeverij as *Allerzielen* in 1998

The right of Cees Nooteboom to be identified as the
author of this work has been asserted by him in accordance
with the Copyright, Designs and Patents Act 1988.

1 3 5 7 9 8 6 4 2

A CIP catalogue record for this book is available from
the British Library.

Printed and bound in Great Britain by
Mackays of Chatham plc, Chatham, Kent

So we beat on, boats against the current, borne back ceaselessly into the past.

—F. Scott Fitzgerald, *The Great Gatsby*

However, the Sirens now possess an even more dreadful weapon than their song, namely their silence.

—Franz Kafka, *The Silence of the Sirens*

All Souls' Day

Arthur Daane was several steps away from Schoeler's Bookstore before he realized that a word had stuck in his head and that he had already translated it into his own language. His brain had registered the German word for history—*Geschichte*—but quickly turned it into the Dutch *geschiedenis*. Somehow it sounded less ominous in Dutch. He wondered if that was because of the last three letters, the suffix *nis,* which also meant "niche." A strange word. Short. Not mean and curt, as short words could be, but comforting. After all, a niche was a place to hide in, a place to find hidden things. Other languages didn't have that. He began to walk faster, hoping to rid himself of the word that way, but his little ploy didn't work, not here, not in this city, for every inch of Berlin was steeped in history. This word was going to be hard to forget. Lately all kinds of words had been getting stuck in his head. "Stuck" was definitely the right word: once they were in there, they stayed put. He could also hear them—there seemed to be a voice attached to the words, even when he hadn't said them aloud. Sometimes they even seemed to echo. The moment you plucked them out of the chain of sentences they belonged to, they would turn, if you were sensitive to that kind of thing, into something so strange, so terrifying that it would be better not to dwell on it too long, otherwise the world would slide out from under you. Too much free time, he thought. Yet he had arranged his life to achieve just that. He remembered reading about "the Javanese" in an old schoolbook: the story of a Javanese man who, once he had earned the equivalent of a quarter, would go and sit under a palm tree. In those long-gone colonial days, you could apparently live for quite a while on that amount, because the man didn't go back to work until he had spent every last penny. A disgraceful custom, according to the book, because you got ahead only by dint of hard work. Arthur Daane had seen the light. He made and produced his own TV documentaries, hired himself out as a cameraman if the subject seemed interesting enough, and every once in a while, if he needed the money or the mood struck, he would make a commercial for a company owned by a friend of his. It was exciting as long as you didn't do it too often, and at the end of a project he would take time off and loaf around for a while. He used to have a wife, and a child, but they'd died in a plane crash. All he had left now were photographs whose images seemed more remote every time he looked at them. Ten long years. One morning they simply took off for Málaga and never came back. A scene he had filmed, but never seen. The blonde woman with the child, a little boy, on her back. Schiphol Airport, the passport line. Actually, the boy is too big to be carried on her back. He calls her name, she turns. Freeze, memory. There they stand, at a ninety-degree angle, for one whole second. She raises her hand, the boy waves, a few short waves. Someone else will film the arrival, which will vanish, along with the bungalow, the swimming pool, and the sea, into the hard, lumpy, blackened mass that swallowed up their lives. He walks over to the line and hands her the small movie camera. One last glimpse, then they disappear. He has closed himself off from the puzzle posed by the pictures. It's too big, he can't take it in. Some dreams are like that—wanting to scream and not being able to, hearing a sound you know you didn't make, the sound of glass. He sold the house, gave away the clothes and toys, as if all their belongings were contaminated. Since then he's been a traveler without a suitcase—a laptop, a portable camera, a cell phone, a world-band travel radio, a couple of books. An answering machine in his apartment in Amsterdam, a fax in a friend's office—a man with machines. Free but tied down, invisible wires connecting him to the world. Voices, messages. Friends, mostly colleagues, who lead the same lives. They use his apartment, he uses theirs. Or else cheap hotels and boardinghouses, a floating universe. New York, Madrid, Berlin. Each of them, it occurs to him now, a niche. He still hasn't shaken off that word. Not the short suffix, and certainly not the long noun to which it does and doesn't belong.

"What is it about Germany that you find so attractive?" his Dutch friends ask him from time to time. They make it sound as if he'd caught a terrible disease.

He'd managed to come up with a trite answer that usually served his purpose. "I like it there. Germans are so serious."

"So they are," they'd say, or something else along those lines. Imagine having to explain the social codes of the Dutch. How could a foreigner, even one who's learned the language, ever understand that a quasi-confirmation of that kind was actually an expression of cynical disbelief?

In the time it took for all these words to go through his head, he had arrived at the liquor store on the corner of Knesebeckstrasse and Mommsenstrasse, the point at which he usually wondered whether he should go on walking or turn back. He stopped, looked at the gleaming cars in the showroom across the street, watched the traffic on the Kurfürstendamm, then caught sight of himself in the mirror of a champagne ad in the liquor-store window. The disgusting servility of mirrors—they go on reflecting your image even when you don't want them to. He had already seen himself once today. Except that this time he was wearing his clothes, his armor. That was different. He had a fairly good idea of who he was and wondered how much of his real self was visible to others. "All and nothing," Erna had said. What was he going to do with Erna, now that she had popped up on the corner of Mommsenstrasse?

"Are you being serious?"

"You bet your boots I am." Only Erna could say a thing like that. So now he had not only Erna, but also her boots to deal with. It had started to snow. In the mirror he could see the powdery flakes clinging to his coat. Good, he thought, now I don't look quite so much like an ad.

"Don't be silly." That, too, was something only Erna would say. They had discussed the subject often enough.

"If you think you look like you've just stepped out of an ad, buy yourself different clothes. Not Armani."

"This isn't Armani."

"Well, it looks like Armani."

"My point exactly. I don't even know what brand it is. I bought it on sale somewhere. Dirt cheap."

"Clothes look good on you."

"Right, that's what I'm saying. I look like an ad."

"You hate yourself, that's all. It happens to a lot of men when they reach middle age."

"No, that's not it. I just don't think I look like the real me."

"You mean you have all kinds of thoughts you don't talk about, and we can't see that?"

"Sort of."

"In that case you ought to get a different haircut. That's not a hairstyle; it's a disguise."

"You see?"

Erna was his oldest friend. He had met his wife through her, and she was the only person he ever talked to about Roelfje. Other men had male friends. He had them too, but Erna was his best friend.

"I don't know if I should take that as a compliment."

4

Sometimes he phoned her, in the middle of the night, from some godforsaken place on the other side of the globe. She was always home. Men came and went in her life, moved in with her, were jealous of him. "That Daane—what a phony. A couple of crummy documentaries, and he walks down the street as if he's Claude Lanzmann." That usually put an end to the relationship. At least she'd got something out of all those men: three children, all of whom looked like her.

"That's what happens when you mate with such nondescript men. An entire gene pool out there, and you pick the losers. You'd have been better off with me."

"Ah, but you're my forbidden fruit."

"The price we pay for the love known as friendship."

"Exactly."

He turned around, which meant no to Kurfürstendamm, yes to Savignyplatz. It also meant passing Schoeler's again. *Nis* was such a handy suffix in Dutch. It cropped up in all kinds of words: *bekommernis, gebeurtenis, belijdenis, besnijdenis*—solicitude, event, creed, circumcision. The snow had started coming down faster. That's what happened when you worked with cameras, he thought—you were constantly looking at yourself when you walked. Not so much out of vanity as amazement. Amazement mixed with, well...that too had been discussed with Erna.

"Why don't you just go ahead and say it?"

"Because I don't know what to call it."

"Nonsense. You know perfectly well what to call it. I can think of the word, so you must be able to as well. You just don't want to say it."

"Okay, so what's the word?"

"Fear. Awe."

He preferred awe.

In one long sweep the camera registered Berlin's snow-covered Knesebeckstrasse, the majestic houses, the handful of pedestrians with their shoulders hunched against the snow. And he was one of them. That's what it was all about—the pure coincidence of that particular moment. The lone figure heading down the street, past Schoeler's Bookstore, past the photo gallery, that's you. Why did such moments always seem so ordinary, and yet sometimes, suddenly, for one amazing second, so unbearable? Weren't you supposed to take them for granted? Unless, of course, you were a lifelong adolescent.

"That doesn't have anything to do with it. Some people never stop to think. But that feeling of wonderment and awe is the source of everything."

"Such as?"

"Art, religion, philosophy. I do pick up the occasional book, you know."

Erna had been a philosophy major for a few years, before switching to literature.

At the corner of Savignyplatz he was almost blown off his feet by a sudden snow flurry. This was getting serious. A continental climate. Another reason he liked Berlin. It always made him feel that he was in the middle of a vast plain stretching deep into the heart of Russia. Berlin, Warsaw, Moscow—mere stops along the way.

He wasn't wearing gloves, and his fingers were feeling frozen. During that same conversation, he'd delivered a lecture on fingers as well.

"Look—what are these?"

"They're fingers, Arthur."

"Yes, but they're also pincers. Watch this."

He picked up a pencil, twirled it around a couple of times.

"Clever, huh? People are amazed by robots, but never by themselves. They see a robot do this and it freaks them out, but they do it themselves all the time without giving it a sec-

6

ond thought. Robots made of flesh and blood—now that ought to freak you out. What a great expression! Anyway, robots can do anything, even reproduce themselves. And those eyes! Cameras and screens all rolled into one. The same instrument used to record and display. I don't know how to phrase it—either we *have* computers or we *are* computers. Electronic commands, chemical reactions, you name it."

"Computers don't have chemical reactions."

"Not yet. Do you know what the really strange part is?"

"No."

"That the people living back in the Middle Ages, people who knew nothing about electronics or neurology—no, farther back than that, the Neanderthals, the ones we think of as primitive—those people were the same advanced machines that we are. Even though they had no way of knowing that when they said something they were using their very own audio system, complete with sound boxes, speakers . . ."

"Oh, Arthur, cut it out."

"I told you, an adolescent. With the same sense of awe."

"But that isn't the kind you meant."

"No."

What I meant, he wanted to say, was a lightning flash of fear, a righteous trembling at the overpowering strangeness of things that presumably never struck other people as strange, things that at his age were supposed to seem normal.

He walked past the bistro owned by his friend Philippe, who didn't even know that he was back in Berlin. He never let anyone know, he just came waltzing in.

At the corner of Kantstrasse the light was red. He looked to the left, to the right, didn't see any cars, and was tempted to cross, but stayed where he was, feeling his body process contradictory commands: an odd kind of neural wave going to the wrong leg, so that one foot stayed on the curb while the other stepped off it. Through the snow he watched the silent group of people waiting on the other side of the crosswalk. At moments like these the difference between the Dutch and the Germans was plainly manifest. As a pedestrian in Amsterdam, you were an idiot if you didn't cross on red, and here you were one if you did, something the Germans didn't hesitate to point out: "Tsk, tsk, there goes another suicidal maniac."

He had asked Victor, a Dutch sculptor now living in Berlin, what he did when there were no cars in sight.

"I cross the street, except when there are children around. Got to set a good example, and all that."

As for himself, he had decided to make use of those odd, empty moments by doing what he called "instant meditation." In Amsterdam no self-respecting bicyclist had headlights, stopped on red, or went the right way down a one-way street. Dutch people always wanted to decide for themselves whether or not a rule applied to them—a mixture of Protestantism and anarchy that produced a stubborn kind of chaos. On his last visit he had noticed that cars, and sometimes even trams, had also started ignoring red lights.

"You've turned into a real German. Rules are rules. There's got to be *Ordnung*. The next time you ride the U-Bahn, listen to how they bark out commands: *Einsteigen bitte! ZURÜCKBLEIBEN!!* Well, we all know where obeying orders got them."

"The Dutch don't like being told what to do." "Germans like discipline." There seemed to be no end to the parade of prejudices.

"In Amsterdam the traffic is downright dangerous."

"Oh, honestly. It's nothing compared to how fast the Germans drive on the autobahn. Now that's aggression, one giant fit of rage."

The light turned green. The six snowy figures on the other side of the street simultaneously set themselves in motion.

Okay, you shouldn't generalize, but there is such a thing as a national character. How had it come about?

"From history," Erna had said.

What he found so fascinating about the idea of history was that it was based on a chemical compound of fate, chance, and design. The combination of these three elements produced a chain of events that produced another chain of events, which were said to be inevitable, or random, or to happen according to a secret plan that was not yet known to us, though by now things were getting pretty esoteric.

For a moment he considered going into the Tintenmaus to read the paper. At least it would be warm inside. He didn't know a single one of the customers, yet every face was familiar. They were people like him, people with time on their hands. Except that they didn't look like ads. There was a plate-glass window across the entire front of the Tintenmaus, with only a few rows of tables between it and the bar. No one ever sat at that bar in the way people usually do—the attraction of the outside world was too great. What you saw from the sidewalk was a row of staring figures, engrossed in one long, slow thought, a silent contemplation so heavy that it could be borne only by the incredibly slow sipping of enormous glasses of beer.

His face felt frozen, but this was one of those days when he welcomed the sensation: a mixture of self-imposed punishment and pleasure, such as one got from walking on the island of Schiermonnikoog in pouring rain or hiking to a deserted village in the Pyrenees in blistering heat. Sometimes joggers had a similar expression of exhaustion on their faces— an almost indecent form of public suffering, like Christs sprinting toward Golgotha. Jogging didn't suit him; it disturbed the rhythm of his thinking, or what he liked to call his thinking. It wasn't really, but back when he was fifteen or sixteen he had decided that it was the best way to describe the process going on in his head. In order for it to work, he needed to withdraw into himself. Ridiculous, of course, but it had become a habit.

In the beginning he had been able to do his thinking only in certain places; now he could do it anywhere. The one prerequisite was not having to talk. Roelfje had understood that. They had been able to walk for hours without saying a word. The two of them had never discussed it; he simply knew that she knew that this process was crucial to whatever was good about his work. He had no idea how the mechanism worked. After one of these sessions it was as if he were able to remember what he wanted to say in a film, not just the concept, but how to go about it. Remember—that was the right word. The camera angles, the lighting, the sequence, everything he did seemed to be accompanied by a strange feeling of déjà vu. Even the handful of movie shorts he'd made with film-school students had come about the same way, much to the despair of anyone who'd ever had to work with him. He'd start out with nothing, then make a death-defying leap—like a figure at the top of a tent hanging suspended in midair for several breathtaking minutes—and eventually land on his feet. The result usually bore little resemblance to the original proposal he'd submitted to get the job or grant, but they forgave him if it was good. Anyway, how could he describe the process? Somehow it involved emptiness—no other word would do. The day had to be empty. For that matter, so did he. Walking, he felt himself emptying out, as if he had become transparent or was no longer there, no longer belonged to the world of others, might as well not exist. Afterward he could never reproduce his thoughts in tangible form, though "thought" was too big a word to describe his indistinct, vague reveries, the jumbled images and snatches of sentences that passed through his head. The whole process resembled a surrealistic painting he'd once seen, whose title he couldn't remember. A female figure composed of fragments, climbing a set of stairs that stretched into infinity. She had not got very far, and the topmost step disappeared somewhere in the clouds. You could tell it was a woman even though the segments weren't connected and parts of her body were missing. Actually, if you stared at it for a while, it was downright creepy. Wisps of fog wound their way through her body where her eyes, her breasts, and her sex should have been. Amorphous software was inserting itself inside her—unrecognizable at this stage—but one day, if all went well, she might be transmuted into something he was unable to conceive of now.

At the corner of Goethestrasse the wind nearly took his breath away. Mommsen, Kant, Goethe—you were always in good company in this neighborhood. He walked past the Turkish espresso bar frequented by Victor, but didn't see him there today. Victor had made a point of what he called "descending deep into the German soul." He had talked to both victims and perpetrators, and also written a book about them without using their names, short pieces that touched the reader deeply because of their complete lack of overt pathos. Arthur was attracted to people who, as he liked to put it, "had more than one person," especially when those persons appeared to be opposites. Victor may have looked casual on the outside, but on the inside he housed an entire cast of characters: a pianist, a mountain climber, a cool observer of human life, a Wagnerian poet steeped in battles and blood, a sculptor, an artist whose eloquent drawings usually consisted of only a few lines and whose titles seemed, even today, to be a commentary on a war that had ended long ago. Berlin and the war had become Victor's hunting grounds. He rarely discussed his work, but when he did he would toss it off as a kind of joke, chalking it up to his childhood in occupied Holland, because "when you're a little boy, soldiers seem very,

very big," and he had seen a lot of soldiers because he and his parents had lived near a German army base. His clothes were vaguely reminiscent of a prewar vaudeville star—check jacket, silk scarf—and he wore a thin, David Niven mustache, shaped like two raised eyebrows. As if his appearance was meant to suggest that there never should have been a war, that the 1930s should have gone on forever.

A walk through Berlin with Victor often began with "Look, you see that? Those bullet holes?" At such moments he seemed to turn into the city itself, to pour forth its memories—a political murder, a roundup, a book-burning, the spot where Rosa Luxemburg had been thrown into the Landwehr Canal, the exact point the Russians had advanced to in 1945. He read the city like a book, a story of unseen buildings swallowed up by history—Gestapo torture chambers, the barren stretch of land where Hitler's plane had been able to land up to the very last day, everything told in a continuous, almost chanted recitative. Arthur had once suggested making a program about Walter Benjamin, which he wanted to call, using one of Benjamin's phrases, "The Soles of Memory." Victor would have been the perfect person to portray the flaneur, the aimless wanderer strolling down the streets of Berlin, because if anyone walked on the soles of memory, Victor did. But Dutch television wasn't interested in a program on Walter Benjamin. He could still picture the producer, a Tilburg University graduate with the usual mix of Marxism and Catholicism still clinging to him like a dirty nimbus—a musty middle-aged man in a musty office in a dried-up dream factory, where Dutch celebrities kept parading through the cafeteria with their carefully acquired indoor tans and throat-cancer voices. Arthur was out of the country so often that he was spared the necessity of remembering their names, but one glance was enough to know who was who.

"I know you have two polar opposites in your . . . head," the producer said (he had been about to say "soul"), "namely, action and reflection. But reflection doesn't get high ratings." The shattered idealism of the Marxist and the wily corruption of the Catholic who had sold himself to the highest bidder for the security of a pension plan—it continued to be an irresistible combination.

"That program you made in Guatemala, the one about the missing union officials, that was absolutely first-rate. And the Rio de Janeiro thing, about those kids shot by the police, the one you got the prize for in Ottawa, that's the kind of thing we're looking for. It cost us a fortune, but I think we finally broke even. The Germans bought it for Channel 3, along with some Swedish station. . . . Walter Benjamin! I used to be able to reel off entire passages . . ."

Arthur saw the bodies of eight or so boys and girls stretched out on marble slabs, grotesque feet poking out from under gray sheets, labels around their ankles, names on pieces of paper that would perish along with them one day, interchangeable, bits of words that had already begun to molder along with the broken bodies they supposedly named.

"Poor Benjamin," the producer continued. "What a tragic fate. And yet, if he hadn't lost hope, there in the Pyrenees, when the Spanish threatened to turn the group over to the Gestapo, he probably would have made it across the border. After all, the Spanish were fascist pigs, yet they didn't hand their Jews over to Hitler. But no, he had to go and kill himself. I don't know why, but suicide has always bothered me. If only he'd waited, he would have made it across, as the others did. Imagine what it would have been like if Benjamin had gone to America, if he'd been there along with Adorno and Horkheimer."

"Yes, just imagine," Arthur said.

"God knows what would have happened," the man mused further. "They probably would have wound up quarreling like the rest of the exiles."

Some people, Arthur thought, manage to look, even when they're fully dressed, as if they're lying in bed in rumpled pajamas and are never going to get up again. He glanced at the figure slumped by the window, then at the view: the opposite wing of the studio. So there's where they produce the crap, the B grade sludge that oozes through the channels and inundates the country, the place where Dutch imitation is mixed with the mud of the mighty transatlantic example. All of his acquaintances swore up and down that they never watched TV, but he could tell from idle bar chat and conversations with friends that they did.

He got up to leave, and the producer opened the door onto a room full of silent figures staring at their computers. Death would be infinitely preferable to this, he later remembered thinking, though that wasn't fair. What did he know about these people?

"What are they doing?" he asked.

"They're writing background material for news programs, panel discussions. The kind of stuff we hand our geniuses when they're obliged to talk about something they know nothing about, which is most of the time. Facts, historical analyses, that kind of thing. We condense the information, spoon-feed it to them."

"A spoonful at a time?"

"Not exactly. Only about a tenth of the material produced in this room ever gets used. Viewers can't handle more than that. The world's getting smaller every day, but most people think it's already too damn big. They wish it would just go away. In any case, they sure as hell don't want to be reminded of it."

"So what about my union officials?"

He could picture them as well. Photos on the desk of a human-rights organization in New York: hard, closed Indian faces.

"You want an honest answer? You're our alibi act. Besides, we've got a bunch of empty time slots that have to be filled. Everyone's sick and tired of Bosnia, but if you're dying to go to Bosnia..."

"I don't want to go back there."

"Then you could come up with something that'll interest at least the select few of a select few. That'll gain us some international prestige in the bargain. An award always looks good in the lobby. It's hard to get approval for Third World stuff these days, but in your case..."

"The Third World will be coming our way soon. Actually, it's already here."

"Nobody wants to hear that. They want to keep it at a distance."

Alibi act. "Boredom is the physical sensation of chaos," he'd read recently. No earthly reason for that to have popped into his head just now. Or was there? The figures in the outer office, those men and women—they weren't human. Flash! That one second of inhuman, bestial boredom, that dislike, hate, or fear, was somehow related to the monitors attached to those bodies: semimechanical dyads with fingers that gently clicked the keys that filled the monitors with words that would soon be scrolled away, but that for one brief moment represented all the chaos in the world. He tried to describe the sound of those keys in the bottomless silence. The nearest he could come was the gentle cluck of a sedated chicken. He watched the immaculate hands move over the keys. They're working, he thought, this was *work*. What had the producer said? Condense, spoon-feed. They dish up the data—fate's latest past tense. Data was Latin for "things that were given." But who gave them to us?

"I still wish I could make a program about Walter Benjamin," he said.

"Try the Germans," the producer replied. "They know you, and they know your work well enough by now."

"They want a program on drugs," Arthur said. "And they want to know why we still hate them."

"I don't hate them."

"If I tell them that, they won't want the program."

"Oh, well, thanks for coming. You know we're always on the lookout for good ideas. Especially yours. Soaring crime rates in Moscow, the Russian Mafia, that kind of thing. Think it over."

The door clicked shut behind him. He walked through the room as if he were walking through a church, with a feeling of total desolation. What right did he have to judge the people sitting there? Once again he was assailed by the same thought that came into his head now, in this other now, here in Berlin: What kind of person would he have been if he hadn't lost his wife and child?

"Thomas." It was Erna's voice. "If you avoid using his name, it means you want him out of your life."

"He is out of my life."

"He has a right to his name." Erna could be firm. Still, he'd never forgotten that conversation.

There was something diabolical about the question. What kind of person would he have been? He certainly wouldn't have had the freedom he had now, which clearly set him apart from others. Just the thought of it was enough to make him feel guilty, without knowing why. By now he was so used to not being tied down that he couldn't imagine any other life. Yet freedom was also barren, destitute. Well, so what? The same could be said of people who did have children and who, as he had once told Erna when he was drunk, "wouldn't have to die alone."

"Spare me the maudlin sentimentality, Arthur. I hate that."

He smiled. All these thoughts had brought him no farther than Steinplatz. Amazing how much you can think in the space of a few hundred yards. On the door of a tall house on Uhlandstrasse he saw a copper doorknob polished to within an inch of its life, with a dab of snow on top, like a dollop of whipped cream on a golden mound of ice cream. ("Aren't you ever going to grow up?") He leaned over to wipe off the snow and caught sight of himself: a plump dumpling, a lumpy midget, the hunchback of Notre-Dame. He inspected his swollen, misshapen nose, his two fish eyes swimming off to the side. He couldn't resist sticking out his tongue, the best way to chase away ghosts. But it wasn't supposed to be that kind of day; otherwise he might as well go get drunk. Today was supposed to be empty. He'd pass the time doing meaningless things, helped out by the snow—that well-known concealer—which would cover the anecdotal and the superfluous in a mantle of white.

Where do sudden urges come from? There were two paintings by Caspar David Friedrich that he had an immediate desire to see. Strange but moving canvases. Had there been a book about Friedrich in Schoeler's window? Not that he could remember. Hmm, Friedrich... He didn't particularly like the man's work, yet he could clearly picture those two paintings. The deserted ruins of an abbey, dripping with symbolism. Death and despair. And the other one—an almost idiotic landscape with purple mountains, mist, a jagged plain, and in the middle a tall, unlikely cliff topped by an even more unlikely cross. A thin cross, a slender cross—how on earth were you supposed to describe the thing? Anyway, it was taller than it should be, and at the foot of the cross was a woman in what appeared to be an evening gown, a lady who looked as if she had fled the ballroom of the Duke of P.

without her cloak and undertaken a grueling journey, in her delicate frock, to that preposterous cliff, where the crucified figure was hanging in unspeakable loneliness, bereft of mother and disciples, of Romans and high priests. It was too far away to see the expression on the faces. The woman was lending a helping hand to a man below her as he climbed the last few steps. She wasn't looking at him, and he had the back of a man who was never going to turn around. The painting seemed to call for either a reverent, ear-splitting silence or an iconoclastic roar of laughter that would bounce derisively off those purple cliffs. But Friedrich's closed world left no room for the latter interpretation—it sprang entirely from his own sullied twentieth-century soul. Not an ounce of irony in the man—the apotheosis of great longing. As he himself had said, Germans were serious people. Even so, one of his friends, who did have a good sense of humor, had written a book about Friedrich. Victor had explained to him why the men in Friedrich's paintings always had their backs to the viewer—something about a farewell gesture, turning your back on the world, he couldn't remember the exact words. Perhaps it would come to him if he looked at the painting, which was on display in Charlottenburg Palace, not far away.

"*Hilfe! Hilfe bitte!*"

A cry for help. He couldn't tell where it was coming from, which meant that whoever was calling—it sounded like a woman's voice—couldn't see him through the snow either, so she wasn't addressing him, but the whole world.

"Help! Help! Can somebody please help me?"

Blindly, he walked through the whirling white flakes to where the sound seemed to be coming from. The first thing the movie director in him noticed was the scene, the absurdity of it: a woman in a Salvation Army uniform kneeling by a black man who might or might not be dead. Homeless people, tramps, drifters, junkies, haranguers—in every part of the globe he went to, the streets were full of them. Ranting and raving, foraging for food, dressed in rags, caked with dirt, hair in matted tangles, they walked through the cities mutely or cursing or begging, like Stone Age creatures come back to remind humanity of something. But what? Something was always dying in this world, and they made it visible. He thought of them as having been transformed into the awe that struck him from time to time, yet he also realized that they exerted a strange, indefinable pull, as if you could simply lie down beside them, crawl into your cardboard box, good night, sleep tight, who knows if you'll wake in the morning. Time—if anything had been eliminated in these lives, it was time. Not the light and dark of day and night, but the premeditated time of purpose and direction. Time that was going somewhere had ceased to exist in these lives. They had surrendered themselves to their gradual decay, which would come sooner or later anyway. One day they would no longer get up, they would have to be picked up out of the gutter, like this man here.

But this one didn't want to be picked up. He lay, a heavy inert mass, in the arms of the Salvation Army woman, who was trying to get him to sit up. She was young, in her late twenties. Blue eyes in the pale face of a medieval saint. Cranach in the snow. Of course this had to happen to him. He fought down the desire to wipe the snow off her bonnet.

"Could you hold him while I phone for help? *Bitte.*"

In the mouths of some women, German was one of the most beautiful sounds on earth, but this was no time for such frivolity. Besides, the man stank. The sister, or whatever they were called in the Salvation Army, was apparently experienced, because the smell didn't seem to bother her, though it was all Arthur could do to keep from throwing up. The man, however, beat him to it, spewing blood and vomit just as he was being transferred to Arthur's arms.

"Oh God," said the woman, and it sounded like a prayer. "I'll be right back."

She disappeared into the blizzard. Arthur had knelt beside the man and pulled him up to a sitting position, his head on his chest. He watched the snowflakes nestle in the kinky gray hair, melt and glisten, only to be replaced by new flakes. With his right hand he scooped up a handful of snow and tried to wipe off the blood and vomit. He heard the traffic, the wet hiss of tires on Hardenbergstrasse. In a few hours there'd be a huge mess everywhere, muddy slush that would freeze as evening fell. Berlin, a village in the tundra. How had she ever found the poor man?

He asked her when she came back.

"When the weather's like this, we go out looking for them. We know where they usually hang out."

"Who did you call just now?"

"My colleagues."

An odd choice of words in this case. Did people ever have affairs with Salvation Army women? Her icy blue eyes looked dangerous. Cut it out, Daane. Here you are on your knees with a half-dead man in your arms. Just this once, try to feel you're part of humanity.

"*Scheisse*," said the black man without a trace of an accent. "*Scheisse, Arschloch, Scheisse.*"

"Calm down," the Salvation Army woman said, then proceeded to clean his mouth with snow.

"*Scheisse.*"

"There's no need for you to stay," she said. "Thanks for helping, but my colleagues will be here soon. I called them on the car phone."

Soldiers of Christ, he thought. There's always a war going on somewhere. The man opened his eyes, two bloodshot ocher-colored orbs. The world as a series of visions. At the end of his life, how many of these epiphanies would he have seen? Where did they all go?

"Beer," said the man.

"All right, all right."

Arthur had noticed before that whenever something unusual happened to him on one of his meditative days, he could think of it only in terms of clichés, the kind of thing everyone thinks—for example, that the strapping black body he had been holding in his arms had once been a child in a country in Africa, or even, God knows, America—all kinds of trite thoughts that led nowhere. It might have been better if the man had been left to die in the snow. They say you don't feel a thing. As it is, the well-meaning Christian soldier would drag him off to a hostel and stick him under a shower.

A black man in the snow—just the kind of thing that might have appealed to Caspar David Friedrich. His canvases always hinted at an abyss that had become obvious only later on in German history. It was as if the painter hadn't yet acquired the vocabulary, so he was forced to make do with peculiar crucifixions on mountaintops and abbey ruins, with monks transformed into bats, the bastard angels of decay. He heard the wail of an approaching siren. Through the snow he could see a vehicle with a rotating blue light.

"Over here!" called the woman in the bonnet. He struggled to his feet. The two men approaching through the snow looked like real soldiers. Time to leave. A quick rum on the corner, then on to Golgotha in the mountains. If you had nothing to do, you should stick to your original plan. He had no trouble visualizing the painting. The ambiguity in art was that it showed both the abyss and the seeming order stretching across it.

He walked toward Schillerstrasse. There were only two cities you absolutely had to see on foot: Paris and Berlin. No, of course that wasn't true. He'd been walking around places his entire life. But Berlin was different. He wondered if that was because of the dividing line between the two halves of the city, which made walking seem like a journey, a pilgrimage. In the case of the Seine, the line was blurred by bridges, yet you always knew you were heading somewhere else, crossing a border, so that, like most Parisians, you tended to stay on your own side of the river, in your own domain. Here, things were different. Berlin had suffered a stroke years ago, and its effects could still be felt. People who went from one side to the other walked through a strange rictus, a scar that would remain visible for a long time to come. Here the dividing element was not water, but that unfinished form of history known as politics, when the paint hasn't yet dried. To anyone attuned to it, the line could almost be experienced as a physical sensation.

He came to the vast plain of Ernst-Reuter-Platz and noticed that the cast-iron streetlights on Bismarckstrasse ("all that was left of Speer"—Victor) were throwing a golden glow onto the whirling, scudding snow beneath them. He shivered, though not from the cold. How long had it been since his first visit to Berlin? He'd been a trainee at the time, and the Dutch public broadcasting service, the NOS, had sent him to report on a conference in East Germany. Already it was hard to explain what things were like back then. It was impossible to imagine if you hadn't lived through it, and you didn't want to be reminded of it if you had. History is full of periods like that—years in which events race ahead of themselves, in which page 398 has long forgotten what was written on page 395 and the reality of a few years ago seems ridiculous rather than dramatic. But he hadn't forgotten it, the chill, the menace. He had obediently stood on a viewing platform along with the rest of the crew and looked across the stretch of no-man's-land to the other world, the one he'd been filming just the day before. Even at the time it had seemed unreal. No; it had been impossible to talk about it rationally then, and it still was. If the telltale stones, the ruins, the construction sites, and the gaps hadn't been there, you could pass it all off as a bizarre figment of your imagination.

Later he had often come back to this imagined city, sometimes for several months at a time. He liked to visit the friends he had made, and he managed to get an occasional assignment from the local broadcaster. Yet this hardly explained why he was secretly attached to Berlin rather than to much more pleasant or exciting cities, like New York or Madrid. It must have something to do with its magnitude; on his walks through Berlin, he knew exactly what he meant by that word, though he'd never been able to explain it satisfactorily to others. *Ich bin überall ein bisshen ungern,* he thought. He could identify with that quote, which is presumably why he'd stored it on the hard disk of his brain. Underlying that "slight feeling of unease" was a strain of melancholy that usually lay untapped. And here in Berlin it seemed as if his own melancholy combined with another, stronger, more dangerous element that could perhaps be thought of as melancholy, but that was on an entirely different scale: broad boulevards big enough to accommodate entire armies, grandiose buildings standing beside oddly vacant lots, the knowledge of what had been said and done in those now-empty lots, an accumulation of the causal and intertwined actions of both victims and perpetrators, a memento you could wander around in for years. The Berliners themselves, probably out of a sense of self-preservation, didn't have time for such reflection. They were too busy bulldozing the scars. What kind of memory would you need to be able to deal with it? It would be unbearable, it would collapse under its own weight, swallow everything in sight, suck the living down with the dead.

The traffic on Otto-Suhr-Allee had thinned to such a trickle that you'd think an emergency warning had gone out, urging people to stay at home. The sidewalks were virtually empty, and the cold Siberian wind had free rein. In the distance he saw the first snowplows, their neurotic lights flashing a deadly amber glow. The few cars that were still on the road also had on their bright lights. Just then the picture of a Greek island floated into his consciousness. Where had that come from? But he was used to it; things like that happened to him all the time. Suddenly, out of nowhere, an image—a church, a country lane, a handful of houses along a deserted coastline— would pop absurdly into his head. The scene would be familiar, something he'd seen before but couldn't quite place, as if he carried a nameless but unforgotten globe around in his head, as if he'd once existed on another planet and the names had been erased. Sometimes, as now, if he put his mind to it, he could force his memory to reveal more than a few vague puzzle pieces from a life masquerading as his own.

He had eaten in a Greek restaurant the night before, so he assumed it had something to do with the music they'd been playing, and he tried to remember the melody of one of the songs he'd hummed along with. A choir of dark, low, beseeching voices, the lyrics half sung, half spoken. His waiter had known the words, had recited them along with the tape. But when he'd asked the man what the song was about, he'd thrown up his hands and said, "It's an old story, very complicated, very sad," and walked off in time to the music, loudly intoning the words, as if to catch up with the voices. All the while, the music had circled around the room— threatening one moment and resigned the next, almost pastoral, melancholy, a commentary on a dramatic event that had taken place long ago, leaving traces of great suffering. Aha, he thought, so that was it, he'd been seeing the coast of Ithaca, the bay of Phorcys, the hills like huge dark animals, the sea incapable of imagining such things as waves, at least not on that particular day, a deceptive onyx that would crack if you set foot on it. The Greeks had a word for that motionless water: *galini*. At last the other thoughts were beginning to come, he was again being "called," as he put it. Not that he would ever tell anyone, not even Erna, or at any rate not in those exact words. Ithaca, the first big trip he and Roelfje had ever made, sometime in the late seventies. "Called"—a ridiculous word. Buried in the mire of the past. She wasn't literally calling him, and yet she was. He knew she was nearby, she had a message for him, she wanted him to think of her.

At first he used to block out her summons, to think of them as a dangerous pitfall, but after a while he started carrying on entire conversations with her, sharing a kind of intimacy that he had with no one else and that took his breath away. She didn't call him often, but she hadn't forgotten him, unlike Eurydice in the Rilke poem Arno had once read to him, the one in which she no longer recognizes Orpheus when he comes to rescue her from the underworld and wonders who the stranger is, in that one poignantly uttered "Who?" Why had he thought of her only now, and not last night, when he'd heard the music? Who was in charge of the timing? And then that other alarming thought: Would he still recognize her? The dead don't grow old, they stay the same age forever. What does change is the possibility to think about them the way you do about a living person. Present, absent. One time she had asked him why he loved her. An impossible question with a thousand different answers, and all he'd been able to come up with was "Because of your tempered gravity." Tempered gravity! But it was perfect. Every image he still had of her fit into those two words. He meant the kind of gravity you sometimes see in Italian Renaissance paintings, delicate fair-haired women who radiate light and yet seem totally remote. If one of those women actually moved, you'd jump.

But it was better to keep thoughts like that to yourself. Also the word "tempered," which got you nowhere even though it fit her to a T. And of course he still remembered her reply, in the form of a question.

"As in *The Well-Tempered Clavier*?"

"Sort of."

They had stayed in a pension, the Mentor, and swum in the cold water of the bay. Not many tourists, no foreign newspapers. While he roamed the hills among the holly oaks and olive trees, he had pretended that nothing had changed since the time of Homer, that Odysseus had walked here and seen the same things that he, Arthur Daane, was now seeing. Of course the sea was wine-dark, of course the ship on the horizon was that of Odysseus, of course the ramshackle hut before them belonged to the swineherd Eumaeus. Roelfje had brought along her copy of *The Odyssey,* and in the sun, on a hillside of poppies and clover, she had read parts of it aloud to him.

In school Odysseus had been his hero, and when he heard the same words and names being spoken in that very place, he understood for the first time the meaning of the expression *genius loci.* Even if it hadn't happened in that exact spot, it had still happened here. In that field with the stones and tumbled-down terraces, that's where the returning king, disguised as a beggar, had visited the swineherd and been reunited with his son.

His son—in what kind of "now" did he find himself? That was the dangerous part of dealing with the dead. Sometimes they gave you back a moment. For one brief instant you felt you could reach out and touch them . . . but then the moment that should have come next turned to dust, disappeared, ran smack into the wall of time. The "now" in Berlin and the "then" in Ithaca, which had briefly wrapped itself in the guise of "now," had tricked him, the "now" of this moment pretending to be a place in "then," just as—such was the power of Homer's epic poem—when he and Roelfje had been there. Instead of reading the adventurous parts he used to admire so much, she had read the scenes that took place in Ithaca, the ones involving the old nurse Euryclea, whom Laertes, the father of Odysseus, had bought for twenty oxen. Years later Telemachus sets off to find his father, Odysseus, and the night before he leaves, Euryclea goes to his room. She packs his clothes, folds them, smoothes out the wrinkles. You can picture her aged hands on the garments, see her leave the room, clasp the silver doorknob. You can hear the bolt slide in the lock. It had been another world, one in which servants were part of the family. You weren't supposed to feel nostalgic about those days, but he had noticed that families had often been torn apart by the departure of their servants. There, in that field, the world had not yet come unraveled. Despite death and destruction, despite the labyrinthine journey, Homer had spun the threads of return. Return, reunification, man and wife, father and son. Arthur quickly suppressed the thought flickering through his mind. Sentimentality, he had quickly learned, got you nowhere with the dead. Once death had struck, they were incapable of action, but since they didn't know it, you couldn't discuss it with them. Natural laws applied only to those who were left behind, which meant that no Telemachus would ever go looking for him, and that he'd somehow have to get the tune from that Greek restaurant out of his head. However, he now knew that one of the ideas he'd been mulling over in that stone-studded field would be with him forever: the thought that the two of them on that hillside had been woven into the story, that the poet had included them in his epic. Not by name, of course, but by virtue of the role they played. It didn't matter whether Odysseus and Eumaeus had ever existed, whether their hands had ever touched those stones. What was important was that they, the future readers who spoke the words in a language the writer could never have known, had been woven into the tale. That's what made the stones, the path, the landscape so magical. That, and not the opposite. It is such moments that make "now" eternal—the old woman over there with her goats is Euryclea, wanting to tell the tale one more time, how the hero came home, how she recognized him, how she watched the son depart, take the path down to the harbor, on a day like today, and therefore today, their day, because a poem is only finished when the last reader has read it or listened to it.

"Slow down, Daane."

Had he thought that, or actually heard it? "Slow down, Daane." In any case it helped—the flood of thoughts was checked. Only bits were given back to you, fragments, never again the whole.

"You'd be smothered." That was Erna. And that other voice, whoever it belonged to, had brought him back from Ithaca to Otto-Suhr-Alle, where a signpost for bus Number 145 was sticking out above the snow. An old woman was sitting in the glassed-in shelter. She waved, and he waved back before it occurred to him that she hadn't been waving, but beckoning him over, and that it was more of an urgent summons than a request. She looked ancient, ninety if she was a day. Ought to stay inside in weather like this. Suppose she really *was* ninety? One hand clutched the plate-glass wall, the other an alpenstock.

"Do you think any more buses are going to come?"

"No. You shouldn't wait any longer."

"I've been waiting for almost an hour."

She said it in the tone of someone who's been through

worse. Had she cheered Goebbels in the Sportpalast? Maybe, maybe not. You never knew. Husband killed on the Eastern Front, house blown to bits by a bomb from a Lancaster. You knew nothing about people. All you could say for sure was that she must have been in her forties back then.

"Do you think the U-Bahn is still running?"

She had a thin, high, imperious voice. Nurse at the front? Or cabaret singer in the twenties?

"I don't know. We can check."

Where are you going? A question he should have asked, but didn't.

"I can take you to the station at Richard-Wagner-Platz."

"Fine."

It's my day to save lives, he thought as he all but lifted her out of the bus shelter. It wasn't far. They walked past Charlottenburg's town hall, keeping as close to it as they could. A tall black building that rose up like a cliff. She held his arm in a firm grip while he cleared a path for her with his right foot.

"Very kind of you."

The sort of remark to which there was no reply. If he'd been a member of the new Romanian Mafia, what would he have done? Except that they didn't go out in this kind of weather.

"They would have snatched her purse." Victor's voice. This snow harbored various ghosts.

"How old are you?"

The question had just slipped out.

"Eighty-nine." She stopped to catch her breath. "But longevity is not a virtue." Then she added, "You're not German."

"No, I'm from Holland."

The hand tugged at his sleeve. "We did you a great injustice."

Not me personally, he wanted to say, but didn't. The

subject was too complicated. He hated it when Germans started talking about guilt, if only because he never knew what to say in return. After all, he wasn't the entire Dutch population and she hadn't done anything to him.

He might have answered that Holland had had the largest contingent of Waffen-SS volunteers of any occupied country. But that wouldn't have been good either.

"I'm too young," he finally replied. "Born in 1953."

She paused by a helmeted dwarf and a giant king with a sword resting at his feet, a warrior.

"My husband was a friend of Ossietzky's," she said. "He died at Dachau."

Actually, the word the Germans always used in these situations was *geblieben*—stayed, also when someone had "fallen" at the front. Fallen, stayed. Had she really said that?

"He was your age."

"A communist?"

She gestured, flicking her wrist as if she were throwing something in the air. Even as the image occurred to him, he knew it wasn't right, because her gesture, which would be impossible to duplicate, had been more subtle, only a slight movement of the hand. Still, something had definitely been disposed of, something that may have referred to all that had happened after the war. She would never say the words, and he wouldn't dream of asking. Just as he could have confided that his father had been a communist, but didn't. They were almost there. Side by side they shuffled past the display window of a tanning salon, where a cardboard cutout of a woman in a yellow bikini was surrendering herself to the piercing rays of the sun. She was beautiful, but had a ridiculous tan.

The old woman stopped at the top of the stairwell. Down below they could hear the thunder of the subway. So it was still running. Someone had sprinkled ashes on the steps.

Civic duties. He escorted her to the platform. No, she didn't need a ticket, she had a pass. He hated to ask, but found himself asking anyway. "Do you know where you're going? I mean, the bus was heading somewhere else."

"Perhaps I wasn't going anywhere, and a detour will get me there just the same."

No argument there.

"And after that?"

"At the other end, somebody will help me, as you did."

She took a few steps, turned and said, "It's all poppycock." She smiled, and, for one split second that no camera could have captured, you could see her face as it once must have been, at some random moment in her life, though he had no idea what that moment might have been. Most of the living were as inaccessible as the dead. Humming "it's all poppycock," he went back up to the snow.

In less than a minute he had been changed back into a vague white shape. Dachau, Napoleon in Moscow, the Two Grenadiers, Stalingrad, Field Marshal Paulus—this was more or less his train of thought as he neared the vanilla walls of Charlottenburg Palace. The cloakroom attendant held his coat as if it had dog shit on it. He peered through the windows in the back, which looked out over the highly regimented ornamental gardens. The circular fountain that children sailed their boats in during the summer wasn't working now. Instead, a hopeless half-erection of gray ice was hanging crookedly from the spout. The path was lined with bushes in planters, now covered up against the winter cold—snowmen in battle array. A bit farther, where Prussian order had less of a hold on nature, tall trees stood like sentries, while an army of grayish black ravens flew back and forth. He had once filmed an interview with Victor in this garden, which is how they got to know each other. The interviewer had been way out of her depth. She had asked him to talk about typical

German traits and elaborate on the differences between the Dutch and the Germans, and Victor had answered that the Germans talked about their blood circulation all the time and the Dutch didn't; on the other hand, the Dutch were prone to back problems and were a major exporter of tasteless tomatoes. The girl had looked helplessly at Arthur and asked if they should shoot the scene over again. He had put his finger to his lips and slowly shaken his head.

"Why not?"

"It'd be a waste of time."

Out of the corner of his eye he watched Victor wander off toward the palace, where he stopped to squint up at something that had caught his eye.

"Why?"

"I don't think he wants to answer stock questions. Everybody always asks about the Germans and the Dutch. It gets to be a bore."

"Look!" said Victor at that moment six years ago. "You see those statues up there?"

High above them, dancing and swaying at the roof's edge, was a row of bare-breasted females in billowing skirts. Each plaster figure was holding an object that was meant to represent the liberal arts—a compass, a lyre, a mask, a book. At that distance he couldn't get a good shot of them, so he filmed Victor instead. Victor holding his hands in front of his face.

"They're faceless—or haven't you noticed?"

"Have they deliberately been effaced? Did the Russians do that?" the interviewer asked.

"The Russians didn't pass through here, sweetheart. No, they were made that way. Ovals without eyes. Just like de Chirico. You don't need a face when you're a symbol. As you can plainly see."

When Victor had uttered those words, he'd been standing only a few yards away from where Arthur was now. One more bit of the past to add to the rest. And not even a very sad or significant bit. If all went well, he'd be seeing Victor tonight, so that couldn't be the reason he was thinking of it now. So what was the reason? It had been a meaningless moment, one scene out of the hundreds of interviews he'd filmed; if he had to remember them all, he'd go crazy. Victor had deliberately screwed up the interview, there was no doubt about that. But it was more important to know why he'd remembered that fragment. Was it because a person's character had been revealed for the first time?

"If you don't mind, I'd like to ask you a few questions about Dutch-German relations anyway. That's my assignment. A lot of Dutch people find the idea of German unity, of a new and even bigger Germany, very threatening...."

"Oh, bah," Victor said. "Isn't it incredible? No face, and yet a mask."

How is it possible for his memory to melt the snow, make the fountain flow, the flowers blossom? The soundman, he recalled, had been wearing a jacket, but he and Victor and the girl had on summer clothes. Of her he had only the vaguest recollection. In other words, she had been faceless. So where does that leave Victor, who never allowed even the slightest sign of emotion to show on his face? The mere sight of that empty spot out there in the snow, where they were no longer standing, had been enough to conjure up that summery conversation. That's how it always went: a world full of empty spots, in which you showed up in a variety of configurations, talking, loving, quarreling, and all the while a ghostly version of yourself hovered over those empty spaces, an invisible, worn-out doppelgänger without any atoms to fill the spaces, a former presence that had become an absence and was now mingling with the other absences on that spot, the others in the realm of the dead and the disappeared. You were only truly dead when you couldn't even remember disappearing.

"In Heaven a million souls can fit into a matchbox." One of Erna's gems.

"Where'd you get that one?"

"From my mother." Erna's mother had been married three or four times, and that had apparently been her answer when Erna had asked her which of her husbands she wanted to be reunited with after her death.

Once the interviewer and the soundman had cleared off—"Thank you; the network's going to be absolutely delighted"—Victor had taken Arthur to the Mausoleum in the park behind the palace.

Spring, darting dogs, a violin player sawing away to the accompaniment of the mechanical orchestra locked inside the ghetto blaster at his feet. ("Tiny little men and women who'll never get out of there. A veritable cesspool of vice and inbreeding. Bah. By the way, you don't play badly.") Victor in an expensive leather jacket that fit him like the finest satin, with a knotted scarf around his neck—blue polka dots this time. Just like Lou Bandy. ("You mean to tell me you know who Lou Bandy was?")

"There's something I'd like to show you. Call it one of life's lessons. And spare us the tears, please."

Lou Bandy—it was indeed a wonder that he knew the singer's name. Old 78s, from way back when. A strange, tinny voice, like the ones in old newsreels, as if people used to have different voices, as if voices could become extinct. Victor knew every single one of his songs.

Oh, I'm in love with Rub-Down Rosie,
She makes me feel so nice and cozy,
For charley horse or achin' spine,
She's got the touch, it's so divine,
Satisfaction guaranteed...

"The 1930s. Turned on the gas and killed himself after the war. Couldn't bear his dwindling popularity. Always that trademark scarf. And brilliantine, eh? Pomade. Pomaded hair—also gone the way of the dodo."

He had recorded the entire sequence, now being replayed without sound. Not only did Victor have a deadpan face, but also he could walk without expression, almost like a robot, and he led Arthur along the back of the palace with that same lack of emotion, as if being followed by the camera was the most ordinary thing in the world. It had been a long time since he'd seen the documentary, but he remembered a shot of long-stemmed geraniums—blood-red, tied up with stakes—which made it seem as though they weren't ordinary flowers, but a rare breed that had been placed there deliberately. A prop for a nightmare. Victor turned down a side path, toward a kind of temple, in front of which were two marble pools with a tangle of rhododendrons planted in a semicircle around them, the blaze of purple so bright it hurt your eyes. The Mausoleum itself was closed. Bronze doors, marbled Doric columns, the rustle of tall trees.

"That's where she's buried," Victor said, and he whipped a postcard out of his pocket, a magic trick. A picture of a young woman. Arthur looked at Victor, but his face was blank. Was he being sentimental, was he laughing at him, or what? He didn't know how he was supposed to react. She was beautiful, but there was also a certain innocence about her. A loosely fitting white gown, gathered under the creamy breasts and tied with a pale-blue ribbon. Victor had thrust the card under his nose so insistently that he'd had to put down the camera. One thing was certain: the woman was looking at you as if she wanted something from you. Tiny curls peeped out from under a heavy, jewel-encrusted crown, and below her face the creamy skin of her neck and breast took on a rosy glow. Straight nose, too-small ears, the mouth a deeper rose, turned up slightly at the corners. Strangest of all were the eyes. A bright blue that matched the gems in her crown and the blue of her cloak, which seemed to slip invitingly off her shoulders. Large, wide-spaced eyes, almost lashless.

He flipped over the postcard. Queen Louisa of Prussia, 1804. Josef Grassi. So what am I supposed to do with the thing? Arthur thought.

"Do you always carry this postcard around with you?"

Only later had he found out that Victor used it to test people, at any rate those he deemed worthy.

"No," said Victor. "You invited me here. And I always visit her when I come here. I have girlfriends all over the world. They're always happy to see me."

His face remained perfectly expressionless.

"I bought that postcard for you. I'm not the jealous type."

Arthur still didn't know how he was supposed to react.

"You're wondering what's left of her," said Victor, pointing toward the sarcophagus. "Not a pleasant sight, I suspect. Probably all dried up. A pity. Nothing lasts forever. But if nobody had painted her, we wouldn't have been able to look at her."

Arthur glanced at the card, and later, after they'd gone inside the palace, at the painting itself. He had to admit, there was something about the woman, and not just her obvious sex appeal. It seemed as if she wanted to step out of the painting, as if she couldn't stand having that frame around her. Of

course the pin on her shoulder had been put there to be un-
clasped, just as the ribbon looked as if it could be untied in
one fluid motion. She wouldn't object, the painting seemed
to say. Or perhaps it was merely the lasciviousness of the
painter, who knew he could rely on the lasciviousness of the
viewer. Unfortunately, she never took her eyes off you.

"It's not as if it's a beautiful painting," Arthur said.

Victor let his remark pass. His head was practically touching the canvas. You saw haircuts like his only in old movies,
thought Arthur. Fred Astaire. Cary Grant. Impeccable, that
was the word for it. Not a hair out of place.

"A lamb being led to slaughter. You don't find her kind of
woman anymore. I don't know a single woman with that
same air. Very confusing. It's become extinct. See for yourself.
Some salamander is dying out, and the world screams bloody
murder. But let a certain facial expression go by the wayside
and you don't hear a peep out of 'em. Things are dying out
all around us. Well, Mr. Cameraman, that ought to give you
pause for thought."

"It does."

No, he hadn't said that. Not then. He'd merely listened.

"Can you imagine how this woman must have walked?"
said Victor. "No, you can't. It's something airhead actresses
in period plays try to imitate. Like the Kleist play I saw last
week. Clothes don't become extinct. They can be copied or
saved, so we're all right on that score. But what does die out
is the way people moved in those clothes. The fabric falls differently when the movement is different. This woman could
never have worn a bikini. She didn't have the right walk for
it, it hadn't been invented yet."

"Who did invent it?"

"Oh," said Victor, "time did. Or capitalism, though that
amounts to the same thing. Working women, the production
process, cars, jeans. Not to mention shorts. Women dressed

like little boys—very peculiar. Smoking, heart attacks. So her kind of expression dies out. Maybe it had to. Take another look. That painting is downright mean."

He leaned closer, near the perfect curve of her right breast.

"A question from the sculptor: Where do you think the nipple is?"

"There," said Arthur, and pointed. Immediately an alarm went off, and a blue-uniformed guard came running over, yelling something in incomprehensible, staccato German.

"That's one thing that hasn't died out," said Victor. "I told you it was mean."

Even before the man had reached them, Victor had turned toward him, the very picture of contrition.

"My friend here is inexperienced. He's not used to museums. I'll make sure it doesn't happen again." After the man had walked away, he continued, "But that was the right place. Mathematically speaking, rather than biologically, since that's impossible to guess. Very soft, very pink, almost a blush. Nipples like that have also become extinct, by the way. The total opposite of those you see on nude beaches today—feisty little nubs. Wind and weather. Or push buttons, as they mutate to mechanical women."

"What do you mean exactly?" Arthur asked. "An obsolete form of submissiveness, or availability, or what?"

"I don't know that I mean anything," Victor said. "Maybe just the past. Besides, the availability is greater these days, or so I'm told."

This sparked a new set of questions that Arthur was reluctant to ask. After all, he barely knew the man. The next day the shoot had taken place in Victor's studio—ominous objects in reddish stone, solid, heavy, rough to the touch. A far cry from the man who made them, and not connected to the past, unless it was to some prehistoric era, the sacred artifacts of a vanished tribe. This man could never have created those objects. Arthur could still recall one figure, that of a horse, made out of what looked like volcanic rock. Its head bent, on the verge of death. No tail, no hooves, a symbolic horse rather than a real one. The blackened surface of the rock gave the animal an aura of sanctity, made it seem like some prehistoric idol.

He had said that, but Victor had looked at him the way you look at a child who's just said "pee" and "poop."

"Not an art connoisseur, I hope?"

Then, then, then. Right now he had the choice of turning left, to the royal chambers, or right, where the Friedrichs were displayed. After all, that's what he had come here for. If he went to the left, he'd be able to see Louisa's portrait again. Indecent, the way paintings stayed the same year after year. He knew exactly what he would feel, and that's not what he was looking for today. He'd been loath to mention it at the time, and maybe it was preposterous, but deep down he believed that Roelfje and this woman might have walked the same way. Demure, that was the word. Demure. Once he said it, he felt that the word no longer existed.

"Dying out," Victor had said. "Packed off to a reservation."

"What is?"

"Oh, Schubert lieder. You have to read the score and imagine what they must have sounded like back then."

"But they're still being sung today."

"Not in the same way. Read a Jane Austen novel. That's where you can still find demure women."

He tore himself away from the window. The sky was nearly black. It seemed to get dark in Berlin earlier than anywhere else. It was only one-thirty in the afternoon, for God's sake. As for the portrait and its resemblance to Roelfje, it wasn't just a matter of demureness. There was something else that had to be taken into account—a certain provocativeness, even if it was only hinted at, even if it was no different than the twentieth-century horniness of a viewer who had never seen a demure look in his entire life. One time someone had said to him, "Your wife makes me think of that parable in the Bible, you know the one about the ten virgins with their lamps," but that reminded him of Amsterdam, and Amsterdam was the last place he wanted to be right now. To the right, then, to Caspar David Friedrich.

It was a Friedrich kind of day, he thought. But it was disappointing, for that very reason. Outside, the sky was getting gloomier by the minute, a perfect match for the paintings he'd come to see. He went toward them as if he were being guided there, though he could feel his body resisting. Why the hell had he wanted to come here? Friedrich's world was a far cry from his own, yet he felt extraordinarily drawn to it.

Another idiot like me, he thought as he stood in front of *Monk by the Sea*. What was the man doing there in that godforsaken landscape? Penance, lonely lamentation? Those thin white stripes on that churning dark-green water—were they seagulls? breakers? rays of light? The man's body was curved at a strange angle. Apparently he was no more anxious to be there than the person staring at him over an abyss of two hundred years. What goes on in a painter's head when he paints a canvas like that? The sand on the dunes was so fine and so white that it looked like snow, the horizon a straight line under a mass of gathering clouds—a barricade cutting off any thoughts of escape. And the woman he had wanted to see again, the luminous figure in his memory—how had she actually reached the mountaintop? Truly an exultation in the most literal sense. She was being held captive by the *craquelé,* a butterfly in a net. Hadn't anyone ever been tempted to take a knife to the painting, if only because they couldn't stand that insufferable lack of irony? Attraction, repulsion—it definitely had something to do with the German soul, whatever that might be. Wilhelm Meister's despair, Nietzsche's weeping on the neck of a coach horse, Friedrich's paintings, Kleist's double suicide, Anselm Kiefer's metal collages, and Botho Strauss's Druidic "goat songs"—they were all related somehow, a dark brooding unsuited to people from the wide-open spaces of Holland. So what was the attraction? The next painting showed a deserted abbey in an oak forest, under a menacing sky.

"You forgot Wagner," Victor said one time when they were discussing it. Victor never missed the Bayreuth Festival if he could help it.

"Can you imagine an English Wagner? Or a Dutch Nietzsche? The Dutch wouldn't know what to do with someone like that. Anything out of the ordinary gets ridiculed."

"That would apply to Hitler too."

"Exactly. He shouted too loud and had a funny mustache. Not the kind of thing that endears you to your neighbors. Even our queen rides a bicycle. Hitler didn't keep his curtains open so the whole world could look in. The Dutch don't like that. We want to know if Mrs. Hitler has vacuumed the living room. As you said, Holland doesn't have mountains. Everything's out in the open. No mountains, no caves. Nothing to hide. No dark places in the soul. Mondrian. Clear colors, straight lines. Canals, dikes, polders. No caverns, no abysses."

"Sometimes it's better to be without."

"Obviously. Anyway, brooding has to be dark. So far there have always been enough antidotes."

"Not during Weimar."

"Time for a history lesson? Do you remember what Hein Donner, the chess grand master, had to say on the subject? That Holland should thank God on bended knee that Germany had been willing to involve it in World War II—because that finally got us out of the nineteenth century. Besides, the Dutch weren't half as heroic as they claim to be. If there are two kinds of people I can't stand, it's Dutch people who think that, just because we've spent the last four hundred years disagreeing with each other, we've invented democracy, and Germans who are always beating their breasts and shouting mea culpa. And before you ask, yes, of course there's such a thing as guilt. But not for those who didn't actually do anything."

"To hear you talk, it just happened to them."

"It just happened to all of us. Egad, this is turning into a real conversation."

"Still, a Voltaire or a Cervantes might have helped."

They were back to where they had started: irony, or the lack of it. Irony had disappeared from Germany along with the Jews. The Germans were left to themselves, not something you'd wish on any society. Irony, distance, breathing space—the discussion had ended with words to that effect. Except for Victor's final comment:

"Boring, eh?"

Once again he stared at the abbey. One wall was still intact. A tall Gothic window let in light that couldn't be explained by that sliver of a moon. Ruins, fallen tombstones, bare ghost-shaped trees, metaphysical light, a cross perched crookedly on a grave—it was all there. Darkness and despair, the hunting grounds of the German soul, which finally, at the close of this mad century, had run out of game. Whether because of the new clarity of thought, the disillusionment of defeat, the double punishment of partition, or simply, as elsewhere, the ultimate triumph of money, he didn't know.

The paintings in the next rooms were inexpressibly dull. Coppery sunsets, harmless forests, bubbling waterfalls, virtuous women, devoted dogs—the world without original sin. You had to grant Friedrich that much: at least he'd had a suspicion. In that sense Victor was probably right. Art is nothing without a sense of foreboding. Not that it had to be beaten into you with a sledgehammer, but the forces of darkness did exist.

"And in that case you need more than irony."

No, it hadn't been Victor who'd said that. He looked at his watch. Two-thirty. He walked to the cloakroom, with no clear idea of what he was going to do next. Through the windows on the south side, he saw another snowplow go by. The rotating amber light seemed to be trying to set the fast and furious snowflakes on fire.

Thomas. There was no protection from the dead, no matter how young they were. Thomas, seeing snow for the first time. He must have been about three. They'd wakened him from his nap and carried him into the backyard to see the miracle. But he'd shrieked and cried and buried his face in Roelfje's chest. Arthur remembered his exact words: "Don't make me look, don't make me look!"

It had been so long ago, yet he could still hear that shrill high voice. Amazing. How could faces gradually disappear, bow out, refuse to show themselves anymore, while one short sentence, one sound bite, could be preserved through all those years?

Outside, and fast. The snow pelted against his body, his hair, his eyes. He wiped away the wet crystals and looked up. He had to. Victor might have his painted mistresses, but he had his golden angel. High above the palace dome, balancing on a golden globe, she danced in the cold, her bare breasts lashed by the snow. Perhaps she could see her sister, the angel of peace atop the column in the Grosser Stern, likewise made of gold. Female symbols, whether they represented Peace or Victory, were always placed as high and as far away as possible.

We always wonder why you wonder so little. We're only here to accompany you, but if we were actually allowed to live, we would spend more time meditating. One thing we can't understand is how you slip into your existence without giving it another thought. And how little you know about the infinite possibilities available to you. No, don't worry—we're not going to interrupt this story often. Only four or five times, and never for long. Bear with us. In the meantime we are able to follow his every move. There are still no buses, though he just noticed a snowplow coming down Spandauer Damm. The plow clears a narrow strip, and he walks in its wake, as if his path is being swept by lackeys. The snow forms a wall on either side of him, so that he seems to be walking through a white trench. However, what we want to say is this: Even though you are mortal, even though you are allotted only a finite amount of time and space, the fact that even one small brain can ponder eternity, or the past, allows you to lay claim to vast amounts of time and space. That's the mystery. Each and every one of you can, if you wish, colonize any part of the world, any era. You're the only creatures in the entire universe who can do that, and all because of your ability to think. Eternity, history, God— all products of your mind. So many, in fact, that you've lost sight of yourselves. Everything is real, and yet at the same time everything is also an illusion. That makes life difficult. To make matters worse, the past is constantly shifting—yesterday's heroes turn into today's villains, as if time is exploding behind you. If you want to find out more, you have to move backward, against the flow of time, while simultaneously moving forward. As a result, you never get anywhere. But you're wondering who *we* are. Think of us as the chorus, as observers who can see further than you can but are powerless to intervene, though perhaps the people and events we're following exist only because we're watching. Look, he's reached Richard-Wagner-Platz, the U-Bahn station where he left the old woman just a few hours ago. In the meantime, she has died, and the homeless man is in critical condition. But the man trudging behind the snowplow has no way of knowing that. That's one of your limitations, and perhaps it's better that way.

Just as Arthur Daane started down the steps to the underworld, he heard an ambulance go by, its siren blaring like a brass band. It was almost pleasant down below—he liked the semidarkness of the U-Bahn, the thundering trains with their whoosh of cold air. Most of all he liked the anonymous fellowship, people sizing each other up with their eyes, creating defensive zones around themselves so that they could explore, classify, and condemn from the safety of their ramparts. The over-your-shoulder readers, the undress-'em-with-your-eyes men, the racists, the autistic lunkheads with Walkmans whose booming drone could be heard in every corner . . . If you sat there long enough, they all put in an appearance sooner or later.

"They're my family," he once told Erna when she was visiting him in Berlin.

"Oh, boo hoo, aren't you the sad one." Erna never beat around the bush. "Shall I pick out a mother and a father for you?"

"No, don't bother."

But ever since then he'd been keeping an eye out for a mother and a father. So far he had a Turkish father, an Angolan sister, a Chinese mother—and scads of German relatives, of course.

"And girlfriends?"

"Those too, but then the game starts to get real."

"So what's your criterion?"

"My latest brother was reading an E. T. A. Hoffmann novella; my latest mother came from East Berlin."

"I bet she was reading something too."

"No, she was crying, and trying to hide it."

This time there were no fathers in the bunch. He changed trains at the Bismarckstrasse station. Actually, he'd been headed toward the Historisches Museum, but two museums in one day was too much. Besides, all of Berlin was a historic museum. No, he'd go to Café Einstein and order a *Glühwein*. Mulled wine would really hit the spot; only now did he realize how cold he was.

In Café Einstein the Germans had been transformed into Europeans. You could swap this place for a café on Place St. Michel in Paris or the Luxembourg in Amsterdam. The customers looked like ads, just as he did. Who knows, maybe they also had families in the U-Bahn. Why else would they be here? Tall blonde waitresses in long aprons that nearly swept the ground. A rack of newspapers on rods, full of the world: *Le Monde, Corriere della Sera, Taz*. His hand reached for *El País* the same time as another, though his was a fraction sooner. He got there first, and she was angry—you could tell. Blazing eyes. Dark. Like the hundreds of eyes he'd seen in the souks of Morocco. Berber eyes. Only later did he remember that this had been his first thought, and realize that he had mysteriously hit the nail on the head. He silently offered her the paper, but she shook her head. So it wasn't about the newspaper, it was about being beaten to the punch, losing. She took *Le Monde* and disappeared around the corner of the bar. He found a place for himself near the window. Not even four o'clock yet, and almost night. "Those that walketh in the darkness." Where had that come from? And did it refer to the nonbelievers? Why wasn't Arno here—he always knew everything. Jot it down, ask him tonight. But he promptly forgot. That face, which had glared at him so indignantly, what kind of face was it? A scar on the right cheekbone. Come to think of it, there had also been a scar on the hand, in that funny fleshy part between the thumb and forefinger. The pencil pad, as Victor liked to call it. When she'd extended her hand, she'd also distended the scar. Shiny, the skin discolored, lighter. The scar on her face was crueler—someone had deliberately jabbed a finger into that cheekbone in order to leave his or her mark. He briefly considered going over to her table and offering her the paper, but that was absurd. If she hadn't glared at him, she'd now be reading *El País* instead of *Le Monde*. The country instead of the world, Spanish instead of French. Definitely not German, not with a face like that. And a sore loser to boot. So forget it, read the paper. Scandals, corruption, González, ETA; he found it hard to concentrate. Was she Spanish? She didn't look Spanish, but that didn't mean anything. In any case, she didn't look like an ad. Ads don't have scars. These days half the human race doesn't look the way it's supposed to look. Jews look like Germans, Dutch like Americans, and then there's Spain, with its Celts, Jews, Moors. Moors? Berber eyes—that had been his first reaction. But enough of this, he chided himself, get your mind back on the newspaper. Countries were like games. Once you knew the rules, you could play from the sidelines. He was trying to learn the rules for Germany. He'd already worked out the ones for Spain. Never enough, but still... You'd obviously grasped the essentials if you could understand the references in the newspaper, could follow the nuances of the latest corruption scandal—and the scandals in Spain were of Byzantine complexity. Generals up to their necks in drug trafficking, the head of the Guardia Civil apprehended in Laos, where he'd fled on forged papers, ministers sending assassination squads across the border, editors photographed in the snare of their own peculiar lusts, not to mention the usual graft—crude stinking money, a muckheap of self-interest and lies that seemed to surprise no one. Perhaps that's why he loved Spain, where this insanity seemed to be part of normal life. Ridiculous, of course. Back in his early twenties, just starting out as a cameraman, he had filmed a couple of programs on tourism. The standard items: the Semana Santa celebration in Seville, the Costa Brava, all the places the Dutch hordes flocked to, Torremolinos, Marbella. All that travel had given him a taste of what really interested him—cities that had managed to preserve their proud heritage while the rest of the country sold itself to the highest bidder, islands of stone in the hard, dry plains of Castile and Estremadura. He had been fascinated by those places, as if part of himself had been preserved there and he had only just discovered it. After that he'd been determined to learn the language, and had accepted any assignment that would take him back to Spain. A few years ago he'd shared a small apartment on Plaza Manuel Becerra, in the shabby part of Madrid, with a Nicaraguan filmmaker named Daniel García. The arrangement suited them both, since Daniel, who had been badly wounded in Angola and gone through years of painful rehabilitation, had started up again as a photographer and was frequently obliged to go to Amsterdam and Berlin. Arthur had traveled around Spain, using Madrid as his base of operations. At that moment the German WDR was considering one of his projects, about monasteries in Spain, and he had suggested that they use Arno Tieck. They'd been kicking the idea around for a year or so—Germany had become almost as bad as Holland in that respect. Anything that seemed even remotely difficult or lasted longer than twenty minutes was suspect. No funds, no interest. "Who'd wanna watch? Less than twenty percent of the population goes to church these days, and how many of them are still Catholic? I mean...*monasteries*? Now if you'd like to do something on Zen monasteries..."

He got up to go to the men's room, making a detour past the bar. She was still sitting there, a picture of concentration. This time he noticed her pale skin. The paper spread out on the table in front of her, her head in her hands, her fists buried in the wiry tufts of her short black hair. Probably felt stiff if you touched it. On his way back to his table he noticed that she hadn't moved.

He wondered if she thought he was Spanish. Under the circumstances, it would have been normal for one of them to have said something, two Spaniards in a foreign country, in a city practically cut off by the snow. But he wasn't Spanish, so maybe she wasn't either. Besides, he'd never been able to do that—cozy up to strangers.

"Not *strangers*, Arthur, *women*." That had to be Erna.

"I just can't."

"Why not?"

"I always put myself in the woman's shoes. Suddenly this asshole comes over and starts handing you some stupid line, when all he wants to do is screw you."

"If that's all you're after, you've got a point."

"And if it isn't?"

"Then she'll notice. It depends on the line."

"I'm shy."

"Oh, right. He trots all over the globe with his camera but is too shy to approach a woman. You're just afraid of making a fool of yourself. Pure vanity. But you're missing out on a lot that way."

"You can say that again."

He skimmed the newspaper. An article on the ETA was accompanied by a picture he'd seen before. A bombed-out car, a body splayed over the front seat, the head tilted back toward the street. A black-and-white photograph, which made the pool of blood on the sidewalk look like tar. The head of a man in his fifties, the mouth slightly open above the impeccable mustache, clipped just that morning. An army officer on his day off. The ETA, on the other hand, never took a day off. To the people living there, fate was always just around the corner. One more corpse to add to this year's death toll, one more for the big book. His name could easily be added to the rest and get swallowed up by the abstract numbers in the book, one tiny fraction of the whole. In a later book the total sum of their names might not add up to more than one line. He studied the faces of the bystanders. They had struck exactly the right pose, as if they had been stage-managed: the woman over there moved a tiny bit to the right, the little girl, the one tugging her father's jacket with an almost clawlike hand, asked to take a step forward, and on every face an expression of horror, grief, sorrow, rage, helplessness. The history machine was at it again, feeding off the blood and pain of human flesh, not only in the photograph on that Spanish street, but also in the city in which he now found himself.

He looked outside. It had stopped snowing. Nobody in his right mind would take pictures at this time of day. All the more reason for him to do it. If he ran home and got his camera, he'd be able to shoot some pictures of the construction site at Potsdamer Platz. In film school, all those years ago, he used to hand in entire sequences shot at dawn and dusk. At first his teachers had merely scoffed, then finally refused to accept them. ("Films are meant to be seen, Daane. If you want to make fading light your specialty, go ahead, but don't do it here, or expect to peddle it to TV later on.") True enough, except sometimes. And that sometimes was what it was all about. In the beginning he'd fought back. ("If that's the only reason, you're ignoring an important part of the day." "That may be, Daane, but we have the technology for dealing with dawn and dusk, or evoking the same atmosphere. You just don't want to make use of it. After all, you can't read a book in the dark either, can you?")

But reading and taking pictures weren't the same thing, and so those hours between day and night and night and day had become his specialty. All the gray nuances, including near invisibility. The most beautiful, he thought, was when the gray took on the color of the film itself, that mysterious celluloid gleam. Darkness slowly creeping up out of the ground or trying to disappear back into it, and in that darkness every imaginable shade of light from the rising or setting sun. Especially when the sun itself could not be seen, or not yet, or not anymore, because that's when the excitement began. Floodlights, the beaming eye of a crane at a construction site, the glow of neon in a deserted street, rotating icy-blue or amber lights that lose none of their tonality when filmed in black and white, the serial lights of speeding trains or slow-moving traffic—the indescribable magic of light in the darkness.

Whenever anyone asked him what he did with all that footage, he found it hard to come up with an honest answer, or at any rate one he was willing to articulate. No, it wasn't the tag end of something else. No, it wasn't part of a project, unless you wanted to call his whole life a project. He took pictures for the same reason a writer takes notes—perhaps that was a valid comparison. In any case he did it solely for himself. Okay, but what did he do with them? Nothing, at least not yet. Except save them. Maybe they'd come in handy one day. Or maybe he was only practicing, like that Chinese or Japanese master who had drawn a lion every day, so that at the end of his life he'd be able to draw a perfect lion in one second. One day he'd film twilight the way nobody else ever had. There was another element that also came into play: that of the chase. Hunting and gathering, like the Aborigines he'd seen in Australia. In the final analysis, it all boiled down to bringing things home. His collection—as he liked to call the stacks of film cans stored in Madrid, Amsterdam, and here in Berlin.

He folded the newspaper and threaded his way through the café, his paper a banner on its rod. Even though he wasn't planning to present her with his flag, he felt both relieved and disappointed when he didn't see her sitting there. Still, it was time to go. As much as he liked the darkness, the feeling wasn't mutual—the darkness never waited for him. He took the U-Bahn at Nollendorfplatz and got off at Deutsche Oper. His apartment was on Sesenheimerstrasse, near the Opera, just off Goethestrasse. A couple of Turkish teenagers were standing forlornly on the corner, shivering in the snow near the playground that mothers took their toddlers to during the summer.

He raced up the stairs, grabbed his camera, left again. Half an hour later he emerged from the U-Bahn at Potsdamer Platz: the place Victor had brought him to after their first meeting, the place where he'd had his first lesson on Berlin. No one who had seen this city when it was divided could ever forget what it had been like. Not forget, not be able to describe it, not be able to tell the real story. Here he was now, alone, out on the hunt, but for what? For something he'd seen then and would never see again? Or perhaps for whatever had been there before, familiar to him only from photographs? He knew what it would look like without the snow: mounds of dredged-up dirt, with construction workers in yellow hard hats rooting around in the soil as if they were looking for the past itself. Bulldozers trundling back and forth like jerky science-fiction machines. The sounds of digging, drilling, scraping.

"As if they're excavating a mass grave." That was Erna.

The first time she came for a visit he had whisked her off to Potsdamer Platz. It was part of the pilgrimage. She was right, except that they weren't going to find any corpses here. Still, with all that digging and grubbing around—the machines gouging the hard dirt with their big steel forks—you couldn't help but feel that they were looking for something, hoping to find a past that could never be retrieved, except in actual physical form, something you could touch, gently lay bare, as if it were impossible that so much past could be reduced to dirt, dust, soil. Hitler's bunker must have been here somewhere, along with the torture chambers of the Gestapo, though that wasn't what he was referring to now, however tangible it might be. No; he meant the things that had been there both before and after the war, the things that had disappeared in its wake and could never be made to reappear again, no matter how deep you dug.

A car was coming. The glare of the headlights lit up the formless shapes of the snow-blanketed bulldozers and Caterpillars, the cubist planes created by the mechanical diggers. It accentuated the depths, momentarily painted the walls of snow a dull black before suddenly transforming them into a dazzling screen. It brought the soundless powdery mass into motion, mingled with the lights shining down from the tall still cranes standing guard over the site. Only when the vehicle was almost upon him did he realize that it was a green-and-white police car. The rotating blue light hadn't been switched on. Too bad. Inside, two officers seemed to be conferring. The woman said something; the man shook his head and shrugged.

The woman stepped out of the car. Her hand moved unthinkingly to her green cap, which the wind was trying to blow off her fluffy blonde hair.

"What are you doing here?"

It sounded more like a rebuke than a question. She was the second uniformed woman to address him today. He held up his camera.

"Yes, I can see that," she said. "But you've gone through the fence. As the sign says, this area is strictly *verboten*. It's been closed off."

That wasn't entirely true. There was a small opening, where the two parts of the chain-link fence came together, and he'd pushed his way through it. Besides, everything was always *verboten*. But he kept his mouth shut.

In Northern Europe female cops were rarely good-looking. Yet a joking tone was out of the question—with this woman too. She stared at him with grave solicitude, which was magnified by the stage lighting around them. He would have liked to film the pair of them: the nameless, one-eyed wanderer and the guardian of the underworld. It was perfectly still; the purr of the engine seemed only to intensify the hush. The man in the car didn't move, just stared.

"There's hardly any light left."

This time it was more of an accusation than a rebuke. They stared at each other through the metal diamonds of the fence. He had kept the camera running, and was now shooting her from the hip. Ridiculous.

"Just enough for the effect I'm looking for, I hope." Dusk is my specialty, he wanted to say, but didn't. She started to reply but was interrupted by the crackle of a voice on her walkie-talkie: another creature, male, seemed to live in the vicinity of her breast. The man in the car answered, then called her over. As you would a dog, Arthur thought.

"You can't stay here," she added, this time in her own voice. "It's dangerous with all those excavation pits."

She raced back to the car and threw it into reverse. The blue light started flashing immediately. She yelled something out the window, but her words got lost in the shriek of the siren. What happened next went so fast that he could barely follow it with his camera. She took off with such speed that she sent the car into a spin. He saw her mouth open wide, her hands frantically turn the steering wheel, her vehicle bang into the lumbering snowplow that had suddenly turned the corner. After the crash, the siren went on wailing. Only after it stopped did he hear a soft, strange moan. He went toward the sound. She had driven right into the V-shaped front, and it had rammed her car like a ship. Upon impact her cap had sailed through the broken windshield and landed on the hood—this time knocked off her head for good. Her face was covered with blood, which was slowly dripping onto the snow. Her partner got out of the car; the driver of the snowplow climbed down from his cabin.

"Well, well, well," he said. "It wasn't my fault. There wasn't any room to maneuver."

Arthur took the cap from the hood and stood there with it in his hands. She groaned softly.

"Can I help?" he asked the two men. The cop looked from him to the camera, as if it were to blame for the whole mess.

"No, you can go. And put that camera away!"

In the meantime it had grown too dark, even for him. He could hear an ambulance coming closer. Three different sets of flashing lights, with musical accompaniment. The city was a work of art, and he was part of it. He watched from a distance as she was lifted onto a stretcher and slid into the ambulance. The police car could still be driven. The two men exchanged information. He was the sole witness, but they didn't need him.

After that they drove away. It was suddenly very quiet. What little traffic there was by the Brandenburg Gate sounded like the dark, soft rustle of a tape deck before the music begins.

"There's hardly any light left," she had said. Just a few minutes ago, she had been standing there, talking. Of course she hadn't understood what he was hoping to capture on film. It had something to do with recording that moment, saving it before it disappeared. He found it hard to describe what he meant, especially to other people. It was somehow mixed up with the world's indifference, what he thought of as its impassiveness, memories vanishing without a trace. What was even more mysterious was the world's wholesale denial. Surely no other century had seen as much murder, slaughter, and genocide as this one. It was common knowledge; so there was no point in bringing it up. Perhaps the worst part was not just the killing itself—the attacks, the executions, the rapes and beheadings, the slaughter of tens of thousands of people—but the amnesia that set in almost immediately afterward, business as usual, as if it were a drop in the bucket to a world population of six billion, as if—and this fascinated him even more—humanity wasn't interested in individual names, only in the blind survival of the species. The woman who happened to be passing by when the bomb exploded in Madrid, the seven Trappist monks whose throats were cut in Algiers, the twenty boys gunned down before their parents' eyes in Colombia, the entire trainful of commuters hacked to death with machetes in a five-minute burst of orgiastic fury in Johannesburg, the two hundred passengers on the plane that exploded above the sea, the two, three, or six thousand men and boys killed in Srebrenica, the hundreds of thousands of women and children slain in Rwanda, Burundi, Liberia, Angola. For one moment, a day, a week, they were front-page news, for several seconds they flowed through cables in every part of the globe, and then it began, the black, delete-button darkness of oblivion that from now on would only get worse. The dead would no longer have names. They would have been erased in the emptiness of evil, each in the separate moment of his or her horrible death. Recent images came to mind: the human form once again wasted, laid bare, dismembered. Skeletons whose wrists were bound with wire, a photo of a child's torso covered with so many flies that you could almost see them moving, the head of a Russian soldier tossed out with the rest of the garbage on a sidewalk in Grozny, a patch of oil on a sea filled with floating suitcases, shoes, bodies. While this last image was being broadcast, a hook had suddenly fished a bra out of the water—that most minimal item of clothing—which a woman had either worn or packed in her suitcase the morning of the day it would be displayed to the entire world, someone whose name had vanished forever though it had been listed in the newspaper along with all the others.

Here in this square it was no different. Not long ago there had been a viewing platform, from which you could look out over the square, from the West to the East. In between was a huge vacant lot with metal barriers placed at geometric intervals, like an early Mondrian, to keep people from fleeing over the border in cars. Uniformed guards used to patrol the area with dogs, men you wouldn't recognize now because they're walking around this same city in ordinary clothes. Another thought you'd be wise to keep to yourself, because people's eyes would glaze with boredom the minute you brought it up. You'd hardly be telling them something they hadn't heard before. They'd already eaten and drunk their daily portion of horror, their daily portion of an indigestible past. It was ridiculous to talk in terms of a new kind of evil being unleashed on the world. After all, evil has been with us since the beginning of time, and just because a technological dimension had been added didn't make it a different type of evil, did it? He could barely formulate this thought. In his futile hunt for images it was more important to know that his attempt was doomed. Other soldiers and other dogs had been here before these soldiers and these dogs; this is where the man whose name would be remembered longer than those of his victims had warned of his deadly crusade in a book the entire world could have read; and this is where he had lived under the ground like a ghost until his despicable death. Arthur had seen the vague contours of a bump, all that was left of the spot where the light planes had continued to land, right up to the last day, with their messages from Hell to the dead, and vice versa. There were photographs of those final days, showing the man, who was merely a shell of his former self, his collar turned up against the winter cold, saluting a row of boys who couldn't have been more than fourteen or fifteen years old, an army of children he would drag down with him into death. The viewing platform had also displayed a blowup of another past, now hidden like the two subsequent pasts under a layer of snow, though this one was in black and white. A square, the same square, glinting in the sunlight, which made the rectangular cars gleam—ash-colored boxes on a white tablecloth. Trams, glistening rails, and, oddest of all, people. Time stands still in every photograph, but for some reason, whether it was the technique or the enlargement of a photo not meant to be enlarged, he had the feeling in this case that a flake of time as hard as marble had been chipped off a block of time. The sun was shining, the same sun that had always shone, but its rays seemed to freeze every person and object they touched. There they stood, caught forever between cars that would never move again, as they headed for sidewalk or tram stop. Not a single yellow star in sight. You couldn't tell the victims from the perpetrators just by looking at the faces, yet those frozen figures, every single one of them, were headed toward their destiny, oblivious to the layers that would be added to their picture in that same century, on that same spot, the space they happened to be occupying at that one never-to-be-undone moment: layer after layer of a deadly spiderweb, complete with parades, improvised pyres, battlefields, a fenced-off wasteland, guards and dogs, and, finally, a snowy construction site, where, at the end of this demonic century, those Mercedes Benzes would be gracing showrooms that at the moment existed only in blueprints. Had he really tried to capture something in the waning light between the bulldozers and the fences that would make the whole thing less of a mystery?

"The past doesn't have any atoms," Arno had said, "and every monument is a falsification. Rather than reminding us of someone's presence, the names on those monuments only serve to reinforce their absence. The message is always that we're expendable, and that's the paradox of monuments, since they claim to do the opposite. Names get in the way of actual truth. It would be better if we didn't have them."

Arthur had felt a strange sense of foreboding in his words, and, as was often the case, he wasn't sure he understood him fully. Arno had a way with words. By comparison, his own thoughts usually inched along like slugs. It wasn't that he distrusted eloquence; it was just that it took him longer to figure things out. Without a name, you only existed as a species, like ants or seagulls.

"Egad," as Victor would say. It was time to join his friends. They had agreed to meet at a *Weinstube* owned by a man named Heinz Schultze, who didn't seem to suit his name, though luckily the food he served did.

The snow had started coming down again, this time in sheets instead of fleecy flakes. It was like trying to walk through a moving wall that you kept having to shove aside. He took the camera back to his apartment and listened to his answering machine. There was only one message—from Erna. The familiar voice filled the empty room, teasing, but concerned.

"What's up? Aren't you ever going to come home?"

He could tell by the way she said "home" that she hadn't really wanted to say it.

There was a slight hesitation, then a laugh.

"Well, in any case, you've got friends here, and they've got phones."

He waited a moment, but there was nothing else. Erna. He wouldn't erase her. Always good to have a voice to come home to at night. Meanwhile, early evening had already turned to night. Muffled sounds, no traffic, black and white, quiet and busy at the same time. *Noche Transfigurada*. He mumbled the Spanish title of Schoenberg's *Verklärte Nacht* like a magic incantation. *Transfigurada* was much more beautiful, as if everything had been thrown upside down and made even more mysterious.

Adenauerplatz wasn't too far from where he lived. The *Weinstube* was located in a hideously modern complex occupied by lawyers and dentists, not the kind of place you'd expect a restaurant to be. First you had to cross a bare courtyard lined with garages, then walk past a series of frosted doors with burglarproof bars and brass plates giving the names and professions of the owners. Only then did you notice a rustic lantern over in the corner. In these surroundings the effect was almost comical, but once you opened the door you suddenly found yourself in a village in the Palatinate. A dark, low-ceilinged room with heavy oak furniture, a dim yellowish light, candles, muffled voices, the tinkling of glasses. He beat the snow off his coat and went inside. Arno and Victor were already seated at their usual table in the far corner. Herr Schultze looked happy to see him.

"So you braved the weather! The Dutch are a hearty lot, not as easily cowed by the elements as Berliners are."

Even from across the room he could see that Arno was in great form. Arno Tieck had not only the gift of speech, but also the gift of what Arthur called enthusiasm. He had told him that one time, and Arno had repeated the phrase. The gift of enthusiasm. Arthur hadn't dared tell him that it had come to him in a dream. For one thing, he could no longer remember the details. All he knew was that there had been a high, clear light, from which a woman had emerged after a long struggle and been declared "the chosen one" because she had "the gift of enthusiasm."

Years ago, when he was filming a Dutch-German coproduction, a short documentary on the house in which Nietzsche had died, he'd immediately realized that the one person to whom this phrase could be applied was this remarkable man, overflowing with stories, anecdotes, theories. Arthur hadn't read much Nietzsche, but what little he had read had stayed with him like the roar of a hurricane—a raving voice on a mountaintop, hurling invective at the nameless slaves below, then switching suddenly into a lonely and misunderstood wail. He knew there had to be more to it than that, but the tragedy of that tormented soul had only hit him with full force when he and his camera had followed Arno Tieck down the hallways and steps of that dilapidated house, filming and listening.

Filming Arno had not been an easy task. Arno's glasses had been specially ground to reflect as much light as possible. He couldn't wear contacts because there was something wrong with his left eye, and the glass on that side looked more like an eye patch than a lens, while the other eye had a disconcerting glint: an asymmetrical Cyclops. Moreover, his thick gray hair stuck out all over, as if in deliberate defiance of the viewfinder, and he moved around constantly as he talked. For the first time in his life, Arthur had finally had an inkling of what it must have been like to be the philosopher-turned-lunatic, or, worse, to have himself been forced to bear the weight of that massive head with that bushy mustache until at last it had laid itself down, weeping, on the neck of that coach horse in Turin and been carried off to the house of his terrible sister. After years of neglect, the house had been in a sorry state. At the time of the filming it had been occupied by an electrician, who hoped it would be turned into a museum one day. But the philosopher of power and violence was not popular in the republic of totalitarian democracy, so it wasn't likely. In any case, Arthur's friendship with Arno dated from that first encounter.

Friendship, Arthur had learned, came in all sorts. The only friendships worth the effort, however, were the ones based on such old-fashioned virtues as mutual respect.

Not until after the shoot, after he and Arno had spent hours together in the cutting room, had he shown Arno a few of his films. His comments had surprised him. It had been one of those rare moments in which he had met someone who actually understood what he was looking for. Arthur was leery of praise. He never knew how to respond, and, besides, Arno's enthusiasm was a double-edged sword: on the one hand he was overflowing with kindness and warmth, and on the other an exacting twin was making a detailed, razor-sharp analysis. Only later had Arthur dared tell him about his other, more private, project, the fragments he'd been filming all these years, the bits of footage without a clear line, at least not to the casual observer, some as short as the one he'd shot tonight in the snow, others longer, bordering on the monotonous, pieces of a giant puzzle only he would be able to fit together.

"If I ever think the time has come, will you write the commentary to go with it?" And before Arno had a chance to reply, he had added, "You realize, of course, that no one in his right mind will be interested in the thing."

Arno had given him a long look, then said that he would consider it a great honor, or something to that effect, in any case a phrase from a Germany that had long ceased to exist but which sounded perfectly natural on Arno's lips, just as he could greet you with an outdated expression like "*Sei mir gegrüsst,*" or use swearwords with an atavistic and rhetorical abandon that also seemed to belong to a bygone era.

After that, they had spent hours going through his collection: icy landscapes in Alaska, *candomblé* ceremonies in San Salvador de Bahia, long lines of POWs, children behind barbed-wire fences, mercenaries, Greek Orthodox monks, street scenes in Amsterdam. Random images that seemed to lack all rhyme or reason, but were connected somehow. A world torn to pieces, filmed from the sidelines, slow, reflective, nonanecdotal—fragments that one day would all come together like a summa. To borrow Arno's word.

Suddenly, in the middle of a sequence shot in a camel market in the southern range of the Atlas Mountains, his new friend had raised his hand at the wrist, a signal for Arthur to stop the film.

"Play that back."

"Why?" But he knew why. He'd been caught.

"Slowly, slowly. That shadow ... yes, that one there, on the ground. There's something strange about it. You held the shot a fraction of a second too long, but I have the feeling you did it on purpose."

"I did."

"Why?"

"Because it's *my* shadow."

"So why don't I see the camera?"

"Because I don't want you to. It's easy enough to do." He demonstrated. "You see?"

"Yes, but why? Correct me if I'm wrong, but haven't you done this on other occasions?"

"Yes. But not out of vanity."

"I understand. It's a way of being in the film without really being in it."

"That's how I meant it to be. Maybe it's childish. I suppose it's because I want to..." He searched for the right word. How on earth could he explain? To leave a mark, to be both visible and invisible. A nameless shadow that nobody, or nobody except this man, would ever notice.

"I suppose it has something to do with anonymity."

He hated words like that. Abstractions. They invariably came out sounding pompous.

"Yet your name is given in the credits?"

"I know, but that's beside the point.... What I mean is..."

Impossible to articulate his feelings. A silhouette in a display window, a footstep in the snow, hold it, hold it, the rustle of a twig or a blossom blown by an unseen person, traces...

"An invisible signature. But that's a paradox."

"You noticed it, didn't you?"

"Is it because you want to go on living after you're dead?"

No. It seemed logical, but that wasn't it.

When nobody knew or noticed his presence, that's when he would no longer be there, would become part of all that had vanished. But you could hardly say you wanted to disappear along with the rest when you were putting together a collection to save them all, could you?

That first time, he had shown Arno only the more recognizable images, the ones you could immediately read a meaning into, assuming that's what you wanted to do. The other, more anonymous, shots—floating water lilies, thistles in a leached field, gale winds lashing a row of poplars, sandpipers scampering along the shore—he still hadn't shown him those.

They were part of the collection too. Maybe I'm just plain crazy, he thought. He walked over to the table.

The conversation between Victor and Arno was of an entirely different character: it was about sausages. Arno had divided sausages into two categories: preliminary and definitive. An important distinction. However, Arthur wasn't quite ready to make the change. It was as if it took his brain longer to process things. The most natural thing in the world would be to say hello, so what was there to think about? Everyone else seemed to live in a faster world, a world in which Arno spread his arms wide and enfolded him in an embrace, while Victor, held back by his customary reserve—the cocoon that surrounded him wherever he went—merely nodded in formal acknowledgment of his arrival. Back in the old days, when a poet or a philosopher traveled from Weimar to Tübingen to visit a friend, people must have greeted each other the way Arno did. Time, distance, and discomfort would have been discounted by a hearty welcome, would have dictated the intensity of the joy on their faces, according to the same equation in which time and distance remained visible in letters from that era. That's why he never phoned Arno: his friend's rhetorical talents, which blossomed in correspondence or physical proximity, withered in the fake proximity of a phone call, just as the virtual simultaneity of fax and e-mail dulls the glow of distance and elapsed time.

"It's all tied up with the mystery of the thing itself—the letter, the object, the fetish."

He'd brought the subject up one time, and that had been Arno's answer. As usual, he'd had to ask for clarification.

"What do you mean?"

Actually, he knew what the answer would be before the question was even out of his mouth. It was hard for him to write letters, especially in German, but for Arno's sake he was willing to make the effort. Arno would just have to put

66

up with his mistakes. After all, gender was arbitrary. Certain objects were feminine in German and masculine in Spanish, while Dutch washed its hands in innocence and looked the other way, not like English, which radically refused to assign any kind of sexuality whatsoever to sun, sea, and death. Dutch had hypocritically sidestepped the issue by slapping a uniform article on masculine and feminine words, so that only a specialist or a dictionary could tell you whether a word should be referred to as a he or a she.

"Don't you think it's funny?" he had asked Arno.

"What?"

"That your words become transsexuals the minute they cross the Rhine? As soon as the moon hits Strasbourg it becomes female, time becomes male, death female, the sun male . . . and so on."

"And in Dutch?"

"The sex markers have been removed. The language was simplified years ago, so now there are only two articles: one for neuter words, and a unisex article for masculine and feminine words. These days nobody knows whether the sea is male or female."

Arno shuddered at the thought.

"That makes it impossible to trace the origins. Heine was wrong. Everything happens fifty years earlier in Holland than it does here. But don't hesitate to write—your voice comes through fine."

So they had corresponded. And of course that's what Arno had meant by the mystery of the thing. You wrote with a pen—neither of them would stoop to using a computer for personal correspondence—as if to emphasize that nothing could replace the written word. Thoughts flowed along with the ink, rather than being objectified by a mechanized typeface. Then all you had to do was fold the letter, stick it in an envelope, add a stamp, lick the flap, seal it, and mail it. He always took it to the mailbox himself. In some countries you tossed your letter into the waiting mouth of a lion, inserting it between a pair of toothless gums whose bronze or copper lips were faintly discolored by the millions of letters that had been shoved between them over the years. After that, he and Arno agreed, the letter was miraculously alone for an unknown period of time. The lion had it, but not for long. It had glided out of your hand, and days would go by before that other hand, the hand of your friend, would be able to touch it. All the other hands, which had taken it from the mailbox, stamped it, sorted it, and delivered it, would remain invisible—unless you happened to bump into the mailman on your doorstep (Arno: "All mailmen are manifestations of Hermes").

And now he was expected to join in a discussion of sausages. According to Arno, preliminary sausages were what Herr Schultze referred to as *"frische Blut- und Leberwurst"*—freshly ground blood and liver sausages. Two condoms loosely packed with juicy ground meat and neatly tied on each end. Sticking your fork into one of those sausages was like jabbing an inner tube—there was a hiss of escaping air, except that in this case the smell of blood or liver inevitably rose to your nostrils and a gray or purply-black liquid gushed out.

"I prefer to drink my blood from a chalice," Victor said. "Haven't you ever wondered, Arno, why you Germans eat these things? The mushy variety, I mean, the ones you call 'preliminary sausages.' You practically have to slurp them up, and that smacks of vampirism. Admit it—you're a bloodthirsty lot. Why don't you just sink your teeth into an uncooked pig? What's the phrase...oh, yes, *le cru et le cuit,* raw or cooked, Lévi-Strauss, that's the crucial difference between the two, isn't it? The French cook the blood first, then let it solidify and cool. They also have a counterpart to your 'definitive sausage'—*boudin*. In case you don't know it, that's French for 'pudding.' Have you ever thought about that? Blood pudding. Liver sausage is just as bad. It's slimy and limp and falls apart on your plate. Come to think of it, a swine is the ideal packaging for a liver. Swine are pretty compact critters. No other animal looks quite so ready, from the outside anyway, for the butcher's knife. Hams, trotters, loins, those cute little ears that just have to be breaded and..."

His monologue was interrupted by Herr Schultze.

"Well, gentlemen, you went through a blizzard to get here tonight, and we appreciate your loyalty. So please allow me to offer you a delightful Grauburgunder—the grapes have soaked up so much southern sun that it's guaranteed to make you forget the snow."

He bowed. Arthur knew what was coming next: the recitation of the menu. Herr Schultze had turned it into an act, which he performed with just a hint of irony. Arno, focusing his one, glinting eye on their host, asked, "Do you have *Saumagen*?"

As Victor had once remarked and couldn't resist repeating now, *Saumagen*—stuffed pig's stomach—was Helmut Kohl's favorite dish.

"Mine too," Arno said. "We're a conservative folk. We don't succumb easily to this trendy idea that meat has to be disguised in order to be eaten. We still communicate directly with the animal world. You eat exactly the same thing I do...."

"Oh, bah," said Victor.

"...Except that you don't want to know it. You're hypocritical eaters. Your frankfurter contains an entire ground-up pig, with the eyes, stomach, intestines, lungs, flour, and water thrown in for good measure, but you turn up your nose at an honest encounter with its sister, the swine. A while ago you were bemoaning the fact that some red-crested bird in

Venezuela was on the verge of extinction. Here we have a dish that's been made in Swabia since the early Middle Ages, and when I point out that it's been edged out by a chunk of ground-up cow's rump that tastes the same from Los Angeles to Sydney, you just shrug your shoulders."

"What do you mean 'you'?" said Arthur. "You don't have to try to convince *us*. Besides, you're throwing Victor's own arguments back at him."

Arno looked crushed, as he always did when interrupted mid-speech. "I didn't mean you personally," he said. "It's just so awful. . . . They can hardly wait until the whole world is eating the same food. And not just the same food. It's a package deal—eat the same, hear the same, see the same, and then, of course, think the same. Or what passes as thinking these days. Farewell to diversity. When that happens, we'll turn this place into a hamburger joint."

He gestured dramatically at his surroundings. In the dim light of the restaurant, he could see small groups of people who had likewise braved the elements to be here tonight. Schultze's son was going from table to table with generous glasses of honey-colored wine. An old-world odor of food wafted from the kitchen and hung in the air beneath the dark, low, beamed ceiling. Murmuring voices, candlelit gestures, conversations he'd never be able to follow, words that would disappear the moment they were spoken, part of the endless chatter around the globe, a tiny portion of the billion words said on any given day. That must be the dream of an insatiable sound engineer: to own a microphone of such cosmic proportions that it can pick up each and every one of those words and record them all. As if that would clarify things, as if the monotony, the repetition, and the incredible diversity of life on earth could be reduced to one equation. Unfortunately, no such equation existed.

"What do you mean by diversity?" Arthur asked.

"Everything that could and does crop up during a conversation."

"In that case all you'd have to do would be to multiply our conversations by a thousand."

"No, that's not what I meant. I mean things like lust, religious mania, murderous intentions, fear, the most extreme examples of human emotion, as expressed in words. Everything...that's intolerable. And secret."

"And we can only be saved by monotony?"

"That's one way of putting it."

"So what's monotony? Our conversations?"

"Repetition. 'How are you?' 'Have you milked the cows today?' 'My car won't start.' 'When's the next appointment?' 'The president has announced that there will be no tax hikes this year.' I'm sure you can come up with your own examples of diversity."

"Do what I say or I'll slit your throat."

"You see, it's easy. Just ordinary words. Except that you don't often hear them in everyday life."

"Throw those bastards into a bus, take 'em somewhere and shoot 'em. Then shoot the guys who shot 'em, chuck 'em in a pit, cover 'em with lime, et cetera, et cetera...."

"Hey, you're good at this."

"I'm a child of the times. We can imagine all sorts of conversations. Those of grave desecrators, child rapists, kamikaze terrorists...It's the other dialogues we have trouble with."

"Why? Whatever for?"

"Because they're so boring. Because of their infinite, stubborn, slow-moving, all-saving normality. 'Did you sleep well?' 'Your retirement check is in the mail.'"

"Stop, stop," Victor said. "Or we'll never get around to ordering. Poor Schultze has already walked off. He was about to launch into his act, but with the two of you spouting off, he couldn't get a word in edgewise."

"Not exactly spouting," said Arno. "Besides, what's your hurry?"

"I'm a one-man monastery, I have fixed hours. Stone won't wait."

"Stone won't wait." Whenever Arthur came back to Berlin, the first item on his agenda was usually a visit to Victor's studio, a gardener's cottage on Heeresallee that had been converted into a lofty white room with skylights. A bed, a chair for visitors, a tall stool that was never more than a few yards away from whatever project he was currently working on, a stereo, and a grand piano that he practiced on for several hours a day. He lived in Kreuzberg, alone. He hated talking about his work. "Not something one should ask about."

He didn't mind having Arthur come to his studio. "But remember the claustral rules—words yes, stories no." It was okay to use his camera. When Victor was busy, or playing the piano, he didn't seem to notice.

"Who's the composer?"

"Shostakovich. Sonatas and preludes."

"Sounds like a meditation." No answer.

The object Victor was working on occupied the center of the room. A heavy chunk of stone, a shade of red Arthur had never seen before. It looked like it was permanently night in that stone. Of course "object" wasn't the right word, but what was?

"Work of art?" Victor scoffed.

"What kind of stone is it?"

"Finnish granite."

He sat in the chair over in the corner and watched as Victor moved his stool around and stared at that chunk of granite. It might take hours or days, but at some point he'd start chiseling. Later on he'd carve and polish until the stone had lost its original shape, no longer resembled its former self. Arthur would be unable to put his finger on it, but somehow a paradoxical change would have taken place.

Victor's one and only comment (and not even about his own work) had been that "it should all be a lot more mysterious and a lot more menacing."

That had to be it, because the more he chipped away at that block of granite, the bigger it seemed to get. Despite the fact that it was now more subtle and polished, it suddenly seemed to radiate a phenomenal power. Perhaps the mystery could be explained by the runes that the sculptor had carved on the side, but who could read them? Hacking, chiseling, grinding, polishing. One time Arthur had recorded the sounds, not because he wanted to synchronize them with the shots of Victor at work, but because he wanted to use them as background for that other, much quieter moment, the moment when the sculpture was finished and the sound had become an anachronism. He had prowled around the sculpture with his camera, just as Victor had. And never, at any time, had Victor asked him what he intended to do with the footage.

Stone won't wait. They called Herr Schultze over, made their apologies.

"I love it when you gentlemen have a serious discussion," said Schultze. "Very few of my customers do."

It was time for his act. Foreigners were always struck by the menu anyway, but it came out sounding even more exotic, thanks to his delivery—a confusing mixture of unexpected stresses and pitches, as if he were making a deliberate statement about his own language. He knew they enjoyed his performance, so he outdid himself in an attempt to lighten the heavy fare with a soupçon of irony, until *Spanferkel, Wellfleisch,* and *Schweinshaxe*—suckling pig, boiled pork, and pig's knuckles—sounded more like a ballet program than the roasted, stewed, and fried bits of animals that had been part of the German diet since Varus brought his Roman soldiers to the Teutoburger Wald, which, by the way, also still exists. Arno ordered *Saumagen,* Victor a *Maultaschen* soup, and Arthur the *Wurst.* The first time he'd ever eaten a blood sausage had been after a memorial service at Dachau, which he'd attended with two of its survivors.

"We'll show you how to eat *real* German food."

The two old men had been filled with an inexplicable nostalgia. They told the most gruesome stories as if they were merely recalling childhood pranks. "And then, after the exercises we'd go back to the barracks, except for the stiffs who were left lying on the parade ground."

In the car on the way there they had sung at the top of their lungs—resistance songs, Communist Party songs, the Horst Wessel song, and, worse, the unrepeatable anti-Semitic lyrics of the former enemy.

"You won't know these; you were born too late." But he did know them. In the camp itself there were hugs, tears, memories—all accompanied by that school-reunion atmosphere. "That's where the gallows used to be. I've got a picture of it. We were lined up here—no, not over there, but here in this corner—so that we couldn't avoid looking at it...."

What kind of chemical reaction had occurred, to change death and suffering into tender recollection and resurrect the voices and faces of those who had disappeared? At Hardtke's in Meineckestrasse the two men had almost barked out their orders. "*Karpfen in Bier gedünstet.* A Pilsener Urquell. A *Bommerlunder...*" Suddenly the words had been charged with a meaning invisible to everyone else in the restaurant. The carp, the beer, everything had tasted of war. The only time they had fallen still had also been the only time he hadn't been allowed to film them: at the border between East and

West Germany. As if even now the green uniforms of the guards, the gleaming boots and belts and caps, and the panting of the chained-up dogs radiated a threat that no *Erbsensuppe* or *Linseneintopf* or *Hackepeter* could assuage. Two elderly Dutch men on vacation in Germany—they had unconsciously moved closer together.

"Our filmmaker friend is off in outer space." He suddenly realized that several minutes of silence had gone by. Before that, they had been talking about . . . well, what had they been talking about?

"Happens to him all the time," said Victor. "Usually means he's filming in his head. He leaves his friends behind and zips through the galaxies. Run into anyone on the way?"

"No," said Arthur. "All of a sudden I was remembering those two concentration-camp survivors I made the Dachau documentary with. You know the ones I mean, Victor."

"*Niet lullen, maar poetsen*," Victor said in Dutch. Reverting to German, he went on. "Impossible to translate, Arno. Dutch is a secret language, you know. We use it to exclude others."

"But I don't get it either," said Arthur.

"Roughly translated, it means 'More work, less play.' The motto of the Military Police. One time I asked the older of the two men how he'd managed to survive three years in Dachau. His answer was, 'More work, less play. That's what we said when I was an MP.' And when I asked him how the other man, the poet, had survived, he said, 'Well, he took it hard, but we pulled him through. We were trained to endure hardship; poets aren't. And when you get right down to it, the Germans had a certain respect for you if they knew you were an officer. . . .'"

"Try telling that to the Poles," Arno said.

But Arthur still wanted to know what they'd been talking about before that.

"The soles of memory."

Oh, right. Strange, that you could hear something even when you weren't listening. There it was again, his abortive documentary on Walter Benjamin.

"How did you get on that subject?" he asked.

"I just bought twenty pfennig's worth of past," Arno said. His Cyclops eye twinkled. Arthur knew that a surprise was in store for them. Friends were reliable that way. Arno had a jubilant kind of intellect that could be triggered by almost anything, after which he needed no further prompting. But first he liked to be secretive. They ordered another bottle of wine. Games. Three grown men, with a cumulative age of one hundred and fifty. Arno placed two printed sheets of paper on the table. A text with a couple of fairly simple illustrations. A broad landscape, one or two primitive huts, a low fence that looked as if it had been woven out of reeds. In the distance you could see hills, a forest, a man carrying a load of hay on his back, a woman in a clearing, stirring something in a kettle. The other drawing was apparently meant to represent a grave. Bones, a skull, pottery.

"I've been in the underworld," said Arno. "After all, memories have to start somewhere. This is Berlin at its earliest, a reconstruction of a Bronze Age settlement. Those people literally lived under our feet. It's what makes the present so arrogant: we refuse to think we'll ever be lying under the feet of others. All Hegel's fault..."

"Why Hegel?"

"Because he thought we'd already reached the end of history. And the idea has stuck. We can't possibly imagine as much future as we have past. Look at that drawing...done out of love, naturally, but it contains a certain element of contempt: the implication is that it could never happen to us. *We* won't ever have to be excavated. *Our* clothes won't ever seem as ridiculous as a bearskin. Nobody wants to imagine the future as a time in which *we* will one day be the butt of jokes, nothing but a bunch of bones in a museum display case. Not us, we're beyond that stage, ha ha. We think either that things will go on like this forever, or that they will end with us. Space travel isn't the answer. It takes years to reach another planet, which means we'll have to engineer, genetically, a different breed of humanity first. But the universe can get along very well without us—that's already been proved once. Who knows, maybe we wouldn't even mind, though we'd never admit it, because the old place would be pretty boring without us. A bunch of clocks ticking on and on, and nobody who gives a damn."

"Rather appealing, with those huts," said Victor. "And with that boat and that fishing net. Cooking over a charcoal fire. No mercury in the fish. Whole-wheat bread every day, the kind with the nice crunchy kernels. And no hassle..."

Arthur picked up the drawing. Printed by the Early History Museum. Also located in Charlottenburg Palace. You could buy it for ten pfennig a sheet. What would it have been like to hear those people talk?

"Take the U-Bahn to Lichterfelde," Arno said, "and you'll find yourself being whizzed through the past. In that sense we're always in the realm of the dead. But those dead people could never have imagined us...."

"Perish the thought."

"I agree, but anyway, from the moment those early inhabitants settled there, communication has never stopped. One long ongoing conversation on the same spot. Mutters, murmurs, centuries-long words and sentences, a vast endless ocean of shouts and whispers, a grammar that keeps perfecting itself, a dictionary that keeps expanding, all on this spot, one layer on top of the other, disappearing and not lost; the words disappear but the language remains, everything we say, the way we say it, all those words and expressions they passed on to us and which we in turn will pass on to..." He gestured toward the dark-brown ceiling, his cigar smoke effectively concealing the unimaginable future.

"...To the poor bastards coming after us," said Victor, finishing his sentence for him. "Thanks to your graphic description, I have the feeling they're standing here with their feet in my soup." He looked at the drawing again. "I wouldn't mind being in someone else's print, being part of someone else's imagined memories. As long as they keep their soles out of my food. I don't see anything wrong with vanishing without a trace. Leaving no trace sounds fine to me. Even comforting."

"So what about the work you're leaving behind?" Arno asked.

"Surely," Victor growled, "you don't believe in the immortality of art. What a laugh. Writers always seem to fall for that one. They're the masters of immortality. Absolutely convinced that they're going to leave their mark, oblivious to the fact that the printed word is plagued by mold and worms. Even when something does get preserved, what kind of time frame are we talking about? Three thousand years? Texts that we interpret through contemporary eyes though they probably meant something entirely different to the people who wrote them..."

He took another look at the drawing. "You see, not a book in sight. I'll tell you what... why don't you take one of Hegel's tomes and trade it for that fish. Tell them you want to do a favor for a friend of yours. They'll understand—Berliners are nice people. I'd like to know what one of those prehistoric fish tastes like."

Herr Schultze brought the *Saumagen*. It looked exactly like a leather sack with stitches.

"Shall I carve it for you?"

"Please do," Arno said. Turning to Victor, he added, "Anyway, back to your work. It's made of stone, so it ought to last a while."

"So what? Someone'll stumble across it one day, and stop and wonder. Or else it'll wind up in one of those revolting display cases...Second half of the twentieth century, artist unknown. Ha! Just like me standing in a museum and looking at an earthenware jug, like the one in that drawing of yours. Oh, I can imagine someone molding the clay, or picture a tall blond Teuton, maybe even a woman I would have been attracted to, taking a sip out of it, but what good does that do the person who made the jug?"

"The fact that it exists. The pleasure of making it."

"Oh, I don't deny that," said Victor. "But that's all there is to it."

Arno raised his glass.

"To our short lives. And to the millions of spirits hovering around us." They drank.

"I like the idea of being surrounded by the dead," Arno said. "Dead queens, dead soldiers, dead prostitutes, dead priests...you're never alone."

He leaned back in his chair, and before long they heard a low drone, a cross between a growl and a hum. Victor and Arthur both recognized the sound: the rumble of distant traffic, a dog that has spotted another canine across the street, a musician testing a bass. It was always a sign that Arno was thinking about something that bothered him.

"Hmm, hmm. Your logic is flawed. Because you're not the one who determines the limits of your immortality."

"There's no such thing as immortality."

"Okay, as a metaphor then. Homer, or the person we think of as Homer, couldn't possibly have known that one day somebody would be able to read his tale in a spaceship.

79

You're hoping you can set a limit, Victor, to be able to say, 'After such and such a date no one will look at my work anymore.' But in fact, the opposite is true."

The lone eye twinkled. Here it came.

"The only reason you say that is out of fear. You're scared of losing control over what people say about your work. It's a kind of escape forward. You're hoping to get a jump on your own nonbeing. But as long as your work exists, it will represent you, even when you're way past knowing it, even when your name has long been forgotten. And do you know why? Because it's a man-made object. It's impossible to set a limit. Hegel accused Kant of that very thing. To Hegel, anyone who sets a limit has already gone beyond the limit, and anyone claiming to be finite does so from the perspective of the infinite. Ha!"

"I know those gentlemen only by name," Victor said. "We haven't actually drunk a cup of coffee together. I'm just an ordinary, pessimistic sculptor."

"There's a difference between something made by Nature and something made by you; don't you agree?"

"In that case aren't I Nature?"

"Okay, let's say for the sake of argument that you're Nature. Imperfect nature, spoiled nature, sublimated nature... you can fill in the blanks yourself. Anyway, there's one thing you can't do, namely, not think while you're making something."

"You mean thinking is unnatural?"

"No, I wouldn't go so far as to say that. I mean that the moment you think about nature, you're above nature. Nature can't think about itself."

"But you could claim that Nature thinks about itself through me...."

At that moment a gust of cold air blew into the room, followed by a heavyset woman in a fur coat. The candles on the tables flickered dangerously. A second later she was standing beside their table.

"Ah, Zenobia," said Arno. "Just let me finish this thought." Turning to Victor, he continued, "You can't call the shots from your grave, no matter how much you'd like to!"

"Goodness, children, what a melancholy conversation... The grave, the grave, the entire city is buried under snow. Watch this! Start counting!"

"Counting what?"

"How long it'll take these snowflakes to turn to tears..."

With her hands in the air, she gazed at the snowflakes melting on her bosom.

"My coat is crying!" She pronounced it "cry-ink."

Zenobia Stejn was the twin sister of Arno's wife, Vera. Only those who knew them well could tell them apart. Both had a strong Russian accent, but Vera, who painted, was silent and introverted, while Zenobia moved through life like a thundercloud. She had a degree in theoretical physics and wrote articles and reviews for Russian magazines. She also had a small photo gallery in Fasanenstrasse, open three afternoons a week or by appointment. Her specialty was German nature photography from the 1920s, Stieglitz's cloud patterns, Alfred Ehrhardt's series of sand grooves, Arvid Gutchow's studies of sand and water. One thing that drew Arthur to Zenobia was the contrast between her exuberant personality and the soundless world of those photographs. All the pictures in her collection seemed to deal with things that had almost vanished but had been caught just in the nick of time. One arbitrary day, more than seventy years ago, a photographer on Sylt, or one of the other islands off the German coast, had picked out that one groove—a narrow, insignificant furrow made by the wind—and the sea had washed over it again and again, filling it with water and forming little rivulets. This tiny, repetitive event had been intensified by the iron light that day, and the photographer had seen it, jotted it down, and kept his notes. The technique of those days made the picture seem dated, yet emphasized a basic contradiction: a timeless picture remained timeless, but also bore the indelible mark of the 1920s. The same was true of Stieglitz's cloud patterns. That one irretrievable cloud drifted through the air, moving slowly over the landscape like a zeppelin, watched by people who were long dead. Yet because of the photograph, that cloud had become all clouds, that nameless mass of water particles, which had been there from the beginning of time, long before mankind had arrived on the scene, had turned into those scudding formations, the stuff of poems and proverbs, usually taken for granted, until one day a photographer came along and gave this most transient of phenomena a paradoxical kind of permanence, and made you realize that a world without clouds is unthinkable and that every cloud, no matter when or where, represents all of the clouds that we have never seen and never will. Pointless thoughts, which nevertheless went through his mind because those photographs, and the effect the photographer was hoping to achieve, had something to do with what he himself was trying to achieve—to save things that didn't need to be saved because they were always there. But that was exactly why he did it: those rivulets, those grooves, had been formed by the wind and the sea, not created by an artist. They had actually existed in time and space, and now, all those years later, that rivulet or that cloud was lying there on the table for you to look at. All you had to do was gently remove the protective sheet of tissue paper, and there, framed by the mat, was a moment in real time, anonymous yet specified, a nameless victory over the ephemeral. No imaginary cloud in a painting by Tiepolo, Ruisdael, or Turner could match that; they merely represented other, real clouds that had never let themselves be captured, not by anyone.

Zenobia placed her chubby hand on his head.

"So what is it pondering? Such a serious head, a thousand miles away. What is it thinking?"

"About clouds."

"Ah, clouds! Clouds are the horses of the Holy Spirit; that's what my chemistry teacher always said when she was trying to explain why they weigh so little. Not very scientific. Clouds supposedly wander all over the world to make sure everything's all right.... Russian education—a combination of fact and superstition."

She shrugged off her coat, apparently taking it for granted that a Herr Schultze would be there to catch it.

"Not to mention that she could have got into serious trouble for saying things like that. Quick," she called to Schultze's retreating back, "a vodka! A double—one for me and one for my soul. Whew, what a day! Just getting here was a major feat! I feel like a cavalry horse. It's going to snow for the next thousand years. I saw those clouds of yours on TV, stretching all the way from the Atlantic to the Urals, just as De Gaulle predicted. De Gaulle—the great meteorologist! At last, a united Europe, united under a huge gray counterpane of thousand-year-old clouds, with us pattering around below on our childish little feet. And Berlin covered in the snow of innocence, differences obliterated, a perfect marriage between East and West, the apotheosis of reconciliation. Snow on German churches, Dutch banks, the dwindling population of Brandenburg, the fiery Poles, snow on Königsberg-Kaliningrad, snow on Kant, snow on the Oder, snow on the dead and dying... Yes, my dear Hansel, you and your cloud demons have set me off. I came in here a happy woman, a whirlwind at my heels, seeking human comfort, even willing to settle for Dutch comfort—sorry, I couldn't resist—and what do I find but three melancholy Wodans. The first word I hear is 'grave.' If you want to bury someone tonight, you'll have to clear off the snow and hack through the frozen ground first!"

"We're game," said Victor. "Anyway, I've got the tools. Who wants to go first?"

Arthur leaned back. Perhaps, he thought, this is the reason I keep coming back to Berlin. For this group of people, for this circle of friends, who need only half a word or a phrase to understand each other, who speak in metaphor and hyperbole or don't need to talk at all, whose nonsense makes sense and doesn't have to be explained unless you feel like it. He also knew how tonight would end. He and Victor would get more and more quiet as the evening wore on, while Arno and Zenobia would feast themselves on Mandelstam and Gottfried Benn, whose entire works they apparently knew by heart. The biographical gap between the two poets, the fact that he and Victor couldn't understand Mandelstam's Russian—they would be long past caring. Russian would ring out through the restaurant, the other patrons would cease to exist, a wave of explosive consonants and fervent vowels would wash over their table, only to crash into Benn's abrupt, agonizing poetry, with its unexpected, un-German rhymes—two tragic lives whose ruin and guilty wounds seemed to sum up the twentieth century. And if they still had a craving for more, they would go over to Arno's, since he lived nearby, and Germany and Russia would dominate there as well, because Arno had a piano on which he'd play Schubert and Schumann, with more feeling than technique, and then Vera and Zenobia would ask Victor to play the Largo from Shostakovich's Piano Sonata No. 2, very slowly, almost a whisper, "the way only a Russian can play it. Shostakovich, that rat. Ah, Victor, admit it, you're a Russian!"

Germany and Russia. At such moments it was as if the two countries felt a kind of homesickness for each other that no Atlantic-born Dutch person would ever understand, as if that vast plain beginning in Berlin exercised a mysterious pull that was bound to have an effect sooner or later, something that wasn't yet apparent, but which would, contrary to present appearances, upset the balance of European history once again, as if that enormous land mass could turn itself around and shake off the entire western periphery.

That nickname business again! Why Zenobia always called him Hansel was a mystery to him, forty-two years old and six feet tall. But he was resigned to it. He felt at ease in the presence of this tempestuous personality, because her radar always picked up his thoughts, yet left him to weave his fantasies in peace. And he knew that "alcohol was the cloud from which her soul sent down snow." More clouds, more snow. That had been Zenobia's description of herself once when she was blind drunk and his steady hand had guided her home.

"I drink to protest facts," she had told him that night, and though he wasn't sure what she meant by that, he felt he understood. She had beat her fists against his chest ("That's what we Russians do") and, in the beam of the porch light, had fixed her blue eyes on his ("There are also blue-eyed Jews").

"The subjective drinks to protest the objective ... Hey, listen to me ..." With that she had swept inside and slammed the door in his face. He could still hear her repeating over and over again in the stairwell, "Hey, listen to me, hey, listen to me!"

Herr Schultze reappeared at their table. Meanwhile his son, who looked like a fallen angel but had the mannerisms of his father ("Assuming it *is* his father," Victor said), had cleared the dishes, and the father was staring at the empty table as if he were suddenly faced with a great metaphysical problem. He pointed at the empty spot, his arm moving with the stiffness of a puppet on a string, and asked them which dish he should bring next. He had a suggestion, and they all knew what it would be. Only the ritual formulation remained.

"The triumph of the peasant?"

"Excellent."

"Grain, pig, and cow?"

"All three."

Soon a board was set before them, containing a crock of lard, several slices of coarse black bread, and a hunk of cheese that looked as if it had been put in a cellar back in the Middle Ages and only recently unearthed. *Handkäse*—a smelly German cheese.

"Actually, it looks more like a bar of soap," Victor said. "Or something you'd use to seal a coffin. How on earth can you people call it cheese?"

"Luther, Hildegard von Bingen, Jakob Böhme, Novalis, and Heidegger have all eaten this cheese," Arno said. "The penetrating odor that you smell is the German version of eternity. And the translucent substance that you see, with the dull sheen of candle wax, might very well represent the mystical heart of my beloved *Vaterland*." He plunged a knife into it. "Are we going to have another round of red, or should we switch to Hefe? Herr Schultze, *bitte,* four glasses of Hefe, from the Eberbach Monastery."

Hefe. Arthur had once looked the word up in the dictionary. "Hefe: yeast, dregs, sediment; used in the expression 'die Hefe des Volkes' to mean 'the scum of the earth.'" Which hardly applied to the delicate, pale gold liquid in the tall glasses on the table in front of him. The spirit of the wine. All around him he heard the gentle murmur of the other diners. It didn't seem possible that they were in the middle of a metropolis, much less that the city was covered in a thick layer of snow that would eventually melt and leave a pool of icy gray slush. Tomorrow morning, at the break of day, he would go to the Grand Hotel Esplanade on Potsdamer Platz and shoot some more pictures.

"Herr Schultze," Zenobia asked, "how is Mr. Galinsky? I assume he didn't try to get here in this blizzard?"

"Then you don't know Galinsky. He's over there in his usual place in the corner."

Over in a far corner was an elderly gentleman, seated at a table by himself, his head turned to them in profile. No one knew exactly how old he was, but he had to be well into his nineties. He came in every night just before closing ("I don't sleep anyway"). Galinsky had lived in a Berlin none of them had known, had worked as a *Stehgeiger* in a café, as the *primas* of a Gypsy orchestra that played at the Adlon...and he had survived it all. Those bare facts were all they knew. He arrived every night at about eleven o'clock, slowly drank a carafe of wine, smoked a cigar, and seemed to be lost in never-ending thought.

"I'm going over to say hello," said Zenobia. But when she came back, they could see that something was wrong.

"What did he say?" Arno asked.

"Nothing, and it doesn't look like he's ever going to say another word."

"Depressed?"

"On the contrary. There's a strange look on his face, a kind of inner fire. He's aglow."

"Russian imagination. Slavic exaggeration."

"Maybe. But I'll make it even more Russian for you. I swear I could almost see a halo. He's turned into an icon. Are you satisfied now?"

They looked over at him.

"I take it you're not referring to the glow of the lamp above his head?"

"No. If you want to see it, you have to stand right in front of him. His eyes are lit up....I know that look."

No further explanation was needed. Zenobia had lived through the siege of Leningrad as a child. She and Arthur had talked about it once, and he had never forgotten her description of what she'd called "quiet death": dying of hunger and cold, giving up, going to lie down in a corner with your face to the wall, as if the world, which had been reduced to just one room, had already slipped away from you, had become a foreign element to which you no longer belonged. In all likelihood, thought Arthur, that was what she had been referring to the night she was drunk and had been babbling on about her "hatred of the facts." He brought it up again one day.

"Oh, that," she said. "That's a typical Hansel question. You should never remind people of what they say when they're drunk. Especially not me, since I'm drunk a lot of the time."

"Why do you always call me Hansel?" he suddenly asked. "I'm hardly a child, and I'm not German either."

"That's beside the point. I call you that because you leave bread crumbs behind you wherever you go. Victor here, he likes to hoard them, while Arno throws out entire loaves. You never say much, but a day or two later I always find a few bread crumbs."

"And what about the facts?"

"You never give up, do you?"

"No."

"Hard to say, hard to say."

"Surely a physicist isn't opposed to facts?"

"I don't mean those kinds of facts. Assuming I can remember what I meant that night. The facts in the sense you mean are always valid, of course."

Silence.

"Yes, I know you're waiting for an answer."

Silence.

"What I mean is...all the suffering in the world is presented as a fact...and that's exactly what makes it so unreal. Whether it's a footnote or a full-length book, it goes down in history as a fact: the siege of Berlin, the siege of Leningrad, from such-and-such a date to such-and-such a date, x number of deaths, heroic population...and nowadays we watch television in exactly the same way...we see people, refugees, whatever, a new group every night, and all of them are facts in the sense that the camps in the Gulag were a fact, but in fact" (she laughed, "listen to this language!"), "in fact all those statistics and news flashes don't help to bring people and events closer; they make them seem even farther away... as if we're looking down from some great height at the camps, the mass graves, the minefields, the massacres, mentally turning away as we watch...We've become desensitized...we aren't moved, we register them as facts, maybe even as symbols of suffering, but no longer as suffering that should concern us...and so the facts, the act of looking at them, has become a kind of armor that shields us from the suffering.... Oh, we ease our conscience with money, or let an abstract government do it for us, but we're no longer touched by the plight of others; they've simply wound up on the wrong page of the history book...because we know, even when it's happening, that it's history—we're experts at that....Amazing, isn't it, history in the making, and we don't want to have anything to do with that either....Arno, what did that stupid Hegel of yours say? 'The days of peace are blank pages in the book of history,' or something to that effect...Well, *we* are those white pages now, and they're truly blank, because we're not there."

"He's sitting as still as a statue," Victor said, coming back from taking a closer look at Galinsky. "I felt a sudden urge to kneel, but I didn't see a glow. He's just sitting there thinking with his eyes closed."

"Then he closed them just in time," said Zenobia. "Call Schultze."

"Ah, an observant table," said Schultze. "I noticed it a while ago, but I thought it was better to leave him where he was. I went over to ask him if he wanted another glass of wine, since I could see he'd finished his carafe, but he was just sitting there, beaming. As if he were listening to distant music. He looked right through me; no, he *smiled* right through me, then put down his cigar and closed his eyes. Since it's nearly closing time, I decided there was no point in alarming the guests. As soon as you're all gone, I'll call an ambulance. There's no need to hurry. He's very happy, and sitting very upright. A perfect customer to the last. A real gentleman. I've brought you another Hefe, on the house." He filled their glasses, a little more than usual, and they raised them in the direction of the dead man.

"*Servus,*" said Victor, and it sounded as if he were singing the melody.

They went outside. The snow was no longer coming down in thick flakes. Instead, a soft dancing powder was swirling beneath the towering streetlights of the Kurfürstendamm. While they were saying their good-byes, they could hear the distant siren of an ambulance.

"Another siren," Arthur said. "I feel as if they've been following me all day."

"Sirens aren't supposed to follow you," said Zenobia. "They're supposed to lure you."

"In that case, my friend," said Arno, "you know what steps to take. Like Odysseus and his crew, you'll have to plug your ears with wax and tie yourself to the mast. After all, the ship must go on."

Without turning around, Arthur could see them going their own ways: Arno to the south, Victor to the north, Zenobia to the east, and he himself to the west, the direction from which the snow seemed to be coming. For the second time that evening they formed a cross in the snowy metropolis— first separately, the four of them coming together to the same place, and now moving away, in unison, from each other. At moments like these Arthur always imagined how a camera, high up in the sky where the whirling flakes were now blocking the view, would record their fourfold journey, all the way from the middle of the cross to those unimportant meanders at the end. After that they would belong to themselves again, alone in their strange stone dwellings, big-city residents whose mouths had suddenly fallen silent. Sometimes he became his own voyeur, a man imagining how another man, himself, would come into his apartment unnoticed and spy on him. Every movement, every action inevitably seemed theatrical, a movie without a plot. A man opens a door, brushes the snow from his coat, takes off the coat, shakes more snow off it, climbs one of those broad Berlin staircases, opens a second door and enters his own apartment. What next? Avoids looking in the mirror—after all, three's a crowd—runs his fingers over his camera, which he can never think of as a mere object, sees a photograph of a woman, a child, the man standing next to them, when, where, how, he ought to look like someone who knows he isn't being watched, no, no, the thought mustn't even enter his mind, but what *does* he look like?

He rifles through his CDs, slides one into his portable player, *Winter Music* by John Cage: silence, sound, silence, frenzied sound, silence, long-drawn-out harmonics. The silences are deliberate, to make you realize that silence is also music—counted beats, bars, composition. It feels like delayed time, if such a thing exists. He's going to use Cage's music with the footage he shot tonight; he knows that already, because any music that can drag out the time can also drag out the image.

He jumps when the phone rings. One o'clock. It had to be Erna.

"So what've you been up to? Where've you been tonight?"

"Out with friends. In a *Weinstube*. One of the customers died."

"Oh. What's that strange music I hear?"

"Cage."

"That won't lull you to sleep."

"I wasn't trying to sleep. I was thinking."

"About what? Or do you have company?"

"No. I was thinking that clocks tick slower when people are alone."

"Feeling sorry for ourselves, are we? I live alone too, you know."

"Not the same. Is it snowing in Amsterdam too?"

"Yes. What do you mean not the same? Because I've got kids?"

"That too. You live with other people."

"Should I be worried about you?"

"Not at all. I've had a very pleasant evening. With three other people, two of whom also live alone. We're in the majority. Loners are the wave of the future. Don't worry."

"Arthur?"

"Yes?"

"Don't you feel even the teeniest bit homesick? The canals are frozen over and covered with snow. We'll be able to go skating tomorrow."

Erna lived on Keizersgracht, one of Amsterdam's main canals. He could picture the view from her third-floor apartment.

"Are you standing by the window?"

"Yes."

"A yellowish glow from the street lamps. Cars covered with snow. Shadowy figures clutching the railing because the bridge is slippery."

"Right. So aren't you homesick?"

"No."

"Are you working on anything? Have you got an assignment?"

"No. Nor do I want one. I can hold out for a while. Something'll turn up. I'm busy."

"Diddling around?" Erna's term for working on his collection.

No answer.

"So what kind of things are you taking pictures of?"

"Streets, snow, sidewalks..."

"You can do that here."

"No. Too beautiful, too picturesque. Not enough history. Or drama."

"Plenty of history, but..."

"Not terrible enough. No power." He was reminded of Zenobia, and of a scene he'd filmed a couple of years ago on his way to Potsdam. He had had to wait at an intersection while a column of Russian soldiers passed by. An endless procession of men heading home on foot, wearing heavy boots, with their caps shoved to the back of their heads. To judge by their faces they came from every corner of the imperium—Kirghiz, Chechens, Tatars, Turkomans—an entire continent filing past, on the way back to their disintegrating empire. He wondered what they were thinking, what thoughts they would take with them as they fanned out over the Asian steppes, returning as losers from a country they had once conquered. But surely that wasn't going to be the end of the story. Maybe that's what kept him in Berlin. Here you felt a constant pull, the coming and going of the tide. Here, more than anywhere else, Europe's fate stood simmering on the burner. He tried to explain his food analogy to Erna.

"Bon appetit."

"Sleep tight."

"Oh, now he's feeling insulted. God, you've grown serious since you've been in Berlin. Go back to Spain. History is turning into an obsession with you. That's no way to live, not even if you're German. You read history the way most people read newspapers. I'd be willing to bet that the minute you pick up a newspaper it turns to marble. But that's ridiculous! Meanwhile, you've forgotten how to live. You've got too much time on your hands, so you start brooding. Go make a commercial. Everybody else walks past a statue without even noticing it, but not you. No, you always have to stop and take a look. It's a kind of tic. You used to . . ."

"I used to what? I used to be different. Isn't that what you were going to say?"

Used to. Before Roelfje died, she meant. No need to explain. But he no longer knew what kind of person he used to be, couldn't remember what he'd been like in the old days, and God knows he'd tried. Actually, it was as if he didn't have a former self. His school years, teachers—very few memories were left. He lived with fragments. It sounded so inane, but it was true: part of the bookkeeping was gone, vanished. Time to bring this conversation to an end. Erna was bound to say something about how he ought to devote more time to his own history, but that wasn't what he wanted to hear. Things were fine the way they were. The man in the photograph could remain a stranger; he himself had something else to do.

"I'll come and stand beside you at the window," he said.

"Your arm around my shoulder?"

"Yes."

"Well, I guess it's beddy-bye time." She hung up. He listened to the silence for several seconds, then went to bed.

And we, watching the strange happenings in their world from our lighted world—what do we see? The four of them lying in their beds, or, as Zenobia likes to put it, the four of them suddenly changing from vertical beings into horizontal beings. "Falling off the edge of the world," she calls it, as if they could leave their world. To us it looks as if they pass their entire existence either unconscious, numb, or asleep, so that the short rest they're having now is actually a duplication. They think of it as resting, and in the context of their rootless lives, it is. But it takes them even further away from us. At least they don't refuse to think, unlike most people. In fact, you might even say that each of them has, in his or her own way, found a large piece of the puzzle, but it's not enough. The wrong doors, the wrong paths. We can do no more. Our power, such as it is, is limited to keeping watch. And to reading thoughts the way you read books. We have no choice but to follow. We turn the pages, listen to the words of their drowsy musings, listen to their thoughts converge as they lie in their dark bedrooms in the snow-packed city, four spiders weaving one web, as impossible as that may seem. They play back the words they spoke tonight, say what they didn't say a few hours ago, snatches, threads, the missing loose ends. Tomorrow, when they wake up, the chemistry of the night will have scrambled the thoughts, unraveled the web, and they will have to start all over again. That's how it goes down there.

A British voice filled the room with the dead and the wounded. Arthur usually woke up to the BBC World Service, as if he couldn't cope with the world in any other language at that hour. Most of the time he was already awake, waiting for a male or female voice to announce his or her name before launching into the news. Perhaps they thought you could deal better with the atrocities, riots, troop movements, attacks, hurricanes, crop failures, floods, earthquakes, train crashes, trials, scandals, and tortures if you knew who they were. A person—an actual person with a name and pattern of speech you gradually began to associate with that name—told you what was happening in Iraq, Afghanistan, Sierra Leone, or Albania, so that it all sounded—just as the robustness of the dollar, the coughing of the yen, or the temporary indisposition of the rupee did—like the latest bit of family gossip.

He remembered hearing somewhere that when World War II broke out, one of those voices had interrupted the program to announce that Britain was now at war, and that five years later, when the war had ended, the same calm, comforting, imperturbable voice—seeming to float above the world—had continued the interrupted program with the words "As I was saying...," thereby reducing the war to a mere hiatus. Just one of those things that happen, have always happened, and will continue to happen.

Nevertheless, this morning Arthur was still asleep when the voice, a woman's this time, burst into his brain at exactly seven o'clock. By the time he switched off the radio, the masked fragments of his dream had been hijacked by a BBC voice with a slight Scottish accent. It was still dark on the other side of the uncurtained window. He lay completely still, to avoid the thoughts that would inevitably come—a ritual soul-searching that would involve not only last night's conversation and the previous day's deeds, but also the time and place in which he now found himself. The daily discipline of a Jesuit, or perhaps it was the opposite: the mental wallowing of a man with no obligations. But he'd deliberately made sure he had a lot of free time, so that he could work on his project. Just what was he hoping to achieve with that never-ending collection of his? How much time should he give himself? Would he ever finish it? Or didn't that matter? Wasn't it necessary to find an exact form for it, a composition? On the other hand, he always worked with whatever material came his way, with whatever images he happened to run across. The unifying element was the fact that he had chosen the images and filmed them. Perhaps, he thought, it was like writing a poem. As far as he could tell from the conflicting statements of poets, they didn't work along established lines either, except that most of them began with an image, or a sentence, or a thought jotted down in a burst of inspiration, often without understanding it themselves. Could he now say with any degree of certainty why he had shot those scenes at Potsdamer Platz last night? Maybe not, but he knew they "fit." Fit what? Still, a poem didn't have to meet the same demands as a film. Except that nobody had asked him to make this film. He was paying for it out of his own pocket, simply because he wanted to make it, so perhaps he actually was more like a poet who wanted to write a poem.

A poem, no matter how short, was about the world. Or did that sound too ridiculous? He was working on a film no one had asked to be made, just as no one, as far as he knew, ever asked that a poem be written. The film—this much he did know for sure—would have to say something about the world as he, Arthur Daane, saw it. That meant that he would also have to disappear in it. He hadn't deliberately set out to deal with such themes as time, anonymity, disappearance, or, however much he despised the word, farewell. It had just happened. The thing had written itself. Germany had also written itself, though you could hardly claim it was anonymous. The trick would be to fit the two together, to get them to rhyme. In the meantime, he'd have to be patient and collect more material. Most of the shots would be filmed here in Berlin, so he'd have to make sure it didn't turn into a documentary. He should stop worrying: after all, it wouldn't be the first time clarity had arisen out of chaos. And if it didn't work, he didn't owe anyone an explanation.

Why the hell Germany? Because it was dogged by the same kind of misfortune as he was? But there was no proof of that. In fact, wasn't it just the opposite now? These days the German economic powerhouse fueled the rest of Europe, the deutsche mark was as solid as a rock, and Germany's geographical position ensured that it would continue to play a pivotal role in European affairs. Still, whenever that enormous body turned over in its sleep, earthquakelike tremors ran through its neighbors. At some point in history each of these countries had suffered injuries that had left an indelible scar on its national psyche. The wounds of occupation, defeat, and humiliation had led to bitterness, suspicion, and distrust. And in the colossus next door these had been combined in turn with grief, penitence, and guilt to produce a melancholy they themselves often called the "German disease"—an unhappiness born of doubt because it was and never will be clear to what extent the nonguilty should have to bear the guilt of the previous generation, and whether there truly is, as some people claim, a fatal flaw in the German soul that might someday rear its ugly head again.

Not that this could usually be seen on the surface. But to anyone with a seismographic sensitivity, it was obvious that beneath the ostentatious wealth and sleek excellence lay a nagging insecurity. Most people managed to deny it or suppress it, but it popped up at the most unexpected moments. He'd lived here long enough to know that, contrary to the claims of its neighbors, Germany was constantly in the throes of self-examination. It took a variety of forms. For example, all you had to do was count the number of times in any given week the words "Jew" or "Jewish" cropped up in the media. This conscious and/or subconscious obsession continued to send tremors through what had long been a modern and successful democracy. What better proof of that than the fact that as a foreigner you weren't even allowed to mention the word "democracy," because every time you did, the very people who were too young to have taken part in the atrocities would warn you not to underestimate their country—not now, not ever. They would cite recent horrors: the arsons, the Angolan who'd been thrown from an East German train, the skinheads who'd nearly beaten a man to death because he'd refused to say "Heil Hitler." And when you pointed out that these attacks were indeed terrible and reprehensible, but that they also occurred in France and England and Sweden, they would accuse you of being deaf to the approaching thunder.

He remembered walking with Victor through the gardens of Sanssouci, before the castle and grounds had been restored. A dark, rainy day. If he'd ever sought images for his collection, that would have been the perfect place: the purple mourning of the rhododendrons by the ruins of the Belvedere; the disfigured statues of women and angels held upright by rusty iron rods; the cracks running through the brick like scars—they all seemed to deny the carefree name that had been bestowed on the palace by the famous king.

"You've got to admit that Frederick the Great did his best," Victor said. "He played the flute, wrote letters in French, wore a powdered wig, invited Voltaire to come here. Not that Voltaire ever really caught on in Prussia. Too light to suit the Germans. They prefer Hegel and Jünger. The Frenchman was weighed and found wanting. An amusing conversationalist, but a kind of butterfly. Not enough gravity. Not enough marble. Too much irony. Oddly enough, the French have now embraced Jünger and Heidegger. They had Diderot and Voltaire, and now they've got Derrida. Too many words. They've lost the way, just like the Germans."

As if to illustrate his point, a few minutes later he performed a brief dance with a German couple. They started down the steps just as Victor, who was a few feet ahead of Arthur, started up them. When Victor took a few steps to the right to avoid a collision, the husband moved to the left, pulling his wife along with him, so that the three of them found themselves face-to-face again. So Victor moved to the left to get out of the way, just as the couple moved to the right. Finally, he stood still, and the other two made a wide circle around him.

"Have you ever noticed that before?" he asked. "Happens to me all the time. Not in New York, not in Amsterdam, but here. They still don't know where they're going. They haven't got any radar."

Arthur denied it, but Victor was adamant.

"I've lived here long enough to know what I'm talking about. Actually, it makes them rather endearing. National insecurities expressed metaphysically as a clumsy pas de deux. Fifty years ago they knew exactly where they were going. That's what's so amazing. They barged in when they weren't invited, and now when they *are* invited, they hesitate because of what happened then. It's like those dance steps. They're skittish."

Later, in the tearoom, they were treated like two "disruptive elements." The Wall had fallen, but the spirit of the GDR was alive and well in Sanssouci. That meant following the unwritten rules—taking your coat to the cloakroom instead of putting it on the chair next to you, not ordering dishes that weren't available even though you had no way of knowing what those might be, and generally assuming a subservient role with respect to the staff.

"These people don't seem to be unduly troubled by the transition," Arthur said. "They know exactly what they want."

"What they don't want, you mean. I can hardly wait to see what happens next. Here in the East they're now going have to sit down on that couch and confess to two pasts. They've been taught that they didn't have anything to do with that other one. It wasn't their past, they weren't Nazis, maybe not even really Germans. No need for *them* to examine their consciences. Now they're going to have to deal with the forty years after the war. Beware of the dog! But I'll miss it. Everything will change. It won't be my Berlin anymore. Before long no one will be able to imagine the pure, unadulterated madness, except for the people who lived through it and a handful of nostalgic crackpots like me. Even if they blow up the Wall tomorrow, it'll always be there. Be careful, my friend: only a few people are needed to create the system; the rest have to live with it. And in this case they were just plain unlucky. Forty years is a lifetime. So that calls for a little humility on our part."

How long ago had that conversation taken place? Five years, maybe six? Light, the first signs of it, had crept up to the window. He could just make out the tall shape of the chestnut in the courtyard. Approximately thirty apartments looked out on that tree. At one time he'd been planning to knock on all thirty doors and ask for permission to film the tree from their windows, but after three people had glared at him in suspicion and turned him down flat, he'd decided against it. Instead, for several years in a row he'd filmed the tree in all four seasons. As soon as it was light enough, that would be the first item on today's agenda. Better to film than to think. More work, less play. He got up and put the coffee on. He could see lights in most of the other windows. They were early risers in this country. Hard workers. He preferred to keep his own light switched off and look at all the people moving around their apartments. He didn't know them, but that didn't matter, or perhaps that's why he was so drawn to them. It made him part of a community, united by the tree.

The only person who'd agreed to let him film from her window had been a little old lady who lived three floors up from him. At that height, you looked directly into the treetop.

"I remember when it was hardly taller than I am. We moved in here before the war. That tree has survived it all—British bombs, everything. My husband died in Stalingrad. Since then I've lived by myself. This is the first time anybody's ever made such a request, but I understand. I talk to my tree and every year it comes closer and closer to me. You can't imagine what it feels like to see new buds and blossoms every spring. Then I know I've lived another year. Oh, we have entire conversations, the tree and I, especially when it starts to get cold. Our winters are so long. By the time it's grown past my window, I'll be dead and gone."

She pointed to her sideboard, to the picture of a young man in an officer's uniform, his blond hair slicked back in a 1930s haircut. He was smiling at the old woman he didn't recognize, and at the young foreigner in his strange clothes.

"I tell him how the tree is doing, how big it's grown. He

can't understand the rest, how everything has turned out. I don't dare tell him."

Every once in a while Arthur would run into her on the stairs. She never gave him the slightest sign of recognition, but merely shuffled past in those sturdy gray shoes that only little old ladies in Germany still wore. A loden coat. A tight-fitting hat with a feather.

The phone rang, but he didn't pick up. No people now, please. All he wanted to do now was wait for the right light. It wouldn't last long, maybe only thirty seconds. A static image, almost a photograph. Still, he was determined to wait. There had to be a certain amount of order in every life, including his. A picture a day keeps the doctor away. He looked at the tree. A tower of snow. Only the hand of a Japanese master could capture that. The snow had redrawn the lines of the tree, almost as if the branches were no longer functional and the tree consisted entirely of snow—a frozen white sculpture carved out of the whitest marble. But he'd have to wait for at least ten minutes. Nothing less than 400 ASA would do.

At that same moment Arno Tieck was debating whether to eat toast or muesli. Then he went back to the thought that had been occupying his mind ever since he first woke up, which was somehow related to the passage from *Purgatory* that he'd fallen asleep over last night. He normally read himself to sleep. He would take a random book from the bookcase and read a random page, regardless of whether he'd had one drink or several, to help escort him into the realm of sleep. He'd read the lines aloud, often hearing his own voice trail off until it seemed to belong to someone else, someone he couldn't see, who was speaking to him from a great distance.

Purgatory was not his favorite Dante book, but at that late hour he'd been struck, as he often was, by the relevance of that chance passage to the essay he was currently working on. He put on his glasses and groped around with his right hand for the book, which must be lying somewhere on the floor beside the bed. He reread the passage:

> O you proud Christians, wretched souls and small,
> Who by the dim lights of your twisted minds,
> Believe you prosper even as you fall,
> Can you not see that we are worms, each one
> Born to become the angelic butterfly,
> That flies defenseless to the Judgment Throne?

And he wondered whether he might be able to use it in his Nietzsche essay. But humanity as a worm wasn't a particularly Nietzschean image, unless you wanted to stretch it to include the despicable Last Man, though of course the Last Man would hardly be concerned about a transcendental world in which he would never be judged. As for the butterfly, even aside from the fact that a worm was biologically incapable of becoming a butterfly, that fragile airiness wasn't the right image either, especially since the poor creature would have to flap its way to the Judgment Throne. No, Dante had let him down. Or perhaps it had been the Hefe. At any rate, he no longer knew why that passage had seemed so meaningful last night.

Neither he nor Zenobia Stejn could have suspected that she was reading that same passage in English just as he was reading it in German. A coincidence of that kind would have struck them both as insanely improbable, though not impossible in a universe that, according to Zenobia, was based entirely on coincidence. In this case, however, coincidence had been helped along by the omnipresence of Dante in all major languages. Zenobia hadn't intended to read Dante, she didn't even own a copy. But this passage had been cited on the last page of a book written by a fellow physicist. Dante's words had made little impression, and she was leery of the metaphysical arguments in the book. But her apartment didn't have central heating, and she didn't feel like getting up to turn on the heater, so she lay in bed a while longer, holding the book in one hand and staring at those six lines. *Infinite in All Directions.* Freeman Dyson was a great theoretical physicist, but why did he have such a need to believe in God? Apparently life without God was unthinkable, even for Einstein and his dice. But she had to admit that there was something appealing about Dyson's concept of an incomplete God—an imperfect being who went on growing alongside his own imperfect creation.

She was a nonbeliever. It didn't really matter whether you lumped the incomprehensible under the heading of "mystery" or "coincidence" or even "God," if that made you feel better. And if you felt the need to believe in something, perhaps it was better to believe in a weak, human God who was searching through all the misery and suffering for his own redemption. Or one who was still growing—assuming that the universe could be said to be growing. Dyson had evidently been told that his ideas were similar to the heretical views of Socinus. That had been the most interesting part of the book. It amused her to think that a person who lived in the same Italy as Galileo and Thomas Aquinas could have come up with the idea of a God who was neither omniscient nor omnipotent. Speculation had always intrigued her, but Dyson had gone way out on a limb. And since he'd been born in the twentieth rather than the sixteenth century, she was inclined to be less forgiving. Such heavy thoughts so early in the morning! It wasn't going to be easy to write an article on Dyson. A God who "grows with the universe as it develops."

That was all well and good, but refusing to differentiate between the mind and God by defining God as that part of the mind that's beyond our understanding—that's where she drew the line. Because in that case whatever we didn't understand would become God. Or, if she'd understood Dyson correctly, if we didn't grow along with God, we would unfortunately get left behind. She'd rather be left behind. Why on earth did he need to believe in anything? The question of God's existence would certainly not be answered in his lifetime, nor any time soon. On the other hand, the idea that humanity was an unfinished product—a good beginning but hardly the last word—had the appeal of the ephemeral. In the distance she caught a faint glimmer of something that not even she was insensitive to, something that went with her photo collection more than her scientific work. Which reminded her of Arthur Daane...and of last night's vodka. One thing was sure—behind that closed Dutch mask a lot was going on that he didn't talk about. You could tell by the way he could spend hours staring at her collection. It must have something to do with what had happened to him. And that, she thought, must somehow be related to his filming. Arno had been very enthusiastic about his project, but Arthur hadn't wanted to show it to her yet. "Later. Right now it's just a series of fragments. I don't know how it's going to turn out." She'd seen the documentary he'd made with Arno, and it was excellent, but she gathered that he was now in search of something else. Arthur had what she called a "second soul." Come to think of it, so did Dyson, though you couldn't prove that any more than you could his ideas. It was apparently impossible to think about these things without lapsing into ridiculous categories: mind, God, soul. Better switch on the heat. But she had to hand it to Dyson, he wrote well. "Matter is the way particles behave when a large number of them are lumped together." That had a certain charm, but butterflies—even Dante's—flapping their way to the Judgment Throne weren't going to do her much good on a cold winter day like this.

Victor Leven had been up for more than an hour by the time Zenobia Stejn and Arno Tieck had reluctantly left their warm beds. The shrill, merciless jangle of the alarm clock must be obeyed. Exercise, shave, ice-cold shower, coffee, no breakfast, no music, no voices, get dressed, as if you were going out, hair impeccably combed, up to the studio, sit on the stool in front of your current project, stare...and keep on staring for at least an hour before you make the first move. He himself didn't know what he thought about during that hour, and that wasn't a matter of chance, but of training.

"I want my mind to be blank," he once told Arthur, "which is damned hard, but you can teach yourself how to do it. You're probably going to tell me it's impossible, because that's what everybody says—'something must be going through your head as you sit there and stare at your work'— but it's not true. Or not anymore. Talking about your work is the height of absurdity, but since it's you, I'll tell you this: I don't think about the object—I *become* the object. Satisfied now? End of conversation."

Once in a while there it was—a light that threw everything into such sharp relief that the sky seemed about to break, like crystal. Potsdamer Platz was now a wide-open plain, transformed by the thick layer of frozen snow on the bulldozers into a cubist landscape. He let the camera roll, struggling against the reflected light. There wasn't a trace of last night left. The policewoman, the ambulance—none of that had happened. Only a few hundred feet of obscure, jerky film remained. Now he'd have to find a way through the fence again. Somebody had shut it. He tried to yank it open, but only succeeded in losing his balance on the ice. This time he was the one who banged his head. He grabbed his camera to protect it, fell on his back to the frozen ground, and felt something slip out of his pocket. He tried to scrabble to his feet, but wound up sitting on his knees and staring at a picture of Thomas that had slid out of his wallet—his son, smiling up at him from a passel of credit cards.

"Do you need any help?" asked a security guard.

"No, thanks."

This was no coincidence. The dead refused to leave him in peace. But he didn't want them just now. Holding on to the fence, he pulled himself to his feet. Then he carefully laid the camera down on the snow so he could pick up Thomas's picture.

"I don't have time," he mumbled. Could you talk to the dead that way? He tucked the picture back in his wallet, but it didn't help. No matter where he went, they would follow.

He was here, and they were everywhere; they didn't have a
home, so they wandered all over; they were no longer bound
by time, so they were always there. "Time means nothing to
them now"—thank God he hadn't been the one to utter that
obnoxious phrase. It's what the priest had said at the funeral.
Her parents had insisted on a Catholic service, and in the
confusion of those days he'd agreed, as he'd also agreed to
have Thomas baptized, though he didn't believe in all that
nonsense. He'd been raised without religion, and Roelfje was
a lapsed Catholic, which her parents always blamed on him.
Before Thomas's baptism he'd never even seen a Catholic rite.
Suddenly the casually dressed man they'd just been talking to
in the rectory entered the church from a side door dressed in
a white embroidered gown. Then his father-in-law took the
baby from Roelfje and repeated, more or less on cue, very
strange answers to a very strange series of questions. Every
time the priest asked something like "Do you renounce Satan
and all his works?" he said, "I do renounce them," repeating
the phrase over and over again because Thomas was too
young to say it himself. Arthur stood beside them and filmed
the whole African rite of exorcism in a kind of rage. All that
pagan mumbo-jumbo made him feel that his child was being
taken away from him. But in this case *he* was the heathen.
That had been clear in the close-ups he'd made of Roelfje,
in the shine of her eyes as she followed the ritual. Afterward
she told him that "it was actually quite beautiful," and that
even though she didn't believe in it anymore, it would have
been very empty without a ceremony, and this way she had
the feeling that Thomas had been welcomed into the world
with a bit of fanfare. If you weren't religious, it didn't matter
one way or the other, but now there'd been a kind of celebration of his birth, and besides it had made her parents
happy. He didn't say what he'd been thinking: namely, that as
far as he could tell she hadn't done it merely to please her

parents, that traces of the old superstition still lingered in her too. As if all that incense-smelling priest had to do was mumble a few magical incantations in his effeminate, exalted voice, and Thomas would be given some kind of extra protection. Perhaps the reason he hadn't said it was that her superstition, her otherworldliness, was one of the things he secretly loved about her. He'd thought of another adjective for her: unhurried. Oh, honestly (Erna)—why don't you just say that you're attracted to her because she's not modern? But that sounded silly and old-fashioned. No; unhurried was better, so that's how he continued to think of her. Roelfje was a person who had decided what her own tempo in life should be. Still, his unhurried wife had died a very swift death. As soon as he heard the news, he'd flown off to Spain. The airline company had asked him to bring dental charts. That was when he'd understood that he would probably not be allowed to see them again. And he hadn't. Bodies burned beyond recognition—that's how the newspapers had described it, but he couldn't bring himself to dwell on the idea. It had been an abstraction, like the X rays, which the identification team had returned to him, as if he needed them for some reason. Shiny gray celluloid teeth in faceless jaws—he'd torn them to shreds in his hotel room. None of it had been real, not even the two white caskets—the big one alongside the little one—in that same church, with the horrible 1930s stained-glass windows and the vaulted ceiling, which had bounced back the words of the priest, the same awful man who'd done the baptism, speaking the words he'd never forget as long as he lived. The priest had called them by their first names, as if they'd been his own wife and child. "Roelfje and Thomas have left us. They have gone on ahead. Time means nothing to them now." That nauseating rhetorical trick, in that sissyish, affected voice of his, that miserable series of past and present tenses, they *have gone* on ahead, time *means* nothing to them now, means, which implies that they were still here, they just lacked that one element, time, something you have or you don't have, like money or bread, something you could buy or go out and get. Time heals all wounds, they say, but that must refer to a different time, one you still had. Another one of those lies, because he hadn't been healed, not as far as he could tell. He stamped his foot so hard that it jarred the base of his skull. Did it never end? The dead were cunning, they caught you when you least expected it. Mourning. For every year you had together there are three years of mourning, Erna had told him. Oh, damn it, Erna. He looked over his shoulder, as if someone was in back of him, thinking all the while, this is pure madness, leave me alone, no milk today, Mr. Milkman. Go. He knew where he was going. He too had his gods. That was also nonsense, but anyway. Quickly, as if he were being followed, he walked toward the Brandenburg Gate, his eyes fastened on the slippery footprints in the frozen snow. He was out of film, so he clicked open his camera and inserted a new cassette. Sidewalks—how odd! So many shades of gray and white. Wide feet, narrow heels, boots. Hordes of people must have passed by here last night and this morning. Each of them had left imprints in the snow, which had frozen along with all the others. Passersby—that's what we call the people who happened by, who left their marks and went on. The bodies that had pressed down on these sidewalks were now somewhere else. He decided to follow a distinctive set of footprints and film it as long as he could, so he started down the street, holding the camera just above the frozen tracks. To his left he could see the leafless trees of the zoo, lined up like a black picket fence with white shadows of snow on the branches. It suddenly occurred to him that he could mix these footprint pictures with the images of the feet going down the steps to the U-Bahn. A crowd heading somewhere, without a visible goal. Movement, like this one, in which an empty image was left behind but kept moving forward into infinity. How long should you hold the shot to suggest infinity? That sounded terrible, but it was somehow at the heart of his project—the insane idea that kept eluding him, wriggling out of his grasp, but which he thought, or hoped, would eventually become clear to him once he had collected enough pictures. After all, he had the time, time still meant something to him.

"All of humanity seen through the prism of Berlin?" That had to be Victor.

"Not just humanity, and not just Berlin."

"Well then," Victor had asked, "what's your criterion?" Always the same question, and never the right answer.

"My own instincts?"

"I hear a question mark. Do you let your instincts be guided by anything?"

Yes, my soul, he thought of saying, but he'd rather bite his tongue off first.

"Myself," he said.

"Can you sum it up in one word?"

No, he couldn't. You could hardly say it was about "contradiction." And yet it was. Those footsteps led somewhere. They had a destination. But at the same time they disappeared into the unknown. Anonymous footsteps, unclear destination, disappearance—a blind force driving people toward something that ended in their disappearance. Only when you realized that this was how the deception worked could you put it to use. And show it. But he didn't say a word.

"Art is precision," Victor went on. Another gem. "Precision and organization. Have you considered the possibility of failure?"

"Yes, but that hasn't stopped me."

"Coming back from the hunt empty-handed? Only in it for the thrill of the chase? Bugles, beaters, barking dogs?"

"Something like that. But on my own. No dogs."

The next day he'd received a small package in the mail. A CD from Victor, the work of a composer he'd never heard of. Ken Volans. The color photograph on the cover depicted a wide, flat landscape, a desert, an empty savanna. He'd immediately associated it with Australia, since he'd once worked there as a cameraman on what had turned out be a very unsuccessful documentary on the Aborigines. The idea had been to use Bruce Chatwin's book to explain what songlines were. But the British director had evidently missed the point of the book and was more interested in the human casualties, the down-and-outers who'd been banished from their tribes and wound up in the gutters of the big cities; black men and women reeking of beer who had lost their place in their own continent and, even if you could understand them, would have had nothing poetic to say about the way their people had once walked thousands of miles through that empty landscape without getting lost because they could sing their way through it. What appeared to the inexperienced eye to be a monotonous sandy plain that you'd never survive on your own actually contained signs that were explained in an endless series of recitatives. Sung maps. There, too, he had wanted to film footsteps. Instead, he'd found himself filming beer bottles.

Hunting, collecting—he could imagine the smile on Victor's face as he'd wrapped up the CD. Only later did he find out that the composer hadn't been inspired by Australia, but by Africa. Still, that didn't change the effect of the music: a continuous, compelling rhythm that went on through the entire piece. You couldn't help but think of people moving through a treeless landscape, people who wouldn't slow their pace for even a second. It sounded to him as if they were all conversing. God knows what they were saying. What did people talk about as they moved through that landscape? The same people who could find water where you saw only drought, and food where you would die of hunger. Men and women, creatures with the power of speech who had an entire continent to themselves, where everything had a name and a soul, a creation made for them alone, in which their ancestors had lived from the beginning of time. Dreamtime, a form of eternity. What would it have been like to live in such a world?

He remembered a night in Alice Springs. Despite the warnings, he'd gone for a walk outside the town. No sooner had he passed the last houses than the sky had fallen down around him—there was no other way of describing it. He'd kept walking because he didn't want to admit to himself that he was scared. Of what? Of nothing, of course. Scared wasn't the right word. It had been pure angst, a gut-level fear of the sizzling silence, the dry, dusty smell of the land, of quick rustles, the sigh of nothingness, a wind-blown leaf—breathing, whispering sounds that had made the silence seem all the more dangerous. And suddenly three figures had appeared out of nowhere, risen up out of the ground. In the light of the half-moon he'd even been able to see the yellow of their eyes in their gleaming black faces, which were a thousand years older than his, because they'd never had to change theirs, because until recently their world had stayed the same. They'd said nothing, he'd said nothing. He'd stood still and looked at them and they'd looked back, without hostility, without curiosity, slightly swaying, as if unable to shake off their continuous motion. They'd smelled of beer, but he didn't think they were drunk.

"You were lucky nothing happened," he was later told, but he didn't believe it. The fear he'd felt before their arrival had suddenly dissolved. Instead, he'd felt humble, because he wasn't part of their world. And inadequate, because he wouldn't have lasted a week out there. Not only because he wouldn't have been able to find food and water, but also because he wouldn't have been protected by spirits, wouldn't have been able to sing his way through that land and, because he was deaf and dumb, would have been lost forever.

Now (now!) he was standing here like an idiot beside the Brandenburg Gate. He walked over to the enormous statue of Pallas Athena in one of the niches and laid his hand on her huge bare foot. The only thing that might seem familiar to an Aborigine, aside from her human shape and the gown falling in chiseled folds over her colossal breasts and mighty knees, would be the owl on her helmet, and possibly her spear. How much past could a person actually accommodate inside himself? There was something vaguely distasteful about being able to switch so quickly from ancestor spirits to a goddess, from naked blacks with white body paint to armored Teutons, from a dry desert to an icy plain. He looked at the statue, at the goddess nobody worshiped anymore. The whole world was a reference, everything pointed back to something: owl, helmet, and spear, laurel wreath, necklace, traces that clung to him, schoolteachers, Greek, Homer. It wasn't just the dead who wouldn't leave him alone; it was the endless span of time that his life could seemingly encompass, the incalculable amount of space that allowed him, a mere ant, to move from an icy Australian desert to the Greek goddess of his schooldays, who had sought momentary refuge—only a couple of hundred years ago—in an arch with Doric columns that had seen Friedrich Wilhelm and Bismarck and Hitler pass through its gate, where she now sat on her ample buttocks proclaiming a message that a triumphant eighteenth century had shouted from the rooftops, but which now fell on deaf ears.

Many troops had come and gone, like the ebb of the tide, through this historical washbasin. When you were twice as old as he was now, it must be almost unbearable. Lost in the labyrinthine web of a computer, there would be no reminders to point you in the right direction. Or was he the only one who noticed? Ghosts! How often had he seen a film of this triumphal gate before he'd actually seen it in reality? The goose-stepping men, their heads all turned in the same direction, the pounding of boots, the perfectly synchronized mechanical movement that had now been halted forever because machines can also die, the open Mercedes, the outstretched arm, the backward rune sign. Owing to primitive film techniques, their predecessors in the previous war had moved in a jerky quickstep, which stripped them even more ruthlessly of their humanity—jittery cogs marching in a rapid tremolo from here to the trenches, as if they were in a hurry to die. And to think that they had walked here and thought things that will be lost to us forever.

He'd gone to see the reopening of the Brandenburg Gate— another moment of euphoria. He must be visible somewhere in those photographs, enveloped in the crowd, a thinking human being like all the others around him, thinking and observing, getting swept up by the euphoria, swept along with the crowd, moving from one side to the other. Once again he'd found himself standing on the viewing platform and looking out over the world that had long been off limits, watching young people dance on top of the Wall, which hadn't been torn down yet. It had been night, the first night, and the dancers had been sprayed by water cannons, but they didn't care; searchlights had lit up the white water shields, and he'd looked at the swirling figures of the dancers, at their indestructible joy, and for a moment he'd had the feeling— for what was probably the first time in his life—that he belonged, not just to these people, but to *all* people. The dancing had continued, not only on the Wall, but also down on the ground, at the foot of the platform, directly behind the

Reichstag, and a young blonde had grabbed him by the hand and dragged him into the whirling mass. Later the two of them had gone to a café, then to a house somewhere in the Kreuzberg district, and afterward he'd walked all the way home, down long, long streets, and had never seen her again. He remembered it as a moment of happiness because for once it hadn't been clouded by other thoughts. Her radiant eyes and jubilant mood had erased the other memories. Her apartment, her furniture, her name—all gone. All that was left was a glow and a whispered farewell. It had been a minor event in the general happiness, something that came naturally when you were part of humanity, almost as if he'd been obeying a law of nature, just as fifty years ago, in this same city, they had burned and plundered and raped.

He paused. Which direction should he take? It would be nice to see the young woman again, but he no longer knew where she lived or what her name was, and, besides, that would be breaking the agreement they hadn't made. Which direction should he take? His Greek teacher had once told him, in reference to Odysseus, that the only people who were completely free were the ones who can always ask themselves the question "Which direction should I take?" He'd never forgotten it. But years had gone by before he'd realized that it wasn't true. Odysseus had been cunning, but not free. Or about as free as he himself was. Our crafty hero had needed to be rescued countless times by Athena, who had come to him in a variety of guises. There she was again—the goddess. But could she still work her magic? On that momentous night, if that girl, that woman, had not been her visible self, if you could believe for even one minute that a divine creature watched over your fate, might she have been that nameless personification—"a young woman," "a shepherd," "an old woman"—someone who had brought him out of his autism for a few brief moments?

He looked up at the statue of Athena, but her eyes looked right past him. Gods never saw you unless they wanted to. Odysseus had been lucky—someone had pointed him in the right direction. She could have come up with a simpler solution, but it wouldn't have made as good a story. He filmed a scene he'd filmed before, a long sweep beginning with Potsdamer Platz, moving slowly over to the Brandenburg Gate and ending by the Reichstag. He held the camera in his hand—there should be a slight wobble. Nothing was stable, especially not here. Actually, when you thought about it, the Germans hadn't been very lucky. They'd always known exactly where they wanted to go, but had come back in defeat.

"Oddly enough, I rather like them for it." Victor.

Oh, if only he didn't have a topographical memory! For it had been here, right on this very spot, that his friend had uttered those exact same words. He'd also used another word that Arthur had remembered all these years, because it had seemed so out of place in these surroundings—the word "powder." Victor's remark, "Oddly enough, I rather like them for it," had been the beginning of a conversation, or, rather, a series of conversations, since Victor's lectures tended to be peripatetic, and this time the walk had included the Scheunenviertel, the synagogue, the Prenzlauer Berg district, the death of the writer Franz Fühmann in the Charité, and naturally the Reichstag and the Brandenburg Gate.

"They don't like themselves, and they don't like each other. So I suppose it's up to me to do it for them."

On such occasions Arthur never knew whether Victor was joking.

"Powder."

"What?"

"It's powder. Here, feel it." He'd held up his hand, rubbed an imaginary substance between his thumb and forefinger and dusted off his hand. Powder.

"Can't you feel that?"

"What am I supposed to feel?"

"You're clearly not a sculptor."

It had been spring. He'd seen the other pedestrians stare as Victor—an impeccably dressed gentleman with gleaming black hair and a silk scarf knotted around his neck—groped in the air, pulled out something that wasn't there, and wiped the invisible stuff from his fingers. A magic trick.

"It's seeped into everything. Including their eyes. Which is why they can't see where they're going. Once again. Re-unification—they don't understand the first thing about it. A whole country is handed to them on a platter, and they don't know where to start. Do you remember the euphoria? The people passing out bananas at Checkpoint Charlie? Welcoming their brothers and sisters from the East? And have you listened to them lately? About how *they* dress, about how *they* behave? Racist jokes about people with the same color of skin. Going on and on about all the things *they* can't do, or are too lazy to do. 'We couldn't afford a vacation in Mallorca after the war, but they're already heading there in droves.' 'Half of the population denounced the other half to the Stasi, and now we're stuck with the whole lot.' 'If it were up to me, the Wall would still be there.' 'You can't make one country out of two, you can't undo forty years, they're not like us.' Etc., etc. The entire repertoire."

"So what do the East Germans say?"

"They feel they've been royally screwed, and who can blame them? First we welcome them with open arms and a hundred marks, then we go check out the old ancestral home. Sell us your factories; we can do it better. Mutual animosity, suspicion, envy, dependence—powder that creeps in everywhere. Have you listened to your enlightened friends in West Berlin? They had such a beautiful enclave. Subsidies could be had for the asking—a theatrical paradise, studios for artists, exemption from military service. All gone. You can tear down the Wall, but it won't go away. And as if that isn't bad enough, there are those in the West who are filled with so much self-hate that they claim the East should have been left the way it was—such a beautiful country, so much solidarity. That may be true, but if you want to see the bourgeois comrades in all their glory, go take a look at the private hunting grounds of the party bosses. Try to imagine what it would have been like to have a so-called independent nation jammed in between Poland and the fat-cat West. Can't you just picture the exodus, the total dismantling? The East really would have been colonized. At least now the West has to pay for the dream, albeit not without a gnashing of teeth. Oh, everybody knows exactly how the other side should have behaved. Every closet is full of skeletons—every report, list, and trial has been documented and is lying in wait in a file somewhere, with all the names and pseudonyms. Someday you ought to take the U-Bahn all the way to the end of the line in the East. A real mind-blower, even now. Make sure to look at the faces of the old people, at the cobwebby bramble-filled heads of those who've survived it all. There aren't many left, but they're there. Think of what this century has been like for them, compared to, say, the Americans: empire, revolution, Versailles, Weimar, depression, Hitler, war, occupation, Ulbricht, Honecker, reunification, democracy. An extraordinary sequence, don't you think? And they're still here in this city. Fanatics and heroes, right and wrong, two, three, and even four pasts that have toppled over on each other, an entire history book etched in those faces. Russian POW camps, resistance and collaboration, disgrace and shame, another loss, everything wiped out, photographs in a museum, flag-waving, memories, powder. Nothing left, except the others who don't understand a single thing. And where are we now? Don't tell me you didn't enjoy my aria."

"So why do you live here?" Arthur asked.

"You haven't understood a word I've been saying. I live here because I want to. This is where it's all happening. Mark my words." And he made the same gesture with his finger that Arthur had made with his camera—the buildings, the empty spaces, the phallic TV tower in Alexanderplatz with that obscene silver swell in the middle. That evening, when Arno joined them, Arthur tried to get Victor to repeat his tirade. He wanted to know how Arno would react. But Victor, who usually talked only in short sentences in the presence of more than one person, seemed to have lost the fire that had fueled him in the morning, and the word "powder" was not mentioned even once.

Just then two young backpackers asked him for directions. They had one of those wretched foldout maps that made the world look as if it had been torn apart before you'd had a chance to find your way. They addressed him in broken German with what was clearly a Spanish accent and didn't seem in the least surprised when he answered in Spanish. Owners—his term for them—of major languages, whether they spoke German, English, or Spanish, always seemed to take it for granted that the less fortunate, who had been saddled with a secret language, would see to it that they could make themselves understood to the rest of the world, despite their initial handicap. Together, the three of them attempted, with frozen fingers, to put the pieces of Berlin back together, and Arthur pointed to the holy places on the map and in reality, as if he worked as a guard at this historical museum and was paid to steer visitors in the right direction. They thanked him profusely ("You Germans are so friendly") and left him with a sudden homesickness for Spain...for other sounds...for other light. Light that wouldn't be harshly reflected by the snow, as it was here, where it seemed to transform everything it touched into the most breakable glass.

The light in Spain could also be fierce at times, so that you had to go through all kinds of contortions to get a decent picture. But it always seemed to be light there, the light a part of the landscape rather than a cause for celebration, as it was today, when everything seemed unreal.

He turned himself around in a circle, as if his camera was still rolling. Those monstrosities built on Otto-Grotewohl-Strasse ("Only party bigwigs were allowed to live that close to the Wall") seemed to be floating on air. He wondered how many cities he knew well enough to be able to walk around blindfolded. He could actually feel the distance between himself and those buildings as a physical sensation—he was organically connected to them, part of a huge body. But why this particular city? A city both triumphant and humiliated, defiant and chastened, royal and common. A city of decrees and revolts and gap-toothed lots. Berlin was a crippled war pilot, a living organism condemned to the past. Time itself had become hopelessly entangled in these buildings, everything seemed to be upside down, accusation and denial had merged shrilly into one—this city didn't grant you a moment's peace. The present building craze would only make it worse. Blatant restorations, like the Gendarmenmarkt, would have to age at least fifty years before poor Schiller and his laurel wreath wouldn't look quite so out of place. No, you didn't get off scot-free when you lived here. Berlin was a guilty city, a captive city. He'd heard the stories—rubble, Allied sectors, airlift—the usual stories, so that there was no need for a constant outpouring of emotion, especially not if you were a foreigner. But once you'd been ensnared in the web, it was hard to extricate yourself.

Years ago he'd filmed the war museum in Canberra. One image had continued to haunt him: a very sinister-looking Lancaster bomber. The plane had filled an entire room, like a prehistoric dinosaur. On the nose cone, just below the cockpit, there had been a series of stripes, one for every successful mission, for every time the plane had returned unscathed from Germany. They'd also shown a documentary. He remembered the slow eerie progress of a squadron across a sky lit up by searchlight beams and tracer bullets, and the ominous, unremitting drone of the engines.

He'd mentioned it to Victor, who'd immediately begun to imitate the sound: a low bass, a long continuous hum that seemed to go on forever.

"My parents used to look up and say, 'They're headed for Berlin.' There was even a popular song that began: 'In the meenie-meenie-moonlight, we're off to bomb Berlin tonight.'"

Years before, Goebbels had sung the aria to this bass continuo in the Sportpalast—his famous "Do you want total war?" speech.

"He asked very politely," Victor said. "It's just that he shouted a bit. But it was so noisy. Such a big crowd. Try it sometime, as an artist—getting so many people together under one roof. He had the voice, all right, but not the looks. A real unsavory character. First he had all those children, then he poisoned them. Clearly a failed artist. Scary types. Just like that other would-be painter. Got to be on your guard." And he'd imitated Goebbels again, so that the people going by had looked up in alarm.

Another walk. This time the Ministry of Aviation. ("Göring hated Lancasters.") Victor had stuck his finger in a bullet hole ("I lay my hand on His wound") and said, "If you think about it, buildings and voices make a city what it is. And that includes the buildings and voices that are no longer here. Every city is a voiceful city. And that's that."

Arthur had never forgotten the phrase: a voiceful city. Of course it was true of all old cities, but that particular question had not been uttered, written, proclaimed, or shouted in any other city. It was one thing to think of a city as a repository of buildings, but voices—that was something else again. How could you even imagine the sheer numbers? The words had vanished into thin air, one step ahead of the dead, yet here in Berlin you had the feeling that they hadn't gone away, that the air was saturated with them, and you found yourself wading through a mass of invisible, inaudible words, for the simple reason that this is where they had been spoken— whispered rumors, execution orders, commands, final words, farewells, interrogations, messages to headquarters. Add to that all the other anonymous words that are always said in cities. It would take you untold hours to string them together again, except that you would die trying—smothered, drowned, suffocated in a surfeit of words. Even today, in this ice palace, the words were everywhere. You could hear them in the bright brittle light, whispering, murmuring, mingling with the new words of the people who happened to be passing by—white noise audible to only the most sensitive of ears, ears which no human being ought to possess because the incessant hum made cities, especially this city, unbearable. In an effort to drown it out, he began to whistle.

"You're in a good mood today," said an elderly gentleman, tugging at the leash of a calf-sized dog, and Arthur suddenly realized that he was. Good mood today, good mood today, he thought, and as he set off again he heard the old man call, "*Achtung*! Be careful, it's slippery!" But the warning came too late, for he had already skittered across the ice, performed a graceless pirouette, and, for the second time that day, wound up flat on his back, hugging the camera to his chest like a baby and staring up at the snowy branches and cracked, icy blue sky. Somebody up there was trying to tell him something. The old man had come over to help, and when he didn't get up, the dog stuck its huge head in his face, so that he found himself staring up into two big wet eyes and a shiny trail of frozen tears.

"I told you to be careful!" said the old man reproachfully. Arthur stood up and brushed off the snow.

"Don't worry. I'm good at falling."

It was true. One time he'd followed the advice of a war correspondent and taken a course in falling. Time well spent.

"There are a number of countries in the world where the ability to switch from a vertical position to a horizontal one in no time flat will come in very handy," the instructor had begun. "There's nothing quite like the sound of a bullet whizzing through the space that you'd been occupying only half a thought ago." Twice Arthur had had the occasion to find out just how true that was: once in Somalia and once during Mardi Gras in Rio. Sudden shots, the amazing whoosh of falling bodies. Except that when everybody got up, there were three people lying on the ground who would never get up again. The course's finale had been a fall down a steep flight of stairs. The instructor, an ex-paratrooper, had turned it into an elaborate act. His helpless body had thumped and banged its way down the stairs, landing at the bottom in a motionless heap. He'd lain there long enough for their faces to be drained of color. Then he stood up, brushed off his clothes, and said, "Pretending to be dead is a useful trick. It gives you the advantage of surprise."

You're in a good mood today, pretending to be dead gives you the advantage of surprise, no, he wasn't going to let anyone or anything rob him of the rest of today. He'd walk over to Alexanderplatz, stop by the Rote Rathaus, put his hand on the knee of the now forsaken Karl Marx, then go over to the U-Bahn and film feet going down stairs. He waved good-bye to the elderly gentleman, patted the dog on its huge head, and walked east, this time a bit more gingerly.

Two hours later he'd done what he'd set out to do. Marx and Engels were still gazing toward the Far East, pretending not to notice the bulge in the TV tower, but there had been a miniature snowman on Marx's lap, and that had suddenly made him seem very human, like an old-fashioned grandpa who'd forgotten to put on his overcoat. Today he'd been less interested in the image of the feet going down to the U-Bahn as in the sound—the continuous squish and squelch in the slushy snow on the top steps, and the drier sound toward the bottom, which was less audible than he had hoped. Boots had all but died out in a sudden epidemic. Apparently nobody wore real shoes these days, just garish sport shoes that contrasted shrilly with their drab clothing. A treadmill, that's what it was, pushing the world away with every step. City people only began to look really strange when you filmed their feet—cogwheels in a faceless factory churning out unknown products twenty-four hours a day.

"They should have put a pedometer on your feet when you were born." Erna. "That way you'd know how many miles you've walked in your lifetime. I don't know anybody who walks as much as you do."

"I'm a pilgrim."

"Aren't we all."

And of course it was true. He looked at the chain of feet going by and didn't worry about whether the people attached to those feet were wondering what the eager eye of the camera was hoping to find down by the filthy yellow wall tiles, in the barren wasteland that was not quite inside and not quite outside. They didn't seem to care—must be some TV program.

Shoes were better at expressing humiliation than any other article of clothing. Worn, wet, muddy, sallow in the sandy neon light, they bore people to their dreary destinations through the grottoes of the underworld, only to be kicked into a dark corner at night or shoved under a bed. Actually, he ought to film the display windows of shoe stores, a whole series of them, so that you could see the shoes in all their pristine glory. Unbroken, without masters, headed nowhere, not yet en route.

A moment later he forgot these thoughts entirely, because in the midst of all those shoes he caught a glimpse of cowhide boots—a pair of red, white, and black boots on two fairly small feet. Boots that compelled him to look up, first at the firm, quick-moving, jean-clad legs, then at the black-and-white check jacket, and finally at the wide wool scarf, the same color as the flag that no longer flew over Berlin, which nicely offset the same pair of Berber eyes he'd seen yesterday. The red scarf was easy to follow. She took the U2 to Ruhleben, switched over to the U15 at Gleisdreieck, got out again at Kurfürstenstrasse.

He followed her up the stairs and walked, right behind her, into the sudden light. He knew, or hoped he did, where she was going. At any rate, she was headed in the right direction. North along Potsdamer Strasse, past the Turkish greengrocer—the purple eggplant and yellow peppers looking as if they'd just been shipped in from the North Pole—past the bakery where he always bought a *Zwiebelbrötchen*. He was in familiar territory; this was *his* usual route. From here he could already see the ocher-colored, odd-shaped building that housed the national library: the Staatsbibliothek. She had a canvas bag that was clearly full of books slung over her shoulder. No, he couldn't be mistaken. There was a break in the traffic, and she crossed the busy street and continued up the sidewalk on the right-hand side, very un-German, not waiting for a light or a crosswalk. Should he keep following her? What the hell was he doing? This was insane! Chasing after a red scarf like a lovesick teenager! There was something distasteful about the inequality of their positions. The person being followed was always the innocent one. In this case she was simply going on her way, thinking her own thoughts, unaware of the invisible line between her and the stranger in back of her. He had the advantage—he had a relationship to her, she had none to him. If he were to turn around, she wouldn't follow him. Of that he was sure.

He slowed his steps and stopped at the bridge over the Landwehr Canal. Gray patches of transparent ice, motionless in the black water. What if she stopped too? But she didn't. Following someone was an invasion of their privacy. This time he hadn't caught a good look at her face. A pale white oval had floated past him. He still remembered the stern face and the scar, from yesterday. This wasn't going to work. Besides, he was too old for such games. He should drop it and simply do what he always did, go upstairs to the cafeteria and have a cup of coffee—it costs only one mark to drink the deadly waters of the Lethe—then go back down to the main reading room, sit next to the big window overlooking the Nationalgalerie, and read the newspaper. There were always a couple of homeless people dozing in the armchairs with a crumpled newspaper spread out over their laps as an alibi.

He handed his camera and coat to the cloakroom attendant, held up his empty hands so the two female guards who inspected everyone going in and out could see that he wasn't hiding anything, and walked up the stairs. It had grown a lot more crowded since the students from the East had started coming here; after all, the Staatsbibliothek was more comfortable than Humboldt University. Coeds of all kinds: Iranians in head scarves, Chinese, Vikings, blacks—an exotic collection of butterflies sucking the nectar from their books in total silence. He didn't see her anywhere.

There was a photo exhibit downstairs—camps and starvation this time. It was as if in some people the inability to mourn—the so-called *Unfähigkeit zu trauern*—had gone to the other extreme and been replaced by a compulsive need for perpetual mourning. As if those poor souls were part of a silent monastic order that had failed to find an answer to evil and were therefore condemned to carry it around with them forever. He stared at the pictures as he went by. To eye something—that was the expression. Suffering and starvation always involved the eyes. Bony skulls staring out at you with a permanent expression of bewilderment. Photographs that aged you as you looked at them. With no effort on their part, the dozing homeless people under the *Herald Tribune* or the *Frankfurter Allgemeine* had become part of the exhibit. That, if nothing else, would clearly date the scene to the late twentieth century. In a flash, he suddenly knew where she would be. If you wanted to read *El País*, you had to go to the Ibero-American Institute, in the adjoining building. There was a connecting passage, so you could get there without having to go outside. One step over the threshold and you found yourself in Spain, a few more steps and you were in Buenos Aires, Lima, or São Paulo. He saw the *Nación Granma, Excelsior*, and *El Mundo*, but no *El País*. She had it.

"You've already read it," she said to him in Spanish. "It's yesterday's paper. They're always a day behind here." And off she went. Black sweater. Shoulders. Small teeth. He focused his eyes on the *Excelsior* without really seeing anything. New murders in Mexico. Statement by Zedillo. Missing witnesses. Dead drug dealer. She didn't have a South American accent, or a Spanish one either. Something seemed vaguely familiar, but he couldn't place it, just as he couldn't think of the right word to describe that face. Compact, clenched...though that was an odd word to use about a face. At least she'd noticed him yesterday; that was something. From a distance he followed her movements with his eyes: she went over to a study desk, switched on the lamp—halo of light on the short fingers—took out the books, arranged them in a neat stack. Orderly type. Pen. Notepad. Back to this side of the room, much too close, but not even a glance in his direction. No, not her. Turned on the computer. Waited for the gray screen to fill with pictures, then words, too far away for him to read. Scrolled down, stared, filled in a form. Walked to the call desk, joined the line, didn't fidget or shuffle her feet like the others. Read, without looking up. Voracious. Those teeth could devour an entire book.

A conversation, years ago, about falling in love. With none other than Erna, who was always falling in love. Like so many of their conversations, this one had been conducted in their favorite spot by the window. Dutch light falling on a Dutch face. Light shining in Vermeer eyes, on Vermeer skin. Vermeer—that mysterious painter—had done something to Dutch women. He had taken their sober pragmatism and cast a spell on it. His women held sway over hidden, closed worlds from which the viewer was excluded. The letters in their hands held the key to immortality. Erna had once had a photograph of Roelfje framed, and in that photograph she was reading a letter, one he'd written to her.

"You were in Africa at the time."

Erna's hair was dark blond, Roelfje's had been a lighter shade. Both of them could have been painted by Vermeer. There were still women like that in Holland: solid and transparent at the same time. Only the painter knew the secret. He had seen something that others hadn't seen, something that gave you the feeling, when you stood in front of one of his paintings—regardless of whether you were in Washington, Vienna, or The Hague—that you were being lured inside, and that if you were to go in, a door would close behind you. An all-consuming intimacy. If other people were standing beside him when he was looking at a Vermeer, he felt very Dutch.

"But why?" Arno had asked. "Great art belongs to us all. What's nationality got to do with it?"

"If she were to look up and say something, I'd understand her, and you wouldn't."

He also knew what kind of voices Vermeer's women would have, though he didn't mention that to Arno. Roelfje's voice had been high and light. Erna's was more hurried, more intense, but maybe, he thought, that's because she's lived longer. Voices aged too. From where he was standing at the window he could see Roelfje's picture. He hadn't wanted to reread his letters to her. Inheriting your own letters—it didn't seem right. But he hadn't been able to bring himself to burn them. Rain scratched at the canal—white needles in the dark-green water.

"What do you mean you can't fall in love again? Because it would be a betrayal?"

"No, that's not it."

And it wasn't. If there was such a thing as betrayal, it would have to be survival itself—the unseemly actions of the living, beginning the moment they turned away from the grave and walked off. No matter how often you came back later on, you could never undo the first time—that moment of separation between the living and the dead that had to be exorcised by an interminable shaking of hands, mumbled condolences, coffee brewed by the dead at night, thin slices of egg-yolk-yellow cake, the food of the underworld. She had been left with the men in black, belonged to strangers now, uncaring desecrators, while only a few hundred yards away the man who should have been lying beside her had let himself be roped into the banalities of helplessness.

"So what is it then?"

"Lack of imagination, I guess."

He'd been tempted to say "loyalty," but that would have brought them back to "betrayal," a word that he of all people had no right to use. Erna knew of his escapades, he had no secrets from her.

"Staying single is even crazier. You'd shrivel up, get all moldy. Someday you might meet somebody who..."

Impossible. Not now. The last thing he wanted was intimacy.

"I'm out of the country half the time."

"You were gone a lot back then too."

"I know, Erna."

Meanwhile, the girl had reached the call desk; it was her turn now. A short discussion. The librarian was doing his best. He rifled through the file until he found the right form, then turned around and grabbed two heavy volumes from a rack filled with similar stacks of wisdom. She checked the contents, nodded and returned to her seat. Now all he could see was her back. Not a Vermeer back, that was for sure. Not with those eyes.

How much could you surmise by looking at a total stranger? Her back wasn't giving off any clues. A black rectangle that deflected any and all questions. What the hell was he doing here with his pitiful Mexican newspaper? Did he have a legitimate reason for being here? To his right he heard the gentle click of computer keys. He loved libraries. You were alone, yet surrounded by other people, all of whom were busily engaged in work. A monastic stillness reigned in this room, and after a while he could distinguish the various sounds—muted footsteps, the thud of heavy books, the rustle of turned pages, a whispered conversation, the brief but recurring whirr of a copier. This was the domain of specialists. Everybody here was working on a project that had something to do with Latin America or Spain. Except for him. The newspapers and magazines were his only alibi. That and the fact that he spoke Spanish.

He was a frequent visitor to the main library upstairs. Special books were kept in closed stacks, but the rest were in the so-called reference library. French, German, and English classics, Dutch magazines, various encyclopedias—you could

spend hours there, which he often did. For all they knew, he
was a student. A bit old, but otherwise inconspicuous. Come
to think of it, he didn't stick out in the Spanish department
either. Olav Rasmussen, specialized in nineteenth-century
Portuguese literature—who would know? He put down the
newspaper, walked through one of the narrow cell-like path-
ways to the open stacks up by the call desk, and opened the
first thick volume he happened to see. D. Abad de Sentillon,
Diccionario de Argentinismos. In that case he'd have to alter
his identity. Philip Humphries, Assistant Professor at Syra-
cuse University, specialist in gaucho literature. He plunked
the fat tome down on his desk and switched on the light to
show that it was occupied. The next time he walked off, it
was as Umberto Viscusi, in search of research material for
his Ph.D. on Spanish mystics. His make-believe quest took
him to the card catalogue, a long row of cabinets, where he
pretended to be looking for something. He found all kinds
of things, and after a few minutes he forgot that it was only
a game. Some of the cards had been written by hand, others
typed on typewriters that had given up the ghost long ago.
He jotted down some random titles from different sections
of the card catalogue, infected by a secret, clerkly pleasure.
Haïm Vidal Sephira, *l'Agonie des judéo-espagnols,* José Or-
landis, *Semblanzas visigodas,* Juan Vernet, *La Ciencia en
Al-Andalus: Cartulario del Monasterio de Santa Maria de
la Huerta,* Menéndez Pidal, *Dichtung und Geschichte in
Spanien.*

This too was a collection—a literal bookkeeping of the
world, a repository of past and present reality. It would be
easy to lose yourself in it. He wondered whether there were
books nobody ever asked for anymore, so that the knowledge
between their covers bided its time in a storage depot, waiting for someone to express an interest in that remote corner

of time—the Jewish quarter of Zaragoza in the thirteenth century, a blow-by-blow account of a battle between long-forgotten medieval rulers, the colonial administration of seventeenth-century Peru, all of them as obsolete as the sand grooves and cloud patterns in Zenobia's photographs, yet preserved for the simple reason that they had once existed, had been part of a living person's reality, had lain dormant for years, like radioactive waste, in dusty books or micro-films, as a partial reflection of the truth, an imperfect double, as if the world itself had been pressed between bindings and could be called to life again—the clash of swords, the secret minutes of a negotiation, all those hopes and schemes stifled and crushed under new layers of leather and rustling paper, awaiting the magic eye to conjure them back to life.

He looked at the people sitting at their desks, absorbed in their work. Each of them was somehow connected to a con-crete reality of time and space that was invisible to him. Li-braries were meant to preserve things, he thought, and of course that included the present, which was turning into the past with every moment that went by. But the act of preser-vation was an expression of something else: the determined struggle of even the most trivial of events to be remembered. And that was none other than the will to survive, the refusal to die. If we let even one part of the past—no matter how in-significant—slip away from us, we too could slip into obliv-ion. This preservation mania of ours was intended to ward off death. It didn't matter whether you wanted to study an obscure branch of Aragon's nobility in the tenth century, the municipal register of Teruel, or the blueprint of the harbor in Santa Cruz de Tenerife. The point was that the past could be accessed and therefore still existed. And it would continue to exist until the act of describing the world ceased to exist, to-gether with the world itself.

He glanced over at the table where she had been sitting: her chair was empty. You idiot, he said to himself, though he didn't know whether it was because he'd let her get away or because he was still playing this childish game. Why do you suppose *she* had come here? Those card catalogues had suddenly piqued his curiosity. Make a bet with yourself. Okay, sociology, probably Latin America. Bound to be a contemporary subject, some hot item. You could tell that from her back—no cobwebs, no *temps perdu,* especially no cloud patterns or anonymity. The position of Guatemalan women in the second half of the twentieth century or some such thing. That face, or what he had seen of it, was certainly not interested in things that had vanished long ago.

He walked over to the table where she'd been sitting, up by the call desk. Pretending to pick up something he'd dropped on the floor, he bent down and sneaked a sideways look at the book lying open on her table: a yellowed Spanish text, the same size as the red linen book beside it: *Archivos Leoneses, 1948.* Hmm, not exactly Latin America. Just as he started to straighten up again, he saw something that really threw him: jutting out of her bag was a copy of a Dutch newspaper, *De Groene Amsterdammer.* Hearing short, quick footsteps behind him, he walked on. At the call desk he asked the librarian what the procedure was for getting books out of the closed stacks.

"To read here or take home?"

"I don't know yet."

"If it's to take home, you need to have proof that you live in Berlin or are a legal alien."

A Dutch accent immediately pegged you as a foreigner. But he hadn't heard hers when she spoke Spanish. Had she heard his? On the other hand, you didn't have to be Dutch to be reading *De Groene Amsterdammer.*

"And you also need a letter of reference."

He thanked the man, took an application form, and wrote on the back, "Could I ask you a favor? I'll be upstairs in the cafeteria at 1:00, next to the window, if you'd care to meet me. It's about a letter of reference. Arthur Daane." And he dropped the note on her desk as he went by.

Two hours later she too had a name. Part of the process of de-alienization, the tentative exploration of common borders. People who don't know each other and find their bodies seated across from each other for the first time are establishing boundaries. Names are not self-evident; you can't possibly know the name of a body you've never laid eyes on before. De-alienization—he liked the sound of that word. As of that moment, the other person was becoming less alien. Once it had started, the process could not be undone. You took note of the voice, the gestures, the mannerisms, the body language—all the personal characteristics you weren't familiar with but which defined someone. Border patrols scurried back and forth; thrills of excitement, curiosity, pleasure. At the moment her body language was clearly defensive.

She was still standing next to the table. He got to his feet. "Do sit down," he said. She hadn't introduced herself. But she knew his name, and for several long seconds her unnamed body was at an advantage. He didn't know why that excited him—a nameless woman, a wary figure in a chair, impatient.

"Would you like a cup of coffee?"

"Yes."

Which meant that he had to get up and stand in line. He was clearly in full view, but she never once looked his way. Instead, she spent the entire time staring out the window at a row of cranes. He waited while heaping portions of *Bockwurst* and *Kartoffelsalat* were loaded on plates for the people ahead of him, then walked carefully back to the table with two large cups of coffee. During the long wait he'd tried out a few names, but nothing seemed right. Annemarie, Claudia, Lucy—it was ridiculous, like parents trying to name their unborn, unseen child. This one could clearly be seen, but no name seemed to fit.

"My name is Elik."

Elik. What kind of name was that? Yet from that moment on it was as if she could never have been called anything else. Elik, of course. The person named Elik was suddenly every inch an Elik—the rough fabric of her dark-gray jeans: Elik. The clear dark-brown eyes: Elik.

"That's an unusual name."

"My mother made three mistakes. The first was going to bed with the man who became my father. The second was not having an abortion. The third was naming me Elik. She heard it God knows where and thought it was a girl's name. Actually, it comes from the Balkans; it's the diminutive form of a man's name."

This was no longer a reconnaissance mission—it was a surprise attack. The invisible line that had started out somewhere in the middle of the table had now been shifted to his side. This was a woman who'd managed to pack a lot of information into a few short sentences, and to utter them in a tone of total indifference. He didn't know how to react. Elik.

"It's a beautiful name."

Silence. Judging by the way she was sitting in her chair, no reply had been necessary. Good, she apparently agreed. No part of her moved. She sat completely still, with her hands on the table. A woman whose preferred method of operation was the ambush. Another nice word.

"Oh God, you and your obsession with words." Erna.

Do you live in Berlin? What are you studying? How long have you been here? I thought you were Spanish. All the things he could have said but didn't.

"Is your mother still alive?"

"No. She drank herself to death."

And your father probably hanged himself, he was about to add, but she needed no prompting. Father unknown. A North African, a Maghreb, a waiter in a bar in Spain, the mother drunk as usual. Elik.

The mother-daughter dialogue got thrown in for good measure:

"What did my father look like?"

"I sure as hell can't remember. I moved out soon after that."

Moved out, but stayed in Spain. Which explains the Spanish.

Maybe it was his turn to talk, but she didn't seem the least bit curious.

"I hope you aren't shocked?" Testing, sarcasm?

"No, not really. But I don't know what to tell you in return. My mother is in her late seventies, lives in Loenen, and enjoys gardening. My father is dead."

He had a vision of a man who looked like her. A mountain village, walls made of red clay. The Rif or the Atlas. Snow on the peaks. Clear, cold air. Berber eyes. It hadn't been a bad guess.

"What are you laughing at?"

He described the scene. She had a different version. A man in a none-too-clean shirt wiping tables with a wet brown rag. Tangier, Marbella.

"Not curious?"

"Not anymore. The only reason he would agree to see me now would be to wangle money out of me for my dear little brothers and sisters in Tinerhir or Zagora or wherever. Or to get him a one-way ticket to Holland."

Zagora, the camel market—he'd filmed the place once. Camels are slaughtered lying down. Or would you call it "sitting"? Maybe "kneeling" was more accurate. Anyway, those camels had been forced to kneel down, so that they were sitting dumbly on the dry dirt with their heads held high, then someone had slit their long throats, and the blood had dripped onto the sand. That wasn't the worst part. The real surprise came when the man stripped their hides in one long movement. The knife cut down the entire length of the animal, through those strange humps on the back, and revealed another camel underneath—a gleaming blue plastic camel, which had laid its head in the sand. This wasn't the right time to tell that story.

"Would you like another cup of coffee?" She follows him with her eyes. He's taller than most of the people in the line.

What she doesn't see. What he doesn't see. Each of those two lives break up into a series of images. The film is played, rewound, stopped at random places. All very ordinary, very familiar—the invisible past exploding into memories until we arrive at exactly this moment: a body, a pose, a strategy, a woman sitting at a table in a cafeteria in Berlin. The journey that began many years ago in Spain has been traveled nonstop. Sleep doesn't count. Sleep is the ford in the river, dreams, mud, crystal. The journey never ends. What doesn't exist is what happens next.

What he doesn't see: a ten-year-old girl sent to Holland and raised by her mother's mother. A loner. That much he can tell. Oh, language, helpful language: alone, a loner. That too he would have recognized in all those stills: at age twelve, fourteen, sixteen, not yet on her own, then by herself, someone who had reached a decision. And before that: an eight-year-old in a thin-walled room in Spain, listening to the sounds next door. The familiar voice, a high-pitched cry, then the other one, the voice of a man she doesn't know, new ones all the time, only occasionally the same. Then one time not the climactic scream or the urgent grunts, sighs, and murmurs, but slaps, moans, footsteps in the hall, a dark figure falling onto her bed, panting, reeking of alcohol, a huge head, a touch that makes you shrink, screams, neighbors in the corridor, pain, a burning pain, her mother's face in the doorway, men in uniform, shrieks, a pain that won't go away, that keeps burning your face, your body, and later, in the cool bedroom in Holland, during those quiet nights, the haunting parade of images, the same ones over and over again. That's how you become the exception, the face in the school picture marked with an x, Elik and the rest of the class, Elik always in profile because she's turned her scar away from the all-seeing eye of the camera.

What she doesn't see: a father who's different from other fathers, a father who comes home from work and sits with his elbows propped up on the table reading books, his lips moving silently over the unaccustomed words, a father who brands his son with a stigma, who comes back from peace conferences held in Bucharest, Moscow, East Berlin, Leipzig, and Havana, who argues with his fifteen-year-old son that it's right to send the tanks into Prague, that anyone trying to get over the Wall should be shot, let them say what they want at school, you should be able to ignore it. One day you'll understand. It's all lies, don't listen to them, just like what's-his-name, and he had no trouble filling in the blanks. He can't get the image out of his mind: the alluring voices, the man bound to the mast, the crew with their ears full of wax. Just as he can't forget that other image: the man on a rainy street corner, his father the clown at the Albert Cuyp market, holding up *The Daily Worker* in a protective plastic bag, and himself hurrying past just like the hundreds of other shoppers who hurried past, making himself invisible so he wouldn't have to witness the scene, wouldn't have to say hello, wouldn't have to be there. In the last years of his life his father had stopped talking. A true believer, and therefore embittered. "So Germany's finally got what it wants and is snapping up the East at bargain prices. Cheaper than war. And who's in charge of the Party in Holland these days? A bunch of loonies, dykes, and faggots, who've never done a decent day's work in their entire lives..."

That's enough for now. We're off.

Cards on the table. Time for a trade. Bargaining chips. Not much on the first day. What she now sees: how he moves. There are various ways of making yourself invisible when you feel you need to. He somehow even manages to make himself disappear in the waiting line, despite his height. A deliberate absence. When he returns with the coffee, he slides one cup over to her, but leaves the other one untouched. He places his hands on the table, two objects, one on top of the other. Years ago on a school trip, she'd seen a bronze cast of a hand in a museum in Paris. "*Voilà, mes enfants,*" the French teacher had said. "The hand of Balzac! He used this hand to write the *Comédie Humaine.*"

"Yeah, and to feel up his mistresses, the fat pig." Had she said that? "And to wipe his ass," another one of her classmates had added, a bit too loudly. Another quiet afternoon in a museum ruined. The bronze hand, dead and resigned, reposing on an open book. Letters had been written with that lifeless, chopped-off hand. Letters in pale ink. Hideous. Realizing for the first time what hands are: instruments, servants, accomplices. Of good and evil. Musicians, surgeons, writers, lovers, murderers. Male hands. She lays hers beside his so she can see the difference. His hand grazes hers, or maybe not really, and he pulls his away. In the conversation that follows he hears for the first time how she uses inflection rather than word order to indicate her questions. Can a question mark be spoken?

?

"Cinematographer. Well, film school. Yes, sometimes. And documentaries. Cameraman. Whatever happens to come my way. My own? Yes, sometimes, yes."

?

"Spanish. Had a head start at any rate. History. Ph.D. An obscure subject. Queen. Middle Ages. León, Asturias. Urraca. Yes, with two r's. Twelfth century."

Every human encounter is political. Who'd said that? Giving and withholding information, bartering. But he doesn't trade his dead wife for her drunken mother. Not yet. Which chambers, caverns, cellars, and attics does she rule over? No further questions, neither of them. Or, rather, one more.

"And the letter of reference?"

"An excuse to talk to you."

She looks at him, not seeing what else he's keeping to himself. Makes what kind of films? He thinks of his last assignment, two or three months ago.

"Yeah, we'd really like you to do it." A Dutch voice. "We're short a cameraman at the moment. But I'll level with you. You've really got to want to do it, 'cause it's a nasty job. Bring a clothespin. You can fly to Belgrade straight from Berlin and meet up with the others there. We'll handle the rest on that end. Aaton Super 16, fine. That's what you always work with, isn't it?" The clothespin hadn't been necessary. As it turned out, the only stench had been that of the mud, draped like a wet greasy blanket over bumps and mounds in the vague shape of bodies, scattered bits, a foot, shoes looking grotesquely large beside the skeletal feet they belonged to, rags, tattered ends, scraps of fabric, a slow drip-drip, gloved hands turning over human remains, rotting arms swathed in bandages, half-chewed wrists bound with wire, a double bracelet, don't look, the camera like a blindfold in front of your eyes, can't help but look, even worse, searching, walking, squelching through the mud over the narrow path

143

beside the ditch, past the disinterred parade of recumbent corpses, eye sockets, preposterous horse teeth without lips. And rain, incessant rain, on a hillocky gray plain, a human landscape, a house wracked by war, the carcass of a mattress, a rusted bed, a broken motorcycle. Someone has to see these things, so someone films the motionless scene in slow motion, someone sets up a tripod at the edge of the ditch and repeats the shot, which slows down the motion even more, the slowest of movements, the shoe with its steadily dripping mud, the ooze of mortality. None of them have names. Memory, storehouse. A duplicate set of memories. Fuji Color negative. Images recorded, played, and replayed on an internal reel, all four hundred feet of film, again and again, always available, ready to go, a clip-by-clip celluloid gleam. The inner twin comes back unannounced, triggered by a certain pose, a look, a nightmare, set off by laughter, a drink, let out of the film cans, shown again, someone has to see these things, but what does it amount to in the end? Two or three minutes, maybe not even that much, living rooms in Oklahoma City, Adelaide, Lyons, Oslo, Assen, instant apocalypse, commercial, pearly white teeth with lips, feet, young, sleek, gently rub it on, yes, also a film, oh, yes, a film can do anything.

"I've got to get back to work."

"It gets dark here so early."

"It stays light a bit longer in Amsterdam, or is that my imagination?"

"It's all that wind. It blows the darkness away."

"Do you know your way around the city? Around Berlin?"

"More or less."

Then he realizes that they each have their own Berlin.

"Elik. What's your last name?"

"You're not going to believe it."

"Tell me."

"Oranje."

144

For the first time they both laugh. The wind rushes through the house, the front door is flung open, a window rattles, there's a riot of blossom, a burst of color, no, that's not true, none of it is, but this was the moment and it's been postponed, it may never happen. That laugh, bewitching. To her, it's the eyes that do it. To him, the mouth—pink, open.

"Are you going back downstairs?"

"Yes, but not for long. I need to check something."

They walk downstairs together, past security, flashing their empty hands at the guards, *schon gut,* past the slate floor tiles, the camps, the hunger, the eyes. Then she disappears. You can usually find me here. Nothing more.

He walks over to the room containing the Spanish encyclopedia and opens it to the letter U.

His room suddenly fills with men's voices. The friend has furnished the apartment with only the bare essentials. A cell rather than a living room. At least it's big. His camera is still there, looking like a small, compact sculpture. Part of the homecoming ritual. Hang up coat. Glance at tree. Check mail (nothing). All done in silence, the outside world having fallen away.

On the U-Bahn he'd thought about showing her (there was no way he was going to think of her as Elik) some of Berlin's highlights. Then he'd caught himself and had to laugh. He'd bought a paper, the *Taz,* and stopped for groceries: corned beef, potatoes, onions. Corned-beef hash— "a typical lonely-hearts meal" (Erna). But it had a certain charm—a lone person moving around his or her room. How many of us do you suppose there were in a city this size? They were united by a secret bond. Boil the potatoes, fry the onions, add a little ginger, pepper, and mustard, mix them all together. He'd made hash in some pretty strange places. You could get cans of corned beef in all four corners of the globe. Argentinian beef, accompanied by its sister, the potato, and its brother, the onion. Eaten in silence, sitting at the table. Afterward, he made himself a cup of tea and thought of the rosy mouth. The way it had opened and briefly laughed. For one small second. She must also be eating somewhere? Stay home tonight, don't make any phone calls. And don't play Cage. His friend had a cupboard full of CDs. He'd already picked out Varèse, that strange chorus in *Ecuatorial,* with the powerful men's voices, as if an entire choir was standing right here in the room. The next piece was short, so he played it over a few times. Fanfares, cracking whips, sirens. Each time it came to an end, the silence was even more intense. Later he heard on the radio that it was starting to thaw, but that it would freeze up again tonight and thaw in the morning. If he went outside now he'd see a winter ballet with chaotic choreography: pirouettes, sudden horizontality—of the sort he'd experienced twice today—undignified positions, slowly gliding cars. Crazy, out of character. Germans aren't supposed to slip and fall. Oops, a prejudice. *Achtung*!, the old man had said, though his warning had come too late. He reread the passage he'd copied from the encyclopedia—such formal Spanish—about Urraca. It suddenly occurred to him that *urraca* meant "magpie." He'd always been fascinated by the names of birds. This one had a nice ring to it, a kind of ricochet, though it sounded more like the cry of a raven or a crow than a magpie. Urraca. The Dutch word for "magpie" was *ekster.* Queen Ekster. Elik. There was something about those short words. . . . Magpies were thieves. They loved to steal anything that glittered. But none of this had been in the encyclopedia. Urraca, the first woman to rule over a Spanish kingdom, civil war, Islam encroaching from the south (how the hell had she come up with this subject?), ruled from 1109 to 1125 (how could you find anything to write about?). La reina Urraca, ra, kra. A sudden longing—for the second time that day—for Spain, space, Aragon, León.

"Can't you even stay in one place for a couple of months at a time?"

"No, Erna, I can't."

He tried—and failed—to think of her as a person writing a dissertation. A Ph.D. with a scar and a pair of cowhide boots. Dr. Magpie. Magpie, the winter bird, black and white. Like the city now. The bird that could suddenly burst into a throaty warble when it was nesting, but otherwise produced a raucous screech, as if it was always angry. Closing his eyes, he could picture a magpie, even the tail looked angry, the way it was always flicking viciously up and down. It had a strange way of flying too, a kind of paddling, so that it could cross a winter landscape—the frozen, snow-covered gardens of Charlottenburg Palace—in a few swift strokes. Had he changed his mind about phoning? No, he wouldn't call anyone. He opened a closet and pulled out various film cans, peering at the labels, and stacked them on the table until he had a tall tower. Then he put Varèse on again, wanting to hear those male voices one more time. Somewhere in that closet there should be sound recordings of a film he and Arno had once made on monasteries—a French-German co-production for Arte television. Until then he'd known virtually nothing about monasteries, and he still wasn't sure how he felt about them. The monks, both young and old, had looked fairly normal. German, French, and Spanish monks. Beuron, Cluny, Veruela, Aula Dei. Benedictines, Trappists, Carthusians—dying breeds. You could distinguish the various orders by their clothes. The Trappists wore black and white, like magpies, except for the choir monks, who sang in white habits. As the robes wore out, they looked even more like aging swans. The Benedictines—black as crows. The Carthusians—also in white. He hadn't been allowed to film them in the choir, though he had been given permission to film them in their cells. The Carthusians, unlike the other orders, always ate alone. There was something very sad about it, especially since the food was shoved through a hatch. He had filmed the cell from the inside looking out, and then from the outside looking in: the bare room, virtually empty, a makeshift altar with a statue of the Virgin Mary, a little garden, a collapsible table folded against the wall beside the food hatch. On the outside of the hatch was a wooden pointer—he could still picture it—that could be turned to three different positions: one loaf of bread, half a loaf, no bread. *Un pan, medio pan, no pan.* So there was always someone who knew exactly how much—or how little—you were eating. That, even more than the closed cell, had made him feel claustrophobic.

Bertrand, the French sound technician, had been able to explain everything: the significance and names of the canonical hours—that compulsive, never-ending cycle of the changeless day, the changeless year, *l'éternité quoi*—which he had related with pride, as if he himself were the owner of that eternity. Once a year Bertrand actually stepped into their eternity. Or, as he himself said, he "became a monk," spending a few weeks in a Benedictine monastery in Normandy, "because they sing more beautifully than the others." Arthur and Arno could well imagine it, since Bertrand had the disconcerting habit of fasting on Fridays. All day long he would only drink a little water.

"Oh, he's famous for that," said the auburn-haired producer. "We call him *Le Moine,* the Monk, but everyone wants to work with him because he's so good."

Which was certainly true. From time to time Arthur played the tape again. But he'd been even more impressed by Bertrand's methods than by his sound techniques, the way the man had lugged his fifteen-pound Nagra around as if it was lighter than a feather—a predator tracking his prey with that fluffy cylinder dangling from the boom like a dead rat, nearly touching the sandals of the monks as they walked to the choir. Nobody ever noticed that quotidian shuffling sound anymore, but he had turned it into a sublime sound, the inevitable overture to the silence and songs that were to follow. And suddenly Bertrand's unusual choice of a vacation spot had no longer seemed so odd to them. They'd watched him as he stood there, a monk among monks, letting the psalms roll over him in waves.

"Why haven't you become a monk, Bertrand?" Arno had asked him in his thick German accent, which almost made it sound like an interrogation.

"Because I'm married and I've got children," Bertrand had replied.

"And a mistress and another child," the producer with the auburn hair had said, "*n'est-ce pas, cher* Bertrand?"

"The mistress isn't the problem," Bertrand said. "My wife is. Since we're Catholics, we can't get divorced, and a married man can't become a monk. A mistress doesn't count. All you have to do is confess and say good-bye. But marriage is a sacrament."

Then and there Arno had thought up a new Maigret and given them a quick synopsis: Bertrand would have to murder his wife, because as a widower he would be allowed to take his vows. But eventually, several years down the line, someone would figure it out and trace him to the monastery. The high point would be the scene in which *le commissaire* gave Bertrand the third degree.

But Bertrand had nixed the idea. Too much of a hassle.

"The last thing I want is to have Maigret breathing down my neck. No, I should have taken orders long ago."

Nothing more had been said about the mistress, and none of the chatter about Bertrand's predicament had made its way onto his small-tape recorder. But Bertrand had captured the Gregorian chants with an awe-inspiring precision. ("Ah, in the old days, when they still sang in Latin! It sounds too effeminate in French. Spanish comes a bit closer.") The recording had even been awarded a Prix de Rome.

"No, no, it has nothing to do with precision. Those chants have been echoing through these churches for hundreds of years. The sound you hear is the breathing of eternity, *aeternitas*. I always hear the aeons. That's the trick, letting both time and timelessness be heard. Someday I'll play you my old recordings so you can hear how it used to be. Don't laugh, but it sounded more eternal in Latin...Listen." He swelled his chest and boomed, "*Domine*...Now compare it to this: *Seigneur*.... Can you hear the difference? It seems to fade away in French, like the voice of a little old lady."

When they came to the monastery in Beuron, he decided that German wasn't so bad either.

"At any rate more masculine than French. But can you imagine what it would sound like if they sang those gutturals in Latin too?" And he tried imitating a German accent in Latin. "*Procul recedant somnia.*"

"Heidegger was a frequent visitor to Beuron," Arno said. "He was raised as a Catholic. Even served as an altar boy in Messkirch, not far from here...Never really did make the break. Carved his initials in a pew once. Here in Beuron someone saw him dip his finger in holy water and cross himself and asked him, 'What are you doing that for? You're no longer a believer, are you?' 'No,' Heidegger replied, 'but so many prayers have been said here that it's filled with the divine.' But what's the divine without God?" And Arno shot them a helpless look through his thick lenses.

The monk assigned to help them suddenly said, "It's not that strange. Even nonbelievers feel comfortable here. And besides, it was Heidegger himself who came up with the idea of

Sein zum Tode. His concept of 'being-unto-death' is, in and of itself, not very mysterious. Here in Beuron we too have to come to grips with mortality. The only difference is that Heidegger deals with fear and we deal with hope. Perhaps heroic fear likes to pay an occasional call on fearful hope, especially when it's accompanied by chants. After all, you can't create a ritual based on fear."

"I'm not so sure," Arno answered. "What about the Nazi rallies in Nuremberg?"

"That proves my point," said the monk. "They aren't being held anymore, are they? This"—and he made a gesture that included the cloister they were standing in, as if he wanted to pull it protectively around his shoulders—"is quite a durable substance.... Whenever I read Heidegger..." He deliberately left the sentence unfinished.

"Then you're grateful you can slip into your choir stall again at night," Arno said.

"That's one way of putting it," the monk replied. "But perhaps it's also because I know that all across the globe others are singing the same chants at exactly the same hour."

"And thinking the same?"

"Perhaps. Not necessarily."

"A sense of security?"

"Oh, absolutely."

"Don't you think it's odd that Heidegger came here to bask in your security when it wasn't something he wanted for himself?"

"Not odd, but perhaps...courageous, if that's the right word."

"Or do you prefer to think that he simply didn't have 'grace'? That's the expression you use, isn't it?"

"Yes. And that's the stock answer...except that I can't quite reconcile that word with Heidegger. However, I shouldn't be thinking that, much less saying it."

On the way home Arno had repeated the gist of the conversation to Bertrand and clarified a few things for Arthur, since the former didn't speak a word of German and the latter had found it difficult to follow at times, especially the bit about grace. Then Arno had hummed a few bars of something that sounded like a cross between a Gregorian chant and diddly-dum, and suddenly cried, "Here's a thought! Try to imagine it: Elfriede dies and Heidegger becomes a Benedictine at Beuron. What a scandal that would have caused! Fantastic! Even better than Voltaire on his deathbed! Still, that monk was closer to the truth than he thought. Heidegger was a metaphysical trapeze artist, performing his flying leaps at the top of the philosophical circus tent, swinging back and forth above the gaping void. And everyone watched in breathless suspense, because they didn't think he had a safety net. He did, but nobody else could see it—naturally he hadn't included it in his ontological system because it wasn't about theology but about religious sentiment. An old man warming himself by another answer to an age-old question, clinging to early memories, to Messkirch and his childhood home, to rituals and traditions that were more important to him than he was willing to admit. Just like Bertrand, n'est-ce pas, Bertrand?"

"Just like Bertrand, but different," Bertrand had replied, and he'd said it in such a way that Arthur, now, several years later, sitting in a room in Berlin, had smiled once again. He switched off the light, continued to stare for a long time at the figures moving back and forth behind the other windows, until they too had turned off their lights. Tomorrow, he didn't think he'd go to the library.

And we—can we do anything? Naturally the whole thing is out of our hands, if it was ever in them. Our eyes rove easily over the icy, frozen, snow-covered city, over the Spree River, over the scar, the gash, where the Wall once stood. We forget nothing. Even the most far-removed fear, mood, or threat from centuries ago seems as fresh to us as if it had happened yesterday, an undeletable fact. We remember when the Pergamon Altar, the one that's now in the museum, was brand-new, a mere two thousand—or was it four thousand—years ago. To us all memories are simultaneous. Museums are power plants, and we, who are so light, know the weight of every object in them. Yes, that smacks of omnipotence, but what would you have us say? It could also be considered a burden. A Cranach painting, a shield from New Guinea, a papyrus roll, the voice of Laforgue reading to Empress Augusta in a castle that no longer exists—as far as we're concerned it's all in the present. Yes, of course you find it annoying not to know who we are, but feel free to call us anything you like. Figments of imagination, if you wish—it's both true and not true. Cause, driving force, simultaneity, it may be a paradox, but it fits in well with the Gedächtniskirche over there. We can see the church as it used to be, before it was bombed, and at the same time we see the ruin, the gaping hole, the hollow monument it is today. There's no need for you to take any notice of us. We and our burden are always here, but you have to deal with us only now, on these pages, in this part of the story, which by the way is only two days old. Now, and only now, when you are hearing our voices or reading our words—otherwise we don't exist for you, except as a possibility. Now, here, on Falkplatz, where the city is darker, where the city is just the same, but different—more run-down, more in need of paint, more vulnerable. A long staircase, a room, a woman lying on a bed, not sleeping, but staring, eyes wide open. Yes, we know every detail, but that's irrelevant; her blank stare says much more. Her hand is resting on the book she's been reading, and it too is sending out signals: vague stories, sudden illuminations, numbers, facts, then back to conjectures and assumptions, since it all happened too long ago. We know the truth, the book does not. It's like an excavation site, in which only a quarter, or less, of what used to be there has been dug up. But if you knew everything we knew, you wouldn't be able to cope with it. You see, we can't summarize, condense, abstract. To us it's all the same length, the same weight. So it's better to keep things simple. It's easy to draw a line between the two silent rooms. After all, something has happened. But as soon as we start to comment on the future, our voices become inaudible, because the future doesn't exist. Or at any rate this explanation will have to do. Do you see her hand moving restlessly while the head is lying so still? Something wants to tug that hand away from that book, but how can you squeeze a living essence, a force, a body out of paper and words, here and now, without stirring up the mold of the past?

Arthur Daane may have been thinking of Elik Oranje, but she was not thinking of him. Elik Oranje's head, which was indeed resting quietly on the pillow, was filled with thoughts of the class she'd attended earlier today in Berlin, part of a ten-week course for which she'd received a grant from the *Deutsche Akademische Austauschdienst*. The professor was a rambling lecturer, but he'd said something that had set her to thinking, something along the lines of "Assume you're sitting in a train...." The course was on Hegel's philosophy of history. Her mind often strayed. She had an inborn Dutch antipathy to what she called "talking in paragraphs," and besides he was as old as the hills and had such a strong Saxon accent that she could understand only half of what he said. But every once in a while something in his voice alerted her to a possible tidbit, an anecdote, a personal note, an escape from the doctrinal straitjacket in which she found herself, here in the same city where young men her age had once hung on the lips of the master himself.

"Assume you're sitting in a train, looking at the other passengers in your compartment instead of out the window. You draw certain conclusions about them, based on what they might have said or what they're reading, but also on their clothes, their general behavior. If you were to write down your conclusions, you'd probably assume that it was a true reflection of reality. After all, you've actually seen them, maybe even talked to them. But now let's turn it around and imagine that they had studied you in as much detail as you had studied them. To what degree would their picture of you be real? You yourself are the best judge of how much you keep hidden from the outside world, what you cover up or choose not to reveal, including things you haven't even begun to define—because people also keep secrets from themselves, things they deny or would rather not know. In addition, there's a whole arsenal of memories, a vast storehouse of everything you've seen and read, a world of secret desires. That train wouldn't be big enough to hold them all. Yet every passenger in that compartment thinks that a...how shall I put it?...that a manifestation of reality has taken place. But has it?"

That had led to a discussion of the introduction of fictional elements into historiography. Even writers who believed that they confined themselves strictly to the facts were guilty of it. But what were the facts? Without turning her head, she picked up the book lying facedown on her stomach and held it up so she could examine it more closely. On the grayish-beige dust jacket was a picture of a river. In the foreground clumps of reeds were swaying in the wind. Hardly a cloud in sight, though maybe they'd been airbrushed away to make room for the title and the author's name: Bernard F. Reilly, *The Kingdom of León-Castilla under Queen Urraca, 1109–1126*. On the far shore a cluster of buildings with empty black windows, the dark shapes of trees, a colonnade, a large square tower—the citadel of Zamora as seen from the south bank of the Duero.

"Whatever made you decide to do a Ph.D.?" her supervisor had asked, as if she'd just made an indecent proposal.

"Teaching jobs are hard to come by at the moment," she'd replied, though that hadn't been the real reason. She'd worked as a substitute teacher a few times and had no intention of going back. She hadn't been able to shake off the feeling that she'd been standing on the wrong side of the classroom, that she'd rather be sitting at a pupil's desk, where everything was still confusing, undefined, immature, chaotic. Especially compared to the unbearable maturity of the teachers' room: her colleagues, with their mapped-out lives. Part of her youth had been stolen from her, so she wanted to stretch the rest of it as long as she could. It was worth living on a shoestring to be free and independent, and her dissertation was the perfect alibi. So was the Hegel course taught by that pompous ass. It had brought her to Berlin, and for that she was prepared to put up with Hegel.

"In light of your background," her supervisor had continued, "I can understand why you chose Spain, but whatever possessed you to pick an obscure medieval queen? And queen of what, by the way?"

She decided to play it safe. "To begin with, because she's a woman." These days no one would dare argue with that. "And also because she's not very well known. Actually, it's very exciting."

And it was, a lone woman among all those men—bishops, lovers, husbands, sons, a constant battle for power and position—the only medieval Spanish queen who had actually ruled in her own right.

"But is there enough material? Which century did you say it was?"

"Early twelfth century. There's scads of material."

"Reliable or iffy? I'm afraid I'm not very familiar with it. After all, it is a rather obscure subject. It also means that I'll have to study up on it as well."

There's no need, she wanted to say, I'll hand it to you on a platter, though I'm going to take my own sweet time with the research. But she wisely kept her mouth shut. This queen was her ticket to freedom—for a couple of years at any rate— and for that she was grateful. Queen Magpie. She had caught herself talking to her. Elik the shield-bearer. What do you suppose she'd looked like? Talk about reality! She'd seen a reproduction of the only known portrait of Urraca in a Spanish book about the queen's friend and foe Diego Gelmírez, the bishop of Santiago, but it had been of little help since she looked more like the queen in a deck of cards than a real person. In her right hand she was holding a kind of banner, on which her name was written with one r and one k: Uraka Regina. The usual regalia—crown, scepter, throne—her knees akimbo so that the pink-slippered feet were resting on a row of intertwining Mozarabic arches, her sky-blue cloak studded with fat stars, the crown perched atop her head like a crooked pillbox, her head itself a stereotype, not the face of anyone who had actually lived, talked, laughed, fought, made love. How could you even begin to understand such lives? And vice versa: what if she had to explain her own anachronistic life to someone from the twelfth century? Berlin, which didn't even exist then. Still, it wouldn't be hard to describe the pure mechanics of power to someone accustomed to wielding it, provided you stayed within the context of the Middle Ages and left out the ideology: the Kaiser, his lost war, the uprisings, the harsh demands of the victors, the rabble-rouser, the next war.... After that it got more complicated. Or did it? Pogroms, Islam, that bit would be easy, even the atom bomb could be explained to a certain extent as a weapon of total destruction.... But a world without religion, that would be unthinkable to someone from the Middle Ages, unless you were referring to Hell. But if there was such a gap between the past and the present, how could you ever hope to understand—much less write about—the reality of the past? Real reality, what bullshit. Better get some sleep. Stop speculating, go to sleep. There was a noise from the courtyard downstairs—she recognized the footsteps of the friend who let her live here for next to nothing. He worked in a bar, and the first couple of nights he'd stumbled into her bedroom, blind drunk, but she'd treated him with such contempt the next day that he'd given up. Only after she'd switched off the light did she remember that strange Dutchman she'd met earlier today. Filmmaker, he'd said, documentaries.

There are many ways to enter the domain of sleep—via images, words, shifts, repetitions. Documents, documentaries. Somebody's creeping up the stairs as quietly as possible. Not much traffic tonight. Silence. City in the middle of a large plain, stretching out toward the east, in such darkness . . .

Days of melting snow, thaw, then suddenly a morning that bursts into the room with a light that seems to be announcing the end of winter. At this time of year, at this latitude and longitude, the light has very few hours at its disposal—and nobody knows that better than a filmmaker. Arthur Daane has spread a map of Berlin out over the floor—the old schizophrenic map, but that doesn't matter, things haven't changed that much, you just have to ignore the thick pink line with the arbitrary zigzags that indicated where the other regime began. The world had been roared at from this city, and the world had retaliated by reducing it to rubble, the populace had devoured itself, but the survivors had crept out of the cellars and ruins only to find new masters who didn't speak their language, then their world had been broken in two, with the weakest half kept alive from the air, and in the wash of human affairs—the waves of good and evil and of guilt and atonement—the city had recovered its wounded, punished, humiliated soul, so that the two short syllables of its name had become synonymous with all the crimes, all the resistance, and all the suffering that had taken place there, just as the one hard syllable and the other soft syllable resonated with all the voices that had ever been heard in that city. But you didn't have to remember these things; the city did it for you, in the form of monuments, neighborhoods, names, so that instead of staring at the map, he ought to enlarge it, blow it up until it was as big as the city itself, he ought to grab his camera, take a taxi to the library, see if she was there, then call Arno and ask to borrow his car so he could take her to the Glienicker Bridge, and to Halensee or Peacock Island.

If he ever needed a few bars of music to give the idea of swiftness, he knew he ought to use something by Shostakovich. Victor had played a couple of pieces for him once, and he'd been able to imagine all sorts of rapid movements—water rushing over rocks, a herd of animals on the run, a chase scene. Not that he'd filmed many of those, but he was trying to put together a list of music that might come in handy one day. Preferably a piece with only a few instruments, like the one he'd heard at Victor's. But Victor hadn't been very cooperative.

"No. 11, No. 12, preludes, fugues, which one do you mean?"

"The first piece you played, the one that sounded as if it were chasing after its own tail."

"That was No. 11, in B major."

"B major doesn't mean anything to me, but I can remember the number 11."

"Planning to mount it on a film, are you? To match sound and image, plink, plank, plunk? Can't the film manage on its own? Background music is an admission of weakness."

"It's supposed to enhance the image, not back it up. Or to serve as a contrast."

"Like Bertolt Brecht. Oppressed masses, great tragedy, and all the while the music goes oom-pah-pah."

"There aren't any oppressed masses in my films."

Victor hadn't answered. Or, rather, he'd shrugged, dryly announced, "No. 13," and put on a quiet, meditative piece. Only after the last measure had faded away had he burst out, as if he'd forgotten that Arthur was in the room, "What an idiot! How can anyone who could compose something like that have written such monstrous symphonies?"

He remembered that now because he'd trundled down the stairs with his camera, gone outside, turned the corner, walked down Wilmersdorfer Strasse and over to Bismarck-strasse—thank goodness there'd been a green light—and had found a taxi just as No. 12 was about to strike the first notes. That meant he'd have all of No. 12 and No. 13 to think about the absurdity of his plan. He knew the series by heart now—No. 14 was short, the whole thing didn't add up to more than half an hour, and then No. 15 would have exactly the right kind of frenzied hammer blows that he'd need if he found her in the library. But the conductor in the cloakroom broke it off in mid-bar.

"You can't take that camera in there. You'll have to put it in a locker."

"I just want to take a quick look."

"Not in Prussia, dodo." Victor.

So he went in without his camera. She stared at him as though he were a ghost. That's the usual expression, but in this case he wasn't the one in the company of ghosts; she was. Her queen has been beaten and almost captured by the man to whom she's married and against whom she's waging war. It's the month of October in the never-to-be-repeated year of 1111. Queen Urraca is on the run from Alfonso el Batallador. The Battler. A magpie and a battler—one day someone will write a book about them.

"The whereabouts of Urraca at this point are an almost insoluble puzzle," she reads. A puzzle that Elik Oranje would like to solve. In the mountains of Galicia, according to one theory. But how were you supposed to imagine the events that were taking place?

"At the moment you shouldn't be imagining anything," her supervisor had told her the last time they'd discussed the problem. "You need to check the source material and dig up information no one else has managed to uncover. Spain has got tons of archives. If there are gaps, just report them. The rest is fiction." But that was the whole point.

"I can't help forming a picture in my mind, can I?"

"That's not a very scholarly approach. What you see are products of your imagination. Letters, deeds, certificates, reports—those are real. You're not writing a novel. Historical novels are the most ridiculous genre on earth. Try to discover the truth, the facts, the reality, no matter how hard it is. Meanwhile, if you find it helpful to imagine knights, pages, and swords, go right ahead. Just don't let yourself get carried away. There probably won't be much danger of that, since you don't strike me as the romantic type. And if you find that you can't resist the temptation, just remember that people used to stink to high heaven back in those days."

No, she wasn't the romantic type. So why did she have such a vivid image of Urraca and her little band of faithful followers in the mountains? On the one hand, she thought, she strongly identified with her research subject, and, on the other hand, there was a deplorable lack of hard facts. In between lay a wide margin for fantasy. One of the most difficult problems was the time factor—the warring factions had always been unsure of each other's movements, which meant that the documents were often unreliable. In those days the fastest means of communication was the horse, and its speed had determined how long it took to find out whether your army had captured a city or been defeated.

"Ah," said her supervisor, "never forget Marc Bloch's wise lesson: 'A historical phenomenon can never be understood outside the moment in time in which it took place.'"

Well said, but as long you weren't allowed to use your imagination it was paradoxical. She would be better off sticking to the maps and trying to follow the actual or presumed movements of the main characters: the king who had taken Palencia and was now advancing on León, the bishop who had lost his battle and gone to Astorga to bring the refugees and the wounded back with him to Santiago, the queen somewhere, but where? To complicate this medieval chess game even further, her son by a previous marriage was now being crowned king in Santiago. As long as he was on her side...And now suddenly this man was standing in front of her. For a moment she couldn't think who he was, and he was saying something, but what was he talking about? All she could see was a pair of steely blue eyes, and she realized that she didn't want to go, didn't want to respond to his invitation—Peacock Island, where the hell was that—observed herself folding up the maps, slamming shut the *Historia Compostelana,* leaving her queen behind in the mountains of Galacia or wherever, walking behind that tossing and pitching figure, out to the street, where the winter sun was bouncing off the swaying building that housed the Berlin Philharmonic.

Elik Oranje was the first woman Arthur Daane had ever taken to Arno Tieck's apartment, and it was even more remarkable, thought Arno, because it was clear that the two of them hadn't know each other very long. He rolled the strange Dutch name around on his tongue and was assured that yes, it meant "orange," and yes, it was the name of the Dutch royal family, but no, she didn't have any royal blood.

A long silence followed, which he finally broke. While he didn't find it difficult to work in silence all day long between those four book-lined walls, you could hardly keep it up when other human beings were sitting across from you.

What he saw was a shy Arthur, who was torn between wanting to leave and wanting to hear his friend's opinion of his companion, though he could hardly expect him to pass judgment in her presence. But if she didn't open her mouth soon, he wouldn't get to know her at all, and it didn't look as though she was going to be the first one to break the silence. Her face was too closed, too obstinate for that.

What he had no way of knowing was that Elik was busy taking her own inventory. Until she got to know the man sitting across from her, she could make him be whatever she wanted him to be, so she turned the stranger with the magically glinting glasses and the nimbus of bushy hair into a master magician—an obscurantist scholar. As if he had sensed her fantasy and immediately decided to comply, Arno burst into a monologue on the symbolism of the color orange.

Arthur knew that his friend was neither occult nor obscurantic, but, as everyone who had been beguiled by his rhetorical talents had discovered, it was difficult not to identify him with his subject. He spoke with passion—the whole of his corpulent body would move to the rhythm of the argument, his hands would flutter through the air to fend off any fallacies that might be waiting to creep into his reasoning before others had even spotted them. Regardless of whether he was talking about Hitler's gnosticism, the vagaries of spelling reform, the magnificence of Jünger's *Der Arbeiter*, the delights of carp in beer batter, the dark side of Proust, regardless of whether his subject was speculative or comic, serious or superficial, sprawling or hermetic, the strategy was usually the same: the optimum use of language, the magical sparkle and musicality of words, everything from prestos, andantes, and machine-gun staccatos to that ultimate rhetorical weapon, the carefully orchestrated silence, so that the two Dutch listeners who had merely come to borrow his car for their first outing were plunged into a panegyric on that mixture of red and yellow that had become the emblematic color of their royal family. In rapid tempo they were whizzed from heavenly gold to chthonic red, from the saffron yellow of Buddhist monks to the orange worn by Dionysus, and thus from loyalty to disloyalty, from sensuality to spirituality—in short, to everything, according to Arno, that was stimulating.

"Don't forget Helen's veil," said Elik. "And the cross of the Knights of the Holy Ghost."

Arthur saw Arno's eyes light up.

"Helen's veil?"

"In Virgil. It's also saffron."

"Ah..."

Another stone had been thrown in the pond, and before long Arno found himself deep in conversation with the surprising Dutch girl his uncommunicative friend Arthur had brought to his apartment.

History (*Gut!*), Hegel course (*Nein!*), dissertation (*Ach!*), Middle Ages (*Herrlich!*)—the conversation flew back and forth like a shuttlecock between the scar and the glinting glasses. Titles, names, theories—topics that left Arthur cold, while out there in the real cold, he thought to himself, the light was becoming more useless by the second. He wanted to go and he wanted to stay. Her voice seemed to take on a darker quality when she spoke German, or maybe it was something in the language itself. She also seemed to become a different person, one who was already slipping away from him. Before he even got to know her, she was gone.

To speak a foreign language, you have to be able to imitate more than just the sound. It requires motivation, observation, mastery of the tonality and stresses, the habitat of the people whose language you want to learn. The motivation was somehow tied up with a desire to blend in, to be inconspicuous and not expose yourself as an outsider, a foreigner. In that sense he was the opposite of Arno, who looked almost naked when he was forced to speak English or French. Naked and defenseless, deprived of his strongest weapon. Not that Arno ever let it deter him—he was too sure of himself for that. Perhaps she was too, though it would be surprising in someone her age.

It was like a symphony. He could tell she was enjoying Arno's attention—she was humming like a cello. Maybe that's why he'd stopped listening to the words and was taking it in as if it were music: a double recitative for alto and baritone. He'd long since dispensed with the song's meaning. As he watched, they began to respond to each other's movements, so that it was turning into a kind of ballet, for God's sake, with the two of them shooting off invisible arrows. No, it was time to put a stop to this.

He waited for the duo to pause briefly so they could look back in satisfaction at their performance. Then he stood up as slowly as he could, indicating with a wave of his camera, which he'd kept by his side, that he had other plans for today.

"Where are you planning to go?" Arno asked.

"To Peacock Island, but first to the Glienicker Bridge."

"Ah, yes. Nostalgia for the gray past. Smiley, VOPOs, threats? The inaccessible other side?"

"Who knows."

When they got to the bridge, he wanted to explain what Arno had meant, but she already knew.

"I've seen the movies."

Movies, movies. Had any movie ever shown exactly what it had been like here, on this same spot, ten years ago? Yes, of course. No, of course not. He leaned over the green railing. The water of the Havel still flowed into the Jungfernsee, just as it had then, but the gray boats of the border patrol were gone. Cars and trucks raced past on their way to Potsdam as though the road had never been blocked. He hunted for the right words.

"I shot a film here once with..." and he mentioned the name of a Dutch writer. "He was standing over there, and we had him walk back and forth at least ten times from East to West and from West to East, and he talked about the border checks, the spy exchanges, what the words 'Glienicker Bridge' meant to some people...and he was doing a good job, but..."

"The past was gone?"

"I suppose so...there's a kind of...inherent lie in a real event that turns into somebody else's story. Certain elements are missing."

"Only because you saw it with your own eyes."

"But that would mean that the more removed we are from events, the more inaccurate they become."

"I'm not so sure about that...but it's impossible to hold on to the past as the past. We don't do it in our personal lives either. Otherwise we'd go crazy. Imagine what would happen if our memories lasted as long as the events themselves. We wouldn't have any time left over to live our lives, and that can't be right. The past has to 'wear out' before we can go on. And that applies not only to our personal lives, but to countries as well." She laughed. "Besides, that's why we've got historians. They spend their lives dealing with the memories of others."

"And so you put up with the lie?"

"What lie? What you mean is that you can't bear to have the past made obsolete. But that's no way to live. Too much past will kill you. Now look who's talking!"

Apparently she didn't feel like pursuing the subject any further. She lit a cigarette.

"How do we get to Peacock Island?"

Before he could even answer, she wheeled around to face him and said, "The film that you made here—is that your real work?"

How could he explain? "I do that kind of stuff only for the money" sounded too banal, and, besides, it wasn't true. He liked what he thought of as the "public" side of his work, whether it was his own or a project in which he hired himself out as a cameraman. Assignments were often valuable learning experiences. The things he did for himself were different. But he didn't know her well enough to go into all that.

They drove back to the Nikolskoe exit. Under the tall bare trees there were still patches of snow—grayish white splotches on a layer of dark damp leaves. He parked the car by the ferry. It was a wonder the thing was still running. Except for an elderly couple, they were the only passengers. It occurred to him that they must also look like a couple to other people. What had she said? The past has to wear out before you can go on. To what extent had Roelfje and Thomas "worn out"? There was something sinister in the sound of that expression—usually only objects wore out. He had the feeling that Roelfje and Thomas were gradually moving farther and farther away from him, though they could be at his side whenever they wanted to be. But why did they come?

The ferry engine began to throb even louder. She put her hand on his thigh, but in such a way that he couldn't tell if she was even aware of it. The boat trip lasted only a few minutes, yet it had been a real trip, with a departure and an arrival— light glinting off the wake, the gentle slap-slap of water reflecting the sharp rays of the winter sun, the aura of mystery that surrounded all islands, no matter how small they were.

Just as they stepped on shore they heard the long, loud, high-pitched screech of a peacock. They stopped, and waited to hear if it was going to repeat its call. But the answer came from much farther away.

"It sounds as if they're crying out for something they'll never get," she said.

There came another cry, and another.

She suddenly started to run. His camera was too heavy; he'd never be able to keep up with her. But that was evidently not her intention.

"I'll see you later," she called.

He watched her go, noticed how fast she ran. In only two minutes, or maybe even less, she'd disappeared from view. Well, it looked as if he'd come to the island by himself. Alone, as usual. The elderly couple was also nowhere to be seen. The last boat would leave at four, the ferryman had said, which meant that there were still two hours to go.

A rustle in the bushes, and suddenly a peacock appeared on the path just a few yards ahead of him. The animal stood still. A second peacock followed, then a third. He stared at their leathery feet and repulsive toes—such a contrast to the extravagant splendor above. There was something all wrong about a peacock: the venomous head with those beady eyes and silly feelers, the thick layer of black and white feathers draped like a comforter over the blue and green body, the eyes in the long tail that trailed behind the male like a limp broom except when it was fanned out in display, that neurotic pecking at the brown leaves.

With a sudden shout he leaped up, and the three animals scattered in all directions. He'd been planning to show her the miniature Doric temple that had been built as a memorial to Queen Louisa—she of the creamy breasts—a hint of ancient Greece in the chillier north, one of those nostalgic structures that nineteenth-century German monarchs had loved to build so they could flaunt their status as the new Athenians.

But she wasn't there. She'd run like a willful child, as fast and as far away from him as her little feet would carry her, away from the man who hadn't even been able to tell her what his real work was. *Real*—that was the key word. What made it *real*? What was so *real* about his work? What would his answer have been if she hadn't run away? No doubt he would have said that he divided the world into two parts: a public part, usually involving people and the things they did with— or, rather, to—each other; and another part, in which the world was simply itself. It's not that there were no people in the second world; it's just that when they did appear, they were nameless and voiceless. That's why he usually filmed only parts of their bodies—their hands, or, as on that day in the U-Bahn, their feet. In any case, anonymous groups, masses. No producer had ever shown the slightest interest in the second world, but perhaps it was just as well, since it was his and his alone. And until he'd found the right form, he ought to keep it to himself. "Ledger entries," Arno had said, and the term had pleased him. It turned him into a regis- trar, a bookkeeper who might or might not reveal his never- ending balance sheet. Whether the first world—the public one of his assignments—would be part of it was far from clear. Because of his maximum availability, he was often sent all over the world, and he let himself be sent whether the call came from Amnesty, Foster Parents, or network TV. He could always film his own things while he was working on the assignment.

"Disaster expert first-class—with honors," Erna had said. "All-around bearer of sad tidings. Death-and- destruction specialist in Her Majesty's service. When are you going to make a real film again?"

"I don't want to make a real film. And nobody wants what I'd really like to make."

"Arthur, I sometimes get the feeling that you use that collection of yours as an alibi. You finance your second world, as you call it, with your first. Oh, we're all familiar with the first one. We see it every night on the evening news: our recommended daily dosage of suffering. But that second one, that second one . . ."

"The second world is about the things that are always there. The things that supposedly aren't worth filming and are shown only as background. The bits that have to be there, but that we take for granted."

"Superfluous things?"

"If you like. The white noise. The things we overlook."

"In other words, everything. Help!" And then, "Don't mind me, I understand what you're aiming at, sort of, but I'm afraid it's a dead end. On the one hand, you see all those atrocities—you've got no idea of what you look like when you come back from one of those trips. And you've told me yourself that you sometimes have nightmares. . . . And . . . you only started filming these things after the accident."

"After the death of Roelfje and Thomas, you mean. You're the one who taught me to call them by their names. But you said 'on the one hand,' so what's the second part?"

"And on the other hand . . . you've never shown me much of your collection."

"Well, what do you remember of what you have seen?"

"Damn it, Arthur, that's not fair. Um . . . an empty sidewalk, feet going down a sidewalk, the whole thing nice and slow, a sidewalk in the rain, a bunch of tree shots, first in spring, then again in winter, and . . . uh . . . oh, yeah, the coot that made its nest here in the canal out of all kinds of junk, God what a dumb bird that was, building a nest with plastic and other bits of garbage, even a condom, and then it started to freeze . . ."

"White noise—I told you. All the little things we take for granted."

"The world according to Arthur Daane. But that includes every little thing, and you can't film every little thing."

"No, you can't." If you can't talk, it's hard to carry on a conversation. That was Erna. And over there, sitting on a wall by that ridiculous white castle, was Elik. She'd taken off her coat, and had her arms clasped around her knees.

"Sorry, but I just had to run."

"Was I walking too slowly?"

"No, too heavily."

She leaped off the wall and imitated the way he walked, jutting her chin forward, wobbling her head as if it wasn't firmly attached to her neck. Doddering. It was quite a performance, since she was trying to make herself seem bigger *and* lumber along like an elephant, both at the same time.

"Do I really walk like that? Like an old man?"

"Draw your own conclusions. Anyway, were you off filming? I've been here for ages."

"No. I took the long way around."

"So why'd you bring your camera? There's not a whole lot of stuff here worth filming, if you ask me. Not to mention that you still haven't answered the question I asked you a while ago."

So his conversation with Erna had been a rehearsal.

"If you don't put your coat back on, you'll catch cold. There's something I'd like to show you, far away from this Disneyland. I used to think the castle was fake, but it's real all right."

They looked at the turrets, the bridge, the plaster facade.

"It was built as a ruin—that must be a German specialty. Not being able to wait, wanting to get a sneak preview on the future past. It's the kind of thing Hitler wanted Speer to build. Oh, I don't mean a kitschy castle, but a grand structure that would be a beautiful ruin in a thousand years. Another form of kitsch, of course. It must have something to do with being in a hurry, not being able to let matters progress at their own speed."

"But..."

He put his finger to his lips and, as if one gesture automatically led to another, very casually placed his left arm around her shoulder. But he felt a certain reluctance, almost a resistance, so he quickly removed his arm, though he did steer her gently, with the lightest of touches, toward the water. Reeds, a pair of ducks, sunlight dappling the surface, and off in the distance, toward the light, the sharp silhouette of a boat and two figures, looking for all the world like an old daguerreotype.

"What do you see?" he asked as the camera rolled.

"Nothing. Well, okay, pure Romanticism. Swaying reeds, ducks, a boat, the opposite shore. And our feet. Satisfied?"

"Don't move."

He filmed their feet. Four shoes in the grass, near the water's edge. Cowhide boots. Nothing special.

"You wanted to know about my real work?"

How long had it taken him to explain it all to this stranger? Not long, because she'd said nothing in return, not even when they'd reached the landing and realized they'd have to wait for the ferry. By now, they were chilled to the bone. And this time they were alone. He sneaked a look at her, at her closed profile. He was sitting on the side with the scar. A sign, he thought. A cruel dark scratch, a letter, a rune, a mute witness to something that would explain why she was maintaining this stubborn silence and why she had so suddenly bolted from him. A key, though perhaps people didn't have keys.

They drank a glass of *Glühwein* in a quiet café by the ferry landing. The wine made her cheeks flush.

"So is that it for today?" she asked abruptly.

"It's up to you. There's something else I'd like to show you."

"Why?" As if she was cross-examining a witness. Elik Oranje was not an easy person to be around.

"You'll understand when you see it. But if we're going, we'd better leave now, before it gets dark. It'll take us a while to drive there. Have you ever been to Lübars?"

"No."

Something she'd said to Arno had given him the idea of taking her to Lübars. He hadn't been following their conversation very closely, but Arno had apparently been going on about historiography as a form of irony and she'd dismissed it as a typical male viewpoint, or some such thing. He wasn't sure, and he certainly wasn't going to ask. Anyway, he wanted to show her one of the things that Berlin had in abundance, and he supposed that "irony" was as good a word as any to describe it; in any case it certainly had something to do with history. It's too bad he wasn't Victor, since Victor was better at putting things into words, though you never knew if he was being ironic. Still, that's what friends were for—to be Victor, or Arno, or Zenobia. She might think they were boring. Though who knows, since the meeting with Arno had gone so well, or at any rate Arno had clearly thought so. Come to think of it, those two had been racing along at a pretty good clip and leaving him by the wayside. Articulate people always seemed to be faster.

"Where is it?"

"On the north side of Berlin. It's actually a village. At the time of the Wall, it was the only village belonging to the West, which made it seem that the city was in the country."

He drove down the Avus, switched to the autobahn at the Funkturm interchange and headed north toward Hamburg, then east toward Waidmannsluster Damm, where they left the city behind them and suddenly found themselves in the countryside: a farmhouse, a girl on a horse, cobblestones, a rustic café, a cluster of graves around a small church. Urban life had melted away. He had often come to Lübars to escape the claustrophobia of Berlin. "There used to be a *Biergarten* here," he said, pointing. "You could sit under that lime tree and look out over the pasture. And there, where it ends, is where the Wall used to be." As usual he couldn't say why he found it so moving. How could anyone do that to a country? A rupture, a wound—it was as if you had insulted the soil itself. But the soil knew nothing, like the birds who flew nonchalantly back and forth without having to ask for permission.

They walked out of the village, continued down a dirt road, then cut through a field on a path that had been turned to mud by last week's snowstorm. She didn't seem to mind, but walked silently by his side. They came to a gently meandering stream with dead leaves floating on the dark water. It was still there.

"Do you see that stake?"

In the middle of the stream was an ordinary wooden stake. Not the kind of thing you'd normally notice.

"Yes. What about it?"

"It used to have a sign nailed to it, informing you that the Western zone ended here, in the middle of this stream."

"So where was the Wall?"

"It was farther back. This was the actual border."

Maybe he was making too big a deal out of it, but it struck him as totally absurd that the border between two worlds had been located in the middle of that piddling stream. Totally absurd, yet there had been a kind of iron logic to it, a logic symbolized by that stake. And deadly, since people had been shot while trying to cross. He did his best to explain it to her.

"Why don't you try to think of it as a comedy?" she said. He frowned in puzzlement.

"What do you mean?"

"A story someone happened to make up. A country begins a war because it lost the last one, and now it loses this one too. You've seen all those Charlie Chaplin movies, where he keeps getting the opposite of what he wants. Well, there's something incredibly funny about that."

"I still don't understand. What about the effect it had on people? I suppose you think that's humorous too?"

She stopped. Piercing, unflinching eyes. He instinctively took a step backward.

"Will it make you feel better if I say it's tragic? I'm perfectly prepared to do that. Of course, it's tragic. But is the absurd comic or tragic? Two hundred years from now, when the sentimentality's worn off, all that will be left is the madness—the claims, the counterarguments, the justifications."

They walked away from the stream, along a furrowed field. It was almost dark.

"Here's where your comical Wall used to be. First a chain-link fence, then the *Todesstreifen* . . ."

"The what?"

"The death strip. Over there, where those bushes are, there used to be an observation tower, and where we're standing now was an asphalt path. On Sundays, people used to come out here and stroll along the path. Every time you stopped, you knew the guard in the tower was looking at you through his binoculars. You stopped, and his arms went up, as though the two of you were connected by a string. I can see the humor in that at any rate."

"That's not what I meant."

"I suppose not. Anyway, on our side you could look through the fence and see the Wall a couple of hundred yards away. Between them was a stretch of sandy dirt, with a watch-

176

tower in the middle, and a patrol road that provided access to the towers. That strip of land was called the *Todesstreifen:* anyone who dared to cross it was shot."

No, he wouldn't say another word about comedy. He stared at the empty field. Every time a girl rode by on horseback, up would go the binoculars. Those guys had been bored stiff. Where do you suppose they were now? It was the kind of thing he often thought about whenever he found himself walking down a street in East Berlin or sitting in the U-Bahn. It was all invisible now. If she had come here by herself, she wouldn't have noticed a thing. Nothing special had happened here, just a comic interlude. History had come and gone without leaving a trace. Only a few memories lingered in the heads of people like him. What had happened had been real, and now not only was it no longer real, but it looked as if it had never been real at all. One day there would be no one left who knew what had really gone on. Hadn't she said something to that effect? That if we had to save everything, the earth would collapse under all those memories? A great starting point for a student of history. And yet he remembered making a film in northern France once, near the Somme, and he'd kept coming across these strange, grayish, ashy pockmarks in the landscape. Even after all these years, the other war was still visible. He couldn't reconcile her two standpoints—historiography couldn't be ironic, but the events themselves could be humorous.

She was walking ahead of him. It was getting dark. And cold. He wondered how she coped with her research subject. If the things he himself had been through could vanish so inexorably—to the extent that they sounded like pure invention whenever you talked about them—then how could you come to grips with an era that had disappeared over the historical horizon centuries ago, that had been tossed on the garbage heap and buried ten times over? How much of what you read was true? If he hadn't run into her, he never would have heard of Urraca and her wars. In any case the drama had worn off, since nobody was moved by those events now. Except maybe her. Slaving away for years on a minor historical figure—surely there was an element of humor in that. Why bother?

"Because it happened."

"Well, this also happened."

She looked at him the way you do at a difficult child.

"We don't have to research this, we know what went on. At the moment there's too much of it. It'll have to wear out first. And of course I meant comic in the sense of the appalling futility of it all. I'm sorry if I didn't make that clear."

Wear out. That expression again. In other words, history only began when the people who'd lived through it were no longer alive, when they could no longer disturb the fictions of the historians. In that case, you'd never know the real story.

"There's no such thing as 'the real story.' And there never has been. Every witness creates his or her own truth. History is denial. On the Internet you can read that the gas chambers never existed."

"According to a bunch of fascists."

"And nuts. But some of those nuts and fascists are historians. Crank theories are also part of the written record."

"So what are you doing back in the Middle Ages?"

"Searching. Scurrying around other people's fictions like a hungry ant. And don't ask me why again. I like turning over rocks to see what's crawling underneath. Solving puzzles. If I wanted to do that here, I'd have to upturn the entire country. It's still teeming with life. It's too big for me."

She looked out over the empty land again. Mist, dusk. In a few minutes it would all disappear. She turned and started to walk away.

"Let's go. I need a drink."

In the café, she ordered a Doornkaat, drank it quickly, then ordered another.

"Don't you want anything to eat?"

"No. I've got to go."

And before he realized what was happening, she'd slipped out of her chair and was moving toward the door.

"Don't you want me to drive you back?"

"There's no need. I noticed that a bus runs here, a Number 22."

When had she seen that? He felt like an idiot. What a bitch! You couldn't just get up and leave! Outside he saw the headlights of the bus sweep the square. So she must've also noticed when the damn thing was leaving. Perfect timing! She hurried back to him, stood on her tiptoes to give him a hasty kiss, her moist lips quickly brushing his, then put her hand on his neck and gave it a slight push with her fingers, and that one gesture in the otherwise empty farewell lingered on as a special caress, a message, a promise that had in no way been sealed with words. Only after the door had swallowed her up—a shadow, a glint on the revolving glass door—and the same shadow had sped toward the bus beneath the chestnut trees and slid into one of the seats, a pale face sitting motionless and erect in the yellowish light—a face that didn't look back—only then did he realize that he still didn't have her address or phone number. Nor did she have his. Not that she'd asked. But for someone who knew, one dark winter evening, what time the bus left from Lübars, a village she'd never been to before, you could expect almost anything. He pushed away his glass of wine and ordered a double Doornkaat. "At least then I'll know what her lips tasted like."

We interrupt. Once again. But our interruptions are going to get shorter and shorter—we promise. Yes, of course we've been following her: the jolting bus ride, the bus stops, the endless stops where nobody gets in or out but the bus stops anyway because it has to stick to its schedule, with or without passengers. This is an orderly country, where time is thought of as dutiful, rather than temperamental. Not exactly a dignified farewell, she thought in the bus. She'd walked off and left him behind like a sinking ship. She crosses over a large square: Falkplatz. He could have told her something about that spot too, the man who knows too much and finds it so hard to express himself. He's taken pictures here as well. A desolate clearing, 1990. East Berlin. They had come from all sides—men and women of good will, innocent children, even VOPOs—and planted trees. An amateurish attempt, tender saplings stuck haphazardly in the ground, in hopes that they would eventually grow into a park or forest. A new forest in an old, derelict city. The people living on the square hadn't joined in the idiocy, but had looked down from the windows of their paintless, pockmarked apartments. With a devastating but inexplicable certainty, they knew that what was happening down there was not the future. Her clicking heels are taking her past row upon row of abandoned trees: a randomly spaced, ragged bunch of orphans, a sad reflection of bankrupt hopes. And since he isn't here to explain it, to tell what happened that day, it too has become part of the formless, invisible history of the things *we* always see because we forget nothing. We look with complete objectivity at the totality of events—something you will luckily never have to do. We have no choice, we follow the labyrinth of egos, fate, chance, design, order, natural phenomena, and death wishes you call history. You are inextricably tied to your own time, which means that what you hear are echoes, what you see are reflections. You never have to shoulder the unbearable burden of the whole picture. Yet all these things have actually happened. Nothing—no act, no nameless traceless event—is ever omitted. And because we know all of these things we hold up the structure you live in. You describe that structure in different ways, depending on the age you live in and the language you use—you who can never detach yourselves from your own time and place, no matter how hard you try. Every book you write is a gross distortion of the book that we read. Whether you call it art, scholarship, satire, or irony, it's still a mirror in which you see only a fraction of what we see. Your greatness lies in the fact that you will keep on trying to the end. You are the true heroes. We haven't got an ounce of heroism.

She's asleep now. As always, we are the only ones awake. Her book is at her side. Yes, of course we knew them all. García, the king of Galicia, Ibn-al-Ahmar, the king of Granada, Joan of Poitiers, Issac Ibn Mayer, Esteban, abbot of la Vid. What does this one live person want with all those dead ones? She's searching, she said. We can't help her. The people in her book, in all those other books, are tossing and turning and muttering under their breath. They're worried about their own version of the truth, but we can't help them either. Voices on the worn-out stairs, creaks in the old house where she lies sleeping, Spanish voices in the wintry Berlin night, voices that want to be heard, that want to tell their story, break the seals, do the impossible. The wind creeps in through the chinks and blows the tattered curtain. Someone should cover her.

The next morning he couldn't remember how he'd found his way home. That hadn't happened to him in years. He had nightmares when he drank too much, so he'd learned to drink in moderation. Apparently there was only a very thin membrane between him and chaos, and last night the sounds and voices had got through, bringing with them images that he hoped he'd never see again. Not like that, with their familiar faces in various stages of decay, disintegration, snatches of a burning plane, scoffing voices, timid approaches followed by a much faster retreat, until his screams woke him up and he groped for the light, only to find himself in a prison cell with belligerently bare walls, while outside a huge monster in the form of a chestnut tree tried to thrust its arms through the window. Did he get drunk because a woman had so unceremoniously dumped him? Probably not. It was more like the act of a person running away from herself. No. Something else was bothering him. He knew what it was and normally guarded against it better. It was his usual reaction to system overload, and it happened whenever he thought too much, saw too much, concluded too much. He'd learned to recognize the early-warning signals: a familiar face he couldn't place, a telephone voice he couldn't identify, a piece of music he'd heard a thousand times that suddenly, all at once, hit him with its full magic. Everything in sharper focus—colors, sounds, faces. The unfamiliarity of the familiar was enough to drive him mad. The best remedy was sleep, or, failing that, staring up at the ceiling. He would lie quietly on the floor, without moving, like a sick dog retreating to its corner, surrounded by a silence that refused to remain silent, but threatened to engulf him. All he could do then was put up with the images that came to him, and pretend he wasn't there, hoping they would pass him by.

He did remember arriving home last night—the phone had glared at him like a giant beetle. No, don't phone, don't play back your messages. Not even Erna's? Not even Erna's. Her voice might sound like someone else's, might say the wrong things. Okay then, the world-band travel radio. But suddenly that black plastic block with its one vicious feeler had looked incredibly menacing, a monster that sucked up disasters—Tamil Tigers lured into a land mine, fourteen dead, interspersed with hit tunes for the German truck drivers still out on the road; autobahn, fog, words, tigers, they all filled the room, and he thought of how those same voices were being heard throughout the world, everywhere tigers were stepping on land mines, flying through the damp ionosphere like astral spirits in search of antennas so they could find a way in; somewhere on the globe the sun had come up, somewhere there was a veranda where tigers were a normal part of breakfast smells, bacon, fried eggs, birds in a jacaranda, a crackling voice in a truck on its way to Phnom Penh, waking up Father Abelard in the leper hospital on Sulawesi, blaring away in an air-conditioned bedroom in the Pacific, tigers, stock certificates, rupees, a fatal injection administered an hour ago in a Texas jail to a man on a hospital bed, like a sick person needing to be cured of life, while his family and the family of his victim followed the proceedings through windows on either side, but he'd switched the radio off hours ago, so how can he have heard that, how can the sounds of the ceaseless world keep on being transmitted?

What had Victor said?

"We're the greatest heroes in history. We should all be decorated when we die. No other generation has ever had to know, see, and hear so much, suffering without catharsis, dragging a heavy load of horror along with us for the new day."

"Unless we deny it. Which we all do, don't we?"

"Or pretend to. We've developed wonderful strategies. We look at things without really seeing them. Still, we can't make them go away. They seep into the secret filing cabinets of our minds, creep into the cellars of our computers. Where do you think all those pictures of yours go? You don't spend your time working on something that vanishes into thin air, do you? And while you're at it, you also try to achieve a kind of beauty, because you're a professional. The aesthetics of atrocity. But there's no point in talking about it, since anything you say sounds like a cliché. I'd rather have the village storyteller: 'Once upon a time in a land that was far, far away....' I can just about hack that. What am I supposed to do with all the human misery that comes my way every day? I want my global suffering to be in rhyme, preferably hexameters, read by John Gielgud—in a velvet smoking jacket—from a slender red volume bound in Moroccan leather with colored etchings of Rubens paintings. And as for you, *you* will be permitted to film only things like ducklings paddling around in a pond that isn't infested with rats, or blond blue-eyed children on their first day of school, setting off with their satchels on their backs, or young lovers with two brand-new pairs of shoes. What do you say, picture-man?"

Picture-man didn't know how to answer; he'd merely imagined what those new shoes would have looked like: a pair of sturdy Dutch brogues beside a sunny duck-filled pond. And now, lying on the floor of his room, he wanted to conjure up the image of those shoes again—two soothing, sleek, brown brogues moving soundlessly over a never-ending path, so that he could count their measured steps all the way to the horizon, where sleep might be awaiting him, along with a veil of clarity to throw over the illusions and create a darkness that would last until the dawn of a new winter day, in which he would slowly awake, cured, at the same time as the gently rumbling city.

Four o'clock, five o'clock, in the outlying districts the S-Bahn trains revved their engines; the first trains of the U-Bahn trundled along the subways with their bellies full of passengers still shrouded in the night; the buses set off on their fixed routes. He lay as motionless as death and listened to it all: the gentle rumbles, the vibrations, the noises of the world to which he belonged.

When he wakes up for the second time, the light is a grayish powder. It's going to be another one of those typical winter days in Berlin, a gray twilight between two nights. "No time to shilly-shally" (Victor), get up, shave, shower, don't turn on the radio, there's no news today, a cup of coffee at the Zoo station, standing at one of those round chest-high tables without chairs that give you such a fine view of the homeless, the Vietnamese cigarette vendors, the security men with their muzzled dogs, the sawdust, the vomit, the Romanian cleanup crews, the junkies, the beggars, the all-pervading smell of sausage, the newspaper hawkers in their down-at-the-heel shoes shouting "*Bildzeitung*," a new day of hustle and bustle, all very real, *Metropolis* employees at work while he was their servant, portraitist, and archivist, drinking his coffee with Bulgakov's cat, standing six feet tall beside him, its furry arm around his shoulder, the long, sharp, curvy nails digging into his flesh. He calls his answering machine. Erna's voice:

"Okay, what's her name? Anyone who hasn't called his best friend for five days must have met a woman." Click.

Zenobia:

"A couple of photographs have come in and I'm sure you'll want to stare at them."

Has she really used the verb *spähen,* to stare? Not bad. More than a look.

At the thought of the photos a sudden calm descends on him. Okay, go home again, a brisk walk in the cold morning air. No. First a short detour past the Autorenbuchhandlung to buy a book for Zenobia. Cook yourself a decent meal. Then stare at the photos.

Arno:

"Where's my car? I need it today!"

Jesus, where was the car? Car, car. White Alfa Romeo, the philosopher's car. But where? He suddenly remembered. In a space reserved for the handicapped. "That can get you the death penalty here" (Victor). "They'll come after you on their crutches and chase you all the way to Hell and back. And even when they've got hooks instead of hands they can dial the police in ten seconds flat."

So much for Zenobia's book. Run.

Dutch NPS television:

"We need a cameraman for Russia—a report on the Mafia, increasing corruption, and all that. Make sure you take a bulletproof vest, ha ha. And since you're in the neighborhood, we might want you to zip over to Abkhazia or whatever it's called..."

With the voice still blabbing in his pocket, he sprints into a subway car, gets off four minutes later at Deutsche Oper, arrives at Goethestrasse completely out of breath, pries the ticket out of the windshield wiper's steely grasp, ignores the angry shouts of a white-haired invalid... *unverschämt, Ar-*

schloch ... and escapes just as a tow truck comes ⟨ corner.

On the staircase to Arno's apartment he suddenly finds himself plunged into the Middle Ages. Ethereal women's voices, accompanied by a single instrument that scarcely changes pitch throughout, a steady, almost nasal tone under the weave of voices. He stops to listen. The front door is wide open, so he walks in and crosses the spacious living room to get to Arno's study—all the while accompanied by the music—and as he steps over the threshold he sees his elderly friend hunched over his desk, his nose nearly touching the book he's copying something out of, like a monk in a scriptorium. Stacks of books on the desk, bookcases bulging with books, piles of books on the floor—how anyone can find his way around here is a mystery.

"Oh, that? Hildegard von Bingen. Exquisite! I feel like the chaplain of a convent. Now wouldn't that be delightful? Me hard at work in my study, and on the other side of that wall the chapel with all those learned, devout women. They're singing the *Studium Divinitatis*—the matins of the feast of St. Ursula, the first song of the morning, the roses still covered with dew, the mist starting to lift down by the river. It's the fault of that girlfriend of yours."

"What's she got to do with it?"

"She was talking about her dissertation yesterday, and after you two had gone I thought I'd check out the music I had from that period."

"Made an impression on you, did she?"

"Anything wrong with that? Yes, I was impressed. And also just the tiniest bit moved. First by her face—such intensity, such distrust. But even more by ... You see, I know so rew young people. Even you aren't exactly young, and you're about the youngest person I know. Oh, I see them out on the street, or on the U-Bahn, or on that box over there, demonstrating or whatever, but then I think, They no longer concern me, their world has almost nothing to do with mine." And he waved his hand in a gesture that seemed to include not only the thousands of books but also the invisible convent in the speakers. "On the rare occasions when I come in contact with students or the children of friends of mine, I'm struck by how little they know. There are incredible gaps in their knowledge. They live in a formless present. To them the world has never existed before now. It's not that they're lazy; they just don't seem to be interested in anything. So when someone like her comes along, it's a welcome relief. Then I think, Tieck, you old fuddy-duddy, you're wrong, they're not all like that."

"So there's hope after all."

"Go ahead and laugh. Look..." He rummaged through his books, revealing a vellum notebook that he'd apparently been writing in, since there was an uncapped fountain pen lying in the crease. Every couple of years another volume of Arno's essays was published: meditations on things he'd done, or books he'd read, travels, thoughts.

"You seemed distracted yesterday. Anxious to get going."

"The light."

"Ah, of course. You weren't really following the conversation, were you?"

"No, not really."

"Well, we were talking about her dissertation. She has rather strong opinions. Apparently she's taking a class on Hegel taught by some old bore, so now she claims that Hegel is worthless. Nothing but pseudo-religious nonsense..."

"I'll have to pass on that one, Arno. I'm the photography department, remember?"

"I know, I know, but still, it isn't that difficult. I wish I could have made her see that there's so much more to Hegel than that.... Naturally I didn't want to bore her with abstract theories, but I did want her to know about that wonderful moment when Hegel heard the distant roar of Napoleon's cannons from his study in Jena and believed that history was entering its final phase, or, rather, that it was already over. Just imagine, history was coming to an end, or so he thought... and he was on hand for the moment of liberation. It would prove his theory, Napoleon's battle would mark the dawn of a new age, there would no longer be masters and servants— an inequality that had existed throughout history...."

"Arno, I just came here to bring back your car."

"I know. She didn't want to hear it either. Anyway, I'm not saying that's how it went. Think of it as a metaphor, if you like. But can you try to imagine how it must have felt when the Napoleonic Code came to a remote corner of Germany... when all citizens were supposed to be autonomous and free? Oh, the excitement of it! Imagine what it would have meant back in those days!"

"My dear friend, you look as if you're standing on a soapbox."

"Sorry." Arno sat down again.

"You don't really think history actually ended then?"

"Of course not. Though there was a sense of finality. The world had reached a turning point.... Something was irrevocably over, and Hegel knew it. After that nothing could remain the same, if for no other reason than the fact that his theories were to have such far-reaching consequences. But I'll spare you the details. Are you going to bring her here again?"

"I don't even have her address."

"Oh. There's something I wanted to give her. About the methodology of historiography. Plutarch railing against Herodotus because he lied. Well, that's the beginning of all controversy: what are your sources, how much have you invented.... She and I touched on that point. I believe she's wrestling with that concept. And of course Lucian, that great part where he says he doesn't want to be the only one without a voice in an age of polyphony... Though I don't know if that would interest her, since she claims that all of our ideas on history have come from dead white males. It may be true, but it's hard to know what to say in reply. After all, I don't know of any female historians of the caliber of Mommsen or Michelet or Macaulay. And if you point that out, you're accused of even more gender bias, since it appears that men have usurped the entire field of history and shaped it to suit their own needs...." He shrugged his shoulders in a gesture of helplessness. "I never know what to say to that one."

"So what does she think we should do?"

"Haven't you had this discussion with her already?"

"Arno, we barely know each other. Actually, we don't know each other at all."

"My, my. You Dutch are an odd lot. Where did you find her? When she came in here I thought that you...that the two of you..."

"Well, we aren't."

"Ah, such a pity..." He suddenly put a finger to his lips. "Did you hear that? Those voices? Listen, here it comes again...."

Arthur knew there must be something special about the music. He shot his friend a quizzical look. All he could hear were those same soprano voices, beautiful, but what did Arno mean?

"There, there it is again. Hildegard von Bingen was such a fantastic composer. And to think that she was also a philosopher and a poet! '*Aer enin volat*... Even as the air flies...' Look, it keeps switching back and forth between D and E...."

We just heard E in the fourth antiphon, and now we hear it again in the seventh. That's the feminine principle. . . . Then there's the sixth, and the eighth. In other words, what they thought of at the time as masculine dignity, female spirituality, male authority. Well, it *was* the early Middle Ages. It's not politically correct to say so in this day and age, but do you hear how beautifully she plays up the contrast? It's lost on us—our modern ears aren't attuned to the nuances."

"Mine certainly aren't. But what did you mean by 'such a pity'?"

"Oh, just that I thought she was special. Just the kind of woman you . . . Well, anyway, in the course of our brief conversation I gathered that I'm not exactly her favorite kind of person. Do you know what she called me? A constructivist! And constructivists—she informed me—are people who think up constructs to support their own theories of reality or history or whatever. A typical male pastime. She intends to stick solely to the niche she's chosen for herself—that medieval queen. . . ."

"So that's why you're playing this music?"

Arno looked a little embarrassed, as though he'd been caught doing something he shouldn't have. For a moment the only voices were those on the CD.

"Yes. I tried to imagine what it was like to have to pick a subject—to choose a time and a place and a person. Of course there's very little left from that period. Only buildings, churches, and manuscripts. And this music, of course—it's from exactly the same era. It provides a little more insight into the people who lived back then . . ."

"But did it sound the same back then? Isn't this just a reconstruction? I mean, aren't we listening to *our* version of the Middle Ages?"

"Oh, I don't know. I tend to think that it's fairly close to the original. Here, just like this card."

He handed Arthur a postcard on which he had jotted down a few notes for Elik.

"You might as well give this to her."

"What's the picture?"

"A fresco from a church in León, just the ceiling. San Isidoro—the pantheon of the early Spanish kings. That Urraca of hers just might be buried there too. At any rate we know it was built in the twelfth century, and it's in the right area."

Arthur realized once again how fond he was of Arno. There must be people like him in Holland, though he'd never met any. Knowledgeable people were a dime a dozen, but it was rare to find a person who could explain things in such a way that you immediately understood, a person who never talked down to you but always made you feel, at least while the conversation lasted, that you could follow every detail. Later, when you replayed it in your head, you discovered how little you really knew, but bits of it always stuck. Over the years he'd learned a lot from Arno. "When did you read all that?" he remembered asking him once.

"When you were off traveling. But what you have to realize is that travel is also a form of reading. The world is a book."

He knew that Arno had meant to console him. Arthur looked at the postcard. A shepherd holding a staff and some kind of squarish wind instrument. Bangs cut straight across his forehead, a robe that came down to the knees, his feet in a pair of buskins. Exactly how people nowadays picture a medieval shepherd. So there was nothing wrong with that. The troubadours who stroll around wine and cheese bars wear the same costume.

"Amazing," said Arno, "when you look at those bodies. They didn't know a thing about human anatomy. Weren't you the one who brought that up a while ago? Electronic impulses, brain stems, enzymes, blood cells, neurons—they didn't have a clue. Must have been wonderful. If they saw anything at all, it was on the battlefield, after they'd chopped off a head or a leg. It wasn't until Vesalius came along in the mid-sixteenth century that they had access to detailed anatomical drawings. But with the exact same brains, they thought different things. Are you going to see her?"

"Look for her, you mean." And he told Arno about last night's farewell fiasco.

"Oh, dear." Arno looked stricken. "Sometimes I feel I'm up in a balloon, looking down on my contemporaries. Or listening to them. Half the time I don't even know what they're talking about."

"They probably say the same about you."

"Great. First life was absurd, now it's hilarious." He sighed. "But what's your next move? Going to look for her? Hmm, where does one begin? It sounds romantic."

Which is why I object to the idea, Arthur thought. He tried hating her, but it wasn't easy. That face. Always as if she was about to take a bite out of something.

"That queen business is still a mystery to me," Arthur said. "How about you? Knowing you, I bet you've done your homework."

"Haven't you?"

"I didn't find much information."

"There isn't a whole lot to be found," Arno said. "Just the basic facts and dates. She was married off to a man from Burgundy when she was eight. I can't remember his name, but even back in those days they all knew each other. She had a son when she was fairly young, but then the husband died and she inherited a kingdom. She married again, this time the king of Aragon, but he beat her and was useless in bed. Not that we're told that in so many words, but you know how it is. A childless marriage. Contemporary sources, et cetera."

"You seem pretty well versed on the subject."

Arno looked slightly guilty. "Well, I researched it yesterday, after you left. I had to go to the University library anyway. I took a quick look at early Spanish history, but didn't get very far. For starters, Spain didn't exist back then. The borders were in a constant state of flux—you'd go crazy if you tried to figure it out. The Muslims and Christians were at daggers, and then there were all kinds of kingdoms and minikingdoms, with everybody killing each other or forming new alliances, and to make it even more complicated, they were all named Alfonso—her father, her second husband, her brother, all of them kings, all of them Alfonsos: Alfonso I, or Alfonso VI, or Alfonso VII. But..."

"But?"

"Well, in the final analysis it all boils down to how you view history. What can we throw overboard? Are major events more important than minor ones? It's the old question of the Bach choir. Or the wine sauce."

"The question of what?"

"The Bach choir. Sixteen sopranos, sixteen basses, et cetera. If one bass is sick, do you notice? The music calls for sixteen, and that's how many there should be. If only one is gone, you don't notice. The conductor might, but you don't. If two are gone, or three... when does it start to make a difference? I'll spare you the wine sauce—you've already had a taste. Let's assume that your lady friend is a good student, that she's hot on the trail of something. But what she and all her fellow researchers are doing is filling up a gap in time that doesn't exist, and yet at the same time it does."

"Something that does and doesn't exist? Help!"

"Just listen. It's not that difficult. The world in its present state has come about through a series of events. None of those events can be left out of consideration, even if we don't know what they are. After all, they did occur."

"But if you don't know something, you can't leave it out."

"I haven't expressed myself clearly. Let me put it this way. The world as we know it is the sum of everything that has ever happened, even though we don't always know *what* happened, or we find out that something we thought happened one way actually went another way. That process of finding out what it is we don't know, or correcting our errors, is the work of historians, or at any rate it should be. Historians are a strange breed. They spend their allotted time here on earth digging up information on one single person or topic. To me, that's unbelievable. Will their work change the course of history? Probably not. Nevertheless, even though nobody cares about it now, at one time Europe's fate was decided in a remote corner of Spain. If a handful of crazy kings hadn't held out against Islam, you and I might very well be called Mohammed."

"Nothing wrong with that."

"Nothing at all."

Arno thought for a moment. "She looks a bit Arabic—have you noticed?"

Arthur didn't feel it was necessary to reply. In the meantime his friend had left the room and come back with a bottle of wine and two glasses.

"Here. Forbidden to us Mohammedans. A Beerenauslese—the finest there is."

"Not for me," Arthur said. "I'm still recovering from last night. If I drink it, this day'll really be down the drain."

"Better to have the day go down the drain than the wine. Here, take a look at that color—liquid gold, nectar. Do you remember what Tucholsky said about wine? That you should be able to caress it. Wonderful! Come on, make yourself a present of this unusual day. And hurry up, because Vera will be home soon, and she thinks I ought to spend my days deep in thought. Do you remember the time we drank that bottle of Poire Williams at Victor's?"

How could he ever forget? Victor's studio, late in the afternoon. The Kunsthaus in Zürich had bought one of Victor's sculptures, and they had been celebrating. "Gentlemen, our mission today is to liberate the pear from the bottle."

After the second glass the tip of the pear bobbed up above the liquid, prompting the great metaphysical question of how it had got in the bottle in the first place, and leading to the much more complex question of how to get it out in one piece. Victor had sworn up and down that he'd seen bottles of Poire Williams growing on trees: "Entire orchards gleaming in the sunlight of the Swiss Alps." His announcement had been met with skepticism. The other two had come up with even more ingenious solutions, but the more the liquid sank and the higher the pear rose—revealing the fruit in all its glory—the more unlikely their theories had become, until the pear had finally lain, a bit pathetic despite its problematic size, at the bottom of the empty bottle.

"What do we do now?" Victor had asked, and he'd turned the bottle upside down. That had sent the pear flying into the neck, where it was impossible to get it out.

"Never underestimate the craftsman," Victor had said. "But before I fetch my tools, let's draw straws to see who gets to eat the pear. No, even better—let's throw dice: the highest number wins."

With great solemnity, they'd tossed the dice. "You see, I *do* play dice," Arno had said, with Einstein's own accent. Arthur had won, whereupon Victor had left the room and come back with a hammer and a wet towel. He then proceeded to wrap the bottle in the towel.

"Here, Arthur, take the hammer. Give the bottle a whack, and a miracle will happen."

So he'd given it a whack, and when he'd unrolled the towel, the broken bottle had lain there like a cracked windshield, with the pear intact.

"Do you remember that Toon Hermans act?" Victor had asked Arthur. "The one with the peach?" And he'd shown Arno how the inimitable Dutch comedian had eaten an invisible peach and how the juice had run down his chin.

The other two had watched in envy as Arthur had picked up the pear with great ceremony and brought it to his mouth. "Ah, the delights of pear juice," Victor had begun. But before he could finish, Arthur's face had turned to a grimace. His teeth had encountered a cold, hard, unripe pear that seemed to be biting him instead of the other way around.

"This is bound to taste better than that pear did," Arno said now, as he tipped his wine glass in Arthur's direction.

"I've got to go to Zenobia's."

"Ah, Zenobia. When you marry a twin, you actually get two wives. Not to mention that in this case you get two Russians, with Art and Science thrown in for good measure! Arthur, if things don't work out with this Spanish Orange, you and I can always go to Russia to find you a twin. I'll line up a documentary, and you can be the cameraman. How about a program on Shestov? Do you know his work?"

"Never heard the name."

"Lev Shestov! *Speculation and Revelation*! Misunderstood, misunderstood..."

"Not now, Arno."

"Oh, sorry."

They sat without talking. The wine seemed to go well with the music. The female voices floated around the room and made further conversation unnecessary. Arthur knew that the rest of the day would trickle away like this and that it could no longer be stopped. He thought about phoning Erna, and about phoning Zenobia to say he wouldn't be dropping by; then he thought about nothing for a while. Suddenly Arno broke off his Gregorian hum to ask, "Tell me, how do you think you produce the people in your dreams? I don't mean the ones you know, but the ones you've never seen before. There must be some kind of mechanism that enables us to manufacture people that don't exist. But how do we do it? They have real faces, yet they're not real."

"Actually, it can be very upsetting," said Arthur.

"Perhaps it upsets them too," Arno mused aloud.

"Just imagine, you don't even exist and suddenly you're called upon to appear in the dream of a total stranger. A kind of command performance..."

The phone rang. A muffled whimper.

"Where'd I put the damn thing? Or is it yours?"

"The beep is coming from your body," Arthur said. "Try your inside pocket."

"Yes. Speaking," Arno said into the receiver. "But who are you?

"Oh, what a coincidence...no, no, not a coincidence, of course not, ha ha. Yes..."

The voice on the other end of the line now took the time to explain something.

"No, I don't think he'll mind," Arno said. "It's Sesenheimerstrasse 33. Oh, you're welcome. Perhaps we'll meet again. By the way, how did you find *my* number? Oh, yes, of course, it's in the phone book. No, there aren't very many Tiecks. Well, good-bye."

"That was my address," Arthur said.

"Yes, it was. You're not looking for her; she's looking for you. I didn't tell her you were here because I didn't think you'd want me too. Or should I have?"

"Didn't she ask for my phone number?"

"No, but of course she'll be able to find it."

"It's listed under another name."

"Then maybe she'll write you a letter."

Or drop by, thought Arthur. But he couldn't imagine it.

"What are you going to do now?"

Before he could answer, the phone rang again.

"Ah, Zenobia. Yes, I've seen him. In fact, I can still see him. Looking the worse for wear. No, the Dutch can't take their liquor.... I'll let you talk to him."

"Arthur?" She wrapped him in her voice like a blanket. Some people sought you out without wanting anything from you. It required no effort on your part. They enveloped you in their warmth, and you knew you could trust them to the bitter end.

"When are you coming over to look at my photographs?"

"Tomorrow, Zenobia. I'll come by tomorrow. This afternoon? No. If it was anyone else, I'd tell a lie. But I'll level with you—I have a date."

"*Obmanshchik!*"

"What's that mean?"

"Two-timer. So who's the lucky woman you have a date with? Is that why you're looking the worse for wear?"

"It's not one, but several."

"Braggart. Who is she? I hope you haven't forgotten my warning. Are we going to have to tie you to the mast? Who is she?"

"She happens to be a lioness."

"I'm also a lioness."

"I know, but this one has real claws. I'm going to the zoo, over in East Berlin. I'll see plenty of females there: ocelots, snakes, lamas..."

"Sure, sure."

"...Elephants, owls, eagles...I can't think of the feminine forms of any animals."

"Tigress, vixen, she-wolf...Are you going to film them?"

"No, not today. I just don't feel like being with people."

"Thanks a lot," said Arno and Zenobia in chorus, and all

three of them laughed. He hung up. They knew what Arthur was like—every now and then he preferred the company of animals to that of people.

"Do you need a ride?" Arno asked. "I'm headed in that direction. I've got to go to a conference in Wittenberg, where I'm giving a lecture on Martin Luther. That's why I wanted my car back. I can drop you off on the way."

"And what about that?" Arthur asked, pointing toward the almost empty bottle.

"Won't do Luther a bit of harm. Are you coming or not?"

"No, no. I want to take a bus. To float above people's heads. Nothing nicer than Berlin from the top of a double-decker. So what are you and that wine-befuddled head of yours going to say about Luther?"

"Darkness and light. And how he was such an incredible stylist. Where would the German language be without Luther? There would be no Goethe, no Mann, no Benn. Oh..." He suddenly stood stock-still, as if enlightenment had struck. "Ha, that's what I was working on, a capriccio, probably nonsense, but anyway imagine Luther in the same room with Derrida and Baudrillard. Their shadowboxing wouldn't stand a chance. He'd knock them right out of the ring. Still...against a Talmudist and a Jesuit..."

"I've got to go," Arthur said. "The animals in the zoo are expecting me. Luckily they don't talk about philosophy."

"Or anything else."

"True." But things were not quite that simple.

The day was still as gray as it had promised to be that morning—the gray of old zinc washtubs, city sidewalks, or enemy uniforms, depending on how much or how little light the overcast sky was letting through. He had walked down

Nestorstrasse, where Arno lived, and was now waiting along with several other shivering people for the bus. No family, not today. When the double-decker finally came, he climbed the spiral staircase to the top. The front seat was empty, so he had the entire city to himself. From this height you were no longer part of it—you could look down at all those heads going so purposefully about their business and register the moment the bus crossed from the West to the East, passing a line that had become invisible to most people, where he always seemed to hold his breath, as if you weren't even supposed to breathe in no-man's-land.

It got even grayer. He had to change buses, which took forever, but he didn't mind, though his head was still fuzzy from the alcohol, the sleepless night, the chitchat, and now the wine. He'd passed through the outskirts of East Berlin many times, yet the sight never failed to surprise him. Block after block of apartment houses with hollow-eyed windows and cheap paint jobs. So this used to be the workers' paradise, he thought. This is where the other half used to live. And still does, though its bizarre government has been shut down and dismantled, its leaders fled, jailed, or hauled into court. It wasn't so much that the rules of the game had changed, as that the game itself had suddenly ceased to exist. People had been lifted out of their own lives, and every aspect of their existence—newspapers, organizations, names, habits—had been changed. All at once forty years had been crumpled into a useless wad of paper, memories of an entire era tainted, twisted, blighted. Could people bear such a burden?

The majority of them had simply been dealt a bad hand. But they had made the best of it, as people usually do: fenced in but free, manipulated but knowing, victims as well as occasional accomplices in a macabre misunderstanding that had resembled the real world—a corrupt utopia that had lasted until the pendulum had swung the other way. Only the pain remained the same, except that this time they also had to put up with the arrogance of those who'd been luckier in the draw.

All but the youngest must have a gap in their lives—a secret document, the crack of a rifle shot by the Wall, or, simply, as in the case of most, a snapshot tucked away in a drawer somewhere, of a young man in the uniform of the now defunct *Volksarmee,* his arm around Frieda or Armgard, in the meantime also ten years older. How did they cope? He was always surprised at how little his friends in the West knew, or wanted to know, about the East's past. Dealing with their own past, which likewise seemed so long ago, had evidently exhausted them—they couldn't take on another, this one was no concern of theirs.

Karl-Marx-Allee, Frankfurter Allee. Rows of cube-shaped apartments looking twice as cheerless in this weather. He caught glimpses of people moving around inside: women in gaudy floral prints, men ambling through the rooms with the slow, aimless gait of the unemployed. Friedrichsfelde. Just ahead he could see the tall trees of the zoo. He bought a ticket—which cost ten times more than it used to—and strolled down the path. He knew what there was to see. Back then there had also been fathers with children, and he'd made up all sorts of fantasies about their lives: subversive poets, army officers on their day off, suspended teachers, party officials...As usual, it had been impossible to tell anything by looking at them. They could have seen from his clothes that he was from the West, or assumed that he was one of the privileged few allowed to travel, but in fact they'd taken no notice of him. They'd had better things to do. They'd lifted up their children to see the polar bear on the other side of the greenish-brown water, and as the children had looked at the animals, he had looked at them. What went on in those little heads? There was one kid who hadn't been able to get enough of a huge snake. You could see his eyes moving along the serpentine body curled up at the bottom of a lighted terrarium, searching among the bulging, sinister coils for the head— the sudden shock of the ridiculously small head and closed eyes—then his unconscious imitation of the motionless snake. The boy had refused to be dragged away by his impatient father. Unable to bear the idea that a living creature could lie as still as death, he'd been determined to wait until the masquerade was over.

Thomas had adored owls, ever since they'd gone to the Amsterdam zoo and he'd seen a large owl with big round eyes rotate its head a hundred and eighty degrees, so that those ocher orbs with their menacing black pupils no longer held the boy's gaze. What did you actually know about a child? Thomas had stored up that mesmerizing gaze, but for what kind of future? Best not to think about it. He had clamored to go back ("Owl! Owl!"), but after that had never said another word, as though he wanted to chew over the images and keep them to himself. Here in the Berlin zoo, the owls had been banished to a far corner, across from a drab monument dedicated to "the victims of the Wuhlheide Camp of the Fascist secret police (Gestapo)...POWs from sixteen countries who were mistreated, forced to work in the armaments industry, and murdered."

They were Turkoman owls, with large heads, delicate beige feathers and eyes that seemed to look straight through you. Never once did they let you see that they were observing you. It was as if you weren't really there. Maybe that's what Thomas had found so fascinating. Arthur suddenly felt an inexplicable urge to see these creatures fly, and he tried to imagine the sound they would make: a sinister swish. It was already evening in Turkmenistan—a green forest on the side of a mountain, the beating of wings at dusk as the heavy body swoops to the ground, the shrill cry of the victim.

He had the feeling that animals knew more than human

beings, but refused to talk about it. The panther avoided your gaze, the lion focused on something next to you, the snake didn't bother to look, the camel looked over your head, the elephant was interested only in the forbidden peanut at the tip of his trunk. They all refused to acknowledge your existence, perhaps out of revenge, but more likely out of such an intense compassion that eye contact would be unbearable. Yet that was also the attraction: all those lives seeking refuge behind quills, shells, horns, scales, carapaces; equipped with fins, pelts, claws; the squawking toucan and the sand-colored insect hiding under a rock—all of these creatures were related to us more than to anything else in the world, because in the course of their shorter or longer lives they were subject to the same laws.

As if in confirmation, the distant hyenas began to howl—piercing, high-pitched cries punctuated by a few hoarse, contemptuous coughs, and then the wailing started again. It sounded like a siren, one that could be turned on and off at will. This time he didn't respond to the call. He looked up at the sky and saw the first streaks of night. It was time to go home. He had shaken off people and their voices—however dear to him they were on other occasions—and if he took the U-Bahn now he'd have just enough time to pick up something for dinner before the stores in his neighborhood closed.

"The lust for loneliness." That's how Victor always described this mood. "Just the thing for a man by himself in a big city. Alone with his ten fingers, his two ears, and his two eyes. Whistling softly in the privacy of his own four walls, surrounded by millions of invisible creatures, alone in a metropolis—the ultimate pleasure."

But things turned out differently. As he climbed the stairs to his apartment he could just make out a female shape in the darkness—Elik Oranje. He turned the key in the lock, and she stood up. Neither of them said a word. He switched on the light and let her go in ahead of him. She was wearing a dark-blue gabardine coat. He merely registered the fact, without thinking. She walked directly over to the window as if she'd been here before, glanced at the tree, and plunked herself down on a square stool that he usually sat on when he was talking on the phone. She hadn't bothered to take off her coat. He hung his in the closet, then put the kettle on. I don't know this woman, he thought, and here she is sitting in my living room. With her coat on and her face as closed as a book. What about yesterday, the revolving door, the pale blur behind the window, the sudden departure?

She'd refused to think about him anymore. He had said too much, and she hadn't let him in. She was going to forget him. Or maybe it wasn't actually what he'd said, but the images he'd evoked—that stream, that field, the whole irrevocable past. He could still conjure them up, but after that they would disappear. They would become part of a vanished history that others would have to discover. All the way home she'd been thinking about this—the long bus ride, the sleeping city glimpsed through the window. A drunk had fallen on top of her, and she'd slapped his face, hard. After that he'd left her alone, slumped over in a corner, swearing steadily under his breath. There hadn't been any other passengers. The driver had watched it all in his mirror, but hadn't moved a muscle.

So I can't see what I'm seeing, she had concluded as she rode through the endless succession of urban neighborhoods. If that's true, then how can you see back over a distance of a thousand years?

She had told him that she was searching, but what did that mean?

All that was left of her queen was a handful of documents and records. Nothing was known of her feelings and thoughts. Oh, there were a few scattered testimonies of her contemporaries—most of them apocryphal—but in any case they dealt with events, not feelings. When she finally arrived home (home! That dump!), she didn't turn on the light. The smell of the damp and mold in the stairwell followed her inside. She got undressed, made her bed into a kind of rabbit hole, and pulled the blankets up under her chin, like a child. Her mind raced. You could search all you wanted, but the documents contradicted each other. Still, Urraca was the only woman in medieval Spain who had any real power. She ruled for seventeen years, alone. At the time of her marriage to the king of Aragon, she was twenty-seven years old, a widow with two children, the queen of Castile and León. King, queen— crazy words. A woman lying in a bed in Berlin thinks about those two bodies uniting three kingdoms in another, hard-to-imagine bed. No, the only thing she could possibly hope to learn would be the facts that were already known or were still waiting to be discovered. No progeny issued from that bed. Had he been impotent? After all, she had already borne children, and he had every reason in the world to want a successor. He used to beat her, the sources said. Thousand-year-old gossip, or the truth, or worse. Their marriage was a disaster. She struck back, but with armies. Anything else you added to that would be fiction, self-delusion.

"I bet I know why you decided to do your Ph.D. on her," her supervisor had said. "The current gender-history rage, right?"

He'd smiled a self-satisfied smile. The smug grin of a man who's sure he's scored a point. She hadn't corrected him— there'd be time later on.

She'd fallen asleep very late, waked up a few times, and the friend who rented her the room had banged on her door and wailed something, but she'd yelled at him to go away. Now here she was sitting across from another man. He poured the hot water over the coffee and brought her a cup.

He wouldn't ask why she'd come. Not this guy. He fished something out of his pocket and handed it to her, "Here, this is for you. From Arno Tieck."

It was a postcard. She nodded, examined the picture. No need to read the message on the back just now. She recognized the scene—they were now on her turf. She had stood in that hushed church, had seen all those sarcophagi with their nearly illegible inscriptions, had wanted to believe that her queen lay buried in one of those stone coffins. The elderly priest who'd been on duty had disabused her of that notion fairly quickly, which is what you get for engaging in such flights of fancy. The man had been almost stone-deaf, so she'd shouted her questions at him and he'd shouted back his answers, and their voices had echoed and reechoed under the low Romanesque arches.

"Napoleon's soldiers had a field day in there," she said to Arthur. "They opened the sarcophagi, tossed out the corpses, or what was left of them, destroyed the inscriptions. The tombs are completely empty now."

"He wrote something on the back," he said.

Now she'd have to read it. She flipped the card over. Plutarch, Lucian. Someone evidently took her seriously. The man with the unruly hair, the Coke-bottle glasses, the face full of hieroglyphs. Hegel, Napoleon, the end of history, queens dragged from their graves, perhaps with reason. She looked at the man who had just sat down across from her again. What could two such different men possibly have in common? The one head full of such impressive cobwebs, the other apparently determined to say as little as possible. Still, all kinds of words had been said yesterday.

"Why don't you put on some music?" she said. And, when he got up to look through his CDs, she said, "No, not something you want me to hear. Play the CD that's in there, the last one you were listening to."

Penderecki's *Stabat Mater.* Incomprehensible words. A series of long-drawn-out notes sung by dark male voices—baritones and basses—followed by high, pleading women's voices, calling from a distance, flowing over the men, whispering, agitating.

"Music from the underworld," she said. "Lost souls."

Sudden screams like the lash of a whip, then mysterious mumbling.

"When did you listen to this? Last night, after you got home?"

"I was drunk when I got home."

"Oh."

"Aren't you going to take off your coat?"

She stood up, took off her coat, and then, as he watched, transfixed, she took off her sweater, then her shoes. Piece by piece she removed every item of clothing she had on and added it to a neat pile, until she was standing in front of the window completely naked. For one long moment she didn't move. Then she turned to face him.

"This is me."

In this light the scar looked almost purple, but that wasn't what took his breath away. Her nudity had transformed it, so that it now stood out against her alabaster skin like a letter, an inscription, forcing him to go over and touch it. She didn't move or reach out her arms, but let his finger explore the indentation, the wound, let his finger trace the outline, then move to her mouth. She placed one hand lightly against his chest, and after he had silently, wordlessly, undressed, the same hand propelled him, mutely but peremptorily, toward the bed, as if he had to be led there, and pushed him down toward the mattress, so that he could feel himself falling back onto the bed in one slow, fluid motion and could see how she appeared above him, how she lay down on top of him with that scar close to his eyes, how she stretched herself out until she seemed to cover him completely, and later on he knew that what he had felt at that moment had been a kind of amazement and disbelief, as if it couldn't be true that this woman was kissing him and caressing him, couldn't be true that she was sliding down his body and taking possession of him, that he was now totally in her power, none of this was really happening to him, maybe that tight face with those closed eyes and that body arching further and further back in ecstasy had forgotten him, and yet a woman was now sitting astride him and mumbling something, over and over again, her voice blending with the funeral chorus in the music, a voice that was about to scream and finally did scream, and at that moment, as if on command, he came with a pain that was immediately smothered—as if it had to be that way—when her body slumped forward onto his, and she lay with her head beside his on the pillow, still mumbling or swearing or whispering.

Only much later did she get up, go to the bathroom, come back. He gestured toward the bed but she shook her head. So he got up and threw his arms around her slender body, which trembled and shook. She slowly detached herself and got dressed. So he too put on his clothes. This was still his room. Why had that thought entered his head? Because he knew the room would never again be the same. She went over to the window and sat down, as though they were reenacting the scene. In a moment she'd take off her clothes again, he'd see that terrible vulnerability again, once more he would be overpowered by that vulnerability, thrown down, taken. Present, absent, these were other laws he'd have to learn. The music had stopped. She stood up and wandered through the room, touching some of the objects with her fingertips.

He could hear her over by his desk, though he couldn't see her because she was standing in the other part of the L-shaped room.

"Who's this?"

He knew without asking. She was looking at the picture of Roelfje and Thomas, the same one that Erna had by her window, only smaller.

"My wife."

"And the little boy?"

"My son."

"Are they in Amsterdam?"

"No. They're dead." There was no other way of putting it. For one small moment there were others in the room. Others?

He waited for her to ask more questions, but there was silence. He slowly walked over to where she was standing, watched her hold the picture to the light, bring it closer to her eyes. She wasn't just looking at it, she was studying it. Gently he took the picture from her hands and put it back where it belonged.

"Would you like something to eat?"

"No. I've got to go. It's not like yesterday, though I'm a world champion when it comes to good-bye. In your case I don't need to think up an excuse." She hesitated. "Are you going to be in Berlin for a while?"

"Until my next assignment."

That reminded him of the message from the NPS. He'd have to call them back. Russia, Mafia.

"But I'll be around until then."

"Good," she said. "So long."

She scooped up her coat with one finger and was out the door. A world champion when it comes to good-bye. He heard her footsteps on the stairs, then the slam of the outside door. She was part of the city now, a mere passerby. It sounded crazy, but he noticed that the room looked surprised. So he wasn't the only one. The chairs, the curtains, the picture, the bed, even his old friend the chestnut tree—they all looked surprised. He had to get out of there.

There were two restaurants that he and his friends liked to frequent: the one belonging to Herr Schultze, and the one belonging to their friend Philippe, which Victor referred to as his "home away from home," since he ate there almost every day.

"Philippe has finely tuned radar," Victor had once said. "He can tell when I'm wrapped in silence. That's not bad for a buccaneer."

Correct on both counts. Victor did seem to have an aura of invisible silence about him when he was brooding, and Philippe did indeed resemble a pirate from St. Malo.

"No," Vera had once claimed, "he looks like one of the three musketeers." And there was something to be said for her theory as well.

"That sad look in his eyes—it's because he misses the other two."

But Philippe was cheerful tonight. He embraced Arthur, who hated it when most people did that, and said, "Victor's sitting in the back." Then without pausing he added, "What's happened to you? You look like you've seen a flying saucer."

So that's what it was, Arthur thought. A flying saucer. He walked to the back. Victor would pretend not to notice him at first. He'd narrow those tiny little eyes of his into slits, faking nearsightedness so that he could open his eyes wide in mock surprise. He'd been reading a book, and Arthur watched him tuck a bookmark in it and hide it under a newspaper.

"Ah, it's you."

All very predictable. They'd never talked about it, but

Arthur knew they both enjoyed the opportunity to speak Dutch.

"It's a beautiful language," Victor had once said to Arno. "Dutch and German are distant relatives, but they've gone their own separate ways. You should have stuck with us. Instead, German has evolved into a language that strikes our Dutch ears as very odd. And very loud, sometimes. That's because your country has so many hills and dales. The sound is always reverberating. Holland is flat, which means that everything's on the surface. We lack depth, but make up for it in clarity. You Germans have to keep a constant eye out for hidden caves, dark forests, shady glens, wooded slopes—no wonder the place is filled with Wagnerian mists, with writers as Druids and poets as high priests. We don't have to worry. The strong wind in our Dutch polders has blown the mist away. Take girl, for example. I mean the word. In German you use the possessive 'its' even when it's a girl '*Das Mädchen hat* seine *Puppe verloren*.' The girl has lost *its* doll. You've got to admit it sounds strange. Makes you think something really terrible has happened to the girl. And that'd be unthinkable in our flat polders—everyone would be able to see it. Holland used to be covered by the sea, so we pumped it dry, let it stand for a while, and built houses on it, and now you can look through the windows. We've got nothing to hide—no mists, no secrets, just a little girl and *her* doll. Girls are feminine where we come from. Have you ever heard Goethe in Dutch?"

And he'd recited a passage from Goethe. In German.

"When you hear that, you can't help but think that Dutch is beautiful."

Tonight Victor was also in a good mood.

"I got chased out of the house," he said. "But what are you doing here? How are we ever going to get our daily portion of global suffering if you're still in Berlin?"

"I'm heading out soon," Arthur said. "Next week Abkhazia. What do you mean you got chased out?"

Since Victor lived alone, there was no one besides himself to chase him out of his house. Arthur put his hand on top of the newspaper and felt around for the book underneath.

"Hiding your book?"

"Not well enough."

"Can I look?"

"It's fast asleep."

"Whose is it?"

"Mine."

"No, that's not what I meant. I mean who wrote it?"

"Ah. Take a guess."

"Do I know the name?"

"I don't know, but he knows yours."

Arthur reached under the paper and produced the book. It was a Bible. He opened it to the page marked by a postcard.

"You've got a nerve," Victor said. "But now that you've gone this far, you might as well help me solve the puzzle." One passage was marked with a small x: "Cast thy bread upon the waters: [a]for thou shalt find it after many days. Give[b] a portion[c] to seven, and also to eight; [d]for thou knowest not what evil shall be upon the earth."

"I understand the first bit and the last bit," Arthur said, "but what's that business about seven and eight? Does it refer to people? And what're those superscripts doing there? I didn't grow up with the Bible."

"Use your eyes. They're cross-references, which are given in the margin: [a]2 Cor. 9:8–10."

"So what's next?"

"The helpless generation. This calls for a gnashing of teeth. Have you ever heard of the apostle Paul, by any chance?"

"Yes."

"Well, this is a letter from the apostle Paul to the church

in Corinth. New Testament. Toward the back. I'll be glad to give you a Bible for your birthday."

Arthur looked it up, read it in silence, and then wanted to go back to the first passage. He looked questioningly at Victor. "Where do I find the first one?"

"Ecclesiastes, chapter 11, verses 1 and 2."

He turned to it, but couldn't see the connection between the two. A bit farther down, a few lines had been underlined.

"As ^{e}thou knowest not what *is* the way of the spirit, *nor* how the bones *do grow* in the ^{f}womb of her that is with child: even so thou knowest not the works of God who maketh all. ^{e}John 3:8 ^{f}Ps. 139:15-16."

"Now you know how it works," Victor said. "What's next to womb?"

"A superscript f."

"Very good. And what does it refer to?"

"Ps. 139:15 and 16."

"Psalms," said Victor. "After Job, before Proverbs. They don't teach you anything these days. We used to have to learn the books of the Bible by heart."

Arthur read.

"Out loud, please," said Victor.

"My substance was not hid from thee, when I was made in secret, *and* curiously wrought in the lowest parts of the earth. Thine eyes did see my substance, yet being unperfect; and in thy book all *my members* were written, *which* in continuance were fashioned, when *as yet there was* none of them."

Victor leaned back.

"Now you're going to ask me why I'm reading this, and I'm going to ask Philippe to bring me a glass of wine so I won't have to answer."

"You don't have to answer. Besides, I didn't ask. I wouldn't

dare. But that business about the bones...and the substance..."

Without thinking he'd removed the postcard that had
served as a bookmark, but Victor now took it out of his hand
and put it back between the same pages of the Bible.

"Let me see that. It was a Hopper, wasn't it?"

"Yep. Better at pictures than at words?"

Arthur was familiar with the painting. Five people were
sitting on a patio, sunning themselves in deck chairs. *People
in the Sun.* You could see part of a house and two windows.
They were closed, but the shutters had been painted the
same yellow as the field of wheat just off the patio. On the
other side of the field was a row of craggy hills, or maybe
they were mountains. The painting projected an atmosphere
of total silence. The lone man in the back was reading a
book, while the four people in the front were staring into
space. They didn't strike Arthur as very pleasant companions. The man nearest the viewer had on white socks and
clunky, light-brown shoes. He was leaning back, his bald
head against a pillow. The woman next to him had on a
broad-brimmed hat, a red scarf trailing down her neck. Beside her was a man who was partially blocking a blonde
woman in a blue suit, so that you couldn't see her face. The
reader in the back had a blue scarf around his neck—the
same blue as the one Victor had on.

"That's me," Victor said. "Do you see our shadows on the
ground?"

The shadows began, Arthur noticed, by the shoes, and
ran, if you could say that about a shadow, out of the canvas
on the left side. Not that they really ran, of course. They actually just lay there on the ground, flat and one-dimensional.

"When you stop and think about it, shadows are creepy,"
Arthur said.

"That they are."

"So what are you reading?"

"Ha ha." He opened his narrowed eyes a bit wider and said, "That's the best painting of eternity that's ever been made. And I've read this particular book a million times."

The door opened, and a bearded young man came in crying, "*Berliner Zeitung!*"

"Is it that late?" Victor asked as he motioned the man over. He immediately bought two papers. "So you'll be spared my eloquence for a while."

No sooner had they started to decipher the first hieroglyphs on bull markets and unemployment than in came Otto Heiland and his shadow. Otto was a painter, his shadow was an art dealer—a man with such an air of gloom that he always looked as if he'd just crawled out of a swamp. Everything about him appeared to drip. "That's not a face; it's a stalactite" (Victor). "Everything droops, his mustache, his moist eyes, ugh. It's a bad sign when an art dealer looks like an artist, especially since artists no longer dress the part. An artist ought to look like a banker on a Sunday afternoon."

Arthur had no idea what that might be, but Otto Heiland always looked like someone whose occupation you'd never be able to guess. Perhaps "sedate" would be the best word to describe him. His outward reserve in no way corresponded to the mysterious, tortured creatures in his paintings.

Victor had known Otto for years. "Would you believe it? The word 'art' has never come up in the course of our conversations. And if you want my opinion, he's got that art dealer only because he feels sorry for him."

"My dear friends, this is your last chance to order. The chef wants to go home."

Suddenly Arthur realized how hungry he was. Today had already lasted much too long.

"I'll have him cook something special for you," said Philippe. "You look tired."

"And preoccupied," said Victor. "His mind's on something else. He's looking at himself through a Cooke and shutting out the rest of us." Cooke was a well-known brand of lenses—telephoto, wide-angle, zoom. One time Victor had asked to look through them. Afterward all he'd said was, "So that's how you fool people."

"We don't fool them; we just give them extra eyes."

"Like Argus?"

"How many did he have?"

"Hundreds, maybe thousands. All over. But things didn't turn out very well for him."

The art dealer grabbed the paper and moaned, "The stock market's up again. . . . If I were an unemployed factory worker I'd smash the place to bits."

"So what are you complaining about?" Victor said. "Part of those profits get invested in art, don't they? There's been a lot of whining in this country lately. You've been weeping and wailing ever since the Wall fell, as if Germany is on the edge of bankruptcy."

"That's easy for you to say. Your lousy country is small."

"The smaller the better."

"Humph, the smaller they are, the more arrogant they get. The Dutch always think they know better."

"That does happen to be an annoying habit of ours. But aside from our tasteless tomatoes, we don't do such a bad job, in my opinion."

"If it's so great, why are you here?"

"You see, that's exactly what I mean. Your first reaction is always to chuck out the foreigners: *Ausländer raus*. And in such an aggrieved tone. Buck up, we all know you're the richest country in Europe."

"And are pea-green with envy."

"Absolutely. So what are you hung up on now?"

Arthur looked over at Otto, who gave him a big wink. He always enjoyed listening to Victor tease his art dealer.

"What do you think, Philippe?" Victor asked.

"Don't ask me. I have French feet, German knees..."

"Oh la la."

"...and a French tongue. Here, taste this. On the house. A white Châteauneuf." He turned to the art dealer. "Do you happen to know the price in euros?"

"Europe hasn't switched over to the euro yet. And if it were up to us, it never would. All our hard-earned savings are going to be squandered on a bunch of money-grubbing Greeks and Italians. Not to mention the Poles and the Czechs—they're already knocking on the door...."

"And to think that fifty years ago you were so anxious to include them!"

"Gentlemen, gentlemen, I'm not giving away my nectar to hear this kind of talk."

"Besides, he doesn't have any savings," said Otto.

Philippe refilled their glasses. Arthur knew what would happen next. Pretty soon Philippe would get that Captain Hook look in his eyes. He'd fetch a new bottle, and two hours from now they'd be sitting in the closed restaurant like a bunch of brigands who'd boarded a ship filled with gold. Victor and Philippe would start singing songs from *The Umbrellas of Cherbourg*, the art dealer would get misty-eyed, and even Otto would be humming along.

"Well," Arthur said as he stood up, "I'm off."

"Party pooper!"

"He's in love," Victor said. "And at his age it could be dangerous. But we must all fulfill our destiny to its appointed end."

Outside, the wind had picked up considerably. For a moment he thought he was going to go flying through the air. What would it be like to soar past those grand edifices? Not like a bird, but like an aimless object, a piece of paper, swept up into the storm, into the swirl of sound, freed from tonight's words, back to that earlier strange and silent hour in which someone had stood across from him in the stillness of his room, someone who had not only overpowered him, but had also raced through his past and shaken it with the force of a gale wind. Could that be true? In such a short amount of time? Was this the start of something new?

At the corner of Leibnizstrasse he was nearly knocked off his feet. The wind must be coming from the Baltic Sea, or from the faraway steppes to the east, plains that could swallow you up without a trace. The wind turned the branches into whips that lashed each other and moaned in pain—a sound that he was to hear all night.

In Falkplatz the wind makes the same noise, yet it's different. First it whooshes through what used to be the barren death strip, where it gathers strength, starts shrieking even louder and attacks an easy enemy: the scrawny trees, the sorry remains of citizen goodwill. Then it turns into more of a hiss and a rustle. By the time Elik Oranje hears it tapping and rattling the one window in her bedroom, it's become a harsh whisper, an oracle, the hoarse mutters of old crones. She's sitting in the lotus position in the middle of her cramped room because she's trying to concentrate, though she's not having much luck. Her thoughts are turning around and around like a weather vane. She keeps coming back to three very different problems, all of which she needs to resolve: the truth about the alleged lovers and miscarriages of her queen, today's Hegel class, and the man who had touched her scar in a way that was more intimate than the act of love itself.

"This is getting me nowhere," she says out loud, and it's true. One by one she plucks at the threads of each thought as if she's unraveling a sweater. And at the same time she keeps repeating them, like a kind of prayer wheel. The scar, which is hers and hers alone, the trial by fire, the pain, the smell of burning flesh, the man grinding out his cigarette, pressing it even deeper into the flesh while crushing her with his insistent weight, tearing her apart, the reek of alcohol from a mouth muttering indistinct words, her scream, her mother who reels into the room and has to hang onto the door with both hands as she takes in the scene—it's all hers. Mine, all mine. Not ever to be talked about. Every other moment passes away, but not this one. It's here to stay. The moment refusal was born. Then, and now. Of what? Refusal. And now another man has touched the scar, gently traced the outline with his finger, as if it could be healed. No. No one has touched it. Tender—that word has been outlawed. As if he knew the whole story. But that was impossible.

And then again, as if the two subjects were somehow related, the other problem. The more she learned about Urraca, the less she knew, because each fact raised new questions. The woman who once was, she called her. A person whose fate she had linked to her own, though that was strictly taboo, because you should never—under any circumstances—identify with your subject. But she knew it was already too late. Unacceptable behavior. She couldn't allow it to show in her writing. It would have to be "as dry as dust." But the more she read—all those contradictory voices, all those gaps—the more she tended to fill those gaps and uncertainties with emotion, as if she herself was fighting for her kingdom, had been beaten, scorned, forced to flee and fight back, to seek the help of men. It was unforgivable, as if she were writing a novel, a trumped-up story in which you could twist the truth to suit your own needs and say, "At that moment Urraca thought . . . ," though you would never, ever know what she'd really been thinking. You could read a dozen books about courtly life in the Middle Ages and still not find out what you wanted to know—what they smelled like, how they talked, how they made love. Whatever you said would be pure speculation. In a novel you could let a medieval queen have an orgasm, but was an orgasm then the same as one now? How different had people been back then? And by the same token, how similar? Their sun had revolved around the earth, the earth had been the center of the cosmos, and the cosmos lay safely in the hands of God; everything was as it should be, the world was part of a divine order and everyone had a place in its hierarchy—all of which was so far removed from our own reality that you could barely understand it, much less empathize with it. On the other hand, aren't there physical constants in the human race that enable you to imagine anything you want? Take the church's crusade against the sins of the flesh, for example—the illustrations she'd seen on those Roman capitals, where the punishment for lust was depicted so graphically that it still made her sick to her stomach. Or the longing in the voices of the troubadours, in which the sexual undertones had just barely been suppressed by the rhythm and rhyme. She rocked back and forth. Her master's thesis had been on Krzysztof Pomian's essay *"Histoire et Fiction."* On the title page she'd cited an Arab proverb that she'd found in Marc Bloch: "People don't resemble their fathers as much as the age in which they were born."

"I could have done without the cliché," her supervisor had said when she showed it to him, "though the use of an epigraph does add a rather professional touch to the thesis." Naturally he'd put his hand on her shoulder and given it a so-called innocent squeeze. She'd removed his hand as if were a foreign object and let it drop. And naturally her punishment had been even more patronizing irony, *"Noli me tangere."*

"That's one way of putting it."

"Fine. In any case, lofty quotes aren't my style. All we're doing here is studying history. If I were you, I'd leave speculation to the big boys."

Just the type to say "boys," of course, but she hadn't even bothered to correct him. Men can't stand being contradicted. Today's Hegel class had been a flop too. She'd been all fired up by Arno Tieck's kindly enthusiasm ("Ah, if only you could have heard Kojève's lectures on Hegel!"). But she still had to wrestle with the great thinker's tortured sentence structure, and the *Herr Professor*'s nasal accent wasn't helping any.

"He sounds just like Ulbricht," one of her fellow students had whispered. She didn't know if that was true, but the man looked like a carrot in a three-piece suit. She'd asked a question that he'd apparently thought was stupid, because he'd said, "I'm aware that Dutch schools pay little or no attention to philosophy, and probably none whatsoever to German philosophy, but ignorance can be taken to extremes. On the other hand, it probably isn't your fault. As Heinrich Heine said, everything happens fifty years later in Holland."

"That must be the reason why Mainz, Hamburg, and Düsseldorf refused to have a statue of Heine in their cities, and why—even as late as 1965—both the Board of Governors and the overwhelming majority of students refused to name this university after Heine."

"I assume you mean because Heine was a Jew?"

"Your words, not mine. *I* think it had more to do with the fact that Heine was sublimely sarcastic. Even a hundred years later—and that's two times fifty, you know—people in this country still can't handle sarcasm. In the meantime New York was delighted at the offer of Heine's statue, and it's been put up in the Bronx. He probably feels more comfortable there anyway. Furthermore, it's my understanding that Heine never made that remark about the fifty years."

In all the excitement she'd forgotten what her question had been. The professor, whom you really still had to address here as *Herr Professor,* had given her a scathing look. None of the other students had spoken up, and he'd gone on with his unintelligible exegesis. She'd been feisty and defiant with Arno Tieck too, but now, here in her room, she was filled with doubt.

Hegel. What on earth were you supposed to do with that enormous mass of words? Every once in a while, a fragment would catch your eye before it swiftly reverted back to rigid dogma or an almost religious attempt at systemization: the utopian organ notes of an unproved prophecy, a future in which the *Weltgeist*—whatever that was—would become, if she had understood it correctly, conscious of itself as free, and then all the contradictions that had plagued the world since time immemorial would be resolved.

It sounded ghastly. She felt an innate resistance to Hegel's mile-long sentences, yet she was forced to admit that some of his formulations were attractive. It was as if a magician was at work—a shaman whose words you couldn't understand but whose help you couldn't refuse. She never had that feeling when she was listening to the *Herr Professor.* Only later, when she was alone in her room or at the library, contemplating the architecture of those endless sentences and underlining important passages, did she have an inkling. Underlining them gave her the feeling that she understood what she was reading, but a few hours later she could barely remember a word. All that remained was an awareness of Hegel's visionary ideas and his basic religiosity. But how the hell could anyone think that "Napoleon was the totally fulfilled person, who in and through his ultimate fulfillment had checked the course of the historical development of mankind"? What had been checked? Still, she couldn't help feeling that the words themselves were not at fault. The reason she failed to be captivated by Hegel was that there was something lacking in her. What had Arno said? "But can't you feel it? Hegel was the first of his era to understand the concept of freedom. In that sense, it really was the end of an era."

Perhaps, but that didn't necessarily mean that history had come to a halt, did it? Because if that was the moment you first realized what freedom meant, if that was when the fairy-tale figures of the master and the servant were supposed to disappear from the stage as they did in a Goldoni play, then it was doubly terrible that the servants—in the very city and country where those words had first been formulated—had become their own masters and let themselves be pressed into the straitjacket of an even worse servitude! Servants who elected their own masters so they could remain servants, with masters they were equal to in name only—what idiot had thought that up! And the madness had spread. Millions of people had died for it.

"That isn't his fault."

Who was she talking to? Wouldn't it be better if she stuck to her queen? If she patiently studied diplomas, folios, primary sources? In other words, if she simply raked her own little garden? By now she realized that the narrow field she'd selected for herself was growing bigger every day. Every time she managed to wade through one thing, another loomed on the horizon: a dissertation on papal missions to Santiago, another one on alliances with Mohammedan kingdoms, and yet another on the influence of the Benedictines. What was the point of treading the well-worn path of that scholarly maze—about which she knew both so much and so little—what was the purpose of all that minimalist, patient ferreting out of minute facts compared to the broad, lofty theories that attracted a much wider audience? What did it all add up to in the end? Slaving away for years to come up with a single crumb for one grand moment of apotheosis?

She stood up and stretched. Again she heard the cries and murmurs of the wind. Ah, the sensation of being alone—no one could explain it. The feeling of total autonomy, of absolute indifference to your surroundings while surrounded by a silence of your own making. A motionless, all-pervasive, healing silence.

In Amsterdam hordes of people spent their time hanging around cafés. She wondered if they'd ever get around to reading something besides newspapers, which got bigger and more boring by the day. Berlin gave you the feeling—perhaps because it was so much larger—that you were anonymous. Whenever she went home, she couldn't help but think that a process of infantilization had set in. A fatal kind of superficial mindlessness had come over people who were apparently trying to prove their individuality by laughing at the same jokes, solving the same cryptograms, buying—but usually not reading—the same books. And all with a smug complacency that was suffocating. Everyone she knew was into yoga, vacationed on Bali, did shiatsu. They were always busy with hundreds of activities that required them to be away from home. Very few people were content to be alone.

"There's no need to get so wound up!"

If she hadn't said it, who had? She went over to the cracked mirror and looked at herself. No, better not to look. What could her eyes tell her? They didn't come from her mother, that's for sure. Two black coals—the contribution of an unknown father. She went to Melilla once and wandered around the city for two days. A horrible place. Spanish but not Spanish, Moroccan but not Moroccan, Islamic but not Islamic. She looked at the men there and decided that she wouldn't want any of them for a father. She saw her eyes reflected a thousandfold, but none of them looked at her the way you would a daughter. A daughter. She moved her hand tentatively toward the scar and gently touched it. Something she never did. Suddenly her whole body froze, as if she'd been reprimanded. Had *she* done that? She could feel herself standing there, as stiff as a doll. Even her eyes looked different. A forbidden line had been crossed.

Us again. Always at night, it seems. The chorus in Sophocles offers its opinion. We don't. The chorus in *Henry V* clamors for judgment. We don't do that either. We pick the night because that's when you're resting. It's the time for thought, a wrap-up, or simply sleep, the time you most closely resemble the dead without actually being dead. Now they're all in place. Arno is reading early history—inspired by Elik. Polybius, to be exact. He's surprised at the perspicacity, the scholarly tone. He notes with interest that he feels like the man's contemporary. He hears the storm outside and continues to read about cultures that devour each other and blend into one. Two thousand years ago someone had thought of history as a fundamental organic unit. The man in Berlin puts his book down for a moment, unsure of whether he agrees. Then he picks it up again and reads until night overtakes him. Zenobia has less stamina. She's fallen asleep over an article she's supposed to be writing on the Surveyor, which in September of this year will have taken 309 days to travel the 466 million miles to Mars. No, we can't tell you if it will get there, nor can we say whether a manned flight will reach Mars in 2012. If you're alive then, you'll find out for yourselves. All you need to know now is that the lines connecting the people and their actions can be represented by a spatial diagram. Arthur sleeps, he's lost to the world, but Victor is sitting in his studio, staring at the fossil remains of a bone that's at least a hundred million years old. "Thou knowest not what is the way of the spirit, nor how the bones do grow." That bone and our not-knowing—the mystery that will determine his next project. He won't say a word on the subject. He's sitting very quietly. He wants to incorporate that mystery in what he's about to make. "All that has been written in this book"—how the days, which didn't exist then, would be formed. We can see it, the thinnest of lines between Arno and the captive Polybius on the desk, continuing on to Zenobia and the first footsteps on Mars, to Elik and Urraca's battle, to Victor and the year in which the bone had been live matter, to Ecclesiastes, to Arthur's absence without images. We are the ones who have to hold all of this together. Your ability to exist in time is limited, your ability to think in time is boundless. Light-years, human years, Polybius, Urraca, Surveyor, a prehistoric bone, lines, a four-dimensional spatial diagram that connects the five to each other—a constellation that will eventually dissolve again, but not just yet. You won't hear much more from us. First just a few sentences, then only a few words. Four, to be exact.

Just as he was waking up he heard the storm subside, quite literally as it turned out. A final gust of wind rattled every branch of the chestnut tree—a sound only brilliant percussionists can make—and seemed to move slowly from top to bottom before finally hitting the ground. One last scrabbling of the dead leaves in the courtyard, a rustle, a whisper, a last word, silence. Within minutes the first pitter-patter of rain. You could count the drops.

There was so much to think about that he didn't want to begin. Be fast, get up, shave, have a quick cup of coffee, hit the pavement. First order of the day: filming. A world champion when it comes to good-bye. How do you film good-bye? Perhaps the pile of leaves downstairs would do. Except that leaves don't fall of their own accord. They *have* to let go, they're "falled." No, it would have to be a different image—a movement of something letting go. The person who leaves always has an advantage over the one who gets left behind.

He grabbed his camera and his Nagra—he wanted optimal sound this time—plus the wind screen, the boom, and the earphones. For what he had in mind it wouldn't be necessary to synchronize the recording. He staggered down the stairs—a human packhorse. Too much, too heavy, as always. Don Quixote, he mumbled to himself, for lack of anything better. He'd wrapped his equipment in plastic because it had started to rain even harder. Good-bye, wheels, the sound of tires on wet asphalt. Rush hour, that's good. He took Wilmersdorfer Strasse to Kantstrasse, which he followed until he came to Lietzensee Park. The park was empty now, but since it was back off the street a bit, he could film the constant stream of tires from there. Just that, and nothing more. You shouldn't be able to see what make the cars were. He wanted only the dynamics of the movement: the turning and splashing, the muddy spray from the revolving wheels. He knew exactly what it would look like—gray, sinister, the outsize tires of trucks and buses, the faster ones of cars, forced to come to a stop, cutting each other off, starting up again, charging ahead, getting stuck behind. Once he had enough footage, he began to record the sounds, standing on the sidewalk and holding the mike as close to the wheels as possible. In his earphones he heard the hiss and slurp of thousands of rubber tires racing through his brain, drowning out the thoughts of a woman who had so suddenly left him for the second time. All that counted now was the sound of rubber on asphalt, an incomprehensible mechanical whisper, a warning he would ignore. Only when he was soaked to the skin did he go home. A few hours later he rang Zenobia's doorbell.

"Who is it? What do you want?" Her voice boomed through the intercom on Bleibtreustrasse.

"It's Arthur!"

"Ah, Hansel!"

"The one and only! As long as I don't have to call you Snow White or Sleeping Beauty!"

"Don't you dare! I've devoted years to acquiring all this flab!"

She waited for him upstairs in the doorway.

"Hey, I thought you were never going to get here. What's this I've heard from Arno? He says she's gorgeous."

He hadn't allowed himself to think in such terms yet. He pictured her hair, braided strands of gossamer-thin wire. It was so springy that when he touched it, his hand bounced back, and you couldn't feel the skull at all. A woven helmet.

"You aren't sure?"

"No."

"Then she must be special."

"Can I come in?"

Inside it was spacious and cool. Functional wood furniture. Bare white walls.

"Walls are not meant to be decorated. If you want to look at something, you should put it on a lectern, so you can study it."

The lectern was standing by itself, about ten feet away from an antique tiled stove, which was purely decorative.

"My personal god. Do you like it?"

"I'm more interested in what's over there."

On the lectern was a photograph of the planet Mars.

"Say something intelligent. What do you see?"

He looked. A pitted surface, bumps, pockmarks, light and dark spots. Mysterious, but how could you describe it?

"An inscription?"

"Not bad. But then in code. Oh, I can't wait!"

"For what?"

She was genuinely shocked.

"Arthur! We're almost there! While you and I are sitting here talking, a lonely spacecraft is on its way to this very spot!"

She jabbed a finger in the middle of the awesome barrenness.

"It's so beautiful. If all goes according to plan, it's going to make a balloon landing on Mars, and then a rover will drive off over the surface. Oh, Arthur, it may look like a toy car, but it can really drive, vroom vroom. It isn't very big. Here, look," she said, holding her hands close together in a reversal of the usual fisherman's tale. "It's this small! But it's going to tell us everything about that code. Here!"

She jammed a couple of computer printouts into his hand. He didn't understand a word.

"Begin Traverse operations. APX5 measurement."

"What's APX5 mean?"

"Alpha Proton X ray. Possible programs. In case it works. To analyze the soil."

The soil! It sounded ridiculous.

"And is it going to work?"

"Absolutely! On July 5th it's going to drive around up there and beam back photographs of the rocks, the boulders, the composition. Look." She reached into a drawer and pulled out a picture of a desolate landscape with a few scattered rocks. The light seemed to be made of lead, and the shadows etched on the boulders only intensified the loneliness.

"Is that Mars?"

"No, dummy. We don't have any pictures of Mars yet. That's the Moon, but Mars is probably similar. There's not a single tree on either one of them."

"Looks lonely. Great place for a bus stop."

"Just give us time, and there will be."

"What do you mean? Have we set our sights on Mars too?"

"Of course. We're going to live there! Ten or fifteen years from now the first person is going to set foot on Mars. Unfortunately, a mission can be launched only once every twenty-six months, because that's when its orbit coincides with ours. This particular little jalopy isn't going to be making the return journey, but give us another eight or nine years and we'll have our very first rocks. Look, here's the rover."

She showed him a photograph of something that looked like a dinky toy.

"Designed by a woman! Would you like a cup of tea? Russian tea? It tastes like gunpowder."

'Yes, please." He sat down.

"Russian tea, Russian *Begeisterung*. A lovely word. German can be beautiful. 'Full of spirits' sounds a lot nicer than 'enthusiasm.' I know what you're thinking: Why is that silly woman going into raptures over a toy car?"

"Nonsense. I'm not thinking that at all."

"Listen, let's be serious for once, yes? Not sentimental. When I was a little girl in Leningrad, during that horrible winter, with people dying all around me and hunger every-where—you simply can't imagine what it feels like to be that hungry—two things happened to me. One was that I thought: If I ever get out of this, I'm never going to stop eating again ... and you've got to admit that I've done a pretty good job of that. The second was that I thought: I want to get out of this world, I want to leave it behind. I swear that's what I thought, even though I was so young. I don't want to live here any-more; that's what I kept thinking, and then one dark winter night—we didn't have any light—I looked up at the stars and I thought: There, up there, this isn't the only world, it can't be the only one, that can't be true, it just can't be ... this smell, this death, this cold. Oh, well, if you want to know how I felt you should take a good look at Vera's paintings. ... We're twins, you know, but she's the so-called pessimist ... the dark side, the shadow side of me. ... But that's not how it was at all. I mean it's because of the same darkness in her paintings that I ... well, that I went into physics ... and it's still because of that same darkness that I ... Anyway I've never been so happy as when Sputnik circled the earth, because I knew then that it was possible, that it was all going to happen. ... I firmly be-lieve that we have a mission in outer space, away from this rotten dung heap. Haven't you ever had that feeling? This world of ours is too old; we've stripped it bare and treated it shamelessly—it's bound to take revenge. We're riddled with memories, everything's polluted. Ah, Zenobia, stop it, give the man his tea. But I mean it, Arthur. Look at the beauty of that spacecraft and compare it to all those bedraggled ... oh, forget it, forget it. You know it's strange, but young people don't seem to be interested in space exploration. I can tell you're laughing at me...."

"No, I'm not. How long is the trip going to take—the first scheduled launch?"

"It's 466 million miles away."

"Thanks."

"Three hundred and nine days."

"And a human being will have to stay in space all that time?"

"I'd go tomorrow. But they wouldn't take me. Too fat."

"Zenobia?..."

"Go ahead and ask. But do me a favor first. Close your eyes and *feel* all those spaceships heading toward their destinations. They're on their way there, right this minute, as we speak! The Voyager, the Pathfinder...and soon the Surveyor..."

"All en route to those barren rocky spheres. Just because they're there?"

"O ye of little faith. We must because we must. Your children will see it all happen."

"I don't have any children."

"Oh. *Glupaya devka*! Forgive me."

"There's no need. I shouldn't have said that. Let me see the pictures you phoned me about."

"Ah." She beamed again. "Like Mars, but then with water."

She brought him a folder. Each photograph was protected by a sheet of tissue paper.

"All vintage prints. Why don't you sit at the table? These two were taken by Wols."

He carefully removed the delicate paper from the first photograph. Penciled on the mat were the words "Wols, *Ohne Titel (Wasser)*." But was that really water? That solidified lavalike mass? Blacks and grays, flecks of light, hollows and grooves on an oily, almost polished surface, sleek yet grainy. That water must have moved, somewhere, sometime. He wanted to run his fingers over it but stopped himself just in time. This was what he was looking for. The anonymous, nonartificial, unnamed world of natural phenomena to counterbalance that other world of names and events. I want to preserve the things that nobody notices, that nobody ever pays attention to. I want to capture the most ordinary things and keep them from disappearing.

"What's wrong, Arthur? You aren't looking."

"I see too much."

"Then try these. They're by Alfred Ehrhardt. 'Das Watt,' the series is called. Mud flats."

What he saw before him was chaos, and at the same time, structure. Incongruities—lines that suddenly forked, branching off at random, then coming back together again. But he couldn't bring himself to say the words "chaos" and "structure." They sounded so awful.

"I'd like to know how he took these pictures. In some of them it looks like he was suspended above the mud, but that's not very likely. His use of light is incredible...but..."

"But what?"

It was an age-old problem. Something in nature, an object that hadn't been designed for that purpose, unintentionally radiated great beauty. Who should be allowed to take credit for that beauty now? Nature, which put it there in the first place, as it had been doing for millions of years before humanity was there to appreciate it? Or the photographer, who was touched by the aesthetics or drama or what he saw and tried to reproduce it as well as he could? Ehrhardt had captured a nonrandom slice of reality, but reality itself was inherently indifferent.

"It has something to do with autonomy. He chose to film it, but it isn't his. He appropriates the landscape, or a portion of it, but basically he can't get inside it. His artistry consists of being able to show that. It remains itself and he preserves it. The water has washed over those mud flats a hundred thousand times and erased every one of those lines, but if I were to go there tomorrow, I'd see the same thing, except that there would be minute changes in nuance...."

Zenobia nodded.

"So is that all there is?"

"No, of course not. Because after that you and I get into the act. But no matter what we do—whether we enlarge the photo or hang it on the wall—it will always remain something that somebody happened to take a picture of on January 21, 1921. Nothing we do will alter that fact."

Zenobia put her hand on his head.

"I can feel things brewing in there. Major events?"

"Probably the opposite."

He had to find a way to end this conversation. What did you call it when a body took possession of yours, took its pleasure on top of yours almost as if you weren't there? It had a name, of course, but while it was going on nature predominated. Physical pleasure made it anonymous. Was that possible, or was that what it was all about? He felt a wave of overwhelming tenderness come over him and stood up.

"How much do they cost?" He pointed to the photographs. "Or, rather, what does one of them cost? I can't afford more than that."

He pictured her vulnerable, ivory body. How could you keep it from disappearing?

"Don't be ridiculous. If you like one, take it."

"Hard to choose. I need more time. I'll come back and do it another day."

He wanted to go to the library.

"I've been asked to go to Russia," he said. "The usual news coverage."

"Oh, great. So everyone can see what a mess we're in?"

"Probably. I'm just the cameraman."

"Go ahead. Nobody ever understands us anyway."

Silence.

"Arthur?"

"Yes?"

"You don't have to choose one right now. I'll give you one that *I* like, but not today. I can tell that you're getting antsy, so go wherever it is you need to go, and I'll go back to Mars. Or to Saturn, since it's next on the list. Maybe I can sign up for the ride. They're sending up a gorgeous probe, just big enough for me. It's been named after one of your fellow countrymen—Huygens."

"When do you leave?"

"October 15th. Arrival date: 2004. Just a hop, skip, and a jump. Huygens and I will catch a ride on board the Cassini. We'll get out on Titan, then float above Saturn for a couple of years. Only nine months to go, I can hardly wait."

"Enough, enough."

"If you want Russian friends, you have to be able to put up with our sentimentality. Saturn is beautiful, much nicer than Mars, which is just one big ice rink. You could fit seven hundred and fifty Earths in Saturn, and it's got all those fabulous light gases. If we had an ocean that was big enough, we could float Saturn in it. Haven't you ever had the feeling that you'd like to be swallowed up by something, to disappear? That's what's so delightful about those numbers. You can't imagine how seductive all those zeroes are."

"I thought that scientists didn't allow themselves to be led astray."

"Scientists are either adding machines or mystics. You decide which. Me, I'm a failed scientist. I stand on the sidelines and write stupid articles."

"I say you're all sentimental Russian mystical adding machines. And now I've got to go."

On the way to get his coat, he paused for a moment in front of her computer. The entire blue screen was filled with the secret language of a mathematical equation.

"What's that?"

"A poem."

He leaned forward. If that was a poem, it expressed a reality far beyond his, a world of terrifying purity that excluded him.

"What's the difference between this and a real poem?"

"The fact that it wasn't written with sadness, or love, or even mud, the way real poems are. It's not based on language, so there's no sentiment. But it's potentially more lethal, despite its beauty, because this same purity has been used to produce some of the world's most horrifying inventions."

She stared at the equation. If you could call what she was doing reading, he'd like to know what she was reading now. She smiled.

"Mathematicians are like ghosts," she said. "They live in a vacuum and write letters to each other in code. It's a world that exists both inside and outside reality. You can't film it. So go to Russia, and remember what I said about Sirens."

"I will."

He didn't have the faintest idea what she was referring to, but didn't want to think about it now. Suddenly, he felt sure that if he hurried, he'd make it to the library in time. She'd be bent over her books, at the same table where he'd first seen her. But when he arrived in the reading room, out of breath, he discovered that her place had been taken by a man with such a patently Indian face that for a moment he thought he'd been catapulted back to the entrance. After checking every room and corridor, he was forced to conclude that she wasn't in the library. He knew then that no indignity would be spared him. The next step would be for him to go to Café Einstein, and she wouldn't be there either. It was like being an adolescent again, when you bicycled past the girl's house, scared to death that she'd see you. He made an about-face, like a soldier on parade. A taxi was cruising nearby—it must be a sign. The driver asked him where he wanted to go, and he realized that he didn't have a clue. Soldiers, parade . . . Aha.

"To the *Neue Wache*—the New Guard House," he said.

Years ago he'd gone there to film the breathtaking boots of the soldiers during the changing of the guard. The men had moved as one, like a large animal, to the click and scrape of the taps on the soles of their shoes. In those days an eternal flame had burned for the victims of Fascism. Now there was a Käthe Kollwitz statue—a pietà, a suffering mother cradling her dead son, whose suffering had been so great that finally their separate suffering had melted into one. He got out of the cab. The men were gone—vanished into thin air. Never again would they march in goose step, snapping the tips of their boots up to the level of their belt buckles. He remembered the captivated stares of the spectators, and still wondered what the source of their fascination had been. The mechanical perfection, which robbed them of their individuality and reduced them to mere machines? It was inconceivable that any of those robots would ever caress a woman, yet there had been an element of eroticism in the scene, God knows why. Perhaps because boots and helmets evoked thoughts of death and destruction. He walked over to the Palast der Republik, the former Parliament building, where he'd been on hand to witness the booing of Egon Krenz—a man who'd ultimately been swept away by the oncoming tide. Within a year, the display cases of the museum on the other side of the street had been filled with the paraphernalia of the ex-rulers—Grotewohl's glasses and Ulbricht's medals— while a zinc-colored statue of Lenin stood guard at the entrance. Larger than life, he stared out at the world with his hands in his pockets and a defiant stare on his face, as if he himself had produced the enormous missile mounted above his head. Images from a past that had been buried with unseemly haste before it had been given a chance to become old. A past shot through and through with ridicule. But of course none of this could be seen on the faces of the visitors. Not then, and not now. That was the paradox: everyone was history, but no one was willing to admit it.

And then? Nothing. He decided not to go looking for her, and he waited. At the end of the fourth day he heard a kind of scratch, the faint sound of nails scraping against his door. He opened it, and she slipped inside like a cat. By the time he turned around she was already sitting in a chair, staring up at him. He didn't tell her that he'd tried to find her, didn't ask her any questions, and she didn't say a word. She avoided using his name, so he avoided hers. It was as if an edict had gone out. She undressed in silence, like the first time. He mumbled something about the pill and condoms, but she waved it away, told him it wasn't necessary. "You don't have AIDS and I don't have AIDS, and I can't have children."

When he asked her why she was so sure she couldn't have children, she said, "Because I don't want any." He was perfectly willing to talk about it, but she had already stretched out on top of him, and when he tried to lift her up, gently to move her to the side, to stroke her, she resisted, as if she'd dug herself in, and muttered no, no, NO, and he understood that if he didn't accept her terms, she would leave, and once again everything was like the first time, except that this time he had let himself sink into it, and the double fire was followed by the same abrupt, silent exit—someone who had come to get something, gotten what she wanted, and then gone home.

In the weeks that followed, she stuck to this routine. He had given up wondering what his own role was. Nor had he been able to answer Erna's questions.

"Loss of confidence?"

"That's not it."

"But you're speechless. Literally, I mean. We've always told each other everything. I'm not prying, I just want to know how you're doing. You sound strange. Something's going on. Arthur?"

"Yes?"

"Yesterday was March 18th."

March 18th was the anniversary of the plane crash.

"And for the first time I neglected to call you. But weren't you the one who always said that it was bound to happen some day?"

"I did. But still . . ."

That was below the belt. Suddenly there were three of them in the room, though the other two were silent. They were farther away than they'd ever been. It must have something to do with their age. They couldn't stand never growing old.

"It's time you left Berlin. That city isn't good for you. You need to get out and do something."

"I'm doing all kinds of things."

"Something real."

"I'm going to Estonia for the BRT. Dutch television wanted to send me to Russia, Belgian television wants me in Estonia. There are Russians there too. Is that busy enough for you?"

After hanging up, he sat for a while without moving. How were you supposed to let someone know that you were going away for a week when she wouldn't give you her address or phone number and never asked any questions? The answer was: you couldn't. He could hardly stick a note on his door. One time he'd asked her why he wasn't allowed to know where she lived.

"It's not another man, if that's what you're thinking."

Oddly enough, it hadn't occurred to him. He told her that.

"Now you're bound to think it. An unsolicited denial is a confirmation. Dr. Freud."

"I don't know about that, but I do know that you come here whenever you want, leave whenever you want... and that we've barely talked. Just that one time on Peacock Island and in Lübars..."

He didn't mention the rest.

"I hate it when people get possessive."

She took a step backward and put her arm up, as if she were fending him off. For several moments they stood locked in that position. She looked as if she were on the verge of saying something, but no words came out. Finally she turned away. "If you think I should stop coming here..." she said. "I... I'm used to being alone."

"You're not alone now." He wanted to fold her in his arms, but he knew it was out of the question. Loneliness, bitterness—it filled him with fear. A person who hid inside herself. Armor, absence.

"As long as you don't get your hopes up." She had actually said that.

"Beat a hasty retreat." That was Victor. He hadn't breathed a word of any of this to him, and yet he had said that. Beat a hasty retreat. But how were you supposed to go about it? He'd done it often enough during dangerous assignments. Without realizing it, you'd go too far and suddenly danger would be everywhere. Sheer panic would follow, until you were safely back where you belonged. So far it had always ended well. But how this was going to end, he didn't know.

On the way to Tallinn the Finns were drunk before the ferry even left Helsinki's harbor. He stood shivering on the deck and filmed the churning wake.

"Your fingers must be frozen to the camera," the Belgian director shouted before going back inside. Arthur had known Hugo Opsomer for years—a friendship requiring few words. He knew that Hugo admired his documentaries and was grateful that he'd never asked him why he agreed to work as a mere cameraman. Hugo would call on him occasionally when he had a last-minute cancellation. Large productions, small productions—it was all the same to him. He liked working with Belgians. None of that forced jollity, and contrary to what most Dutch people think, the polite distance Belgians maintained had something to do with their respect for others. Every time he worked on a Dutch production he was struck by how often and especially by how long he'd been away from Holland—he didn't know who today's heroes were, what the latest running gag might be or who was being imitated. He was part of the gang, and yet in a strange way he wasn't. But the Belgians merely chalked his little lapses up to the fact that he was Dutch.

Once the ferry had cleared the harbor, the sea got choppier. He watched the collapse and swell of the icy gray waves. Icy gray, or green gray? In any event the water looked bitterly cold. This is how it must have looked, he thought, when that ferry sank with eight hundred people on board. Big news at the time, now forgotten. The thin membrane between himself and chaos—in less than an hour it was possible to vanish from the face of the earth. Brief images of horror and destruction, helicopters circling above the oblivious white-capped

water, and after that the victims were so ear-splittingly forgotten that it was as though they had never existed.

Estonia. He'd been there once before. Lutheran churches
decorated with the coats of arms of Baltic barons, Russian
Orthodox churches filled with incense and Byzantine chants,
potholed roads and brand-new highways, years of neglect
and a sudden building boom, Russian whores and leather-
jacketed pimps with cell phones. The Soviets had gone on a
rampage, deporting nearly half the population and replacing
them with ethnic Russians. The behemoth next door still cast
its shadow over the tiny country. On the street you heard
just as much Russian as you did Estonian—a language that
seemed to be wrapped in mystery, because there wasn't one
familiar sound to cling to. Maybe that's why he'd agreed to
come. Of course the crew would be speaking Dutch, but for
the rest of the time he'd be freed of the burden of compre-
hension. After she had let several days go by without coming
over, he had immediately accepted Opsomer's sudden invitation and canceled the NPS job. All that compulsive waiting
was wearing him down. Soon after that she showed up on his
doorstep, but he paid her back by not telling her about the
trip. "Tit for tat" was a stupid way of describing it, but he
couldn't deny having felt a certain vindictive pleasure.

To judge by the sudden wave of drunken shouts, someone
had come on deck.

"We were worried about you," Hugo Opsomer said. "A
frozen cameraman won't do us much good. God, you look
like a . . ." But he never found out what, since the analogy got
lost in a sudden gust of wind. The lounge was overheated.
Mindless chatter, slot machines, a blaring TV. What did you
have to do to escape the world's vulgarity?

"Come on, have a vodka. Rejoin the world of the living."

He couldn't shake off his thoughts. Were some people actually in love? All we ever heard was how they stabbed,

stalked, or shot each other in a fit of jealous rage—but love? It wasn't a word that applied to her; she'd scoff if you used it. But what else did you call it when you spent night after night in Berlin waiting to hear a scratch at the door? And why her—a woman who barely said a word, who talked to others but not to him, whose eyes looked right through him, whose closed face and white body he could picture here among the hundreds of drunken slobs, though it seemed to pull away from him when he tried to hold it, a body that took possession of him as if it had a right to, that used him as a stud horse in reverse, while he let himself be used, in spite of it all, and longed for her return because of what happened to him in that room—a kind of sorcery performed without words, especially not the words whose acknowledgment would mean the betrayal of an earlier life, a life that had never known such intensity.

"So what's first on the agenda for tomorrow?"

Hugo Opsomer pulled a book out of his bag and showed him a statue of Stalin, lying face up in the middle of a weed-choked lot. He stared at the picture for a while, trying to figure out what it was that bothered him so much. He finally asked Opsomer.

"It's the cap," he said.

"Oh, of course. Normally speaking, it should have fallen off, but in this case it's still firmly on his head."

"Let's hope the statue hasn't been put back in place in the meantime, or we won't be able to use it."

"Don't worry, it hasn't been. Not even the Russians in Tallinn would go to all that trouble."

He was right. If anything could illustrate what Estonia and its neighbors had been through, it was that statue. Not just because it was Stalin, but because something that was supposed to be standing up was lying down. The world was topsy-turvy. The man with the Napoleonic hand between the two bronze buttons of his tunic looked ridiculous, and all because his cap hadn't been knocked off during his fall. He'd been exposed as an imposter, a powerless idol that couldn't obey even the simplest laws of nature. There he lay, amid the weeds and litter, like the country he had occupied and ruthlessly governed. The nightmare of his reign would gradually fade and be forgotten, until nothing remained but an expletive. It was finally over, the bear had danced its last dance. The millions who had died, who had been slain, executed, or starved to death, had now been swallowed by the earth, like the passengers on the ferry that had sunk in this same sea. Just as final, and just as invisible.

He would spend the next two weeks living and filming among people who either chose to remember every detail or preferred not to—survivors, descendants, later generations whose children would one day learn about the past in schoolbooks. Homework, lessons. But by then it would resemble the swirling surface of the sea more than the never-to-be fathomed death below.

Twice Elik Oranje had applied her cat scratch to Arthur Daane's door, and twice she had heard a silence that betokened absence. She considered calling Arno Tieck, but decided against it. Maybe later.

Now that she was back in her room, she forbade herself to think about the futile trip to his apartment. Instead, she stared at the Gothic letters in the German book in front of her, *Die Urkunden Kaisers Alfonso VII. von Spanien,* and tried to concentrate. Cobwebs! During Urraca's reign her son had referred to himself as emperor only once; apart from that there was no evidence that he had used the title again until after her death. However, the only source for that one time was a document drawn up by a notary from Sahagún, a monk who must have been close to her court. The archbishop of Toledo, the bishops of León, Salamanca, Oviedo, and Astorga, and a number of other great lords had affixed their seal to the document on December 9, 1117. The date struck her as absurd, conjuring up images of offices, secretaries, e-mail, computers. What were you supposed to do with an arbitrary number like that? She tried to imagine a calendar bearing the date December 9, 1117. And yet there really had been such a day: a group of dignitaries had come together in a monastery in Sahagún and set their stylized signatures at the bottom of the document that the monk had so laboriously copied out. The event had actually taken place, yet it didn't seem real. Her supervisor had made a remark—no, an intentionally sickening remark—that kept nagging her brain: "I need to warn you once again that you can get bogged down in history projects like these—they're absolute quagmires. I had a look at that Reilly book of yours, and the bibliography alone was enough to send me up the wall. Are you sure you want to get mixed up in this? You speak Spanish, of course, so this stuff won't seem so obscure to you, but still... Some of the pages contain more footnotes than text, not that that should scare you off, but most of the documents aren't available here, not even in sourcebooks. You'll have to go to Cluny, and Santiago, and Porto, and to the National Archives in Madrid.... Not to mention all those Arabic sources. You'll have to consult an Arabist for those. As you can see, I won't be of much help. I'll have to find people to fill *me* in—there's someone in Louvain who knows considerably more than I do—but as I've told you from the start, this isn't my specialty and I can't spend too much time on it. After all, I've got my own book to think of.... Still, I OK'd your proposal because you were so eager to do it. But one day you'll find yourself sitting in front of a mountain of paper and wondering what on earth you're doing. Wondering whether it's relevant. Mommsen"—she knew what was coming next; it was his favorite quote—"said: 'He who writes history must politically educate his readers,' and I don't see that happening here. What I mean is that you need to think of the impact on others. When you go back that far in time, you have to remind yourself that even the simplest of things had different connotations. For instance, a road wasn't a road, and distance wasn't distance. When *you* think of a road, you mean the one you see outside this window. And you're used to thinking of distance in relation to a unit of time that's totally unrealistic.... Let me cite an example to explain what I mean. Toward the end of 1118 Pope Gelasius sent a new papal legate to Spain, Cardinal Deusdedit—wonderful name. Can you imagine how long it took? First he had to invite the bishops of Iberia to a council in Auvergne. At the same time he was also trying to keep the fragile truce between Alfonso and Urraca—in other words, between Aragon and Castile—from blowing up in his face, so that Alfonso would be free to take Zaragoza back from the Muslims. But he was also carrying a message for Diego Gelmírez, the bishop of Santiago, who also happened to be Urraca's ally. Gelmírez had been hoping to go to the council, but in order to do that he needed a letter of safe conduct from Alfonso, which he doesn't get. He heard the news while he was in, uh..."

"Sahagún."

"Of course, you already know all this. Still, I'm just using it as an example to illustrate my point. So anyway, while Gelmírez was waiting around Sahagún to see if Alfonso was going to give him a letter of safe conduct, the Pope died in Cluny. By then it was 1119, which is what I mean about time and distance.... Not to mention that you're going to have to check all this out, since half the time the documents contradict each other, and there's far too much room for speculation."

"But can't you say the same about events that took place a few hundred years later? If a ship was bound for Chile, it took a year before Charles V knew whether it had arrived safely. Surely that shouldn't come as a surprise to a historian?"

"Except that we know more about later periods."

"That's exactly why I'm doing this—to provide more information. Except for Reilly, nobody has ever really written anything about her."

"Aha! Ambition!"

"If you want to call it that."

"It's still an illusion. So when you're drowning in paper, don't come complaining to me. This project is going to take you, and to some extent me, at least ten years. I didn't know your generation thought in such long periods of time. By then

I'll probably be close to retirement." The man was obviously obsessed with time. There was either too much of it or not enough of it, but in any case you couldn't measure it by the same yardstick.

Only after she'd thoroughly pondered this problem did Elik Oranje allow herself to think about Arthur Daane. But she felt such a humiliating restlessness that she promptly called Arno Tieck. Arthur was, as his friend put it, "off globe-trotting through Finland and/or Estonia and wouldn't be back until next week." What he couldn't see was that, after hanging up the phone, Elik Oranje took the *Crónica de los príncipes de Asturias*, the *Relaciones genealógicas de la Casa de los Marqueses de Trocifal*, and Peter Rassow's *Die Urkunden Kaisers Alfonso VII. von Spanien*, and hurled them, one by one, across the room. Then she switched off the light and sat for a long time in the dark without moving.

The day Arthur Daane returned to Berlin there was a frivolous hint of spring in the air. The Finnair plane from Helsinki had flown over the glaring scar that still ran through the city—that trace of no-man's-land slowly filling up with new buildings, new streets, new patches of green. He could even see the horse-drawn chariot on top of the Brandenburg Gate—which after fifty years was now racing toward the west again, as if it was in a hurry to reach the Atlantic Ocean—and the place where the dancers had cavorted on the Wall in a nimbus of silver water.

Two hours later he was reminding Victor of that momentous night. They knew each other's memories, but liked to dredge them up again from time to time, especially in front of Philippe, since he always listened with the wide-eyed look of a child who can hear the same story a hundred times.

Victor had spent that historic day "like a lonely spermatozoid," fighting his way upstream against the surging masses, since he had gone to the East to visit an old friend: "an antihistorical exercise." The man—a sculptor who'd been partially paralyzed after a heart attack—had sat in the middle of his studio in a wheelchair "like the Commendatore, though without the heavy footsteps." The two of them had watched the big exodus to the West on television.

"To think that last May they were waving flags and cheering Gorbachev and Honecker."

"Maybe not the same people?"

"It doesn't matter. It's always the same people. People can go in two directions. All you have to do is tell them which way. Look at the pure joy on those faces! They don't know what's in store for them. They just want to collect their hundred marks. A pity Bertolt Brecht didn't live to see this. But he's sleeping his eternal sleep. So what are you doing here? You walked against the tide of history!"

The friend used to design stage sets for the Berliner Ensemble.

"Me? Just out for a stroll. We'll all have to go back home tonight."

"It'll give them time to think about how long they'll have a home to go back to. But I expect the present regime to hang on until I've kicked the bucket."

"I didn't know you were so fond of them. You've always referred to them as 'those bastards.'"

"Yes, but they were *my* bastards. I was used to them. Besides, life over here was more pleasant than you think."

"For you, yes."

"Humph, trading the trash you know for the trash you don't know—is that all there is to it? I've already done that three times. First Weimar, then Hitler, then Ulbricht. And now this. I just want to be left in peace. Take a look at all those suckers. Lining up for a banana. Like monkeys in a zoo."

"You had bananas."

"I don't even like bananas. Such a ridiculous shape, and that stupid yellow skirt that you have to peel off. Now if they were square...Hey, look at that!"

The TV showed a fat woman stuffing a banana in her mouth.

"Pure pornography. Some things ought to be against the law. Can I get you a cognac?"

On the way back Victor had also been given a banana

and a pack of chewing gum as he passed through Checkpoint Charlie.

"A gift from history," he said. He had waved it in front of the TV cameras, in hopes that his friend would see it.

It was quiet in bistro l'Alsace.

"God, the place is dead."

"Soccer," said Philippe. "Have you been on another planet or something? Whenever there's an important match, it's like the bomb has been dropped. No cars, no customers, no crime. So how's your love life? The mysterious lady you've been keeping from us?"

"Beats me."

"Why don't you bring her here sometime?"

"Philippe, I don't even know where she lives."

"Not to worry," Victor sang. "If you want to see her, come with me to Schultze's tonight. I gather she thinks of Arno as her guru. Or her sparring partner. They're always arguing, but about lofty subjects. History as history, or history as religion, that kind of thing. Minor events versus great thoughts, data versus ideas, Braudel versus Hegel. Useless, but amusing. She's always accusing him of a male bias. Arno likes that. Gives him a chance to say mea culpa. Anyway, she can hold her own."

"So what do you think?" He heard the eagerness in his voice.

"Beautiful. A real person. If you don't mind my saying so. Or would you rather I hadn't seen her?"

Very perceptive of Victor, and to some extent true. Her high visibility was indeed annoying. It was the last thing you expected from a person who never came when you wanted her to and then suddenly popped up at night on your doorstep like a ghost.

"Beware."

This time Victor wasn't kidding, and Arthur could feel himself getting angry. Somebody was trespassing on what was his. But he knew that Victor had said it out of friendship.

He looked at his friends: Victor, who had lowered his eyes, and Philippe, who hadn't been able to follow the conversation but knew that it was about women, which was always exciting. One man from the 1930s and the other from the eighteenth century. Philippe stood up to light the candles on the tables. That only made it worse. "A musketeer who misses the other two." Vera had been right. Melancholy, but cheerful.

"If you want to go to Schultze's, we'd better get going," Victor said.

"Didn't you just get through telling me to beware?"

"You won't listen anyway. Because we must all fulfill ..."

"... our destiny to its appointed end," the other two finished for him.

"You certainly know your classics."

"Before you leave for my competitor's, let me offer you a glass of champagne," said Philippe. "A cascade."

He stacked up three low, wide champagne glasses and, holding the bottle high in the air, let the champagne run quickly into the top glass. It bubbled over the edge and into the two glasses below. Just as they were about to overflow, he stopped pouring and slid them apart.

"*À nos amours,*" he said. They took a sip.

"And to spring."

"When are you leaving again?" Philippe asked Arthur.

"He just got back."

"The day after tomorrow," Arthur said. On the last day of shooting, Hugo Opsomer had come over to him with a fax in his hand.

"Finally! After two years of haggling, I've been given the

green light on an old project. Something I've always wanted to do."

"What is it?"

"The Eighty-Eight Temple Pilgrimage in Japan. And I'm allowed to pick my own cameraman."

He'd said yes and almost immediately regretted it. Still, he would have regretted it if he'd said no.

"Eighty-eight temples," Philippe said dreamily. "How long are you going to be gone?"

"A couple of weeks, maybe longer. I'm not sure yet."

"And when you come back you'll be a new man."

"Who knows."

They left.

Outside, on Kantstrasse, Victor paused for a moment.

"Do you remember the time we saw all those Poles standing over there by the Aldi superstore? Lugging around those huge boxes with TVs and VCRs? How long ago was that—maybe seven years? And now they're all rich. You've got to admit it's strange. Gorbachev came here, gave Honecker a kiss, and the whole house of cards collapsed. And then? The Poles went home and started making their own TVs. There we were clustered around the bed of world history, but it seems that the patient was under narcosis—and is still trying to snap out of it."

"Who's the patient?"

"Us. You and me. Everyone. Can't you feel it—the sleepiness? Of course there's a bustle of activity, economic recovery, democracy, elections, Treuhand. But also a kind of stupor, as if it isn't true, as if they're waiting for something else. I think I'd rather not know what that might be. There's a general feeling of malaise, *mal à l'aise,* literally 'ill at ease,' and nobody feels at ease these days, especially not here. We were living in such a quiet house, then suddenly the back wall fell out, and now the wind is whistling through and all sorts of strange people are walking in and out. A dreamlike state, waiting-room jitters . . . But behind all that activity and enterprise, behind all those Mercedes Benzes and Audis, there lurks a nagging doubt: it's going so well and it's going so badly, what did we do wrong?"

"Maybe you've lived here too long?"

"Could be. It's contagious. But I've always suffered from *Weltschmerz*."

What could he say? At the moment he was troubled by a different kind of lethargy. His could be attributed to this morning's early start, the ferry to Helsinki, the Finnish vodka in the plane, the thought of the far too sudden trip to Japan, the idea that she might be in the *Weinstube* tonight. He noticed that he was still avoiding her name. Erna had told him to use names. Because . . . why? Because otherwise you kept people at a distance. Maybe that's what he was trying to do? Did he want her to be at Schultze's or not? No, not tonight, not surrounded by the others. But he was disappointed when he didn't see her.

"Hansel!" Zenobia cried. "Come sit here next to me. Tell me, how many Russians did you see?"

"I've brought you something."

Zenobia studied the two postcards he handed her. The first one showed a blushing boy with cherry-red lips and a big fur hat, tilted at a rakish angle above the childish face. His Imperial Majesty the Crown Prince. She sighed. The other one was a picture of the first electric tram in St. Petersburg. A bridge over the Neva, officers on a bicycle.

"*Da capo ad infinitum*. Poor Russians. Now they can go right back to where they started. For the last seventy years His Imperial Majesty has been lying quietly in a mass grave. Soon they're going to rebury him, preferably with Yeltsin in attendance. The Romanovs, Rasputin, Orthodox patriarchs, incense, Dostoevsky—the process of rehabilitation can begin.

And once again it's bound to end with that row of men on that big balcony. Herr Schultze, a vodka, please. Did you at least see any gorgeous Russian women?"

"He's practically on his way to Japan," Victor said.

Herr Schultze appeared at their table and bowed toward Arno.

"Herr Tieck," he said. "I recently read that your book on our great philosopher Hegel has been translated into Spanish."

"Oh, God," Victor muttered, but Schultze was not to be deterred.

"Therefore, I would like to present you and your friends with a Beerenauslese." He turned to Arthur. "The Dutch aren't very familiar with this wine."

"No. In Holland *Beeren* are bears," Victor muttered.

"The last grapes on the vine—the *Beeren*—have been carefully plucked by hand, one by one. The French call it *pourriture noble*...noble, blissful rot. It's the least I can serve you on such an occasion. Together with my special goose pâté. How does that sound? Just a small portion, because after that I have a real treat for you, assuming you all order it together. As a farewell to winter, darkness, and cold—my sausage cathedral! And to go with it, not a Beerenauslese, but a..."

"Just how much is all this going to cost?"

"No swearing allowed on the premises."

They ate, they drank.

"Hegel in Spanish?" Zenobia asked.

Arno blushed. "Well, I wrote it a long time ago. I tried to read the Spanish translation. But it's like trying to make an eagle sing."

"A crow, you mean," Zenobia said. "Kant is an eagle."

"No, Kant is a giraffe."

"A giraffe? Why a giraffe?"

257

"Ortega y Gasset says somewhere"—Arno knew everything—"that he was a loyal Kantian for twenty years, but after that he only read him from time to time, 'the way you go to the zoo to look at the giraffes.' "

"Wonderful animals," said Vera, who rarely said anything. "Can you imagine what the other animals look like from that height?"

The sausage cathedral was an impressive work of art. Plump gray sausages, purply sausages, delicate white rounds, thin red ribbons, sausages of every shape and kind stacked on top of each other, clasping each other—a steaming basilica with buttresses and belfries, portals and transepts, resting on a colorful base of shredded cabbage: light-green, dark-green, red, and Savoy.

"But I'm an atheist," Victor said softly.

"All the better," said Arno. "We need to attack this with a certain iconoclastic fervor."

Half an hour later the cathedral lay in ruins. They had watched it slowly collapse. The walls had shuddered and glided away in their own grease, the colors of the nave had run together, and finally all that was left was a mass of congealed blood, pink marbled meat, empty casings, and bits of cabbage.

"The blood of the martyrs," said Zenobia. "Arthur! Wake up! You young people don't have an ounce of stamina. A sausage has more staying power than you do."

It was true. The candles, the dark room, the voices, the remains of the massacre on the earthenware platter, the glasses of Rhine wine—everything around him began to sway gently back and forth. He felt as if he were back on the boat that had borne him over the Baltic Sea in the early hours of the morning, an incredible exhaustion that must have something to do with all the images he'd seen in the last few weeks: the people, the streets, the landscapes he'd filmed—another form of indigestion. And now the sausage cathedral had been added to the rest. After a few days the images would begin to trickle away, but only after the remains had been buried in the flat round cans, somehow laid to rest, dead and delivered to the editor who would chop them up on the cutting table and relegate most of them to the garbage heap. By that time he'd be in Japan. He recognized the feeling that was coming over him and knew that people in his profession couldn't afford to have it, for what he felt was nausea—the nausea of anxiety and panic, a revolt against newness, against the speed at which he would be transported to the other side of the world, leaving his soul thousands of miles behind. ("You set yourself up for this. Time after time." Erna.) And he knew that the feeling would fade, that he would soon be wending his way through the silence of those temples, that the room in which he was now sitting with his friends would seem far away. He left his life behind, time after time, because another life was waiting for him over there, wherever "there" was, and all he had to do was step into it, become another person who also happened to be him, so that he didn't have to change himself, just his world, his surroundings. Sometimes the transition, the transmigration, was painful, but only until he became wrapped up in the reality of the new place, became the seeing eye that saw, recorded, collected—another person and yet the same one, a person who allowed himself to be moved by his new surroundings, an invisible figure gliding unseen among the lives of others.

"This ought to wake him up."

It was Arno's voice, with an unfamiliar note of excitement.

He could feel them all looking at him. Among the illuminated lanterns of their faces he could make out a new face, one that hadn't been there a moment ago but was now staring at him as well.

Later he was to play back the events of that night over

and over again in his head. A film that kept changing—
bizarre shots, a blurry cast of characters, bright overex-
posures followed by huge blowups, a random sequence of
images, her face among the others, set apart somehow, lighter,
as if she were in a spotlight and everyone else had to make do
with candles, a dreamy, flickering light, filled with shadows,
because the living flame had fluttered in a blast of air, the
opening of a door, a sudden movement.

Herr Schultze's voice, a good-bye, Victor's gaze, the gleam
of Arno's glasses, the amazing duplication of Vera and Zenobia, Otto Heiland taking in the scene as if he wanted to use it
somehow—the moment itself, which belonged to them as
much as it did to him, was long gone, but they would hold on
to it, would remember how he, who had just come back, had
sat dozing at their table, maybe even dreaming, how he had
been summoned, without a word or a command, how a young
woman had appeared among them (like one of the Fates,
Vera later said) and had ordered him with her eyes to rise up
out of his circle of friends, how they had felt his fate hanging
in the balance (as you would with the Fates), and although
they had no proof, they knew that a strange thing had
happened, because why else would a man, swaying slightly
on his feet, have gone over to a woman who—they couldn't
agree on this point—had looked cruel (Zenobia), compelling
(Victor), forlorn (Arno), fateful (Vera), stunning (Otto, who
would later use the scar in a painting), and had all but clung
to her, so that they could tell from his back that he was already gone, had left them, disappeared into the hollow black-
ness of the city—a tall figure that was framed briefly in the
doorway before he followed a small, tightly clenched figure
into the night, from which, as they later confirmed themselves, all traces of spring had vanished. The final farewell
had been a gust of wind that had blown out the candles and

let in a few outside sounds—traffic, a bus, footsteps, voices, then nothing, silence, the confirmation of absence, the scraping of chairs, their renewed, now so different, conversation.

The sequence of *his* images would always begin with that exit, with his friends who would fly with him over Siberia, over arctic landscapes, streams, empty plains, images he wanted to take with him to the island of the temples. But there too the door would shut behind him, and he would begin to walk, with the pace set by her feet, in the same shoes she'd been wearing on the U-Bahn, the black and white cowhide boots, except that this time the film would be moving at an impossible speed, a rapid staccato with vocal accompaniment. Suddenly there would be a voice, talk, thoughts, someone telling him about her world, though he didn't know whether he was being lured into it or driven out of it, two different people talking out of the same mouth, one who longed, or admitted to having longed, and one who pushed him away, demanded solitude, erected barricades, refused, tightened up, invoked the past with dark, dangerous snatches of memory and rage, then fled to a future, a torrent of stories about her Spanish queen that had astonished him, someone with her own past as the present, and someone else's past as the future. He'd tried to imagine years of a future filled with bishops, battles, Muslims, pilgrims, a world that had nothing to do with him and never would, and meanwhile he had recorded that face, had filmed without a camera, enlarging the mouth that talked about the things that did have something to do with him, the white gleam of teeth, the sentries that let the words escape, the distortion of her lips when certain words were emphasized. There was nothing he failed to notice, nothing, the lamplight that crept up and died away on her face as they walked, the eyes that he had once, the very first time, thought of as Berber eyes—his first glimpse of a woman who had wanted to snatch a paper out from under his nose—that one moment in which every action, every scene, every ending had already been taken into account.

He stopped next to the Bellevue, unable to go on anymore, and the flow of words finally came to a halt. He leaned against a pillar, and only after a long while, as if she suddenly remembered his presence, did she ask about his trip, asking what had struck him most. A ridiculous question, the kind of thing you were asked in an interview, a telltale sign of feigned interest, and he remembered speaking slowly, as you would to a child or a none-too-bright interviewer, telling her (and himself) about a conversation they had recorded with a very old woman, the last of her people to speak a dead—or dying—variation of Ugric. About how strange it had been to think that one day soon those sounds would never again be heard from a living mouth. Even more mysteriously, the final moment before she died would be the last time anyone would think in that language. Inaudible words that no one would ever be able to record.

They began walking again, not quite as fast this time. Footsteps, two clocks running at different speeds, Unter den Linden, Friedrichstrasse, Tucholskystrasse, the gold dome of the synagogue, green-uniformed men with machine guns, shivers, stringy silence. He mentally turned around to look at the image again, to fix it in his mind, but she had kept on walking, talking, drawing him in, twists and turns, meanders, hoarse, breathy, a change in rhetoric, a conversation in a mountain village, a Berber woman along the road, Monbijoustrasse, Hackescher Markt, he had long ago given up listening to the words, seeing only gaping courtyards, shadowy buildings, faint light. Where she was headed he didn't know, but he could feel that they were almost there. A door, a man with a shaved head whose face he didn't trust, a mechanical beat coming from downstairs, light from the underworld, unsavory characters leaning against a bar—*Gegenmenschen,* he called them, a new subspecies of humanity. Their voices didn't sound like those of his friends. They spoke in evil drawls, the language of caves.

She seemed to know them, to assume a different voice, a kind of shout to be heard above the music, heavy metal, the sound of a factory producing nothing but noise, pounding figures on a dance floor, slave laborers working on an absent product, contorted bodies moving in time to a merciless beat, writhing with every lash of the whip, screaming along with what they seemed to recognize as words, a German chorus from Hell, raw voices scraped over jagged iron, poisonous metal.

Gegenmenschen—people who hated silence. XTC users, speed freaks, cokeheads, vanitas faces with thin bodies in chic rags. She suddenly handed him her coat, mumbled something, and the next thing he knew the woman who only a few minutes ago had been flying along on wings had thrown herself into the witch's brew, and he had retreated to a corner with a lukewarm glass of beer that a wraith had shoved into his hands, not wanting to see anything, especially not her, twisting and turning in the orange and purple glow of the revolving light on the darkened dance floor, working herself into a frenzy like a Maenad, a humiliated madwoman, a stranger, a person he saw again only after another beer-swilling skinhead had lurched over and shouted something at him that he didn't understand. He saw the man point at her. She was now dancing by herself under the flashing lights, and she seemed to have a hundred arms, stretching out in all directions, one minute flowing sinuously and the next jerking spasmodically, a desert dance that chased everyone else off the floor, so that they formed a circle around her, grinning and leering, and only then did it dawn on him that the man with the stinking breath had been saying, *Ausländer, Ausländer,* foreigner, and

263

making vomiting sounds. Then suddenly there was a fight, some guy punched him in the jaw, knocked him down, gave him a swift kick in the ribs, but by then it had turned into a free-for-all and everybody was beating up everybody else, almost in time to the music, and he saw her fell a big brute with a single karate chop, extricate herself from the tangle of wrestling bodies, come over to him, and drag him away. The bouncer by the door put out his arm to stop them, but he took one look at her face and moved aside. In the distance they heard a police siren.

"*Scheisse,*" said the bouncer, but by then they were already outside. She led him behind a stone wall, and from there they watched the cops rush into the courtyard.

"You're bleeding," she said, but he knew it wasn't serious. She started to wipe his face, but this time he was the one who pushed her away. She shrugged her shoulders and walked off toward a bus stop. He looked at the schedule to see when the bus was leaving, but since he didn't know where they were going and didn't want to ask, it was useless. There was no one else at the bus stop. He moved a few steps away and looked at her as if she were a stranger. So this was the woman he'd slept with—no, who'd slept with him, though such things weren't visible. Two strangers at a bus stop, standing several feet apart. A woman who was freezing, with her hands jammed into the pockets of her gabardine coat and her arms held tightly to her sides. A man who took another step away from her, so that the woman was even more alone. Impossible to know what she was thinking. Nobody could have guessed that only fifteen minutes ago she had felled a man with a karate chop, or that only thirty minutes ago she had been dancing in a disreputable dive like a woman possessed. He walked down to the corner to see what street they were on. Rosenthaler Strasse. Where the hell was that? Rosenthaler Strasse, Sophienstrasse, it sounded familiar but he couldn't place it. He turned to go back and noticed that a bus had pulled up and she was getting in. What? Why was he so slow, why were other people always so fast? Waving his arms, he ran toward the bus and got there just as it was starting to take off. The driver stopped, opened the door to let him in, and then accelerated suddenly, so that Arthur found himself sprawled in the middle of the aisle. Never before had he been so close to those cowhide boots.

"Had a few too many?" the driver called.

"No. I got an early start this morning," Arthur said. He was about to add that he'd just come from Estonia, but realized in time how stupid it would sound.

"I've just come from Estonia." Not the kind of thing you say to a Berlin bus driver, but to a closed-faced woman in an empty bus who was staring out the window and seemed to be headed somewhere, though he had no idea where. If the driver hadn't stopped for him, he'd still be standing at the bus stop. He sat down on the seat across from her. Karate expert, Maenad, history student, world champion in good-bye. As for himself, how many different guises had he assumed that day? A man who'd shaved in Tallinn, waited on a cold wind-whipped dock, leaned over a railing, sat in an airplane, dined with friends, walked for miles through Berlin at a woman's side. And now he was a man in a bus staring at a woman. Nobody ever got the entire film, just a series of clips. She pressed the stop button. Was he supposed to get out or not? He stayed in his seat and watched her move to the door. Only after the bus had stopped and she had stepped out did she look back over her shoulder and say, "We're here." The door closed behind her.

"Hold it!" he said to the driver.

"Definitely a few too many," the driver said, but he opened the door again.

This time she waited. In fact she was standing so close to the exit that he bumped into her.

"You're still bleeding," she said. "Hold still."

She pulled out a handkerchief and dabbed his face with it. Then she brought a corner of it to her lips, moistened it and rubbed the spot again. For the first time he felt the pain.

"A cut," he said.

"You're lucky. That guy had a broken glass in his hand. He just missed your eye."

His right eye. A one-eyed cameraman. But it hadn't happened.

"Why do you go to that place?"

"Because I'm not welcome there. Could you understand the lyrics?"

No, he hadn't understood the lyrics, but he had heard how the music ripped everything to pieces.

"Could you understand them? Your German can't be that good."

How could anyone make out the words in that raw aggressive roar?

"Good enough. Especially when someone takes the trouble to explain them."

"I bet they love doing that."

"Absolutely. But they've never hassled me."

"Up to now."

"Because I've always been on my own before."

"So it's my fault."

"Of course not. I provoked it."

"But why do you go there?"

"The first time I was simply curious. Then I thought of it as a challenge. I like music that doesn't like me. Especially when I can dance to it."

"You call that dancing? It looked more like a fit of rage."

She stopped suddenly and looked at him.

"You're beginning to understand," she said.

266

He wasn't sure he wanted to, so he didn't answer.

Milastrasse, Gaudystrasse. The street names were some-how familiar, but he couldn't place them. Pockmarked houses, peeling woodwork, flaking stucco. They came to an open area and a large building that looked like a gym. Inside, a dim light shone down on an empty handball court. There were three aluminum flagpoles out front, jingling in the wind. He suddenly realized where he was. She turned to the right and started walking through a park. It was pitch dark, but she was sure of the way. Falkplatz. The gym must have been built after the trees had been planted. He wondered how they were doing, but it was impossible to tell in the dark.

She crossed a street, went around a corner, and opened a large, heavy door. They walked through a hallway that smelled of wet newsprint, mold, and God knows what else—a smell that he would never forget. Later, he realized how amazing it was. Out of all that had happened to him that night, out of all the impressions, images, and sounds, the first one that always came back to him was the smell of damp and decay—as if time itself had been rotting away. Those newspapers had been meant to say something, to tell what happened in the world, to serve as a record, but in this case the dank sheets of newsprint had stuck together and the ink had started to run, so that the opposite had been achieved: instead of recording events for posterity, they had been only one step ahead of oblivion. News bulletins, editorial opinions, reviews—everything was a soppy wet gray, reeking of decay.

Up a flight of stairs, an unpainted door with a No Trespassing sign in Dutch: *Verboden Toegang*. Books spread out in a circle on the floor, with an empty space in the middle. She began picking them up so that he would have room to move around. She could have said any of the things people usually say—sorry the room is such a mess, so small, so tacky, but she said nothing, just hung her coat in the closet and held out her hand for his, which she folded up neatly and placed in a corner by the door.

Would you like a cup of coffee?

No, she didn't say that either. Nor did she tell him that this was the first time she had ever let anyone come here. She said nothing, he said nothing. They simply stood there staring at each other. He didn't know that two people could make so little noise. There was a predictable precision to it all. The silence was part of a choreography that went on until the tension became unbearable, until she moved her hand, touched his shirt, gave it a gentle tug—a small gesture, but one that meant that they should take off their clothes—the rustle of garments falling to the floor, being folded up. She lay on the bed, looking at him, then held out her hand. Tentative, hesitant, demure—a word that Victor had once used, a long time ago, in Charlottenburg Palace. So this was what it meant. A kind of hesitation. He knew that what was going to happen next would not go unpunished, that this woman had made up her mind, would no longer avoid him or run away, that he wasn't alone in his feelings, but that he was in a danger zone and would have to tread lightly, knowing that he had been allowed in, that he had to be present so that she could be absent, that nothing less than total oblivion would do, and that he could only let himself be carried away once she had reached that state of absence and the two bodies in that room had let go of their personalities, until sometime later a man would lift his head from the shoulder of a woman, look at the head under his and see tears on a turned-away face, a glistening scar, a body that curls itself up as if it wants to sleep forever but will be gone when he wakes up in the morning, when the gray Berlin light creeps through the uncurtained window and he observes the silence, the books, the dismal dungeon of a room. For a while he thinks she'll come back, then he's certain she won't. He gets up, naked and large, an animal in alien territory. He washes himself at the sink, but every sound he makes is too loud, every move he makes is trespassing. Nevertheless, he picks up the books one by one and inspects her handwriting. It looks like he thought it would: wiry, like her hair. Crossed-out sentences, the lines like swords, razor sharp. Names, dates, words that make him feel like an outsider, until he finally lets himself out. The last thing he sees is a photograph on the windowsill beside the bed. An elderly woman with a stern, typically Dutch face. Not much of a resemblance, except for the intensity of the stare. He walks down the stairs, but since he's a cameraman, he thinks of it in rewind.

"But that's impossible. In that case you'd have to be going down the stairs backward." Erna. He remembered a conversation they'd had many times before. Erna, more than anyone he knew, didn't believe in clinging to the past.

"It has nothing to offer you. You've already been there. And if you're always longing to go back *there*, you can't be *here*."

"I can't deny the past."

"You don't have to. But you take it to extremes. You're always trying to turn the present into the past. You've got your tenses all wrong. As a result, you're not here, you're not there, you're nowhere."

He knew he had to go past the moldy newspapers again, so he got himself outside as quickly as he could. He looked up and down the street in the hope of seeing her, trying to reconstruct the events of last night. Falkplatz. He drank a venomous cup of coffee in a corner café, then walked over to the gym. Peering in the window, he saw a bunch of kids playing handball, and for several minutes he watched them run and jump, and wondered how old they were. Thirteen...fourteen at the outside. In other words, mere kindergartners when the

Wall had fallen, back before this gym had been built. So this was the first generation of new Germans. He watched them laugh and leap into the air, boys and girls together, weaving their way across the court with a complete freedom of movement, and he was reminded, as he always was, of Thomas. He turned around so that he was facing the park. It was hard to imagine a sorrier sight. The people had apparently fared better than the trees. Thin, scraggly saplings with not enough space in between, empty patches of dirt—a bankrupt utopia. But maybe he was the only one who still remembered the tree planting. He'd filmed that too. Now he would have to superimpose those images on today's images. It was all so pathetic— a pond with a stack of cubes in the middle, an insultingly innocent grassy knoll where the death strip used to be. He walked down Schwedter Strasse into the dimly lit, once forbidden Gleim Tunnel: the yellowish glow of gaslight, cobblestones, damp—it was 1870 in here, a rat-infested cave. He started breathing again only when he reached the other side. Now to find the quickest way home.

A chorus of voices on the answering machine. Arno wondering if he would have time to drop by before he went to Japan, Zenobia asking him to phone her back, Victor telling him to enlighten himself in Koyasan, Hugo Opsomer informing him that the Japan trip would have to be postponed for at least a week to give them more preparation time, the NPS looking for someone to film minefields in Cambodia, Erna, who swore and told him that if he didn't get his ass over to Amsterdam soon she'd come to Berlin, and finally Hugo Opsomer again to ask if he could fly to Brussels so they could work out the details together and drive up to the Museum of Ethnology in Leiden, "because that's where Robert van Gulik's son works. He's an expert on Japan, and he'll be able to point us in the right direction. Just think of it, my friend, eighty-eight temples, some of them accessible only on foot! We'll have to get in shape first!"

But the voice he was hoping to hear wasn't among them. No need to call Victor back just yet. He phoned Erna and asked her to tell the NPS that he wouldn't be available. Then he recorded a message saying that he'd be gone for at least two months, phoned Sabena to book a flight to Brussels, and began to pack his bags. Yet all the time he knew that his swift action was meant to mask a slow indecision, a longing to flee in the opposite direction, back to the rat-infested tunnel in the underworld, to the square with the hapless trees where children raced across a handball court, to the darkened hallway that smelled of mold and rotting newsprint, where he had followed a woman up a flight of stairs, a woman he would have to go looking for when he got back from all those temples. Then he called Arno to say that he would stop by on his way to the airport.

"Ah, you've already left us, I see," said Arno with a note of concern in his voice. Arthur had come in, plunked his worldly possessions down in the hall, and joined Arno in the study. It was strange how friends could sometimes sense your mood. Arno was right—he had packed his bags and was as good as gone. His whole being was taken up with the trip. From now on things would go very quickly. The taxi, the airplane, the glimpses of the landscape below, the days in Brussels, the visit to the museum in Leiden to get information on their trip to Shikoku, the photos of the temples they were to visit, the discussions of the ancient pilgrimages—everything would dissolve, fade into the background the moment he started shooting the first pictures. He tried explaining it to Arno, and he had the feeling that Arno understood.

"You're here and you're not here," he said. "That has a nice Zen ring to it. Very appropriate, considering where you're going. According to the Buddhists, everything is an illusion, so I might as well spend the next twenty minutes talking to an illusion. Afterward I can wonder if you were actually here. I envy you. I'd love to go to Japan. Some of those Buddhist sects have been claiming for centuries that the visible world is an illusion. And they've got beautiful chants. You know, thundering drums and deep hums, very dramatic. Anyway, they never said Galileo was wrong. Why should they? Meanwhile, after an endless search, we've discovered that everything we used to think of as solid consists of empty space, and that we would need a pair of glasses bigger than anything we can currently conceive of to be able to observe all the invisible and unpredictable particles that make up our so-called matter. They were right. We *are* transparent, even though we look so substantial! Ha! Now that we've found out how much of our world consists of appearances, we could turn it into a religion, except that the Buddhists have beat us to it. We humans barely exist. We shouldn't even have names. Have you ever thought about that? Things would be a lot clearer if we didn't have names. We'd simply be a bit of ephemeral matter with a glimmer of awareness. Apparitions who come, and shortly thereafter, go. But because we have names we think we really amount to something. We even expect names to confer a kind of protection. Yet who knows the names of all the billions of people who were here before us?

"I'll be honest with you. I'm usually amazed by everything I read, but I try not to let myself get carried away. It would be pointless. I stick to the facts as I see them; otherwise I'd go mad. My name is Arno Tieck, though that's neither here nor there, and I'm as firmly rooted in reality as I am in this chair. Science is busy unraveling the mysteries of the world, and naturally that's difficult to accept. After all, we just want to be ourselves. But every once in a while, when the outer reaches of our world have been pushed back a bit farther, my head begins to swim: more zeroes, more exploding galaxies, more light-years. And then there's the opposite direction. Instead of expanding, our world is getting smaller, as we hone in on superstrings, antimatter, atoms that belie their own name, digging deeper and deeper until there's nothing more to see and yet there's still something there. Reality on a rasp. In the meantime we continue to give ourselves names as if we've got everything under control! Nietzsche was right about one thing: we ought to treat nature's mysteries with more respect. But do we listen? No, we go poking around the darkest recesses of the universe, stripping off layer after layer until nothing more is visible. One day we ourselves are going to be swallowed up by all those secrets, because our miserable brains won't be able to grasp them. But, my dear friend, when it all gets to be too much for me, when the waves come crashing over me, I think of this. Do you remember my convent? Hildegard von Bingen? If the universe is a question, then mysticism is an answer, and her music is mysticism in song. No answer is ever complete, but I opt for art. When you're in Japan and you've had enough of those somber male voices, listen to her music: one certainty pitted against another—the certainty of nothingness, of the subsumed self in Nirvana versus the certainty of the soul next to God for all eternity, humming along with the harmony of the spheres. Holy basses versus holy sopranos! You've got to admit it's fantastic—whatever horror or abyss, redemption or ecstasy you give people, they make music out of it. Thousands of years ago the planets sang God's praise in perfect harmony, but they've apparently stopped—probably because they knew we were on the way. We've been banished to the far corners of the cosmos, and at the same time our world has shrunk. But we were given music to console us—harmony as well as heart-rending dissonance. Have you got one of those portable CD players you can use on the plane?"

Arthur did.

"When you've climbed to an altitude of about thirty thousand feet, listen to my medieval choir. Then you'll be close to where they thought the music was coming from. Here."

Arthur took the CD. The cover illustration, he read, was an illuminated drawing from the *Codex Latinus*. A young, dark-haired woman in a medieval gown holding up two stone tablets, like Moses with the Ten Commandments, except that these were blank. *Voice of the Blood*. He didn't like the title.

"It's typical of the Middle Ages," Arno said. "The blood refers to the martyr St. Ursula—one of the great legends of the Middle Ages—who was the inspiration for this music. But it leads us to an age-old question: How are you supposed to imagine a past that you're incapable of imagining? Those people had the same brain structure we do, but different software. This music is a perfect expression of that, since it sprang from an emotion we no longer share. What makes Gregorian chants and Hildegard von Bingen so popular nowadays? Nostalgia! The source of the music no longer exists, but the music itself does. These are the puzzles your girlfriend will also have to solve. Her queen lived in exactly the same period. Hildegard von Bingen wrote this music because she was moved by Ursula and her eleven thousand virgins. They seemed real to her. In the Accademia in Venice you can see Carpaccio's version of the Ursula story. But by then the Renaissance had begun. Style and outward appearance had taken on more importance. They're beautiful paintings, but not as devout. And it wasn't long, only a few centuries, before the first lenses were being ground, thanks to the efforts of your compatriots—assuming you count Spinoza as a Dutchman. So one leg was already being sawed off the mighty throne. Have you said good-bye?"

Arthur understood that he was referring to Elik.

"You can hardly call it that. She doesn't even know I'm leaving."

Arno didn't answer.

"Maybe you can tell her for me? I didn't get a chance to."

"I will if she comes by. I think her time here in Berlin is almost over. I'll be sorry to see her go, because I've become rather attached to her. She's so, so . . ."

"What?"

"Different. Different from most young people I meet these days. She's got an inner fire, but every once in a while it rages out of control. Sometimes she's cool and rational, and then you can get a really good discussion going, and other times I don't understand why she even bothers to come, since she's her own worst enemy. Besides, she's as stubborn as a mule. I've noticed that she's thought about some of the things I've said, but her first reaction is always to reject my argument. Nobody's obliged to listen to me, and I personally consider healthy skepticism to be one of the great motors of rational thought, but she's turned it into an art form. Anything she regards as speculative is suspect. And according to her, speculation is a typically male pastime." He chuckled.

"What's so funny?"

"I told her the other day that women had become the men of the second millennium. But she wouldn't hear of it. 'God forbid,' she said. 'I hope you don't mean it as a compliment. Just let me get on with my work. I've found my niche, my own bit of turf, so let me stick to it. I'll leave no stone unturned, even if it takes me years.'"

"And what did you say?"

"That if you reject everything that smacks of the transcendent, you'll have trouble writing about the Middle Ages. . . . Anyway, she'll find that out for herself. It's just that . . ."

"What?"

"I worry about her. I sense that she's very vulnerable beneath all that armor. Sometimes she reminds me of Zenobia.... No, not the Zenobia you know now, but the one of forty years ago. You may not believe it, but she was a demon back then. It was as if she was being pulled in a hundred different directions. Now she's... now she's found... a certain equilibrium."

Arthur stood up.

"I need to call her."

"You can call her from here."

"No, I'll do it from Tempelhof."

"Tempelhof? You mean that airport is still being used? It always reminds me of the airlift."

"Yes. Sabena flies in and out of there. In those small airplanes I like so much."

"I'm jealous. When will you be back?"

"In six or eight weeks."

"Ah well, we're used to such long absences in your case. Take good care of yourself. And bring me some music from one of those Zen monasteries. And, uh, please don't tell Zenobia."

"Don't tell her what?"

"You know, those things I told you, about how she used to be. She was more than I could handle, back then."

He actually seemed to blush.

"So I chose Vera. Just like Zeno, you know, in that book by Italo Svevo."

Arthur didn't know.

"He was in love with one sister, then another, and he finally married the third sister. A very happy marriage. But that's not what I meant. She's actually the one who's worried."

"About Elik? But she hardly knows her."

"No, she's worried about you. Because she recognizes so much of herself in Elik. After all, she saw her last night. We were all there when you were kidnapped. Anyway, don't mind me, I'm just talking off the top of my head. Come back safe and sound."

"I'll try."

"Are you going to work on your own project?"

"I always do."

He could see that Arno wasn't through, so he paused in the doorway.

"I've been thinking quite a bit recently about the fragments you showed me. They're...they've stayed with me. But that was a while ago. Are you still planning to do something with them?"

"Yes."

"Good. Then it isn't necessary for me to say what I wanted to say. I was going to tell you not to lose faith. For what it's worth, I see it—and forgive me for expressing it in these terms, but I suppose it comes with the job—as a weaving of the historical and the ahistorical world. No, don't roll your eyes.... It's related to what I was just talking about. The historical world is the world of events, the things you've filmed in the course of your career, no matter where you were, no matter whether or not you were on assignment: Bosnia, Africa, and of course Berlin. Names, facts, dates, dramas. But that other world, the everyday world of the unseen, of the anonymous—or whatever word you used—the little insignificant things that nobody notices because they're always there...I was reminded of it last night when I came across something Camus said about how he had been taught to classify the world, to see how it all fits together, to deal with the world of knowledge and of facts, but that he no longer knew why he'd had to learn all those things.... I can't remember the exact wording, but then he suddenly said, 'I understand much more when I look at the rolling hills.' I remember the bit about the rolling hills, and then there was something else, about evening and restlessness, but it was the rolling hills that made me think of you. You'll bring me a few of those rolling hills from Japan, won't you?"

—   With that, he gently and firmly shut the door, and for a moment Arthur felt as if he'd been thrown out. He tried to phone Zenobia from Tempelhof, but there was no answer. An hour later, after the plane had leapfrogged over a heavy cloud, he saw the city spread out below him for the second time in two days. Pressing his forehead to the window, he tried to find Falkplatz, Schwedter Strasse, and the Gleim Tunnel, but the clouds got in his way. So he slid the CD that Arno had given him into his portable CD player and listened to the soprano voices, which seemed to want to soar higher than the airplane itself.

Before and after. The ancient Greeks didn't like showing the influence of time on emotion and mood. Yes, we know that because we need to. Of course we're still here. It's not in our nature to let go of things. Too much and too little is happening. In Euripides's *Medea* the chorus is allowed to comment on what comes next. In Sophocles it may ask and even beseech, but not foretell. As for us—we can't spin webs, but we can see them. We skip easily from one time zone to the next. Night and day flow over the earth like a kind of liquid, but we hardly notice. We never sleep. All we do is watch. Victor is playing the piano in his nocturnal studio—a piece so slow that time itself can barely stand to be measured in such intimate increments. As he plays he thinks of Arthur, who has now been gone for six weeks. Does he miss him? We would only know that if Victor allowed himself to think in those terms, which he doesn't. He simply thinks of his absent friend, acknowledges his existence somewhere in the world. The friend himself isn't thinking of Victor, but of Arno. Because at this very moment he's looking at a long row of monks. Sixteen, to be exact, but they're not chanting, they're meditating. Za Zen. Sixteen men sitting in the lotus position, with their hands resting in such a way that the thumbs are always on top. Exactly like the hundreds of statues he's seen in the last few weeks, except that these statues are made of flesh and blood. It's dark, and the faces above the black robes are closed tight, locked in concentration, so that they reveal nothing. Yes, if you must know, we also know their thoughts, but that's not important now. They're seeking absence, and that's hard to find, even for them. Arthur registers their stillness, the low platforms they're sitting on, the darkly gleaming wood, the scant light coming through the rice-paper panels, the zoris lined up neatly on the floor tiles in front of each monk. He's not allowed to film them, which is why he sees so much more. Soon they'll start to chant, though you can hardly call it that; it's more of a buzz, the sound of thousands of bumblebees, a long sustained drone containing hidden words, which wrap him in a cocoon of incomprehensibility. What had Arno said? Something about invisibility, transparence. The sound reverberates to the depths of his being, nestles itself inside the weeks he's been here: pilgrim paths, sacred mountaintops, devotion, vulgarity, moss-covered stones, sacred objects, gongs giving off almost visible vibrations, cedars wreathed with cords as if they were also holy men, cherry trees so full of blossoms that he couldn't help but think of the snow-covered chestnut tree in Berlin. Up and down all those trails his camera had borne down on him, as though he were carrying a stone monkey on his shoulder, but most of the time he had felt as if he were floating, as if he were not quite real. How he wished he could have answered Arno those many weeks ago, but as usual he hadn't been fast enough: he needed to chew over new ideas. So only now did he realize that transparence could be felt as a physical sensation. His two dead spirits and that one living one were still with him, the way his friends were also with him, despite the immeasurable distance between them. He was here now, but they would wait for him until he no longer strove for absence, until the world cried out to him with its grief and longing. The monks would go on chanting, but he would have departed, if for no other reason than because he didn't know what kind of person you had to be to stay behind. A gong sounded, and the buzz began again—to produce such a sound these men must have underground caverns somewhere in their bodies. Hugo Opsomer had given him the text of the sutras they were chanting, but the words didn't bring him any nearer the truth. They sounded true as they were being chanted, simply because they were being chanted. Yet they continued to elude him. He had never been able to find the right words to describe his thoughts. "You think with your eyes," Erna had told him once. We watch him as he gets up from his cramped position on the floor and picks up his camera. Later he'll be able to see what he's been thinking all this time. Those aren't our words, but his. No, of course he hasn't said them to anyone. Only to himself. You people are always saying that you were just thinking of someone. "Yesterday I suddenly had the feeling you were thinking of me. Were you?" Sometimes it's true, sometimes you lie.

In the night train to Hendaye, Elik Oranje is thinking about Arthur Daane. She's wide awake. She couldn't sleep then, and she can't sleep now. This time it's because she's being tossed in a narrow berth, because the man in the lower berth is snoring, because the train is hurling her backward as well as forward—away from what she doesn't want and can't have and toward what she has to do next. Her books have been sent to a general delivery address in Madrid, where she can pick them up as soon as she's found a place to stay. She's free. The train is racing between Orléans and Bordeaux, the wheels are beating out the rhythm of her thoughts—I'm free, I'm free. So why can't she get him out of her head? You leave a bed because it's not wide enough for two, because you wake up in an unconscious embrace that imprisons you more cruelly with every heartbeat. You see a strange face too close to yours and realize that you don't want that closeness and that you never will, no matter how much you might long for it from time to time. You've broken your own code, the one that was branded into you, the one sealed by fire, the decision that was made before you were even allowed to make your own decisions. If this was a story in a history book, she thought, I'd have burst out laughing. But it's my own story and I'll decide how it ends. I've never capitulated before and I'm not about to now. This should never have happened. She's clenched her fists so hard that her nails have dug into the flesh. She can picture the book beneath her pillow, the only one she's brought with her. The grayish-beige cover, the citadel of Zamora, the dates, the name of the queen, which also happens to be the name of a bird, two syllables in her own language, a name that sounds like the dull chink of pebbles being struck together. She's alone again, she's free. An unwanted item has been disposed of. And what do we see? A pianist playing a prelude late at night, a philosopher reading a short farewell note from Elik Oranje that says something other than what it says, a twilight glow by the Myōshinji Temple toward the end of a journey, a chain of dimmed lights moving through the deserted landscape of the Dordogne— we can't let go of anything for so much as a moment, not even the lone woman in her living room staring at a photograph of a cloud that floated above a beach in Helgoland seventy years ago. A letter that doesn't say what it says—what kind of nonsense is that? But if it's nonsense, why does he dwell on it? We don't make judgments, so that's not it. Perhaps it's sadness, sadness because of the fact that something means too much to one person and not enough to the other. We shall see. Just because we observe and follow every move doesn't mean we're obliged to tell what happens. Thank goodness. Once upon a time queens and heroes were the subject of myths and tragedies. You had an Oedipus for punishment, a Medea for revenge, an Antigone for resistance. But you are no longer kings, or king's daughters. Your stories are trivial, except to yourselves. Continuing episodes, news items, soap operas. Never again will your grief be used to coin a wealth of words that others can dip into during the limited amount of eternity available to you. That makes you more superficial, ephemeral, and, in our opinion, more tragic. You have no echo. No audience. Yes, that's another way of putting it, though that's not what we meant. Besides, this has been the last time you'll hear from us. Except for those last four words.

"You were gone before you actually left," said Arno, "and now that you're back, you're not really back yet. Tell me all about it."

"It's too soon," Arthur said. "My head's still reeling. Here." He handed him the CD that he'd bought in Kyoto. "Men in exchange for women, just as you asked."

No, he couldn't talk about it yet. Again he had flown in a small plane over Berlin, just as he had two months ago, and again he had tried to locate Falkplatz. But every time he thought he'd spotted the arched roof of the gym, a racing cloud had come between him and the world below.

"When can I see something?"

"You can't. Not yet. I left the reels in Brussels, and sent the footage I made for myself to Amsterdam. I'll be away from Berlin for a while."

"Oh." Arno sounded disappointed. "But what did you film?"

"Silence. Motionlessness. Stairways leading up to temples. Feet on the stairs. The usual things."

Arno nodded and waited.

"The same shots I made for the official film, only slower. And longer."

Somehow that made it sound as if he'd moved around when he was filming, though he hadn't. At some of the smaller temples he'd sat totally still, usually beside a pond or a garden with moss-covered rocks and raked gravel. He would sit on a wooden walkway and focus the camera directly at an object, from the lowest possible angle. The secret was to stare at it for a long time, until you could feel the fullness of the rock, until the silence became ominous. But you couldn't say things like that, not even to Arno. Later he would see it for himself. Everything in a Zen garden had a meaning. You knew what it was without knowing it. That was for the others, the explainers. He was perfectly satisfied with just looking.

He wanted to ask Arno about Elik, but wasn't sure how to broach the subject. After the plane had landed, he'd gone straight home, put down his bags, and looked out at the chestnut tree. He'd been relieved to see that it already had its first leaves, because at least something had changed. No. Actually, what had caused him to stand for several long minutes without moving had been the sight of his room. Two kinds of time—change and changelessness—could apparently exist side by side. He was an orderly type. Before going away, he always put on his desk the things he wanted to be reminded of when he got home—a date book, a list of names, a note for the friend who'd lent him this apartment, in case he came back unexpectedly. Plus a few miscellaneous objects—a stone, a seashell, a miniature Chinese statue of a monkey holding a platter, the picture of Roelfje and Thomas—the things he liked to have around him when he stayed somewhere for a long period of time. Nothing had moved. He'd flown to the other side of the world, had sat in buses and trains and temples, had seen what must have been a million Japanese, and all that time the stone and the seashell hadn't moved an inch, the monkey had continued to clutch its platter, and his wife and child had stared into the room with their frozen smiles. Once, ten years ago, they had laughed into the camera and now those smiles would be there forever. He slid the monkey and the photo off to the side, opened the window, which rustled the papers on the desk, and listened to his answering machine. There was a message from Erna.

"I know this is totally ridiculous, since you aren't there, but it's one of those nights. I was watching a boat go down the canal, and there was just one man in it. It had a captain's wheel—you know, the kind with the handles—and a motor that went chuk-chuk-chuk, and the man was steering that thing for all he was worth, as if he was piloting a real ship. Well, actually, it wasn't a chuk-chuk-chuk, it was a duller sound, more of a put-put-put. Anyway, you know what I mean. Can you hear it? It's funny—you're in Japan now, but by the time you get this message, it'll be another 'now.' So call me when it's now."

Her voice had been followed by other, male, voices: a possible assignment, something about an old program being shown again. And in between those messages there had been a listening silence, then a click. Someone had wanted to get in touch with him, but not badly enough to say anything. His next step was to go to Falkplatz. Handball, jingling flagpoles, green leaves on misshapen trees. He tried to find her door, but which one was it? He didn't know the number, but it must have been on Schwedter Strasse. Or had it been Gleimstrasse? Either way the building had been near a corner. He tried one door, then another. A stack of rotting newspapers. The same one? Couldn't be. Must be other papers, yet the same. You could make a fortune growing mushrooms in the hallway. The second door off the courtyard had an intercom. This is where she'd gone up the stairs ahead of him. Cowhide boots. She couldn't be here, she must have left ages ago, gone to Holland, or to Spain. But where exactly? Madrid, Santiago, Zamora? He rang every doorbell on the intercom. For a long time there was no answer. Then a crackle and the voice of an old lady. He asked for Elik Oranje. Her name sounded strange in that empty courtyard. Stinking garbage cans, a rusty tricycle.

"She's not on the list, so she's not here!"

It sounded like "she doesn't exist." So she didn't exist.

He rang the other bells again. This time a male voice answered, sleepy, hostile.

"She took off. Won't be coming back." Crackle.

"You're lost in thought," Arno said. He stood up, went over to his desk and came back with a letter, or, rather, an empty envelope.

"Here."

Arthur read the return address. Elik Oranje, c/o Aaf Oranje, Westeinde, De Rijp. Ah, a small village north of Amsterdam. The familiar handwriting, like iron filings.

"And the letter?"

"It was addressed to me. Nothing special: thanks, enjoyed the discussions, good-bye, maybe we'll meet again. The usual things."

"Didn't she say where she was going?"

"No, but my guess is Spain. She said in her letter that she had to do some fieldwork, so I assume that means Spain, though it could be anywhere."

"Nothing about me?" He hated to ask but did anyway.

Arno shook his head.

"It was a short note. Actually, I was surprised. But I think the address was meant for you."

Arthur stood up.

"I have to go."

So that was what he had to do. He had to go. To Holland, to Erna, to De Rijp, to Spain. The Japan trip had merely postponed things, or maybe just temporarily numbed his feelings. It was inevitable. She had gone into hiding, but she'd left a clue. Presumably for him. A crumb, or, rather, two crumbs: Aaf Oranje, a name like a rifle shot, and De Rijp, another one. Either you're Hansel or you're not.

"Wait a minute," Arno said. "Zenobia and I were planning to meet at Schultze's for a glass of wine. What if I phone Victor? I haven't seen him for a while, though that's not unusual—it means he's working on something. But if he knows you're going to be there, he'll come."

A repeat of other dinners. Sausage, *Saumagen,* bacon, *Handkäse.* He thinks back to the last time he was here, to how he'd been spirited away. What was the word Arno had used? Kidnapped. He'd been kidnapped, then released without ransom. He looked around at his friends. This time it was the intervening interval that seemed to shrink. Monasteries, temples, trails—all that had been left behind. He'd gone away and come back. Japan was still somewhere inside him, but for the moment he didn't know where.

Victor examined the *Saumagen.*

"It looks like marble. Great forces of nature have been at work here. A randomly selected pig has been dismembered, its sweet little face cut open, its lips bent out of shape, its cheeks, its feet, its stomach—everything rearranged, until it finds itself lying on a platter beside a potato, though they've never met before."

"You're forgetting the salt mine," said Herr Schultze. "And the pepper tree, the laurel tree, the grapevines...The whole world comes together here, in all its simplicity."

"Wonderful," said Victor. "First order, then chaos, then order again."

"Chaos..." Arno began dreamily, but Zenobia cut him off.

"Arno, don't get started again!" To Arthur she said, "Surely he must have told you that you're actually invisible? It's his latest obsession—a combination of science and mysticism. There's nothing wrong with that. We can't forbid it. After all, it occurs even in the best of families. A sudden interest in the mind of God, that kind of thing. At least other people know what they're talking about. I don't begrudge them their little foibles, as long as they don't romanticize things. But whenever my dear brother-in-law reads about chaos or particles or the unpredictability of matter, he goes off the deep end. To him it's poetry. Of the worst kind. What was it you said recently, Arno? Oh, I remember: 'The universe has been ruined by creation! Cast out of a state of holy unity, thrown out of perfect, exquisite equilibrium.' Arno! You make it sound like a fairy tale."

"I owe it all to you," said Arno. "There's nothing wrong with fairy tales. Besides, it's like other creation stories. First the world was whole and perfect, then we ruined it and were banished, and now we want back in. And I don't mean just a poor lyrical poet like me, but your scientific colleagues as well. Too late!"

"Not all of my colleagues."

Victor broke in. "There's much to be said about this loaf of bread. It's on the verge of extinction. Here, take a look."

He held it under the lamp.

"Millions of Russians still eat this kind of bread," said Zenobia, "especially in the countryside."

"It's the color of the soil."

"Yes, of course, it doesn't make a detour through a bread factory. Soil and wheat kernels, finely ground between two millstones. That's the way *we* do it."

Herr Schultze came running over.

"Is there a problem?"

"No, no."

"This bread comes all the way from Saxony. From a small bakery that makes it the way it used to be made in the Middle Ages. It's a very old recipe. It tastes especially good with *Handkäse*. But most of my customers don't dare order a smelly cheese like that."

"People stank back in the Middle Ages," said Victor, "so they probably didn't notice."

"I'd like a glass of Hefe," Zenobia said to Schultze.

"But *Frau Doktor*! You're still drinking wine!"

"I can't help that. I was suddenly reminded of Mr. Galinsky. It's my brother-in-law's fault, for bringing up the subject of invisibility."

"I didn't bring it up."

She pointed to the corner where the old man always used to sit.

"Do you suppose anyone ever thinks of him?"

"I do," said Herr Schultze.

The conversation suddenly took off in all directions. The irrevocable disappearance of people and things, what might have happened to Galinsky's violin, an article about him in the *Tagesspiegel* . . . how had the poor man actually managed to survive the war?

Arthur thought about the sonorous notes of the violin that had once rung out in the city's grand hotels: the Kranzler, the Adlon. If there was one thing that knew how to make itself disappear, it was music.

"Like me," Zenobia said. "War is one long wait. We all waited for it to end. And now it's finally ended."

"Compassion."

Arno had said it. Or had he used the German word *Mitleid*? And was *Mitleid* the same as compassion?

Arthur asked Victor.

"It's the same as the Dutch *mededogen*. To feel someone else's suffering. A mixture of pity and love. A mantel to wrap around someone else, like St. Martin."

"My meaning exactly," said Arno. He tried pronouncing the word. "*Mededogen*."

"But compassion for what?" Zenobia asked.

"For the past. For that loaf of bread. And for Galinsky. For things that die, that die out. The last time I talked to..." He looked over at Arthur.

"Elik. It's all right to say her name!"

"OK, Elik. She and I were talking about the concept of compassion. She mentioned all those books she has to read, the names, the facts, that entire corpus of extant material.... And she told me that she thought of her research as a form of compassion. It wasn't meant to sound sentimental; it's just that she can't stand having things buried, in paper, in archives. She wishes she had the power to bring it all back to life.... Yet she also knows that the past can never be resurrected, and that it can be used—or misused—to achieve a certain end. There's the rub, because a book or a project ostensibly aimed at discovering the truth eventually finds itself smack dab in the middle of a lie. The past has been reduced to rubble, and every attempt to pick up the pieces..."

"To sum up the discussion in one word—mortality," Victor said. "Excuse my language. I don't like to swear."

"My cheese should probably be on the list of endangered species," said Herr Schultze. "Along with my bread and my *Saumagen*. We never heard Galinsky play the violin, though he played it his entire life. But the best remedy for a bad case of mortality is Schultze's famous *Apfelstrudel*. 'Food for the gods,' that's how it was written up in last year's *Feinschmecker*. And, as you all know better than I do, the gods are immortal."

Zenobia wasn't through.

"You can feel compassion for things that are gone. But no matter how formless, unknown, or forgotten the past may be, the present is still made up of the past, whether we're aware of it or not. So what difference does it make? We're doomed to be our own past anyway."

"A comforting thought," said Victor. "So are we supposed to patiently join the line?"

"There's not much else we can do."

Zenobia swirled the Hefe around in her glass, then drank it down in one gulp.

"Actually, the present and the past are at odds with each other. We can't avoid the past. We have to carry it around with us wherever we go. We can't put it down even for a moment, because we ourselves are the past. But it's an exercise in futility, since you can't live with your head turned backward."

"Unless you're a historian," said Arno.

Herr Schultze brought the *Apfelstrudel*.

"You can't live with your head turned backward." The words stung Arthur like an angry hornet. Is that what he'd been doing for the last ten years? But wasn't it inevitable when you were surrounded by the dead?

"Do you remember when you and I were looking at those Caspar David Friedrich paintings?" Victor asked.

He did.

"Why do you ask?"

"Because when you look at those canvases, you look back in time. Friedrich himself looked forward."

"Well, what did he see?"

"Munch's *Scream*. Listen carefully, and you'll be able to hear it."

Arthur stood up. "*Arrivederci tutti*," he said, much to his own surprise. They all looked at him.

"Are you leaving us?" Zenobia asked.

"I'll be back," he said. "I always come back."

"Where are you off to?"

"Holland."

"Ah, too bad," said Victor. "I understand it's pretty crowded there."

"Then on to Spain."

"My, my."

I'm back to where I started, Arthur thought. A summer day, rhododendrons. Ten years, or had it been nine years ago? He bent down to kiss Zenobia good-bye, but she grabbed his wrist in an iron grip.

"Sit down!"

It was an order. She might as well have said "Down, boy!"

"It's not fair. You come and go. And you haven't told us a blessed thing about your trip." She grabbed his other wrist. "At least tell us about one beautiful thing you saw! The most beautiful, or the most moving. And whether you thought about us. And if you did, whether you thought, 'What a pity they aren't here to see this?'"

"Not see—hear."

He put his hands on either side of his mouth and imitated a sound that here, in this enclosed space, could never equal the original. A plaintive blast, a mournful howl that needed to roll across the world, to resound against hills and mountains, to infect everything in its path with its wailing lament. It was impossible to imitate.

"You've got to imagine it ten times louder," he said helplessly. "And in the mountains."

"I can feel it here!" said Zenobia, patting her breastbone.

"A conch shell?" asked Victor.

Arthur nodded. It had taken him longer to figure it out. He'd climbed for hours, an agonizing trail that wound its way through a mountain forest. After every curve it looked as if the trail would go on into infinity. Then suddenly he heard the sound, mysterious and far away, and it had mingled with his exhaustion, the drizzling rain, the slow ascent, the impenetrable green of the trees that blocked his view of the monastery, which he knew must lie somewhere up above. Back and forth it had gone, a call echoing between the mountain he was on and the invisible one on the other side—two prehistoric animals calling out to each other, plaintive laments, statements that summed up the world, wordless voices expressing the inexpressible. Only later, when he was much closer, had he seen him, the monk, still a young man, sitting in the lotus position in a pavilion overlooking a valley. The mountain sloped away and climbed back up again to a mist-shrouded mountain on the other side, which is where the answer, the counter-lament, was coming from. Every time it stopped or faded away, the monk picked up his conch shell, waited for one brief moment, in what suddenly became an unbearable silence, then blew it again. A human breath was forced through what had once been the curved corridors of a mighty mollusk, until the sound made the mountain tremble. It had filled him with fear. Perhaps that's why he had thought of the three people he was now preparing to say good-bye to. He gave Zenobia a kiss, hugged Arno, bowed toward Victor, because Victor didn't like being touched, then turned quickly, almost a pirouette, and left the *Weinstube* without a backward glance. Only when he was outside did he remember that he'd forgotten to say good-bye to Herr Schultze.

After that everything needed to go quickly. And it did go quickly. The next afternoon he was in De Rijp.

"Holland? Oh, too bad," Victor had said. He had a point.

"De Rijp?" Erna. "For God's sake, why do you want to go there? It must have something to do with a woman. I can't think of any other reason anyone would go to De Rijp. Does she live there?"

"I don't know."

"Don't be so secretive. You sound like a teeny-bopper."

"I didn't know people still used that word."

"Shall I go with you?"

"No."

"You see!"

Now, here he was alone. A long street lined with houses. You could look right through them to the gardens in the back. Victor's "oh, too bad" had not been an expression of pity, but of something more complex. Villages like De Rijp were the epitome of the past, of a Holland that no longer existed. There they lay amid neat green polders, blissfully unaware of the encroaching cities around them, greedily lapping up every morsel of land, like a lesser version of Los Angeles. In fact, they were little more than open-air museums in an imitation landscape.

He walked past the modest brick houses, noting the plants on the windowsills, the dazzling-white curtains, the sofas, the shining copper pots, the Persian rugs on the ball-footed refectory tables—bourgeois versions of interiors painted by the Dutch Masters. On the other side of the spotless windows people were moving with easy assurance through their minuscule domains. He found it embarrassingly touching. He wanted to look inside, and at the same time hesitated. Don't look, because it was all too intimate. Do look, because of the express invitation: here we are, stare all you want, we have nothing to hide.

Aaf Oranje's house was no different. A varnished oak door with a white enamel nameplate. Aaf Oranje. A sticker on the mailbox: No advertisements. Red bricks, glossy woodwork. He rang the copper bellpull and waited for the sound of footsteps, but none came. He looked through the window. Rubber plant, sword plant, cactus, hanging lamp, Persian rug on the dining table with a bowl of oranges on top of it, a row of books on a buffet, a photograph of a young girl with a scar, a photograph of a man in a suit that had been fashionable thirty years ago. So this is where she had lived after Spain. What an insane transition. He waited a moment, then walked down the cobblestone street in the direction of the church. When you looked through the houses you could see cows grazing in the meadows on the other side. Down Rechtestraat, over to Oosteinde, past the town hall with its step gable. In the churchyard he read the names: Nibbering, Taam, Commandeur, Oudejans, Zaal. An old man in the middle of a white bridge was feeding the swans. He wound his way through the graves, reading the birth and death dates of those bygone lives, the inscriptions:

> *The silence hath us all addressed,*
> *'Tis evening now and time to rest.*

He sat for a while on a bench, then stood up again. Time to rest. What had Erna said? "You're walking strangely. I can always tell when you're tired. One of these days that camera is going to wear you down to the bone."

But it wasn't the camera—it was Japan, it was Berlin, or, rather, a combination of the two, plus someone appearing in his life and then suddenly disappearing without his being able to do a damn thing about it. He'd come here to get closer to her; now he was farther away than ever. Maybe she hadn't wanted him to follow up on the return address. After all, the letter had been addressed to Arno, not to him.

"Why don't you stay in Amsterdam for a while? You've got a place here too."

But there was no "here." Here had now become wherever

she was. Besides, his apartment was driving him crazy. He lived on the ninth floor, and his living-room window faced north, so that he could clearly see the polder on the outskirts of the city. Every time he looked at that orderly green oasis he was reminded of what he had come here for, so he had finally decided to go to De Rijp. He rang the bell again, knowing that he was being watched from across the street. People could look in, but they could also look out. Footsteps, then the door opened. An old woman, white hair pulled into a tight knot, clear blue eyes. Ah, he thought, the Berber eyes had won.

The blue ones showed no hint of surprise. He had apparently been expected. He wasn't sure what that meant, except that the return address had been written on the envelope for a reason. Or was this some kind of game?

An hour later he was standing outside again, feeling that he had just concluded a session with a master statesman. Aaf Oranje had sat across from him and not divulged any more information than she had planned to—no address, no shared confidences. He had been weighed and, he believed, not found wanting. Yet at the same time she had tacitly argued her granddaughter's case by telling him only as much as he needed to know to follow her explanation, without ever indicating that she knew exactly what had happened between him and Elik. No apologies were extended. The whole thing had resembled a mission carried out to perfection. Here was a person who had long ago resigned herself to the fact that the daughter of her unhappy daughter was someone who charted her own course. It might be against her better judgment, but the grandmother's approval was irrelevant. Suffering, she seemed to suggest, had repercussions, and even if it led to more suffering, the solidarity between grandmother and granddaughter, or perhaps simply between one woman and another, required total support. There would be no pact between this elderly lady and the not-so-young man across from her, even if she wanted one. Elik had come back from Berlin, there had been some kind of problem which the grandmother wasn't authorized to discuss, and now Elik was in Spain, a country that had been the undoing of her mother. Years ago the woman sitting across from him had gone there to fetch her half-wild granddaughter, to raise her here because the mother had been declared unfit and the father had vanished without a trace. And she had done it all on her own, since her husband—she pointed to the buffet—had died young, just like Elik's mother. No, she didn't have a new address, and even if she did, she wouldn't give it to him without Elik's permission. A strong will, he thought. It had skipped a generation in this family—there was a lot of Holland in those Berber eyes.

The whistle of a teakettle, the silence in the suddenly empty room when the grandmother went to the kitchen, a longing to get up and touch the face in the silver frame, to stretch out on the sofa and make himself at home, if only for a few hours, the smell of Dutch coffee, the familiar cookies in the cookie tin, an insufferable homesickness, the traveler reduced to his true, secret proportions, the impossible. His impossible question left unasked: What had she said about him? A question of that sort would be out of place at such a high-level meeting. That left only one question, which he finally asked when he realized there would be no further explanations, no attempts at mediation, no promises: "How did you know I'd be coming?"

"She didn't want it to be a surprise."

Not very informative, but it would have to do. So that's how the game was played. Righteousness, he thought. That's the word that went with those eyes. You could look into those eyes until you saw truth itself, but that didn't mean you'd get an answer to your question.

"She's in Spain." Suddenly the conversation took an unexpected turn. "But," she added, "I'm not sure I'm doing you a favor by telling you that."

He swallowed and didn't know what to say. Suddenly he realized that this woman also knew about Roelfje and Thomas. She might not know their names, but she knew. She also had two dead to contend with.

In the hallway there was another light, not as clear. She held the door open so that she stood in the shadow, where she couldn't be seen from the street. A hand briefly touched his arm.

"Be careful. She's going through a difficult period."

Difficult—but the door had already been shut. So that was the message. He heard himself set off over the cobblestones, on his way to Spain. There was a long road ahead, but he was used to long roads. Even when you bridged the distance quickly, it was a long road.

"You're crazy," said Erna.

She was standing by the window overlooking the canal.

"You just got back from Berlin, Japan, and before that—Russia?"

"Estonia. We've already been through all this."

"It's as if you've got the devil at your heels."

"Perhaps the other way around."

"Arthur, why don't you just tell me what's going on? I'm your oldest friend. It's not just curiosity."

He told her. When he was through, she didn't say a word. He noticed that the trees on the canal were full of leaves. It was mid-June—time was going fast. The streetlights had come on and were casting an amber glow. They heard a boat. A small boat with a single light on the bow. It was coming from the bridge on Reguliersgracht, and there was a tall man at the helm.

"There he is again," said Erna. "I wish he'd sing."

"His boat is doing all the singing. Put-put-put—your imitation was good. But why do you want him to sing?"

"Because your story makes me so sad."

They stood quietly for a while. He looked over at her. Still a Vermeer.

"You're inspecting me. Checking to see if I'm getting older."

"You're not."

"Like hell I'm not."

Silence. The sound of the boat died away in the distance.

"Arthur."

He said nothing.

"If you add up all the hours, how much time have you actually spent with this woman?" When he didn't answer, she said, "Well?"

"I'm counting.... One day. One long day."

That couldn't be right. It had been years—long years. Time was utter nonsense. Dalí had understood that when he painted his melting watch. Nonsense that slid out of your grasp, even when you felt it in every fiber of your being.

"Why don't you wait a bit?"

"I'm beyond that stage."

She's going to tell me I'm too old for this kind of stuff, Arthur thought. But she said something entirely different.

"Arthur, this girl is bad news."

"You have no right to say that!"

Erna took a step backward.

"This is the first time you've ever yelled at me. For a moment I thought you were going to hit me. You've turned absolutely white."

"I'd never hit you. But you're passing judgment on someone you don't even know."

"I'm not offering an opinion. I'm just reacting to what you told me."

"Well, what am I supposed to call it? A prediction? Female intuition?"

"Call it whatever you want. I'm worried about you, that's all."

"Can't you hear how ridiculous that sounds? I'm entitled to make my own mistakes—assuming this is one. Don't worry. It won't kill me."

She shrugged.

"Maybe we ought to go out and have a drink." There was a short pause. "When are you leaving? Do you need to do any laundry before you go? You can use my washing machine. You know I'm a good ironer."

He took a deep breath.

"I didn't mean to yell at you. But what made you say that?" He repeated her words, with the same rhythm and intonation: "this girl is bad news."

She looked at him. Beyond her, he could see Roelfje. Sentimental bullshit maybe, but true. Someone else had warned him. But who?

"You told your story too well," Erna said. "I got a good picture of her as you talked. I mean..." Instead of finishing her sentence, she added weakly, "Well, you might as well try your luck. How are you going to get there?"

"By car."

"In that old wreck?" He had an ancient Volvo Amazon.

"Yes."

"And when are you going to leave?"

"Now."

"Get real. You have to arrange all kinds of stuff first, don't you?"

He held up his cell phone.

"Can you stay in that apartment in Madrid? Have you already phoned your friend?"

When calling Daniel García, you had to let the phone ring a long time, because, as Daniel himself put it, he'd left part of his body behind in Angola.

"You know, the strangest thing about it is that disaster struck from the ground. It's always a possibility, of course, but somehow it's the last thing you expect. Land mines— now they're truly flowers of evil. There are two types of disaster: horizontal and vertical. Bullets are horizontal, bombs are vertical. But in the latter case they shouldn't come from the ground up. You either fall into something or something falls on you, but fate shouldn't strike from the same place as the grave. You're supposed to go to *it*; it's not supposed to come to *you*. There's something indecent about it when it does." He was known in the trade as Daniel the Philosopher, and Arthur wholeheartedly agreed. The world took on a new light after Daniel got through describing it. To him a land mine was an underground plant that could burst hideously into blossom in one fateful second—a carnivorous bloom of death and destruction that had taken his left hand and part of his left leg to a place "where I couldn't follow. God knows where they hang out these days." His loss had led to radical changes in his life.

"CNN paid well for the missing parts. I'll give them credit for that."

After months of rehabilitation, he had moved to Madrid ("I'm less conspicuous here"). He had bought a large-format camera, and now, despite his handicap, he was one of the most sought-after special-assignment photographers. His first report had been about the victims of land mines in Cambodia, Iraq, and, naturally, Angola. ("You should always stick to what you know best.")

But there was no answer now, which made Arthur realize how much he'd been looking forward to hearing Daniel's dark voice and Nicaraguan accent.

Daniel García was a sturdily built man with a body that was almost square ("Chalk it up to my love of math") and he had thick, dark-gray, kinky hair ("Over there in Surinam you folks call that *kroesoewierie*. You didn't know that, did you? What'd you go and have a colony for if you don't know the first thing about it?").

"Surinam is no longer a Dutch colony."

"Hey, I'm not going to let you off the hook that easily. Once a colonizer, always a colonizer."

They first met at a documentary film festival, where they'd both been awarded a prize by the European Community—a miniature gold-leaf laurel wreath in a Plexiglas holder. It had come in a large purple velvet box. ("I'm not going to travel with that damned beauty case. It'll attract every drag queen within miles. Give me a hammer and we'll get that gold out of there in no time.")

"So what now?" Erna asked.

"I'll try again tonight."

"Let's go out for drinks, and after that we'll go over to your place."

"To do what?"

"Wash, iron, pack. You can't imagine how much I enjoy sending a man on his way."

"I don't have an ironing board."

"So I'll use the kitchen table. And quit whining."

While she busied herself, he spread the map of Spain out on his desk. He knew that the longing he now felt had nothing to do with Elik Oranje. What route should he take? He whispered the names to himself as his finger moved over the map: Olite, Santo Domingo de la Calzada, Uncastillo, San Millán de Suso, Ejea de los Caballeros. . . . Almost every town evoked a memory.

"You're humming."

"Come look. You see all those empty spaces? Spain is the emptiest country in Europe."

"And you like that?"

Like wasn't exactly the right word. But what was the right word to describe the appeal of that desertlike landscape—the leathery, bleached, chalky, sand-colored, petrified mesas of the high plains? It was a physical sensation that was somehow connected with his love of the language.

"Give me Italian any day," said Erna. "Spanish is a macho language."

"Which is why it sounds so beautiful in the mouth of a woman. Here"—he pointed with his finger—"here's how I'm going to drive. From Oloron-Sainte-Marie I'll head south, then up over the Pyrenees, and down to Jaca, Puente de la Reina, Sos, Sádaba, Tauste . . . taking only back roads—these little yellow and white lines—then on to Serranía de Cuenca and finally to Madrid."

"That's the scenic route. So you're not in a big hurry after all. Or are you scared?"

"I might be. I haven't thought about it."

"So why are you going?"

"To deliver a newspaper."

"You're hopeless."

Yes, he was hopeless. Daniel still hadn't answered the phone, the Volvo Amazon broke down somewhere in Les Landes, and the days inched slowly toward the end of the month while he waited for a spare part. All he could see from his hotel room was a depressingly well-ordered wood that would never turn into a decent forest. He nearly went crazy staring at that Limbo of scrawny pines. When he phoned Erna, she seemed to find his situation amusing.

"So you've finally got time to think things over. But of course you're not doing it. Mr. Impatience himself. Men aren't good at self-reflection. What are you doing?"

"Filming pinecones."

Two days later the car was finally ready. The Amazon raced up the Pyrenees as if it knew it had to make up for lost time. On the other side of the mountains the landscape changed—a vast expanse spread itself out before him, shimmered in the heat waves, forced him to slow down. The last sounds of French gave way to rapid-fire Castilian. The soil here was older, crueler, more steeped in history, and as usual his spirits soared. At the same time, his heart sank, because there was a catch: while the landscape drew itself up protectively around his shoulders, the daily news took its toll. It sucked you in, whether you wanted it to or not. Other countries had a two-party system; here it was a constant battle based on poison, lies, perjury, insinuation, scandal. The papers were at each other's throats, judges were biased, money could buy anything, yet it was also grand theater, opera buffa, editors filmed in women's underwear, the government as a bumbling kidnapper, ministers who were convicted but never went to jail, Grand Guignol, a long-standing problem, a habit that was hard to kick though everyone was fed up with it.

The real problem lay elsewhere, in a band of determined killers whose bombs, executions, extortion practices, and hate-filled followers dominated everyday life—a deadly gang that held the nation in a grip of fear and wouldn't let go until the seeds of destruction had been sown throughout the entire country, and probably not even then. He read the names of the latest victims, heard the frenzied voices of the broadcasters and commentators as he drove down the deserted back roads, and wondered if that was why he had slowed his pace, why he sometimes parked the car on the side of the road and walked into the empty guiltless land, filming and recording its sounds. Dryness, desolation, the rush of wind through the thistles, a faraway tractor, the hooting of a barn owl. In the evening he stopped at small hotels and watched the TV in the lounge along with the other guests. A demonstration for a man who'd been held captive in an underground hideout for more than five hundred days, a counterdemonstration of masked supporters throwing rocks and Molotov cocktails. No country, he thought, could be worth so much blood and hate. One night they showed this year's death toll—a series of grisly corpses and burned-out cars. In a perverse way, the cars were sometimes a better illustration of the ETA's orgiastic destructive urges than the mangled, helpless, mutilated bodies of the victims.

How long ago had it been since he'd had that conversation with Elik in Lübars? An eternity, three months? How had she put it? "Try to think of it as a comedy." He hadn't understood her at the time and he still didn't, but apparently he wasn't the only one. In the dusky hotel lounge the screen was filled with red blood and pink flesh, but the sound was even more horrifying—stone walls, tiled floors, no wallpaper, no carpets, nothing to absorb the hard mechanical voices, a shrill echo mixed with the oaths and sighs of the guests. Surrounded by an invisible chorus, he sat in the lounge and thought of the answer she had given him.

"Will it make you feel better if I say it's tragic?" And: "Two hundred years from now, when the sentimentality's worn off, all that will be left is the madness—the claims, the counterarguments, the justifications."

That much was true, he wanted to say to her, but did it help us to know that? Surely it only made things worse? It was bad enough that you had to suffer now, but, even worse, one day your suffering would be meaningless. Life wasn't measured in her two hundred years, but in the five hundred days that someone had been locked in his own grave. Historical time was an obscene abstraction compared to someone whose brains had been blown out in a restaurant. Of course, unlike the people in the lounge, the abstract generations of the future wouldn't have to see that brain-spattered restaurant on their TVs. They would have their historical tidbits served up as statistics, enigmatic ciphers, footnotes in a scholarly review. And the bill would have been paid long ago. But that too had been figured into her calculations. One day nobody would know anything about it at all, and then the comedy could really begin. He wondered if she was seeing the same images on her TV, but he knew that in order to ask her he'd have to find her first. She had vanished, like that night in Lübars, when she'd left him sitting in the café like an idiot. The old woman in the chair next to his, who had been watching TV all evening with a handkerchief clutched in her hand, stood up and came back with a drink for herself and a criminally full glass of cognac for him.

"*En este mundo no hay remedio,*" she said, "*vivimos siempre entre asesinos y demonios.*"

Demons. In Spanish the word suddenly took on extra meaning, so that it sounded as if demons were part of the human race, shared the same space, looked like us. They might be sitting next to you in an airplane or a bar, so sure of themselves that they carried death—their own and that of others—with them wherever they went.

The next morning he phoned Daniel and finally got him.

"Where are you? You've got a great sense of timing. Have you been watching TV? The whole country is in an uproar."

"I'm very close—just outside Sigüenza."

"Take your time. I've got a houseful of people I can't get

rid of. I need a couple of days, because they haven't got any ID papers. In the meantime, why don't you pay a visit to the *Doncel* and ask if you can borrow his book. You know who I mean, don't you?"

"Yes."

The *Doncel* was a marble sculpture in the cathedral of Sigüenza—a young man sitting on top of his own tomb, reading a book.

"Give me about three days. Then you can move in here. Have you got enough money?"

"Don't worry about that."

"Until then you can stay at the Hotel de Mediodía. It looks expensive, but it's not. Won't cost more than about five thousand pesetas. It's worth it just for the name. I'll call you there, or you can call me. What brings you here? Something special?"

"No, no. Just the usual."

That wasn't true, and he could hear it in his voice. Daniel too, because he said, "Is there anything else I can do for you?"

Arthur hesitated.

"Where would you go to look for someone who's working on a history project?"

"It depends on what the subject is. This country's got a lot of history, as you know. The national archives are here in Madrid, on Calle de Serrano. You can also find a lot of stuff in Simancas, but that's about a hundred and twenty miles away. Most of Spain is stored there, except for the Middle Ages, I think. And of course there are all kinds of municipal and provincial archives and church records. The Civil War is someplace else. Not to mention the labor movement, et cetera, et cetera. Mountains of paper. You're welcome to it. It just depends on what you're looking for. *We* are in Seville, in the Archivo Real de las Indias. But I assume that's not what you had in mind."

It wasn't a question, he took it for granted. By "we" he meant Nicaragua. If Arthur didn't want to tell him what was going on, Daniel wouldn't ask. But he must have felt that something was up, because he said reassuringly, "Okay, *cabrón,* I'll let you go. I've got to take care of my children. Begin at the beginning, on the Serrano. For one thing, it's the closest. And you might get lucky. After all, someone always wins the lottery, even though it's only one number off from the people who don't win—a mystery. *Suerte,* we'll be in touch."

His "children" were illegal immigrants trying to find work in Spain. Daniel was a kind of a modern-day saint ("I'm trying to live up to my middle name, Jesús"), though if he had a hand instead of a prosthesis he'd probably punch him one for saying that. *Cabrón* meant "bastard," but it was OK when Daniel said it.

As he drove into Sigüenza he caught sight of the cathedral dome. The *Doncel,* why not?

"Another delaying tactic!" Erna's voice. She was laughing at him, but she was right. His fantasy was about to become reality. Of course he'd find her. Among those millions of Spaniards, he'd somehow find her. He didn't doubt it for a minute. And then?

It was dusky in the cathedral. Oddly enough, you had to go down a flight of stairs to get inside, as if that huge edifice was so heavy it had sunk into the ground. Some kind of Mass was going on. The choir stalls were filled with priests in black and red, and their singsong chant echoed throughout the hollow interior. He watched their white faces, the mouths forming the words that the eyes above no longer needed to read. It was a familiar sight, as old as the tombs lining the walls, and he walked over to one of them now. The *Doncel* hadn't moved a muscle since the last time he'd been here. Arthur remembered every feature of the young man's face. The former page of Queen Isabella the Catholic lay on top of his tomb, propped up on one elbow, and hadn't turned a page of his book in the last five hundred years. Killed in the siege of Granada in 1486. A casualty of war, we'd call him nowadays, though his body could never have resembled the victims whose only monument was a grainy photograph on a flimsy sheet of newsprint. No one will be looking at *them* in five hundred years. Nor will they ever be able to achieve the same dreamy, lost-to-the-world look of repose. This boy had forgotten his death centuries ago. His effigy lay in the cathedral like that strip of land outside Lübars—as a reminder, though the *Doncel* himself no longer knew of what.

Arthur went back outside and was blinded by the light. Supposing his fantasy did become reality, would it be able to withstand the fierce light of Spain? He made an absurdly wide circle around Madrid ("Another delaying tactic!"), driving through Alcalá de Henares and Aranjuez, and finally entered the city via the Puerta de Toledo at the hottest hour of the day. The hotel was located directly across from the Atocha railroad station. He double-parked to unload his camera and bags, and the cars behind him immediately began to honk their horns. So he had to contend not only with the heat, which hammered down on him like a bizarre form of physical violence, but also with the staccato blare of vehicles that had been whipped into an even greater frenzy by the siren of an ambulance.

He dumped his bags and rushed back to park his car. As he hurried back to the hotel he saw that it was over a hundred degrees. His room, which faced the station, didn't have an air conditioner, and when he opened the door to the balcony, the noise was deafening. Sitting on the edge of his bed, he studied the map of Madrid. A set of railroad tracks came up from the south and dead-ended at Atocha station. On the other side of that was a green rectangle with a dab of blue in the middle—Retiro Park. Though he couldn't see the lake from his window, he knew that it was often full of rented rowboats. At the upper left corner of the park was Plaza de la Independencia, which ran into Calle de Serrano. His ultimate destination, but not just yet.

He spent the rest of the day wandering through the labyrinth of the old city. From a phone booth he tried to call Zenobia and Erna, but neither was home. He didn't leave messages. What on earth could he have said? I've come to the end of a walk that started one snowy day in Berlin and will be concluded—one way or another—in the sunny streets of Madrid, where I've nearly been snow-blinded by the light. Copies of *El País* could be seen in every kiosk and on every café table, and today's headline story about yet another bombing only added to his tension. Things weren't going right; he needed to calm down, but he couldn't. He kept reminding himself why he had come here. If he didn't feel up to it, he ought to get his car out of the garage and drive away. But where to? Amsterdam? Berlin? No. He had a couple of things to figure out first. Like whether he ought to go looking for her, and what the meaning of her wordless disappearance, her refusal to face him really was. Had he been relegated to the scrap heap? Had those few mysterious nights been declared null and void? Or had they never taken place at all? Cobwebs, nothingness, moments that had been erased, had become a vague memory, a strange episode with a woman who had stretched out her hand a second too late for a newspaper, who was a world champion in good-byes, who didn't know—and even if she did, she wouldn't care—that he was sitting here like the village idiot staring at a statue of Tirso de Molina, surrounded by a bunch of homeless drunks with liter bottles of lukewarm beer in their dirt-caked hands—his companions, the new savages of the metropolis, staring with unseeing eyes from beneath a tangle of matted hair, muttering, swearing, begging for cigarettes. Suddenly the lone female, a woman with orange hair, staggered to her feet and lifted her skirt, showing one of the men an incredibly filthy pair of underpants, and he couldn't help but see it as a parody, a comment on his bravely begun mission. He shouldn't be here. His presence was a betrayal. Of what? A certain someone—he couldn't even say her name to himself—had interrupted his long mourning, had shaken him out of his rest and reduced him to humiliating restlessness. How were things supposed to end when it wasn't a story or a film? Why had she sent her grandmother's address to Arno? Why had her grandmother been expecting him? If he could only figure these things out, he could cross them off, delete them, and then drive off into that vast, empty, scorching countryside with his camera beside him on the front seat of the car, having been liberated, given back to himself.

Taxi, Serrano, shops, the latest fashion, well-dressed men and women in display windows, their arms in midair, a doomed existence, motionless. That's how it should be—distance, a ready supply of new clothes, no conversations, no scars, no mourning, no lust.

The Archivo Histórico Nacional was closed; it would be open again—unless the world came to an end—tomorrow morning. He let the taxi go and started walking up the long avenue, looking at the shoes of the passersby, at the briskly stepping pace of the post-siesta, at feet that had been born a second time that day and knew where they were going. Years ago he had read a sentence that impressed him so much he had never forgotten it: "Lisette Model put her camera at nearly ground level to achieve a worm's-eye view of pedestrians." The world as seen from the ground, from ground zero. Giant figures that ruled the city, that marched across the world with great confidence because it was their domain. And among all those giants there was one, a female, that he would have to find tomorrow. He felt sure he would.

He returned to the hotel to find hordes of screaming children running up and down the halls. His own body seemed strangely tall beside those noisy dwarfs. However, they didn't seem to notice, and went on chasing each other until long after bedtime. He slept fitfully and woke up in the middle of the night, soaked in sweat, unable to remember what he'd been dreaming. His life was racing out of control, and he was powerless to stop it.

The heat hangs heavily in the sparsely furnished room. He opens the door, which doesn't lead to a real balcony, only to a balustrade that you can lean on. There's still a lot of traffic. It's bound to go on like this all night.

He switches on the tiny TV mounted in the corner and sees a blurry black-and-white image of people kissing each other. To judge by their clothes, the actors must have been dead for at least twenty years. He leaves the sound off, and the next time he wakes up he sees snatches of the morning news. The hostage who has finally been freed from his 532-day ordeal looks into the light as if he's seeing the world for the first time. The pupils of his eyes look even larger because of the heavy glasses above his white, sunken cheeks. He switches off the TV, he can't bear it yet, the demon hour hasn't yet begun. The room has cooled down a bit, now that the early-morning air has reached the city from the high plains. Leaning over the balustrade, he can see the winged horses on the roof of the Ministry of Agriculture and the winged lion on the station across the street—animals from a nonexistent past, a time when horses and lions could fly through the air, dreamtime, someone else's imagination. In other words, now.

And we? No opinions, no judgments. That's our mandate. Oh, we do feel an occasional touch of surprise at your incomprehensible ways, though we should be used to them by now. The elusiveness of your actions, the connection between events and emotions. The myths, stories, and theories you devise by way of explanation, your attempts at knowledge, your numerous detours through the absurd, the loose ends, the surprising moment in which you suddenly see someone else standing before you in the mirror. Bus 64 that goes from Atocha over to Paseo del Prado, then to Plaza de las Cibeles, Paseo Recoletos, Plaza de Colón, and Paseo de la Castellana, to where the man we once followed behind a snowplow over Spandauer Damn gets out, walks over to a large building on Calle de Serrano, passes through the gate, under the granite portal, and into the lobby, where a uniformed guard is seated behind a row of monitors. We know the place well. After all, we were there when Elik Oranje first entered with her letter of introduction, when she was first given her instructions, when she was first allowed to sit down at the long table beside her fellow researchers, scholars, diggers, moles, who had barely looked up in the all-encompassing silence, who had buried themselves in their folios, registers, treaties, and deeds, peering at the letters and numbers in all those ancient documents, the runes and hieroglyphs of a long-ago past. Naturally we know how thrilled she was, how readily she threw her supervisor's advice to the winds. For the first time she will be able to lay her hands, literally, on the letters written by the magpie queen herself. This is her big moment. She'll never come any closer than this. Up to now it's all been an abstraction, but it's about to become concrete, to become true. This is what she's wanted all along, and she's not going to let anything get in her way. Something's happened to her; she's been hurt, and according to your sometimes twisted logic, she's entitled to hurt back. No, we're not passing judgment. Besides, it's over and done with, and despite what she says, we know the price she's had to pay. But now is not the right moment to go into that, since we're following two lives, not one.

Today is no longer the first day, but the excitement has remained. She's mastered the names—the lovers, the advisers, the enemies. She's living in two centuries. Sometimes it's incredibly oppressive, as if she's in a diving bell, descending through the murky waters of the past in search of hidden secrets. The eye of the camera registers the empty table in front of her. It bothered her in the beginning, but she's used to it now. The guard upstairs sees her without really seeing her. The dead eye sweeps the room—the scholars with their papal bulls, diplomas, lists, maps, scrolls, index cards. When her name is called the eye follows her movements—today just as it did the first day, already a month ago, when she first plunked down the *carpeta,* which was almost as big as she was, on the long table, so that the others had to move over to make room for it. She runs her hands over the shiny calfskin, now more than eight hundred years old, seeing with her own eyes the combination of lines and curlicues that form Urraca's stylized signature—a series of arabesques that were once slowly and laboriously set under a treaty, a grant, a will. The vellum takes up the entire width of the table. She gently runs her finger over the writing: *Ego adefondus dei gra rex unu cum coniuge meu uracha regina fecimus...*

The silence in the room is absolute, as if a single sound

might cause the accumulated past to crumble or evaporate . . . a cough, the scratch of a pen, the turning of a parchment page. The silence has become the citadel she returns to each day with a passion that makes up for the rest—the noisy guest house, the droning TV, the din of the busy street below, the daily subway rides, the heat, the newspaper headlines that have a strangely inverse effect on her: she's so absorbed by the things that everyone else has lost interest in that she's lost interest in the things that absorb everyone else; she reads the words and hears the conversations, but she doesn't read and doesn't listen; it's too raw, too big, not worn enough, not condensed, not yet boiled down by time, still brimming over the edges—one of those newspapers contains more words than the book she will write and almost no one will read.

It will be an act of love. She will rescue the woman from her suffocating obscurity, extricate her from her grave of documents and depositions. The thought of it makes her face glow, and it's that face that the man upstairs sees on the monitor, just as he's about to address the guard. She's sitting with the good side of her face toward him—an almost unbearable moment—and the camera nearly captures her in a close-up, so that he wishes he could zoom in more. He sees her total absorption, and his first instinct is to turn around and walk away. But he stays and watches as her hands move over the documents, smooth a curled corner, jot down a note, and he's so fascinated that he barely hears the guard's repeated question. No, he can't go in there, he hasn't been authorized, and he, the guard, can't authorize him, but a message can be sent downstairs. A few minutes later they both see a woman go over to her and whisper something in her ear, and they also see her unwilling surprise, her perturbed frown, the slowness with which she gets up from her chair, so that he already knows he shouldn't have come. You, she says when she's standing before him, her voice sharpened by the distance she's had to travel from the world she belongs to now, a world that no longer includes him, a man from Berlin, a man who's sparked something inside her that he can't even begin to suspect, a man who represents a threat because he's found a weak spot she wants to forget. He can tell by the way she goes back down the stairs, by the treacherous magnification of her image on the monitor: an actress who escalates the drama, turns it into fiction, a woman who almost angrily closes the *carpeta,* rearranges the papers, almost stroking them, looks back at the empty table, disappears from the screen on which he'll never see her again and into the startling reality of those who live outside the monitor, until she's standing before him once more.

We are too close. It takes our breath away. That's not how it should be. We're not supposed to get involved, but it's easier said than done. We promised to keep things short, and they've grown longer. We told you we wouldn't interrupt again, but we have. This time, though, we really are going to withdraw—the all-seeing eye must keep its distance. Still, we can't let go of them, not just yet. We'll follow them from afar. No, not as in the theater, though that might make it easier for you to understand. You see, that's the puzzle—how you people, given the same facts, have come up with an endless number of variations on the same theme, a man and a woman, which all seem to parody each other. The clichés of passion, a quantum number of possibilities that only stir the emotions of those involved. We leave it up to you to decide what you want to call it. We'll be back just one more time, but don't expect too much from our last four words. Think of them as a gesture, a sign of our inability to act. No, we can't intervene. That's not allowed either.

"Where are we going?"

Then, without waiting for an answer, "I wish you hadn't come."

"That sounds hostile."

She stopped.

"I didn't mean it to be. It's just that...this is hardly the right time or place. I think it's better to say that up front."

He didn't answer.

"Where were you going?"

"Maybe we could go to Retiro Park for a cup of coffee?"

"Fine." They walked side by side for several minutes in silence, after which she said, "You went to De Rijp. To see my grandmother."

So she'd heard.

"You sent the address to Arno Tieck."

"That was then."

So it was that simple. There was a "then" and a "now." "Then" was impossibly far away, there was no going back, his passport had expired. For the second time in an hour he suppressed the urge to walk away. But no, this cup would have to be drained to the last dregs. This was the woman who had scratched at his door, sat on his doorstep in a blue gabardine raincoat, walked through nighttime Berlin at his side. To reach the park they had to pass through a tunnel that ran underneath Alcalá. A black man in a filthy djellaba was banging a battery of bongos so hard that it sounded as though he wanted to beat them into the ground. On the other side of the tunnel—sudden silence, trees, shadows. Still cool. The mottled bark of the plane trees, the leaves etched in the sand, an intricate weave. He looked at the profile next to him. Alabaster. Offhand he couldn't think of a better word. A face that you could film in near-darkness, because it would continue to give off light.

"That was then." She had clammed up entirely since she'd said that. Knowing her, the only way he could get her to open her mouth again would be to pry it open. He said nothing. After all, two could play at that game. The paths in the park were named after Spanish-speaking republics— Cuba, Uruguay, Bolivia, Honduras. They kept on walking, through an entire continent. Past the dark water of the lake. Past a row of tarot-card readers, dictating destiny on the basis of the cards. Love, divorce, illness spread out on a filthy rug. The voice of one of them was weaving a web around the head of a woman who was keeping her anxious eyes on his mouth. So he wasn't the only person dying to know something.

"After that night in Berlin, I thought we'd see each other again."

"While you were off in Japan, I found out I was pregnant."

There was also a woman reading palms. He watched her take the hand of her victim in her own tawny, leathery hand. She peered into the other, whiter, hand with her mouth hanging open as if it were the first time she'd ever seen such a thing—a drunken network of merging and diverging lines, notches and grooves. Without looking at her, he said, "And you aren't anymore."

It wasn't a question. He didn't need palms or cards to tell him that. A ball bounced into him, green and blue, a plastic globe, and quickly rolled away. They kept walking, still not speaking, beside the rectangular lake. Rowboats, couples, wheelchairs, songs, applause. They sat down on one of the stone benches by the Lion Monument, two tourists looking small and insignificant beside the monstrous statues. Someone took a snapshot. He could tell by the angle of the camera that the two of them would be on it, mere background scenery, their silence invisible.

So now there's another spirit to add to the other two, he thought, but it seemed blasphemous. Someone who hadn't had the chance to become more than an amorphous blob wasn't really anyone yet. To be a spirit, or to be counted as one, you had to have more of a past. A possibility was invisible, something only fantasy could fill in, though in this case it was better not to. Was there such a thing as somebody who wasn't anybody?

She was sitting very still, staring straight ahead. He started to put his hand on her arm, but she moved away from him.

"It was no big deal," she said. "I made the decision, and not just for myself. After all, I had a good look at that photograph of yours in Berlin. That's no life for me. I could never have given you a substitute child."

Thomas. He felt a rage come over him, a lashing fury.

"I didn't ask you to. There's no question of a substitute."

"My point exactly," she said.

"I don't think of abortion as murder," he said, "but somehow you're surrounded by death."

"Always have been."

She suddenly turned her face toward him so that the scar was close by, an angry, purple, gaping mouth that cursed and accused him more than the other one, the mouth speaking in a different voice, lower, colder, hoarser, saying something about how he must have been watching some of those American antiabortion films, with their pictures of crushed skulls and buckets of fetuses, flagrant propaganda, and he was suddenly reminded of the face he had seen the night she'd danced, the face of the Maenad. He couldn't really take in the words, something about how she didn't need anybody, not now, not ever, how she should never have become mixed up with him, should never have let herself... unfinished sentences and phrases that ended with go away, just get the hell out of here, phony, intruder, then she herself bolted off, turned around, came back, slapped him across the face, swearing and moaning and wailing until she suddenly stopped, so that the image that stayed with him was that of a woman standing in front of him with her mouth wide open, screaming soundlessly, but he would never know how long it went on because he sat frozen to the stone bench long after she had gone, a man among the pillars and lions and winged females with stony breasts.

He saw a couple of children staring at him, totally transfixed, so he got up and left, knowing all the while that he wasn't walking away, but running away, and that he would spend the rest of the day in flight. It was impossible to switch off the machine in his head.

He should never have made that remark about death; it was unforgivable, but why hadn't she told him? After all, it was—or would have been—his child. And if she didn't want to have anything to do with it, he could have raised it. But there was no baby; he was supposed to forget it had ever happened. There had never been any such thing. Something in her past made it impossible, forbidden, something that happened long ago, but sooner or later you had to pay the price, and there's nothing comical about that, not even the second or third time around. The bill is presented over and over again, one parody follows another, someone isn't born because... But there was that word again—someone! There was no someone, there was only a past that kept contaminating the future. Except that countries, unlike people, could take a thousand years.

He walked past the Botanical Gardens toward the train station. Once he was there, he went upstairs and sat in the glass-canopied waiting area where old men went to read the papers. He picked up a front page that had fallen to the ground. Another kidnap victim. No sooner had one been set free than they had the next one, though this time it wasn't for the ransom money. He crumpled the paper into a wad and walked away. It was hopeless; they'd have to deal with it themselves. After this hostage there would be another, and another. Behind a large picture window was a fake jungle, an artificial landscape travelers had to pass through on their way to catch the fast train to Seville, Alicante, or Valencia. But he didn't want to go to Alicante, he wanted to go home. Erna had warned him that she was bad news. Women always figured these things out faster. Home? He didn't have a home. Not like other people. Had this been an attempt to get one? What he had to get was out of here, out of this city. He couldn't handle Spain just now. Go see if there was an assignment for him up north. Maybe there was even a nice little war somewhere. This was definitely not the right moment to be filming his anonymous world. He ordered a cognac at the station bar—at least they gave you a glass strong enough to fell an ox. What was she going to do now? Don't think about it. She was gone. He'd never see her again. Serves him right for snatching a paper out from under a woman's nose. What had the grandmother said? Be careful. She's going through a difficult period. You don't say. Erna wouldn't approve of what he'd done. But what had he done? Some of the decisions that had a bearing on your life had been made in other lives. And not just today, but ten or twenty years ago, or in some prehistoric era that had taken place long before you entered the scene. They lay dormant, like germs, waiting to be passed on to someone else, filling the world with ineradicable forms of evil, leading a secret life—invisible wounds, pathogens ready to strike at any moment. Guilt had nothing to do with it. At one time, back at the beginning of the chain, it had been possible to apportion blame, but since then it had been growing unchecked. No one was immune, everyone got a share. "I could never have given you a substitute child." "My point exactly." Stop wallowing in self-pity, get up, go into town, say good-bye. Rejected lover downs another glass. The usual remedy.

A Hopper painting—a man in a bar. Where's my hat? The men in Hopper paintings are always wearing hats. And smoking. He could see the hotel from where he was sitting. Go to bed—that was the solution. Hadn't slept a wink last night. Mission accomplished. The heat in his room practically knocked him off his feet. TV, pictures of the latest hostage, a young man. He'd be shot within forty-eight hours unless the government agreed to do whatever it was they naturally couldn't agree to do. In other words, a death sentence. His sister. His fiancée—blond, a broad face, a Greek tragedy mask. The drama had already left its mark and would never be erased: a barbaric expression of grief and fate, too much for a human face. There was no escaping it—this was real. Don't watch. He perched on the edge of the bed and watched. Thick blond hair sprouting from her forehead. How do you get a mouth like that, open in a wide O, all those teeth, of course they're going to kill the man, they always do, everything always comes true. He was already dead before he was born. Sooner or later, his death would be avenged.

He must have fallen asleep, because when he woke up the TV was still on, a car commercial, a naked girl in a car tossing her panties out the window. Not a tragedy mask, but the bland, denuded face of paid actors. You look as if you've stepped out of an ad. Had Erna said that? No, he'd said it about himself—I look like an ad. Next a detergent smiled at him, then a translucent row of prawns, shimmering under a thin layer of frost created by a winter machine. It was already dark outside, and thousands of neon suns had come up around the plaza. He phoned Daniel. No answer. Fine. Where was that bar Daniel usually went to? The Nicaragua? You could just about squeeze three people in there. Not in the best of neighborhoods, especially at night, but not too bad. God, the cognac hadn't worn off yet. Take the camera? You never know. Madrid at night... beautiful. So take it. In the meantime the number of drunks by the statue of Tirso de Molina had doubled. The monk-cum-writer towered above them like the dreaded Commendatore in his own play. The woman with the orange hair was still there. She stood directly in front of the camera and stuck her two forefingers in the corners of her mouth and pulled it wide open. He walked away to the sound of jeers, taking flight for the second time that day, and turned down a side street. Damn it, Calle de Toledo had to be around here somewhere, why had he dragged that heavy camera with him, it was already too dark out, even for him, and these streets were so badly lit that it looked as if they were still using gaslight, he was back in the nineteenth century, just like that tunnel, the morning he left her house, the hallway stacked with newspapers, he should have stayed in Japan, those monks didn't have any worries, all they had to do was sit there and chant, not go wandering down narrow alleys and side streets, suddenly it seemed that everyone was out to get him, but no, there was the familiar plaza, a triumphal arch in a neon glare, a hideous chalky light, again not right. The bar was just down that way, cross the street, turn left, basically a living room, even smaller than he remembered, he and his camera could barely fit in. The three barstools were already taken. No Daniel. "That's where I always go when I want to look for my leg."

The conversation halted abruptly when he came in, a crazy man, a foreigner, what was he doing here? The three men on the barstools had the same accent as Daniel, exiles, old men. He ordered a cognac, offered them a round, said he was a friend of Daniel's, that he'd been here before, a long time ago. Ah, Daniel, they said, Daniel, and they drank to his health, their hard serious faces lined with war. This place, a few square feet of space, belonged to them, and he was an interloper whose presence was briefly tolerated. Daniel, one of them said, of course they knew Daniel—he was a man who had lost something, a man who knew how to appreciate life. Their words had the ring of truth, and the conversation went on without him, other names, other events, their world lay elsewhere.

He stared at a map of Nicaragua hanging on the wall— ten years of international solidarity, a woman in a swimsuit standing up to her knees in blue water and waving to a relief ship while a shark or dolphin, it was hard to tell which, sipped soda through a straw and a band of cartridge-belted contras lay camouflaged on the banks of a river. Jungles, swamps, villages, palm trees, *Sandino vive!* The same map that he had seen eight years ago, five years ago. Unconsciously he had stored up each and every one of those details—forgotten them and yet not forgotten them. A real war, a forgotten war. And all that time the map had been tucked away in his brain, waiting for the sight of it to jog his memory. How many other things—facts, faces, words—did he know without knowing? Half your life disappeared while you were still living it—a kind of advance on the oblivion that was to follow. Jesus, he was drunk, he ought to clear out, get into the car tomorrow morning and drive away. This had been a sidetrack, a detour leading to a dead end. A laugh, really.

He stood up and staggered toward the door. *Cuidado,* the men said. And they started talking to him as if he were a child, speaking kiddie Spanish, pointing to his camera, pantomiming no, be careful, dangerous here, but as it turned out it wasn't a warning, but a prediction, a forecast of the future that took place ten minutes later, when he had almost reached the safety of the underworld, the Latina subway station, and was called back by an image, the cry of a dream figure, a lion on a pedestal with its paw resting on a huge granite ball, a sense of curiosity, the usual yearning, an image that might be an image for tomorrow, the tomorrow of his departure, but the lion lured him back into the spell of the prediction, toward two men, two skinheads who shoved him, sent him sprawling to the ground, tried to snatch his camera, stomped on his neck when he wouldn't let go, beat him on the back and hands with an iron rod, but still he held on. They smashed his fingers and he was afraid they were broken, but he scrambled to his feet, his neck in his shoulders, and since he couldn't hit back, he tried to hold them off by kicking, tried to buy time, tried to scream, but just as in a nightmare, no real sound came out, he couldn't scream either, only a strangled cry choked off by an iron grip around his throat, a metal claw forcing him down toward the sharp stony edge of the monument, and later he knew that he'd seen letters, it had all gone incredibly slowly, a breathless, slow-motion silence broken by a cracking skull, an inner explosion, the grit-filled crunch of nails and heels, a grinding and splitting sound, and then a silence that could be compared to nothing on earth, in which he was lifted up so that he could see the entire scene, himself at the foot of the monument, the winged lion, a man in a puddle of blood clutching a camera to his chest, and then the distant sound of a siren that was coming to fetch him, that would receive him, envelop him, embrace him, until he lay in the exact middle of that sound, until he himself had become the siren and flown away and nothing would ever hold him back again.

Reluctance. His first thought. Light. A woman's voice, coming from far away. No, make it dim again. But something tugs and calls. Don't listen. Hide. No light. I don't want light. Silence. Can you hear me? Rustling. Spanish voices. I don't want to hear. I curl up. "He can hear us." A familiar voice. Daniel? "Perhaps you should try it, sir." "Does he understand Spanish?"

I say nothing. I stay where I am. There's something in my nose. I'm strapped down. Pain everywhere. Go back to sleep. Where I've been, you will never follow. Endless crowds, packed streets. I hear them, but I don't say it. I say nothing. Rustles. Veils. I've flown. It must be night. The same woman again, no, another. A face bending over mine, I can feel her breath. A hand on my wrist. Whispers. He lies very still. Endless exhaustion.

"He doesn't want to yet."

"That's normal."

He hears it very clearly. It's true, he wants to go back, to the all-enveloping light, to stay there. Not this pain.

"Arturo?"

It's Daniel's voice.

"Arturo?"

Now the world is coming to him.

"There's no need for you to stay, sir. It could take a long time."

"No, no."

Doors opening. Other voices. Light...semidarkness...
light. As if it was gradually becoming morning.

Later they told him that he'd been in a coma for nearly
two weeks. "You didn't want to come back."

"Where's my camera?"

"It almost cost you your life."

"Are you finally awake?"

Now he saw Daniel's face for the first time, so close, directly above his, big eyes, pores.

"You're back."

"Don't move." A woman's voice.

He felt his eyes filling with tears, felt the tears trickle
down his cheeks. His hands were wrapped in bandages. He
held them up toward Daniel, who took them between his.

"Where's my camera?"

He felt Daniel let go of his hands, heard steps outside his
field of vision, saw his friend hold up the camera, between
the one real hand and the other one in the black leather glove,
which suddenly seemed so big.

"He needs to rest."

"Does it hurt?"

Had that been the same day, or much later? Time had
ceased to exist—there was only sleep, and oblivion, and periods of twilight and waking up, until the day they were finally
able to talk.

"How long do I have to stay here?"

"A couple of weeks at least. After that, you can come to
my place. It's already been arranged."

"How did you know? That I was here, I mean."

"It was in the newspaper. Dutch cinematographer
mugged. I didn't know you'd made so many documentaries."

"Long ago."

"Don't tire him out."

Afterward, memory was put to work. The sharp crack,

328

the inner explosion. But memory was also reluctant to come back. Daniel told him that he'd received lots of letters, messages from people in Berlin, phone calls from Erna and from his mother, who hadn't even known he was in Madrid, a drawing from Otto Heiland, flowers from the NPS, from Arte.

"Didn't expect that, did you? And a German sausage from Berlin, a liverwurst. You couldn't eat it, so I did. It was delicious. I told everybody that you weren't allowed to have visitors yet."

Hesitation. Then he asked.

"Some guy from the embassy. One time. But you were still in hibernation. He left a card."

Hibernation. *Sueño invernal.* In Spanish it meant "winter sleep." Winter, snow, Berlin, the scream that had ended in silence. So be it. Bears went into hibernation. What did it feel like? As if you'd come back from the deep freeze of death? Tortoises too. But they were already part fossil. No wonder they grew so old—they spent half their lives not living. He sank back into sleep.

"You still don't want to wake up, do you?"

Was that the same day? A woman had also come to visit. Had Daniel just told him that, or had he said it before? Daniel had found her sitting by his bedside, but she'd left without saying a word. She'd nodded, slid past him, made herself invisible.

"Some people are like that. They move without making a sound, and when they're gone, it's as if they'd never even been there."

Arthur pointed to his cheek. Daniel nodded. That was the nice thing about friends—they immediately understood what you meant, so that there was no need for an explanation.

He wasn't allowed to read or watch TV.

"What happened to the man who was kidnapped?"

"Miguel Angel Blanco? He's dead, they killed him. Here. They won't let you read, but they didn't say anything about photographs."

Daniel held up the newspaper he'd been reading. Arthur saw a picture of a dark-haired young man, asleep. Long eyelashes, lips like Buddha, full, curved. Despite his indescribable suffering, he was at peace, in total repose... impossible.

"While you were in a coma, all of Spain took to the streets. Huge protest marches against his murder, against the ETA. Millions of people in every major city. Nothing like it has ever happened here. I taped it. I'll show you the video someday."

"I heard."

"Who told you?"

"No. I mean I heard the march from here."

"But you couldn't have."

He didn't argue, it would be pointless. But he had heard it. The footsteps of thousands, no hundreds of thousands of people, murmurs, shouts, a billowing swell of voices, rhythmic, chanted slogans. Of course he couldn't have heard it, but he did hear it, he was sure of that. Better not say any more about it. He looked at the photo again.

"How?"

"A bullet to the back of the neck. Their trademark."

"But he's sleeping."

What made him look so peaceful? How could his killers even look at that picture without fear? Could the dead take revenge? But this man was beyond all that. Slaughtered like an animal, yet there wasn't a trace of pain or fear on his face, only immeasurable sadness, and that impenetrable repose. In the split second of his death, this man had already been somewhere else, and he had an idea of where that might be. It was light there, and you could hear things that the living weren't allowed to hear. It was impossible to explain, and it would be useless to try. He had the feeling that it was forbidden. You weren't supposed to come back. It left you with an inexpressible longing. You didn't belong there, but you didn't belong here anymore either. No, words couldn't describe it. All he had were those ridiculous tears that he could no longer control, that kept flowing down his face, that wouldn't stop. The nurse came in and wiped them away.

"Not now," she said. "Some people are waiting to see you."

"Could I have a word with you outside?" This to Daniel.

"Four is too many. I don't speak English, so would you tell the visitors that they can stay for only fifteen minutes? And that they mustn't upset him, as you did just now, with that picture. You see the effect it has had on him."

Arthur listened to the words at the door, to the silence in which they were received. Then his Berlin friends entered the room—the Magi.

Arno, Zenobia, Victor.

They said nothing, looked at the tubes, at the bandages around his head, his hands. Zenobia gently touched his shoulder, Arno opened his mouth to say something, decided not to, reached instead into his pocket and produced a package, which he placed on the bed.

"Real German sausage, from the Pfalz. A gift from Herr Schultze. He said that he'd already sent you one, but that he didn't trust the Spanish postal service."

Again Arthur felt himself fighting back tears, but what happened next was even more difficult to bear. Victor, who'd been standing back behind the others, walked over to the corner where Arthur could see him, adjusted his polka-dot scarf, straightened his jacket, bowed to him, seemed to count off a few beats, and then began to tap-dance, keeping his eyes on Arthur the whole time. The nurse rushed in a moment later and put an end to it, but Arthur knew he would never forget that moment: the click of the taps on the tiled floor, the feet he couldn't see, the subtle arm movements, the silence in which the whole thing had been performed. It had been a ceremonial dance, an exorcism, a clarion call—at the sound of the clickety-clack, he was supposed to get up and walk, to let his feet carry him away from here, to leave behind all the terrible things that had happened to him. This wordless message had been clearer than any words could have been. A person, Victor, had danced him back to life, and he had understood. It would take a long time—he would have to learn to walk again, and the bandages on his head would have to be replaced countless times before then—but he was on his way. The nurse wiped away his tears again. The clickety-clack of Victor's patent-leather shoes. He never even knew that Victor could tap-dance.

Arthur apologized to the nurse, in a kind of sign language, for the tears.

"It's part of the healing process," she said. "*Es completamente natural.*"

There followed a discussion of tears, weeping, and crying. All that was missing was the wine, the *Saumagen*, and Herr Schultze.

"And the vodka," said Zenobia.

Arno was currently working on an essay about tears in literature. That was a coincidence. What did Nietzsche have to say on the subject? Surely Nietzsche had said something.

"He who does not weep is not a genius," said Victor. "I know my proverbs."

"OK, OK, but what about: 'I can't distinguish between music and tears.'"

"Your time is up, ladies and gentlemen."

"In my humble opinion," Arno said, "the last time anyone wept was in Stendhal. Everybody weeps in *The Charter-*

house of Parma: duchesses, marquises, countesses, bishops—one big vale of tears. At least Flaubert put a stop to that."

"No Dutch person would be caught dead weeping in the twentieth century. Only Germans still weep." That was Victor. "We Dutch don't weep, we cry. We've been crying since the 1920s. In German you call it *heulen,* which is more like howling, or wailing."

"Russians are always wailing," said Zenobia. Except that she pronounced it "wail-ink."

He could feel the words gradually slipping away from him. What had he done, a moment ago, after Victor's tap dance—had that been weeping or crying? "Russians are always wail-ink."

He could feel how tired he was. The words kept circling around, wanting to say something to him, but unable to. He waited for the sounds to fade, melt, dissipate, until only a soft breathy sigh remained, the sound of his own breathing... which was sleep.

Erna arrived the day he was due to be released from the hospital.

"At least you don't look like an ad anymore." So she hadn't forgotten his words either. Together they looked in the mirror. A man with a bald head, a person who resembled someone he used to know.

"You'd fit right into a monastery."

She and Daniel helped him up the stairs to the apartment. Daniel had changed it somehow. It seemed lighter.

In the room he was going to sleep in, Daniel had hung up two color prints—almost the size of paintings. Women walking through a misty landscape with flowers in their hands, women in a graveyard. The mist permeated everything, even seeming to dull the colors of the flowers. The graveyard was so big that you couldn't see where it ended. Pale patches of winter sunlight shone down through the mist, and in those places the women didn't seem to be walking, but, rather, to be floating or drifting between the tombs, between the cypresses and the acacias—a dream world stretching out to the horizon. There were hundreds of women. Some of them were bending over as if they were talking to someone, others were arranging flowers in a jar or embracing each other. It looked like a feast was about to begin. In another minute they would start dancing to an inaudible tune. A few fingers were pointing to something in the distance, showing the children something the viewer couldn't see. Perhaps the graveyard itself was floating, sailing like a ship of joy through the air. Any moment now it would rise up and take the women, the children, and the flowers on a journey through space.

"Where is it?" Arthur asked.

"Porto. It was a cold day, the mist never cleared. But I thought you'd like it. I made it last fall."

"What's happening?" asked Erna. "It's very festive, but what are they all doing there?"

"It's All Souls' Day."

"Oh. Is that some Catholic holiday? I've heard the term before, but what's it about?"

"That's when the souls of the dead are commemorated. On November second. The dead wait all year for that day."

"Sure. And at night, when all the people have gone home, they come out and dance."

Daniel looked at her.

"How did you know? I took some pictures of the dancing too, but when I developed them, they were blank."

After Daniel and Erna had left, Arthur lay for a while looking at the pictures. All Souls. He didn't know exactly what went on that day, but the words seemed to him to have more to do with the living than with the dead.

But the dead were still there too. They had to be some-where—you couldn't get rid of them entirely, you had to bring them flowers. Perhaps they had even seen him when he was so close to them. But it was better not to say anything. After all, they had gone out of fashion. Except that those women in Porto didn't seem to know it. When he fell asleep ("You need to rest"), the room would slowly fill with mist. Far away he could hear the traffic on Plaza Manuel Becerra, the sounds of a city, horns, a siren, a loudspeaker extolling the virtues of something, though he would never find out what.

Approximately six weeks later, if you had been looking down from a nonexistent observation post above the earth, you would have been able to see an old Volvo join the traffic flow by Atocha station and head north. The driver had a short stubble of hair, and beside him on the front seat was a camera, a book on the history of Asturias, a guidebook about Santiago and a map of Spain, with a large X by Aranda de Duero—his first scheduled stop. ("Short distances to begin with.") Just outside Aranda was a small riverside inn, where he was planning to spend the night. Before he left he'd asked his friend, just once, if he was sure that the woman who'd come to visit him in the hospital hadn't spoken. His friend had averted his face and said, "I wish you hadn't asked. But since you did, she told me that she had to go to Santiago to do some research."

"Didn't she give an address?"

"No. That's all she said."

Evening had set in. It wasn't quite dark yet. The man came out of the inn and walked down to the river. He began filming something, though it was hard to see what it might be, unless it was the dancing light as the sun's last rays bounced off the water, silvery glints that slowly dissolved in the approaching twilight. After that he went back inside. In the night he was awakened by a desperate wail, a hoarse cry that answered itself and was so unmistakably mournful that our language even has a separate verb for it, so that the man in the inn wanted to throw his arms around the donkey's neck and comfort him.

After breakfast he filmed the river in exactly the same place, then drove on, taking the N122 toward the west, then heading north at the junction with the N1. Only the inconceivable eye up above could have seen the car hesitate at the crossroads, then finally turn away from the west and keep going until Basque names began to appear on the traffic signs, and the broad skies of the north became visible beyond the foothills of the Pyrenees.

A̲nd we? Ah, we...

The historiography of recent decades—in its preoccupation with the most irrelevant trivia, in its capacity to absorb whole shelves of documents on the verge of crumbling, investigations never read by anyone, not even by the clerk who transcribed them—has proceeded along this path, even if it has tended to delude itself about its motives. Myriad researchers thought they were coming closer to certainty as they waded through oceans of paper; or actually believed, as they compiled numbers and charts, that their methods resembled those of science. Yet the greater the accumulation of raw data, the more it became clear that every historical trail was a mute puzzle. Behind those names, those notarial acts, those judicial files, stretched the immense aphasia of life, closed in upon itself, lacking all contact with a before and an after.

Robert Callaso, *The Ruin of Kasch*